Heather Hay was born [in?] Scotland and England. [...] and two sons and lives [...] kept pigs, goats, and chi[...] marketable pies and pât[...] that led to her catering for Orient Express tours on trips to Penshurst Place, the stately home of Lord De L'Isle in Kent. During this time she started work on her first book, *Country Enterprise*, which was published in 1983.

By the same author

Country Enterprise
Heritage
The Business

HEATHER HAY

Honour

GRAFTON BOOKS

A Division of the Collins Publishing Group

LONDON GLASGOW
TORONTO SYDNEY AUCKLAND

Grafton Books
A Division of the Collins Publishing Group
8 Grafton Street, London W1X 3LA

A Grafton Paperback Original 1989

ISBN 0-586-20418-0

Printed and bound in Great Britain by
Collins, Glasgow

Set in Sabon

To my family, as always.

Acknowledgements

The Montford family, who began their lives in *Heritage*, still owe their origins to the special atmosphere of Penshurst Place, Kent, stately home of Viscount De L'Isle, VC KG.

In my own continuing saga, my children, Joanna, Alexander and Rex, and my husband Jonathan are a continuing source of inspiration. As is of course my mother, who despite my efforts, is still better than me at spelling. Jane Judd, my agent, and Judith Kendra, my editor, have my continued gratitude for their hard work and enthusiasm.

For their help in my search for the 'heady gaiety' of the 1920s I would especially like to thank Bob Willis, MBE, Chairman of In Style Promotions, and Robert Burness, Executive Director of the Café Royal.

Part One

Honour's a mistress all mankind pursue.
Paul Whitehead (1710–74)

Pencombe, England, 1921

The scarlet Bugatti sports car wheeled to an elegant halt in front of the Norman porch of the country church. The driver leaned forward to switch off the engine and grimaced at the solemn organ music he could hear. It proved he was late for the service. He shrugged off his heavy tweed driving coat, revealing a slim, young figure in a black suit, very Savile Row. Young Eli Bradbury would have liked a cigarette to fortify him against the overwhelming odour of sanctity that he was sure was awaiting him, but instead he straightened his shoulders and brushed an invisible fleck of dust from his sleeve. It wasn't every day a fellow attended the funeral of a viscount, especially one who was part of the family.

Isabella had heard the crunch of wheels on the gravel. She could relax a little now because it meant that her young half-brother had arrived, even if he was ten minutes late. Isabella shivered. The chill of the church struck through the light wool of her coat and it would be comforting to pull the fur collar up and cut off the draught that was on her neck, but it wouldn't be right. The cold was making her skin even paler than usual, the black of her mourning clothes was very severe against her fair hair and blue eyes.

The vases in the chancel ahead of her were overflowing with autumn chrysanthemums, all of them tones of brown, emblems of death and decay. It was too sombre for the last rites of a man who had lived happily and healthily until his ninety-second year. Lord Montford, Isabella's father-in-law, had lived a life that many would envy. Only during his last few weeks had he even contemplated the end of his mortal existence, and then he'd said to Michael that he was at peace, he had no ambitions left, except perhaps – and here the old man had allowed himself a moment of self-pity – he would have liked to see Johnnie, his younger son, just once more.

Michael and Johnnie, Isabella's husband and his brother, the dead Earl's sons, had both survived the Great War. The Montford line had been more fortunate than some of the other aristocratic families of Kent whose sons had never come home from France. There was young Billy Soames: he was killed at Arles; Teddy de Knowles was lost at Ypres. Ypres, that was where Timmy's wife of only a few weeks had died. Isabella could just see her nephew Timmy, his tall, spare figure standing apart from the mass of his brothers and sisters. He always looked alone these days, even in a crowd.

For many of the congregation, villagers as well as gentry, memories of death were too poignant; it was not simply an old man that they were remembering today. Isabella felt her sister tapping on her shoulder and looked round at Lucinda who was in the pew behind her.

'Have you got a handkerchief?' Lucinda whispered. Her eyes were damp, her plump cheeks shining with tears. Isabella passed her a scrap of embroidered muslin. Victoria, Lucinda's only daughter, was beside her mother, her face registering irritation at the display of emotion. Isabella smiled briefly at the girl, who at nineteen was almost a woman, then turned back to look again towards the altar. The choir was rustling with self-importance, their black robes under white surplices crackling with starch. Lord Montford's passing was an event of monumental importance in the village, an event that summoned extra choir practice and had the bell-ringers filling the evenings with exploratory peals. Michael, who overnight had become a lord, and Isabella his Lady, were now their property. The new incumbent was in early middle age and his wife was only just turned forty. It was reasonable for the villagers to assume that the great house of Pencombe would face an age of restoration, that the tenants on the farms could look forward to their landlord investing in their futures. Only the family and their advisers knew differently: the estate was impoverished, it might be necessary to dispose of acreage to cover death duties, and that would signal the beginning of the end.

Isabella wished that she felt closer to her husband. Over the past few years they'd begun a gradual drifting apart. Looking back to the war, the only times they'd had together had been Michael's leaves and every precious second had been filled with love, with tears and laughter. It had been a level of emotion that peacetime, and a return to a normal married life, could never sustain.

Johnnie? What would Johnnie be like now? Isabella was happy not to dwell on her own marriage. She leaned forwards to look across the aisle. Adele, Johnnie's wife, was there with her daughter and her brother Bill. She was still very pretty, with a bright, brittle polish that was most particularly American. She was very pale, though. As a girl she'd always had a high colour; now her skin was pale cream, the loop of hair that escaped fashionably from her neat cloche hat still a deep chestnut. The black of mourning suited her. Isabella put a hand up to check that her own hair was smoothly restrained in the knot that she now wore low on the back of her neck. Her own hat was a wide beret shape, a useful hat, one suited to the life that Isabella foresaw ahead of her.

At last the rector began the closing phrases. Isabella felt a sudden, almost passionate, longing to be away, out of the confined affinity with death. She closed her eyes, squeezed them almost painfully tight. Breathing in the chilled air made her shudder and Michael felt it. He put his hand gently on her arm. He was sorry for her; he knew she had been close to the old man in these past years. Certainly closer than he himself had been. Michael did not feel close to anyone now. It was as if the friends he'd lost, even the men he'd never known who'd died, had made a shell around his feelings, scar tissue over an open wound, sealing him from hurt. Scars — that brought him back to thinking of Johnnie. A car accident had ruined his brother's face — and after coming through such a glorious war without a scratch, that's what they'd all said, such a gallant, glorious war for Johnnie.

Young Eli had found a place in the very last pew. He was positioned for a quick exit. This was a definite bore. He stared down morosely at his shining patent leather shoes. Michael would probably make a comment as to their unsuitability, but it would only be half-hearted; Isabella's husband didn't carry the kind of weight needed to make a gay blade like Young Eli toe the line. He smiled to himself, the corners of his lips lifting in the way that made the young girls flutter. He was quite a ladies' man, he liked them, and they liked him, and that was pretty much how it should be. The car helped, too, the shining scarlet machine that waited his attention after this compulsory drag was over. The best thing he'd ever done was to rent out Linstone, the magnificent house high on the Kent Weald that he'd inherited from his father. That had funded the car, which he'd bought direct from the factory at Strasbourg, and contributed to his high-flying London lifestyle that required more than the trust fund allowed him.

There was a party in town this evening, but he had the afternoon to fill in first. He fancied a touch of fresh air, after all this. He had no intention of hanging around for the funereal meats. He could do with some company though, but the boys were all still wet behind the ears, except for Timmy. Young Eli glared at the back of Timmy's head. He had been the age to go off and do his bit, the rest of them weren't. That was no big deal, but the family always acted as if it was.

The pallbearers were taking their places. He could see Michael walking slowly to his appointed corner; Thomas Cade, Lucinda's husband, stepped out from his pew; Bill, Adele's brother, was taking the place that would have been Johnnie's, and Timmy, of course, specially asked for by the old man, before he'd had the decency to go to his Maker at last. Amongst all the backs that met his gaze, one face was turned palely in his direction, his sole ally in the camp. Young Eli sighed to himself at the unfairness of it all. He was such a dashing fellow, too much for these country bumpkins. But at least Herbert, the butler's son to whom he winked slowly in greeting, held him in awe. Herbert, who was whipper-in for the mangy remains of the once thriving pack of hounds, was also the provider of nubile young village girls for a gentleman's pleasures. Yes, Herbert could accompany him this afternoon; they'd pick up a couple of floosies and drive off for some tea, somewhere jolly, after a little fun of course, somewhere nice and private. A country lane, a pretty girl and a open-top car. What could be nicer?

The organ began the asthmatic wheezing that signalled the beginning of the funeral march. Young Eli rearranged his face carefully. But the composed saturnine expression was wasted on all of them except Isabella and Michael's younger son, Eddy. 'Silly ass,' the boy hissed in his brother's ear as he nodded in their uncle's direction. Both boys stared at him with all the superiority that a fourteen- and a sixteen-year-old, down on special leave from school, feel for their elders.

* * *

It was as well that Isabella had brought in extra domestic help from the village. Maude had become used to the leisurely routine of housekeeping for an invalid; her progress in laying out the cold buffet for lunch provided proof of that.

'Let me give you a hand, Maude,' Isabella said, despairing of the housekeeper's infinitesimally slow placing of a salver of sliced ham.

'Oh, no, your Ladyship, I couldn't possibly.' Maude was serenely unaware of her mistress's rising irritation. 'You go back to the drawing room, we'll manage fine in here. Mr Dove's pourin' out the sherry now. Off you go, there's nothing you need fret about, not today, your Ladyship.'

Once more, if Maude called her 'your Ladyship' only once more, Isabella would scream. She would insist on being called 'ma'am' tomorrow; it didn't matter what book of outdated etiquette the servants went by, Isabella intended to go by her own. Breathing deliberately slowly to calm herself she walked back towards the room where the family was gathered, everyone except Young Eli, whom she hadn't seen after the service, and Victoria who'd gone straight to her room with a headache. At least there was a fire in the drawing room. The stone-walled hall was draughty despite the heating system that was working at full blast today. It had been installed by Johnnie and Adele when they'd lived here at Pencombe before the war. To American heiresses a central heating system in a draughty castle was a basic necessity, as had been the tons of coke to fire it. When their guests left, Isabella and Michael would have to make do with the heat from the wide open fireplaces and 'sensible' clothing, as had all Michael's ancestors.

Isabella's expression softened as she passed the portrait of one of her favourites among the long line of Montfords past the Cavalier whose likeness hung at the base of the staircase, its gilt frame glowing against the honey stone. She rested her hand lightly on the carved oak finial of the banister as she paused. She thought of him as her friend. He was very handsome with his dark, wavy hair and bright brown eyes. He sported a splendid moustache above his pink-painted lips, but she really liked him for the sympathy of his smile. He seemed to be telling her that he understood. He knew all about cold rooms, tenants whose roofs needed mending before your own, rent rolls that seemed pitiful compared to the awful expense of maintaining a stately pile that you didn't want to live in anyway.

'Ah, Isabella! We all wondered where you'd got to.' Lucinda was coming towards her, arms outstretched. 'You weren't too upset, were you, dear? He was an old man, I only hope we all live as long.'

Isabella smiled at Lucinda's concern. They hadn't seen much of each other in recent years, even though they lived less than a dozen miles apart. It seemed that inheriting a title brought even relatives hurrying back, but that wasn't a kind thought and Isabella quickly dismissed it. 'No, no,' she said, 'it was time for him to go. He wouldn't have been happy to drag on, not after he became – ' she paused, she'd nearly said 'incontinent', but that wouldn't do ' – so poorly,' she finished.

'Come and have a sherry, Isabella.' Michael was beckoning her towards the tray. It was on a side table close by the fire that roared in the stone-framed hearth and he knew she felt the cold. The bright light of the flames reflected off the yellow-painted panelled walls, the gold upholstery, the gilt chandelier, more legacies of Adele's money. 'All well in the dining room?' he murmured as he handed her a glass, and she nodded. He raised his voice, relaxing a little now that domestic problems appeared shelved.

'Adele,' he said, 'it was a pity you only arrived this

morning, it would have been nice to have had a chance to talk before the service. I think,' he looked down, studying his glass intently, 'I think we were all hoping Johnnie would change his mind and come.'

'Change his mind?' Adele's voice was high, acute. 'Now, you can't have forgotten your own brother that much, Michael. Johnnie has never changed his mind in his life. He sets off on a course and then sticks to it. Like he used to when we would go out hunting, nothing would change his direction, he'd take anything in his way, gates, ditches, why I remember . . .' But her voice broke suddenly, and she was reaching into her handbag. 'I'm sorry.' The words were muffled by the handkerchief. 'I hate funerals. Come on, Michael, for goodness sake give me a drink. No, not a sherry, I want a real drink.'

Michael poured her a neat whisky and she drank it quickly then held the glass out for a refill. 'Thanks,' she said. 'I seem to drink a lot these days, since the accident. There doesn't seem to be that much else to do any more.' She became suddenly aware of the silence in the room, of her daughter Belle and the other children watching her. 'Go on, go off and play somewhere, can't you?' she cried. 'Go and see the hounds, go and talk to the grooms. You've still got grooms, haven't you, Michael, even though my money's not here anymore?'

'I think we still run to a groom or two, Adele.' Michael smiled wanly. 'Go on, you youngsters, clear off for a bit. We'll call you when lunch is ready.'

They trooped out, long-faced until reaching the sanctuary of the hall, then relief touched them all, and, as Timmy checked that the door was closed behind them, a cry like a Red Indian's echoed down the corridors. That would be Eddy, Isabella smiled, he was a little devil.

The room was depleted by the younger generation's absence. Thomas and Lucinda sat side by side on a wide, hard-stuffed sofa. Michael remained standing close to the fire and Isabella sat uneasily on the long needleworked stool. Adele had unnerved her, even though she'd expected her sister-in-law to be overwrought, that was understandable, all things considered.

'Is Johnnie feeling any better in himself?' Isabella asked.

'I don't think he's in pain, if that's what you mean.' Adele was looking uncertainly from the black japanned side chairs near the windows to the tapestry-covered wing chair close to the fire that the late Lord Montford had made his own. In the end she sat down gingerly on the latter. Isabella realized that she was holding her breath; no one had used that seat since the old man had taken to his bed. 'At least, he says it doesn't hurt any more,' Adele continued. 'But how he is in himself? Well, that depends on who you think he is. If you met him today I don't suppose you'd recognize him. And I don't just mean for the scars on his face.'

Isabella looked quickly at Michael. Her husband's face was drawn as if he himself were in pain. He couldn't stand the thought of Johnnie's face so badly burnt; it had made him cry when he'd first heard, the only tears she'd ever seen him shed.

'He's become quite a different person,' Adele continued. 'He won't go anywhere, won't see any of our old friends. Reads a lot, shuts himself up in the library for hours and hours. Drinks too much, although he won't allow me to drink in front of him. I have to keep my spirits up in private – I think he'd go mad if he knew. But what am I saying? Go mad? Why, I think he's quite mad already.' She stood up very deliberately and carefully put the empty glass down on a wine table. 'Bill can tell you anything more you want to know. I'm tired, tired from the journey down here. I always thought it was a drag to have to come all the way down here from town, and that was in the good old days, when we all were young. Principal guest suite I assume, Isabella? I'll just go on up, Maudie can help me. Ring for her for me, Michael.' She walked slowly to the door, the centre of all their attention. She seemed to carry with her the most awful vision of Johnnie, their bright handsome Johnnie, whose face was ruined and who'd ruined this woman, his wife, whom they'd all remembered as a vivacious little thing who would dance until dawn. The door closed behind her and Isabella felt the tension drain from her; she felt almost limp.

'How utterly awful!' Lucinda said huddling closer to her husband. 'Thomas, that woman's like a stranger, I've never seen anyone change so much.'

'That, my dear,' said Thomas, 'is probably only because you haven't seen Johnnie. I think he must have changed beyond anything any of us can imagine.'

'It isn't just how he's changed.' Bill's American accent was harsher than his sister's. 'There's something else, something about the accident that made Adele like this. It's nothing any of us can talk about. I thought coming over here might help, but it just seems to have made it worse. I'm sorry if it's embarrassed you.'

'No, no, of course it hasn't embarrassed us, Bill.' Isabella stood up as she spoke. 'We're family, we're concerned that's all; it might do Adele good to stay here with us for a few days. She's very welcome, as are you and Belle, of course. I'll just check if everything's ready, then I think it would be a good idea if we went in to lunch. I'm afraid this sort of occasion is always difficult, isn't it?' She smiled in a rather lopsided fashion. She hadn't felt like crying herself until now.

Timmy stood on the broad, brick doorstep of Reason Hill and breathed deeply. The vast panorama that spread out below him was tinged with the orange reds of autumn hedgerows that outlined the rich brown of ploughed fields and green rectangles of pasture. The wooden scaffolding of the hop fields in the distance made islands of feverish activity where the harvest was coming to a quick climax; the far-off hoppers were ant-like in their hurry. It was almost the view he would have had from an aeroplane. Almost, but not quite, because here standing in front of the farmhouse, he was anchored to the ground. He could feel the surging longing that came whenever he thought of flying; there were the remembered sensations impelling him.

'Get a move on, come on, Timmy, bloody day-dreaming as usual.' The gruff tones of his brother Tom brought him back to reality.

'Come on, old man, we'll miss it if you don't get a move on.' Albert's voice was lighter, but that was to be expected, he was only seventeen. As Timmy turned to walk alongside them, it was clear that, although Timmy was taller than both of them – Thomas was five foot ten, Albert was some two inches shorter – they were peas from the same pod. Both had the dark, thick hair and broad faces and hands of their father, Thomas Cade, and the bright flashing eyes of their mother, Lucinda. Timmy didn't look like his brothers because he was Thomas Cade's adopted son, and although he'd lived at Reason Hill since he was six, his body had never thickened with the good living.

'With luck, it'll be a heifer this time,' Albert said. 'I'm not cutting the poor little bugger's balls off if it's not.'

Tom smiled in his superiority of years. 'You're soft, Albert. It's as well father doesn't go into milk, or you'd be crying your eyes out all the time.'

'I didn't cry last time, that's a lie.' Albert hurried on ahead of them, his shoulders stiff with irritation, as Tom and Timmy continued at a more leisurely pace towards the building where their father would be with Daisy, their much-loved house cow. Thomas might have gone out of livestock farming, but he was a stock man all the same and Daisy wouldn't come to harm in his hands. Two of the cow's last three calves had been bulls that had needed their manhood removing to be fattened for the table. Albert was too soft for that kind of thing, not that it seemed to put him off his roast beef on Sundays.

They walked on to the group of wooden-sided buildings that provided cover for the machinery, space for hay and grain and, at calving, a stable for Daisy. There were never horses over here because there was a legacy of ringworm in the wood. It didn't matter too much if the cattle picked it up, but Thomas was desperately proud of his horses, he wouldn't have them contaminated.

'I thought you'd miss it.' Thomas looked up at them from where he was squatting on the floor, companionably placed beside Daisy's head. She was breathing heavily, her eyes wide with surprise, her sides heaving, but there was no air of panic in the warm atmosphere. 'Come in, but be quiet about it,' Thomas continued, laying a calming hand on Daisy's neck as she turned her head to look at the visitors. 'Keep back over there against the wall. She's not got long to go.' He stroked long and soothingly over her rich brown coat. 'I can never get over the miracle; birth is a wonderful thing.' He stared down at the cow; he was fond of her and he knew that was stupid. It was a fault in him, his liking for animals. That was why over the years he'd gone out of livestock, preferring to concentrate all his energies on grain and hop production. He had more than enough to do with that and his other business enterprises. Last to go had been the sheep and finally he'd relaxed, content to admit to himself, but to no one else, that he thought them unintelligent creatures. And that too was an odd emotion for a farmer, who after all should look at his stock in terms of profit or loss rather than character. But Daisy was different, he wouldn't part with her.

Timmy squatted down, leaning back lightly against the wall. He loved his adoptive father, and this was a rare moment to see the real person who existed beneath the polished veneer of the highly successful man of the land, man of business. Timmy was sorry that he couldn't feel for Reason Hill the way that Thomas did. The pride and love of the farm was an overwhelming motivation for the years of care that had been lavished on its land. The farm would come to Timmy when Thomas died. It had all been arranged long ago. Reason Hill was Timmy's, and Thomas's natural sons would have other parts of the Cade empire. Tom already worked much of his time on Bull-stone Farm just two miles away, down on the flat land bordering the Ashford road which would be his legacy. Albert's farm-to-be was further out, near Tenterden, with a fine black and white house that had once been a weaver's, and it was close to the land that had been bought for young Jonathan, who at fourteen was more concerned with his current hobby of fishing than thinking of the new house that his father was having built for his future.

Having thought through the boys' inheritances, it was natural for Timmy to think of his sister Victoria. She was nineteen, slim and beautiful in a strained, fragile way, like a filly that was too finely bred. As Timmy watched the placid progress towards birth his forehead creased. He didn't understand Victoria any more. Once she'd been easy to talk to and they'd been friends as well as relations. Now she was too gay, too charged with bright hard laughter.

'Careful now, girl, take it easy there.' Thomas had got to his feet smoothly and quietly. He wanted to check the presentation of the calf, and was encouraged to see a pair of small hooves shoot into view at the end of Daisy's effort. Quickly the forelegs appeared up to the knees.

Thomas held his breath for an instant, then he saw the muzzle of the calf and he could relax, it was to be an easy birth. Daisy's sides were heaving with her exertions; a shaft of sun struck through the open stable door and the steam from her breath shone like silver. With a gentle, slithering sound the whole top half of the calf appeared, shining with the iridescent skin-coat that Thomas briskly rubbed off its face. There was mucous round the soft warm nose and he wiped that clear. The little body twitched with the first, shuddering breath of life, damp eyelashes fluttered, then bright brown eyes opened, suddenly aware. It was the miracle of life. Thomas rocked back on to his heels, content to watch for a moment as Daisy summoned her energies for a final push.

The calf was a heifer. Albert grinned widely, a bull calf would inevitably have been castrated and then fattened for beef. 'You'll have to buy your meat from the butcher in a couple of years' time, Father.'

Thomas smiled too. This was good; he'd decided that if it was a heifer he'd let it grow on, here at Reason Hill, as a successor to Daisy one day. He stood to pull the calf round to Daisy's front, and the cow dropped her head slowly to focus her great soft eyes on this new being she had created. Slowly she began to nuzzle the dark brown coat, gently licking it clean with her steaming tongue. The men stood back to watch.

'We'll leave her to it,' Thomas said, 'have a cup of tea and then come back to check she'll stand for it to suckle. Come on.' He put his arms round the nearest shoulders, Tom's and Timmy's. Albert opened the door for them to leave and then bolted it with care behind them. He was so pleased that Daisy had done what he'd wanted and produced a girl; he felt himself blush, a girl indeed! But he had his own ideas as to his future. He hated the practice of castration, hated growing animals for meat. He'd worked out a plan for himself, to breed bulls. He would sell them as first-rate breeding stock. That way nothing he produced would be wasted. But he wouldn't tell his father or brother yet, though; they'd think he was mad.

Lucinda presided over her tea table with a matronly grace. She poured the strong orange tea that Thomas favoured into blue and red patterned cups that shone with good living. The kitchen was large and friendly, with a gleaming black cooking range in the inglenook fireplace and copper pans hanging on the whitewashed walls. The stone-flagged floor was covered by an assortment of coloured rugs that went right under the long oak-topped table and the well-polished Windsor chairs. There was a wide dresser on the wall opposite the fire that was weighed down by the remainder of the twelve-place china service that matched the tea things. Geraniums in pots sat on the two tile-edged window sills, and a ginger cat slept curled up on a cushion on one of the pair of fine high-back chairs flanking the range. A grandmother clock ticked the seconds to complete the atmosphere of the room that was secure, amiable, at peace.

The feeling as the four men came in, having left their yard boots in the back hall, was anything but peaceful. Victoria was standing with her back against the dresser, her cheeks were flaming and her eyes over-bright. She had her hair pulled back tightly into a knot that made her cheekbones even more prominent than usual. Her voice had echoed along the corridor to meet them.

'Doesn't anything ever affect you, Mother, anything? Not ever? I don't understand you, you're . . .' Her father had walked into the room and she'd stopped at once.

Lucinda had asked how the calving had gone, and smiled her well-practised smile at the result. She loved her husband and it was clear in every gesture, every movement

23

she made, that she lived to please him. He liked his home life ordered, placid, he liked her inner fires reserved for when they were alone.

'Pass me the sugar will you, Victoria?' Thomas asked, his voice low and strong, unmoved by Victoria's emotion.

Timmy felt disturbed by the tension that came from the girl, but, looking round at the others, they seemed oblivious of it. He hardly tasted the seed cake that was handed to him and in his concern took too big a mouthful of hot sweet tea and stung his mouth. It was silent at the table and soon, without his meaning to, he let his thoughts drift off, back to Lizzy. He could see her so clearly, his beautiful bride with her short bright blonde curly hair, her pale fine skin, her eyes ... He realized suddenly that they were looking at him and felt a flush of embarrassment. For him to be caught thinking of Lizzy was like being found out naked. Then as he looked quickly at each of them, at their concern and, for Albert at least, a kindred embarrassment, he wondered how they'd known his thoughts. If he'd asked Lucinda she could have told him how clearly he showed his feelings. It was the only time he looked truly happy nowadays, when he was thinking of the wife he'd once had, and she would have been glad for him to think of the girl if it hadn't been for the aftermath, for the price he always paid for the sweet memories, by reviving the pain of his loss.

Lucinda stared down at the tea she was making swirl in her cup. Round and round she stirred with the silver apostle spoon, even though the sugar had long dissolved. She was so worried about Victoria. The girl was impossible to talk to, and impossible to fathom. Lucinda would very much have liked to sigh with exasperation, but long ago she'd found that the only way to cope with her busy life, with her children and her darling Thomas, was to adopt an air of tranquillity. A small smile hovered at the corners

24

of her lips as she remembered what she'd once been like; she'd been a hellcat, and Thomas had loved it. But he'd told her quite plainly after they'd married that tantrums were for children, and she was a woman with a woman's pleasures. She looked across the table at him. He was still so very handsome. He'd been forty-six last birthday and there was grey in his hair now, a very becoming dash of white at each temple. He felt her gaze and looked up and they could smile at each other, a slow secret smile. If ever Lucinda remembered that she'd once been going to marry Michael, to have been Lady Montford herself, if ever and whenever the memory came, it only needed Thomas to love her and she knew she wouldn't have traded places with Isabella for anything in the world.

The clatter of the teacup falling to the floor was loud.

'Oh damn!' Albert jumped to his feet as the hot tea poured over his trousers.

'Albert!' Lucinda wouldn't stand foul language from the boys. 'What a mess, what on earth were you thinking of? Go and get changed at once. Go on, hurry up.'

Albert hesitated for an instant. He would have liked to point out that he'd only spilt the tea because Victoria had stuck her bony elbow savagely into his ribs. All because he'd made a face at her, which she deserved because she was always going on, nagging at them all except father. Albert decided he was glad to leave the kitchen. He went out past the scullery where the girl Maggy was peeling potatoes. She stuck her tongue out as he passed and he leered at her. If it wasn't for Maggy he wouldn't like girls at all, he thought. Perhaps he'd go and find Jonathan who was off fishing in the stream. Albert knew he'd have to watch out or Jonathan would end up a better fly fisherman than he was himself. Yes, he'd go and find Jonathan and they'd compare notes on what a scratchy cat their sister was.

* * *

25

'We'll see to ourselves now, thank you, Maude.' Michael put the cover back over the scrambled eggs that he'd helped himself to sparingly. The sideboard at Pencombe was loaded with enough breakfast to feed a couple of dozen hungry foxhunters rather than the four adults it was intended for, whose appetites had been dulled by the war years.

'Michael, be a dear and bring me a piece of toast.' Adele in her flowery wrap made a pretty addition to the mahogany-dark dining room, but Michael would be happier when she left them and he could have the heating turned off.

Isabella was, as always at breakfast, already dressed for the day. 'You can bring me a piece as well, Michael,' she said. 'It's as well you men are off today. It doesn't matter what I say to Maude, but she seems convinced that she must perform this morning magnificence while you're in the house. I hope your appetite picks up with the sea air at Falmouth.' She was becoming concerned about Michael; his lean good looks were on the verge of appearing strained.

'I can't wait to get down there.' Bill sat back in his chair, pushing the plate away from him. 'Apart from anything else, it's further south and that must mean it's warmer. I freeze in this house, Isabella, I don't know how you stand it.'

'Well then, I suggest you always give me plenty of warning before paying a visit. If you came here when the central heating wasn't on you'd risk frostbite.'

Maude came back into the room without knocking, surprising them all by her fluster.

'Oh, ma'am, oh! Miss Isabella!' In her agitation she'd gone back to addressing Isabella as she had some twenty years ago. 'It's come, oh! You should see it!'

Michael pushed his chair back and stood up smiling. 'I

think this must be your present,' he said. 'I'm glad it arrived before we left. Come on, Issy, let's see what the old boy got you.'

They abandoned their breakfasts and followed Maude who led the way outside through the magnificent front door instead of the usual humbler door to the small courtyard. Isabella had taken Michael's arm in her excitement. Her father-in-law, Lord Montford, had left her a special bequest. Out of a nest egg of his own, set aside from the usual formalities of inheritance, it was a present in gratitude for her attention and love during his last years. It was something for Isabella to enjoy, it had said in the will, a little independence. The words had sounded strange coming from the parchment-dry lawyer's lips, but they'd nearly brought tears to Isabella's eyes. She knew quite well what Lordie had meant by them. He'd told her often that, as he became gradually more chairbound, he realized the most precious gift of all was that of mobility, an independence he'd once taken so much for granted, until at the end when it was no longer attainable.

They stood back to let Isabella walk towards his gift on her own. It was a car, a small one as befitted a lady, and it was quite perfect. The beetle black model T Ford had a touring top that was folded down, it was jaunty in the sun that shone on them on the gravelled drive. The salesman who had delivered it ushered her in to the driving seat and, as she slid in, the sweet fresh smell of leather enveloped her. The dials on the dashboard were bright, pristine. She ran her hand slowly over the smoothness of the steering wheel. She hadn't felt so excited in years.

Dear Lordie, dear sweet Lordie to think of it, she thought. All her memories of him now were happy ones. His cantankerous fights against her tenderness faded away.

Michael came towards her. Seeing his wife so excited, like a young girl again, had made him realize how rarely he actually looked at her now. They had become too used to each other recently, treating each other like relatives rather than lovers. He watched her as she listened to the salesman's instructions. She was slimly elegant in a maroon day dress that was set off by the double row of pearls he had given her for an anniversary. She was a wife any man would be proud of. He wished suddenly that they had more time before he left, another day, another night.

'Issy?' He touched her hand as it rested on the steering wheel. 'Issy, will you come down to Cornwall? I can't say come and stay with me, you know that, but come closer, take a cottage at Boscastle. I used to stay there as a child, and I know you'll love it. I can visit you there – say you'll come.'

Isabella looked at her husband. She had made plans for filling the time he would be away, the weeks, possibly months she'd imagined stretching ahead of them, and she realized with an ache that she'd been looking forward to being alone again. To facing some of the challenges of owning Pencombe on her own. She loved Michael, she always had and always would, but he had become withdrawn since the war. She was concerned that at times she said the wrong things when they were together, then a shadow would cross his face and he would be further away from her than ever. Now that he was asking her to come towards him she realized it was easier for her to love him when they were apart. What had changed over the years? Once, a day without him had been too long.

'Of course, I'll come,' she answered and she laughed, sounding almost nervous. 'I'll drive down.'

Michael felt such a relief when she agreed that he realized he hadn't been sure she would. He was no longer certain of their relationship. He turned away from Isabella, worried she would see the doubt in his eyes and he looked at Adele, who was pulling her wrap tightly about her, and he noticed for the first time that she was smoking. Posed against the baronial door behind her, the long, slim cigarette holder held lightly between her fingers, she was a brittle picture of elegance, and from the expression on the face of the young car salesman he clearly thought the same.

It was time to break all this up. Michael looked obviously at his watch, 'Sorry to have to spoil your fun, Isabella, but we'll have to get ready. Bill and I can't afford to miss the Truro connection.'

So they went back into the house, leaving Isabella's present of independence waiting on the gravel.

When it was all over – the goodbyes at the little station, the settling into their seats and then settling back to become engrossed in the newspaper – Michael decided to think briefly of his home life before he set himself to concentrate on the task ahead of him. There was something missing in his marriage. It was ridiculous. They had two fine sons and now there was Pencombe; the mere fact of having it as a responsibility should pull him closer to Isabella, but he knew that they were slipping further apart. It wasn't simply that their lives were taking different paths. He knew he could have turned down the Falmouth assignment – he had been offered that option – but he'd been determined to follow up his involvement with submarine development. He would be running a team of a dozen experts and assistants. Their brief was to improve the quality of air in the underwater vessels, the final hurdle in submarine development. He had felt that his organizational abilities had been underused during the war. Now, in peacetime, it seemed that the 'powers that be' were more prepared to accept that he had the requisite talents to mould a team. More than the prospect of leadership excited him, he was fascinated by the submarines themselves, convinced that they could be used as a positive force for peace, and he felt he owed himself the opportunity to make a constructive contribution to that. He was suddenly irritated at himself for thinking so pompously. The truth was he'd grasped at the opportunity to get away from Pencombe where the prospect of having to break up the estate filled him with dread. He tried vainly to read some of his newspaper but eventually he allowed his thoughts to come back to what he knew was at the root of their problems. His war had been almost sedentary. Certainly there had been moments of glory, but of a secretive, hidden kind. Mostly he remembered those years, when his friends had been mentioned in despatches, when Johnnie had been oh so glorious, as a succession of arguments. He seemed to have been continually at loggerheads with his superiors. The eternal bickering, the constant compromise – it wasn't enough for him, he felt cheated.

His marriage to Isabella had always been based on such high ideals. It had begun in a rush of passion, of excitement that had lasted as the boys had been born, and then grown. His career in politics had absorbed them both and their love had blossomed stronger than he'd ever dreamed possible. Then that bloody war. They'd been parted for months, and leaves had been short bursts of pure sensual pleasure, impossible to sustain when it was all over and they'd had the prospect of forever together again. It seemed to him that Isabella was always so sure of her role in life, it made his own disillusion so much greater by comparison. He had kept his doubts hidden; if only he'd had Johnnie to talk to. He missed his brother.

The train wheels turned rhythmically and his eyes closed behind the raised newspaper. He could remember Johnnie's face so well. The bright brown eyes smiling, the pink cheeks of the sportsman. He couldn't make himself imagine the Johnnie that Adele described, bitter and scarred.

Bill cleared his throat sharply, rustling his paper as he turned the pages. Michael couldn't talk to Bill, not about his own worries. To begin with, he had to woo Bill's attendance on the Falmouth project. It had seemed the most tremendous good luck when the American had revealed that he had been involved with the American submarine venture that achieved the first ever underwater crossing of the Atlantic Ocean. When he said he wanted to stay in England for a few months, it had been only natural to ask him to add his expertise to that of the team. And now, Bill had another reason than his interest in underwater exploration to make him stay. Arabella Foster was a beautiful young girl, clever and well-educated and Michael had been happy when she was appointed as his stenographer. His happiness had faded a little when she and Bill had met and so obviously fallen in love. It was understandable, Bill was attractively American, forceful and bright. He had an invalid wife far away who, if one believed Adele, made his life a misery. Although Michael hadn't known it, Arabella had been on the verge of falling in love with him when Bill swept her off her feet. But it complicated things, it was bound to. Now Arabella and Bill would be down at Falmouth together, and however much they would try to keep their personal feelings from intruding on their work it was bound to happen.

As the train pulled into Charing Cross station, Michael very deliberately turned his thoughts to the development programme. He must make his team into a unit that would function effectively. He stood to straighten his coat and smiled at Bill who smiled happily back. For Bill the thought of Falmouth was inextricably tied up with thoughts of Arabella. Simply thinking of her made his pulse race. He hadn't been so happy in years.

Chicago, Illinois

Johnnie stretched out a hand towards the decanter. It was positioned so that he had to lean fractionally forwards in his chair to reach it and the similarly deep-cut crystal glass beside it. Johnnie was very particular how things were placed on his wide mahogany desk. Having poured himself a generous measure of best Scotch whisky, he settled back against the deep-buttoned hide of his chair. The walls around him were lined with books and the room had the atmosphere of a library, an under-used library. But the atmosphere was misleading; it was calculated to mislead.

The hand that held the glass was the least scarred, so Johnnie did not cover it with a glove when he was at home. His other hand was quite different; even he could not relax in its company and it was continually encased in soft black leather. Johnnie was waiting for the house to empty. Soon, the muted sounds through the study door would inform him that only the servants remained, and of course Mary, Bill's wife. Mary never left the house and Johnnie liked it that way. As always when he was alone in his sanctum the photograph of Adele was lying face down in its silver frame; the simple act of turning it over gave him a surge of pleasure. By the time he had finished his drink, the first of the day, it was ten o'clock and he reckoned Adele's brother and mother had left. The routine was rigid. The Macaul men, David, and Bill when he was at home, left every morning for the office and Betsy Macaul, the family matriarch, began her round of social calls. Betsy was a pillar of Chicago society. Like many of her friends she dispensed charity abroad with as much enthusiasm as she dispensed vindictiveness at home.

He stood swiftly, enjoying being able to move around normally when away from the family's scrutiny. The act he performed for them, the limp, the slow drawling speech, he abandoned in front of Mary. Even on bad days when he would have liked to favour the leg that had been so badly broken, he never allowed himself to appear crippled in front of her. It was a game he played to pretend that he was in no way incapacitated. After all, although it had taken him a long time to see it, the accident had done him a service. At first he had wanted to die, just to escape from the horror that stared back at him from mirrors, but then gradually he had realized, and Mary had helped him, that this way he was free to concentrate. Cut off from his fellow men, violently repelling friendships he'd once enjoyed, it had given him a new chance at life. He had constructed his own rules; slowly and meticulously in a retreat from pain he had made a different person inside himself, with new goals, new visions. But he had to be cautious; although he had forbidden the servants from his study at this hour of the day, they could still be in Mary's room or the hall between and he never stopped being careful.

Johnnie picked up the stick he habitually carried and went out of his lair. He didn't knock on Mary's door but pushed it open ahead of him, dominating the feminine room with his aggression. Mary smiled slowly up at him from the sofa. She was ethereally beautiful, delicately appealing. Her skin was unmarked, unbroken – she had been flung from the car before it had exploded into a ball of flame – but her back had been broken and she would never walk again. They made a fine pair, Johnnie thought as always, as he bent to kiss her on the lips. In their different ways they were parodies of people, and now, unlike the days when their passion had been with bodies entwined, now it was their minds that merged. He had brought the books of their joint adventuring with him for Mary's enjoyment, the columns that added up their fortune, the figures of properties acquired and properties sold. It was important to them that as their love affair had once been secret, so should this acquisition of riches be hidden from the family. Alone in the column-fronted mansion on the hill, Mary knew that when Johnnie drove off in the afternoons it was to further their enterprise, with strange men whom the honourable gentlemen of the Macaul family would have wanted kicked into the gutter.

Mary stroked her pink-nailed fingers slowly over the thick ridged scars on the back of Johnnie's hand then lifted it slowly to her lips. Her eyes glittered: this was the only man she had ever loved, now the only man she would ever love, and for her he was changing the world, bringing it to her isolation and manipulating it for her enjoyment. In the afternoons when he was away she would listen to the radio, eager for the names she knew from their ledgers, Capone, Bertiolie, and tonight, when she was at last lying between her smooth silken sheets, she would weave more dreams in her head that Johnnie would go out and turn into reality. Sometimes, when she had one too many dry martinis or, even worse, one too few, she wondered if life would have been as perfect if there had never been the accident. She had just the slightest memory that she had been growing bored with Johnnie and his eternal pursuit of pleasure in those days. But now they were tied together forever, as no man and wife could ever be, as no one who has not been perfect, and then been broken, could be.

Lucinda was quite annoyed. The hat she'd tried on last at the Bond Street milliners had caught in her hair. The girl had tugged at it, loosening the carefully knotted arrangement, never mind that Lucinda had snapped irritably at the silly child and that the modiste had endeavoured to repair the disarray. Lucinda was meeting a friend for lunch, and it was utterly infuriating that now she wouldn't look her best. She felt positively aggrieved and began comparing her imperfection with the coiffures of every woman she passed. They were all perfect, shining and elegant as was inevitable in such a fashionable part of London. Across the road she caught sight of a particularly attractive style, worn by a young woman not much older than Victoria who was dressed in army uniform. Her shining brown hair was swept up into a roll, not a hair out of place and the man with her was paying the utmost attention to every word that came from her pink lips. Lucinda found herself smiling, it was such a pretty picture of affection – and then suddenly her smile faded. The man was Michael, their Michael. She couldn't believe it. She blinked hard, convinced she must be making a mistake, but no, it was certainly Michael and he was talking so determinedly and yet smiling, the very picture of the attentive male. Lucinda felt suddenly quite old. What on earth should she do? She forgot about her hair, she forgot about her friend who waited in vain at a table for two in the Ritz. She took the train home, trying all the way to compose the words that she'd have to use to tell her sister that Michael was being unfaithful.

'C'm up, Moonlight. Here, Star.' Herbert quickly shovelled the blood-rich minced pigs' lights out of the pail and into the trough as he called to the hounds. He was eager to get them fed this morning and then he'd be free to begin the fun of the day. He whistled melodiously as he poured a bucket full of skimmed milk carefully in front of the hounds' busy heads. Usually he wasn't too fussy about splashing the animals' coats, but when Eli was at Pen-combe he took extra care. If Herbert had a hero, then it was Eli. He admired everything about him: the fast car, the women, the careless abandon with other people's property. All those traits proved to Herbert that Eli was a toff, a swell, and today he was to be in sole command at Pencombe – this would be the best 'do' yet. Old Hermione, Lord Montford's aged aunt, had been left in charge in the Montfords' absence; conveniently, she had now been confined to her bed by the doctor.

Herbert gave her little sympathy as he wielded a quick but effective brush in the corners where the old bitches who couldn't wait until they were let out in the morning had left their deposits. Hermione was old, very old, and it was only natural that she should be ill, natural and very well-timed because today's shooting would have been a lot tamer with her ruling the roost.

Herbert pulled off the brown twill coat that he had worn to protect his best tweeds and stepped out of the kennel and into the sunshine. He squinted up at the brilliant blue sky. The air smelt sharp and tangy, there was only the slightest wisp of white cloud high above him – a perfect day, the birds would fly with a will, there'd be good sport. He patted the greaseproof-wrapped pack of sandwiches in his pocket that his mother had provided for his lunch. Fat lot she knew about things: Herbert would be eating finer fare than his mother's potted ham today. In the meantime, he unwrapped the packet as he walked on to the beginnings of the copse that separated the kennels from the field where the beaters would be assembling. He munched steadily as he walked the dry mud path, careful to take quiet steps and not send the pheasants up. They'd get plenty of exercise later.

* * *

Victoria had been up since dawn, and dressed carefully a good hour before anyone else in the house was stirring. She had pulled a chair close to the window and sat in perfect stillness to watch the beginning of the day. She had seen the dark clouds pull back, letting the early morning sun shine through to reveal the green and gold beauty of the land stretching up the slope ahead of her. Beneath the mature oak trees dotting the park, carpets of fallen leaves were like early shadows. She watched the pigeons flying out in search of grain and looked down at the crunch of gravel that heralded the progress of the head gardener patrolling his domain. Her eyes saw it all, but in her heart none of it registered. It was all Timmy, Timmy. She was unable to break the circle, the thought of him and then the empty longing, as always she felt the lonely desperation. She needed him, needed to be in his arms, but he didn't know. Timmy, Timmy.

At eight o'clock her cousin William knocked on her door on his way to breakfast. She stood up and checked her dress in the cheval mirror, then turned to admire the slimness of her ankles in the low suede boots, smoothed the straight slimness of the green tweed skirt and ran her hands around the tightly belted waist. She stepped up close to the mirror to check the minutely thin pencil line outlining her eyes, and smiled slowly, secretively, at the new pink lipstick she was so taken with. There would be no one to tell her to wipe it off today, because her mother wouldn't be here, and now, thank heavens, neither would Hermione. She walked quickly down to breakfast, suddenly breathless with excitement: perhaps he was here already.

It was unusual for cigar smoke to perfume the dining room during breakfast at Pencombe and Maude coughed irritably, trying to make the point, but no one paid her any attention. William and Edward were down on exeat from

Harrow. To them, a skivvy was a skivvy, never mind how long she'd worked for the family. Eli, whose habit of enjoying a cigar with his breakfast was as established a part of his routine as breathing, was amused by Maude's reaction and puffed twice as hard as usual to make his point. There were a couple of carloads of chums motoring down from London for the shoot and a spot of lunch and he was looking forward immensely to his day. For once he was most definitely lord of all he surveyed.

'Pass me the mushroom ketchup, Willy.' Eli gestured with his cigar, sprinkling ash over the damask cloth. 'You know, Teddy, you eat like a bloody sparrow.'

Edward grinned at him, excitement making him pale. 'Can't help it, I'll make up for it later.'

'For God's sake don't encourage him to eat, Eli.' William pulled a face as he looked at his brother. 'He'll throw up everywhere if you do, he's always like this when he's got something on. He puked all over the table last term when . . .' He broke off as Victoria came into the room and looked suddenly self-conscious. He wasn't quite comfortable in the presence of girls, not even his cousin. Come to think of it, as he ran an appreciative eye over Victoria's nifty costume, he was very uncomfortable in her presence. He flashed a look at Edward who'd gone so far as to stand up as she entered the room, not that it got him an acknowledgement.

'Oh! No one else arrived yet?' Victoria's voice was high, almost squeaky, William thought.

Eli drawled a reply. 'No, you've got us all to yourselves, darling. Aren't you the lucky girl?'

Victoria tossed her head in a way that might have indicated she was annoyed by Eli's flippancy, but William was learning the ways of young women and he understood that she was in fact pleased.

'Come and sit beside me, Viccy.' Eli indicated the vacant

chair beside him. 'You don't want to sit near the babes of the family.'

'And I certainly don't want to perfume my clothes with your cigar so you might do me a favour and put it out.' Victoria raised her immaculately thin eyebrows at Eli and with a smirk he obeyed her request by grinding the cigar to pieces on the edge of the butter dish.

'God, you're a slob, Eli.' Victoria patted him on the shoulder as she took the chair beside him. 'But at least you know how to do things in style. Heavens, I'm bored.' She yawned slowly like a satisfied cat. She was enjoying parading herself in front of the boys, even if they were only that – boys instead of men.

'I'm simply parched,' she continued, 'desperate for bubbly.' She turned to look again at Eli and he perked up at the suggestion. Champagne at breakfast? Why hadn't he thought of that?

'Maude!' he bellowed. 'Maude, get your old man to bring us in some fizz, will you? And,' he continued, in the face of her obvious horror, 'tell him to bring up a couple of dozen bottles, we'll want them at lunch.'

Victoria felt herself begin to relax. Champagne would take the edge off her nerves. She reached into her envelope handbag and took out the slim silver cigarette case that she kept hidden from her mother. Eli was quick to delve for his lighter; Viccy amused him although he was glad he didn't see her too often. He had the feeling she led her brothers a hell of a dance. She'd be happier living in town, he thought, and she was bright enough to keep up the pace – needed it, probably. Yes, that was it. He watched as she inhaled the cigarette smoke deeply and saw how she closed her eyes to savour the sensation. Her eyelids were almost translucent. He saw her clearly for what she was, understanding what the others didn't see, that she was a sensual animal, the type to get her claws into a man and God help him when she did. Another few years and she could be a very dangerous woman, unless she married one of those hick-type farmers that she claimed she despised, but that would be the only thing to tame her, a brood of children, otherwise . . .

Eli held out his hand to her, clicking his fingers for the cigarette case lying on the table. When a scandalized Dove entered bearing a bottle of champagne on his tray, Eli was lighting a cigarette with the practised disdain of a man about town. William and Edward both hurried to the sideboard, pretending to help themselves to some more breakfast. Their father would be livid when he heard of this, but there was nothing they could do. William stabbed savagely at a sausage that slid away from his fork. There was nothing he could do, and nothing he would want to do anyway. When his father was at Pencombe it was unutterably boring, low-key, not the kind of life a chap needed at all. After all, his pals at school had home lives that positively zinged. He kept his back firmly to the room until he heard Dove leave, closing the door with an audible bang, then he turned round. 'Us too, Eli,' he said, 'we'll all drink to the day's shoot, jolly good fun, what?' As he lifted the foaming glass to his lips a cheerful hoot of a car horn announced the arrival of the visitors from town and they went out, glasses in their hands, to greet them.

Herbert stamped his feet impatiently. He wanted the beaters to start, wanted to savour the moment when the men and boys from the estate began their task of flushing the birds to fly high overhead for the guests to shoot. He wanted to enjoy the exquisite sensation of being a guest himself. Young Eli was on one side of him in the line, and Edward on the other. It had given him a moment's qualm being next to Edward who was only a kid, but seeing him handle a gun he realized the boy knew all about it – which

40

was more than could be said for Victoria, who was on the far side of Edward. She was a stunner, Herbert thought; with her clever make-up she was the closest he'd ever come to seeing a real flapper. Eli had put Timmy on the other side of her, to steady her he'd said, but her voice had got higher and higher and if she giggled any more Herbert would have thought she'd had too much to drink, which at eleven o'clock in the morning was ridiculous.

With a distant shout it began, the primitive rhythm of stick on tree, the regular tread of men in heavy boots flattening the undergrowth. Suddenly, "Ware cock!" and up it flew, the first bird of the day, whirring above them, its tail streaming back, all the colours of autumn. Then more cries, another bird, another, and the firing started, punctuating the perfection of the morning with the acrid smell of shot.

Timmy raised his shotgun, eyeing a bird that flew high and straight, tipping the barrel up, following its line so swiftly as to be almost without thought. Then the squeeze on the trigger, the clap of thunder and the recoil hard on the shoulder, following through with the gun. He'd fired as he'd been taught and then his eyes were stinging as the sounds around him brought that vile remembered stench of wet mud to his nostrils. Must keep his eyes open, open wide, mustn't slip back to remembering. He lowered the gun slowly, then turned, only half-seeing, to hand it to the loader behind him. The man said nothing; he remembered mud too.

'Timmy, oh Timmy, you got one. I saw it fall. God, I can't hit a thing.' Victoria threw the barrel of her gun up wildly and pulled the trigger before she had the stock tight against her shoulder. 'Oh!' she cried. 'That hurt!'

'Give it to me.' Timmy reached out for the gun that was now pointing earthwards, dangerously loose in her hand.

'It's still loaded, idiot.' He'd spoken sharply, without thinking, still sick at his stomach.

'Idiot, idiot, am I?' Victoria's pallor was ghastly, the pain in her shoulder underlining the white make-up she wore. She clutched the gun up to her; he shouldn't take it from her as if she were a child.

Timmy spoke to her gently now. 'I'm sorry, I didn't mean that, give it to me, Viccy, please, I'll help you with your grip if you like.' He held out his hand to her. She flushed suddenly. He'd have to hold her in his arms to show her how to shoot, she knew that, she'd seen other coaches at work. The champagne flared in her, he shouldn't have spoken to her like that.

'No, thank you, Timmy, please don't disturb your own sport.' She turned to her loader. 'I say, I'm not shooting with just one barrel, it's much too slow. Be an angel and load it up again, will you?' She handed the gun back to the man who looked pleadingly at Timmy. He didn't fancy standing behind a girl as excited as that as she let off a couple of barrels, but Timmy didn't say anything. After all, he reasoned with himself, he was overreacting. The loader handed the charged gun back to Victoria and she smiled in satisfaction, then turned away from Timmy to look once more over to the wood.

''Ware cock!' The cry rang out again. Victoria was alone in being ready, Edward had stepped back to his loader and Timmy had no gun. Along the line Herbert watched as the fascinating Victoria went for the kill. She aimed for the first bird, which was winging high and fast, flying straight towards her. She fastened her sights on it, determined to get this one. She followed it and the gun head rose higher and higher. It was almost directly above her when she fired and the recoil blasted down on her shoulder like a massive hammer. The tiny heel of her elegant day-boot spun on a damp piece of mud and her body slewed round. She was squeezing the trigger, ready for the second barrel as she fell, she saw the sky bright blue as she twisted, the trees, the green and the gold, then another almighty recoil and there was red, bright red splashing over it all as the second barrel burst into life discharging death into the narrow chest of Herbert, turned fully towards her in his admiration.

The ringing in her ears turned into the most awful silence. There were no words, none, as her eyes closed and she slumped down on to the ground while all around her chaos broke out.

Isabella had come back to a madhouse, at least, that was how Pencombe had seemed at first. Lucinda had said on the telephone that there had been an accident, that Victoria had slipped and accidently shot and killed Maude's son, Herbert, but now, according to a desperately taut-faced William, it seemed that it had been Edward who had fired the gun.

'I don't understand,' Isabella repeated herself to William. 'Your aunt said . . .'

'It doesn't matter what Aunt Lucinda said, she wasn't here when it happened, Mama. It was Edward who had the accident. It's nothing to do with Victoria, she's just overwrought, that's all. The doctor's given her something.'

It had been an enormous relief when the loudly sobbing Victoria had been taken off upstairs and Edward had been able to sink down into an armchair and drop his head into his hands. He was so tired. He had acted instantly in grabbing the gun from his cousin Victoria as she lay cowering on the ground, driven by an overwhelming protective instinct to shield her, and now it couldn't be undone.

Isabella dropped on her knees beside the boy and

stretched out her hands towards him. 'Teddy, Teddy,' she said, 'it's all right, I'm here now. Come on, old chap.'

Edward sat bolt upright and stared at her. He looked almost a stranger, fierce with an adult determination she had never seen before.

'Don't pet me, Mother, I'm not a child. Please, go and see to Maude or something, it'll be easier for me on my own. Please don't worry,' he added, seeing the hurt in her eyes. 'William'll stay with me, please go and see Maude. Go on, you've got to.'

Isabella stood slowly and for a moment looked down at him, her younger son, and she felt she didn't know him any more. Then she shook her head briskly; it was the shock affecting him, of course. 'Yes, I'll go and see Maude,' she said, 'but first I'll see Victoria. If the doctor's still with her I'll send him down to you. Even if you don't want my attention, you'll have to put up with his.' She walked out of the room and Edward looked up at William; they'd manage to carry it off between them. He smiled thinly. He was glad he wasn't the elder brother. He needed William to lean on sometimes. Both boys turned quickly at the knock on the door and stiffened as the local policeman came in to the room. Suddenly he was not simply a friendly bobby who kept the poachers' activities from becoming too obvious, suddenly he was the daunting representative of law and order.

'Master Edward, the inspector'll see you now,' he said.

William stepped forwards to go with his brother but was stopped short. 'Not your turn yet, Master William.'

Edward didn't look back as he left the room. He couldn't bear to. Suddenly he wished very much that he hadn't interfered.

Isabella knocked gently on the bedroom door. She could hear voices, and thought the doctor might still be with

Victoria, but it was Lucinda's voice that called out, 'Come in!'

The sisters embraced, holding each other a little longer than usual, both needing comfort.

'Victoria had a nasty shock,' Lucinda whispered. 'She was standing next to Edward, you see.' Lucinda's face flushed with concern for Isabella.

'Have you seen Maude?' Isabella asked.

'Yes, it was awful, quite awful. Thank God you've come, Issy.' Lucinda meant that wholeheartedly, it was much more Isabella's place to deal with Maude and her husband. Lucinda still felt sick from those first desperate minutes when she'd misunderstood and thought it had been Victoria who'd . . . who'd . . . no, she couldn't bear to think of it.

'How are you feeling, Victoria?' Isabella walked over to the lace-draped bed where Victoria lay listlessly, propped up on heaped pillows. Her hair was loose and she looked very young. Victoria didn't answer but pulled restlessly at the sheet; her cheeks were burning. She looked for a moment at Isabella and then her eyes slid away. Isabella reached out and patted the small white hand that held so tightly on to the bedcovers.

'Try and sleep, dear,' she said. 'It'll all seem a lot better tomorrow, you'll see.' She turned away from the bed. 'Lucinda, has Victoria been given a good, strong sedative? She really should sleep. Where's Dr Groke now, is he with Hermione?'

Lucinda nodded distractedly. Victoria was starting to cry again.

Isabella paused in the middle of the room, she couldn't stay, she had to go to Maude; perhaps, she thought, Lucinda would find it easier on her own with her daughter. 'I hope it works soon,' she said. 'I'll go and see Maude now. If you go to Hermione, Lucinda, don't let her know

45

I'm back, not right away. She mustn't get to hear any of this.' Isabella left her sister and niece and went down by the back stairs. She was breathing slowly and deeply, trying to fortify herself for what she was certain would be an ordeal. She wished Michael was here.

'Maude, Maude, I'm so sorry. So very, very sorry.' Isabella went to the shrunken figure sitting in the chair by the range and bent down to put her arms around her house-keeper. It was silent in the dim kitchen apart from the crackling of the fire in the grate. Dove stood looking out through the window, his back to Isabella and his wife.

'Maude, is there anything I can do?' Isabella could feel tears on her own cheeks. It was so desperately sad, all of it, such an awful waste.

'Nothing to do,' Maude's voice was muffled against Isabella's shoulder, 'nothing will bring him back, nothing.' She struggled in Isabella's grip. 'If that wicked creature hadn't sent for the champagne none of it would have happened, none of it.'

'The champagne? What champagne? What are you talking about? I don't understand.' Isabella stood up and turned to Dove. 'What's this about champagne?' Her voice had risen. The butler turned slowly to face her and she almost recoiled from the sorrow in his face.

'Master Eli had me bring up champagne at the breakfast, and then they went on drinking it until Mr Cade's family arrived. They'd had too much, much too much, but I couldn't tell them, could I?' He asked the question more of his wife than Isabella.

'Do you mean – ' Isabella had to struggle for breath, she felt suddenly overwhelmed by the implications of what she was hearing, ' – do you mean that my son Edward had too much to drink, and that was how Herbert came to be – '

46

she paused, hardly able to say the word, but it had to be said ' – shot?'

'It wasn't Master Edward who had the accident, ma'am,' Dove said, 'it was Miss Victoria. Master Edward's just trying to save her, just doin' the gentlemanly thing like.' His lips twisted in a parody of a smile.

'Oh my God!' Isabella couldn't think what to do, what on earth should she do? Then Maude spoke from her chair.

'It doesn't matter who fired the shot, it was that Young Eli's doing, all of it, and I curse him, I curse him for it.' She broke into loud sobbing and her husband went to her, glad to be able to bend his head and hide his own emotion.

'I . . . I don't know what to do,' Isabella whispered. Dove's voice cut through her confused thoughts.

'Leave it as it is, your Ladyship, as long as Master Edward isn't going to come to harm, just leave it as it is. Nothing's going to bring back our Herbert.'

The room sunk back to silence. Isabella stayed a little longer, trying to arrange her confused thoughts. What would Michael have done, she kept asking herself. She should telephone him. But then she realized how difficult it would be, it would be a long-distance call and there would be interference on the line. It would be impossible to explain it all clearly to Michael. They were just excuses, she realized that, but Michael, with his desperately rigid code of honour, may decide not to allow Edward's innocent subterfuge. The police had been told that it was Eddy, to change that now might cause awful problems. After all, the shooting had been an accident. She straightened her shoulders, steeling herself for what had to be done.

The inspector was very gentle with her. She benefited greatly from his having been in the same regiment as her brother-in-law Johnnie during the war. He gave her a small lecture on the inadvisability of allowing shooting parties without adequate supervision. He appreciated, he said, that her aunt's sudden illness was unavoidable, but all the same . . . he looked at her almost tentatively, as if he wished her to lead him, so she did. 'It was all quite deplorable,' she said. 'I'm sure my husband will take steps to ensure it never happens again. He will instruct the factor that in future all arrangements for a shoot must be confirmed by himself.' Her voice was chill with authority and it had its effect.

'There are still some formalities, Lady Montford,' the inspector concluded, 'but as this was an accident, they won't take too long, and then if I were you I'd get your son back to school as quickly as possible. It won't do him any good dwelling on it.'

'Three frames, best of three.' Edward almost ran to beat his brother to the rack of cues hanging on the wall beside the fire.

'No way, best of nine at the very least. I don't like chance and three frames is too chancy.'

'You're yellow, that's what you are William, through and through.' Edward grinned widely. He was full of go, feeling wonderful. With the resilience of youth the news that they were to go back to school in the morning had transformed him. This was the first time they'd gone into the billiard room since the day of the shooting party. Usually they almost lived in it on exeats. The table played brilliantly, far better than the one at school, and they both agreed that the hours they spent practising on it were more than worthwhile. The Montfords had quite a reputation to keep up at school for their skill at snooker.

'I thought you'd be here,' Victoria said as she came into the room.

The boys looked up quickly from the table and Edward's

48

face drained of colour. He hadn't seen his cousin since the accident, she'd stayed up in her room, and he didn't want to see her now.

'Your mother suggested I came to see you.' Victoria's face was scarlet and she held her head high. 'She thought I might like to say goodbye, since you're going back to school tomorrow.'

'I wonder if she thought you ought to say thank you.' William's face was also flushed. 'I think she knows. She hasn't said anything, but I think she does.'

Edward began rolling the balls on the table in front of him. The reds followed each other swiftly, colliding with the colours, creating chaos where a moment before there had been order.

'Your mother can only know if you told her.' Victoria's voice was sharp, but William had no intention of being quelled by it.

'You know perfectly well we wouldn't tell. Don't you understand, Viccy? Don't you understand at all what Teddy did for you?'

Victoria stood very still. She wanted to run away, wanted desperately to convince herself that the past few days had been a dream, a bad dream. She stared hard at Edward, willing herself to see him as hateful, someone with the power to hurt her. His cheeks were pink now, his hair tousled from his agitation, he was still rolling the snooker balls, but more slowly. He was a child – she saw it suddenly – a child who'd done something big and very brave to help her. She walked forward towards him, very stiffly, like a marionette. He stood quite still as she leaned forwards and kissed him on his cheek. 'Thank you, Teddy,' she said. Then she turned and went out of the room.

'Bloody hell!' William whispered.

'Yuk,' Edward said as he wiped the kiss off with the back of his hand. 'I hate girls.'

'Still . . .' said his brother.

'Yeah, still. Come on, silly ass, how about a game?'

'As long as it's best of nine.'

'All right.'

Victoria realized that she had one last visit to make before it was all over. She went upstairs slowly, summoning her energies. She disliked sickrooms, but more importantly she disliked the fact that her aunt Isabella might know.

'Come in,' Isabella called softly. Hermione seemed to be asleep, although since she'd collapsed on the day of the accident it was difficult to tell what was sleeping and what was waking for the frail old lady lying in the magnificent bed. Years ago it had surprised Isabella that the newly widowed Hermione had been so determined to have as her own the Pencombe bedroom that housed the vast ancestral bed of the Montfords. Isabella thought it a horrible monstrosity, with its swagged maroon curtains, its ostrich plumes and fat carved posts. Hermione had moved into Pencombe after her beloved husband had died on the *Titanic*. Poor George, he'd always loved good living and it had been the death of him. Hermione would be the bed's last occupant. When she died it would be put in one of the public rooms, it would herald the end of an era.

Victoria came quietly into the room. It was dim and fusty and she felt contaminated by decay.

'I just came to say that I've said goodbye to the boys, and that I'll go back to Reason Hill in a little while. My father is coming to get me.'

Isabella smiled grimly, glad that her face would not be easy to scrutinize in the gloom. Victoria was guilty. Guilty, that was the wrong word, Isabella realized. Whoever had shot Herbert, it had been an accident. But Isabella wouldn't like to think a child of hers would stand by silently and let another take the blame. However, it was all over and done now, the only thing was to act as though nothing had ever happened.

'Come and kiss me goodbye then,' Isabella said, and Victoria came towards her quickly, glad that she wasn't to be asked to stay in the room. She had turned and was walking back towards the door, when Isabella's voice made her stop.

'And don't forget to kiss Aunt Hermione, dear.'

Victoria was frozen to the spot. How horrid, she wouldn't do it. She turned round to face Isabella, her eyes were now adjusted to the light. Edward's mother knew; Victoria could see that now. She went very deliberately up to the old woman in the bed and held her breath as she bent to kiss the withered lips. Then she stood and looked again at Isabella. She had performed her penance.

Thomas walked purposefully across the small foyer towards the reception desk. He wasn't used to visiting modest London hotels in quiet backstreets. He'd taken after Lucinda's father and made a rule that if a man must patronize a hotel, then it should at least be the best that money could buy.

'I believe you have a Mr Jones staying here?' he asked the elderly receptionist whose sparse grey moustache quivered in time with his bobbing Adam's apple. 'A Mr Luke Jones.'

'Ah, you must be Mr Cade. Mr Jones is waiting on you in our lounge, if you would just follow the boy.' The man banged his hand on the desk bell and almost simultaneously a tiny bellhop appeared. Although the boy was very small his uniform was even smaller, the trousers finished a good two inches above the black boots, but he smiled cheerfully at Thomas as he ushered him into the mediocrity of loomed tapestry-covered chairs and machine-lace doilies that rejoiced in the title of Residents'

Lounge. Thomas tipped the boy a few pennies as he took in the new, older Luke Jones who put down a newspaper and rose to greet him.

The years had been kind to Luke, Thomas thought. In his youth the man had had an almost gypsyish appearance, now there was a sleekness in the dark hair that was greying at the temples and the healthy bronzed skin that was at once opulent and strong. Luke must be nearing fifty, just a few years older than Thomas himself, but Thomas had a feeling that Luke's lifestyle was a lot faster. He did not have the appearance of a middle-aged married man; in fact, if Lucinda had been with him, Thomas would have felt that she might need protection from such an obvious charmer.

'Thomas, I can't tell you how pleased I am to see you!' Luke shook hands firmly, goodwill sparkling in his dark eyes. The twang of his transatlantic accent matched the dashing cut of his coat. 'It was good of you to come out of your way to meet me here. I would have liked to visit you at Reason Hill, but there are too many memories down there for me. I still feel the lure of the old country at times.'

Thomas doubted if Luke really thought of the sleepy lands of Kent overmuch, but he acknowledged the civility of the greeting. Having accepted the offer of a whisky and soda Thomas sat down and waited. Luke had been most persuasive on the telephone, he had said there was money in 'a venture' he wanted to discuss. Thomas would be interested if there was, for however much he disliked admitting it to himself, he was stretched for liquid cash.

'I understand you've acquired a distillery, Thomas?' Luke began and Thomas's heart sank. One word loomed instantly in his thoughts: 'prohibition'.

'I bought two, actually,' he replied. 'I picked them up for next to nothing during the war.'

'Yes,' agreed Luke, 'I expect you did.' He'd kicked

himself for not doing the same, for not seeing the opportunity. The only excuse he had was that he had been overwhelmingly involved during those years in assembling the foundations of his fortune. Luke had flourished in the cut and thrust of America. He'd begun in New Orleans where his gypsy looks and fluent French had given him a head start, then he'd uprooted to Chicago, the big time. He had made himself powerful enough to exist in relative peace and harmony alongside the Mafia-based gangsters, but every now and again he liked to perform them a service, a gesture of goodwill. That was why he was here now. It would be an excellent move, he reckoned, to ship a boatload of good Scotch whisky to his friends and acquaintances. Thomas, he was sure, could be just the man to supply it and, after all, Thomas owed him.

'But how rude I'm being,' Luke struck himself on the thigh, a gesture of apparent disbelief at his own stupidity. 'I should have asked at once, how is your beautiful wife, Lucinda, and those lovely children I hear she's given you?' That was the debt he could call: he'd been the one who'd saved Lucinda from drowning, many many years ago, and she'd gone on to marry Thomas, spurning Michael and his title. Thomas would owe Luke until his dying day; after all, it had been Luke who'd put Lucinda, quite literally, into Thomas's arms in the isolated barn. That had been the night that they'd become lovers, began their future together. Luke smiled, showing his perfect strong white teeth.

The two men talked for over an hour. They talked in veiled terms, but understanding each other. Thomas explained how he could not, under any circumstances, allow himself to be seen to be involved in illegal whisky running to the US. He had ambitions that made it essential he avoided such risks; Luke did not have to be a genius to appreciate that Thomas was aiming for a knighthood. The farmer was being charitably disposed to his poorer brethren and lending himself for public service, all things that could end with the final, great accolade. And, of course, being the kind of man he was, he no doubt wanted to provide his wife with the title she had thrown over for his sake.

Luke was content with the meeting. He had sown in Thomas's mind the seeds of avarice. There were fortunes to be made flouting the prohibition laws, quick fortunes. Thomas wouldn't have stayed for over an hour if he hadn't wanted to sound out the possibilities. That meant that Thomas might not be as financially sound as he would like to appear. Luke saw his visitor to the door of the hotel and smiled to himself as he walked back to retrieve his hat from the lounge. It would be easy enough to find out Thomas's position; he would start this afternoon. After giving the receptionist the promised five pound note that had bought him the services of the reception room for the morning, he stepped out into the London backstreet and, walking swiftly, soon found a cab. He sank back into the seat and relaxed. Soon he would be at his hotel. He would get his secretary to set up some enquiries, then he would be just in time for his lunch date with a delicious young starlet who was setting the town alight. The doorman of the Dorchester stepped forward to open the cab door and saluted respectfully: Luke was always a generous tipper.

Isabella steered the car in to the side of the road and stopped to read the signpost. She was glad of a brief respite from driving and rubbed hard on the base of her neck. It was aching, and she would be stiff as a board tomorrow. *Boscastle three miles*, painted in peeling black on white; thank goodness, she was nearly there. Evening was coming quickly. She slid the engine into gear and with a quick glance over her shoulder pulled out into the crown of the narrow road. Above her the sky was still a deep bright blue but ahead, on the horizon where the sea must be, she could see the dark gathering clouds of night.

She was so tired that she wound the window down beside her, needing the air to keep her from dozing. There was a tang of salt on the breeze, vital and invigorating. She gave the car more throttle as it slowed on the increasing gradient. On either side of her loomed hedges of wind-swept blackthorn that leaned drunkenly back towards the land, away from the sea wind that rushed in at her. She reached the brow of the hill at last, there was a bend in the road, and then suddenly, magnificently, stretched out before her there was the sea. She slowed to a crawl, rejoicing in the glory of it all. The sea was a deep slate blue, touched with purple shadows that stretched off to the far horizon where fat cushions of dark clouds piled on top of each other to reach up to the clear celestial blue.

Isabella let the car roll to a stop, and pulled on the handbrake. It was so beautiful it was breathtaking. Opening the car door she got out stiffly, stretching her arms up, delighting in the freedom of the wind around her. At once she was in a new land. There were crows cawing, crying their passage home, and there was a brief bleating of sheep from far off, carried to her on the wind. It was all so alive, all of it moving, grass heads tossing, the bushes bending. It was impossible for her to stand motionless, she must hurry down into it, to become a part of the village that she could just see nestling in the fold of hills that made the valley below her.

The car seemed to soar down the narrow lane, she was almost afraid at their speed. What if something was coming up out of the village towards them? But it was impossible in her present mood to slow down, she was exhilarated by the rush of the high banks and drawn by the stone cottages rushing up to meet her, smoke from their crowded chimneys scenting the evening air.

She drove on, past the high-faced grey stone pub, the comfortable-looking hotel and then on to the track beside the fast-running river, always towards the sea. The car jolted on the uneven surface and eventually she brought it to a standstill. Very slowly and deliberately she reached forwards to turn off the engine. She sat for a moment, leaning back in the seat, willing the pain away from the base of her neck as the engine cooled and the clicking metal kept her company. But she couldn't wait; there was still enough light to see her way. The way that Michael had described to her in his letter, when he'd written telling her of the cottage he had rented for them. She stepped out on to the rough flint track and closed the door gently behind her. Protected from the winds, deep between the hillsides that led steeply up behind the precariously banked cottages, she was immersed at once in the peace of it all. She looked along the regulated rows of houses, doll-like in their neatness, facing each other over the river beside her. She began to walk, her stride free and unrestrained. The thought of the open sea beckoned her, but she must get beyond the towering hills that cupped the harbour ahead of her in a giant embrace. The tide was out and granite dark rocks reached into the tiny harbour to stand proud in the smooth grey-green mud. There was a sprinkling of boats leaning crazily, high and dry, their mooring ropes looped to the harbour wall. She walked on until the path ended and she could go no further but the view ahead was still blocked by the bulk of the harbour wall that had been built on the far side of the river from her. She realized now that she should have walked on the other side. From here she couldn't see out to the open sea. For an instant she considered retracing her steps, crossing the stone bridge she could see back beyond the car, but then she smiled.

She was acting like a child, the sea would still be there tomorrow. She took a last look at the gulls searching diligently in the pools on the harbour bottom, disdaining to acknowledge her presence, then she turned and walked back. It was all so utterly peaceful, she felt as though she were coming home.

Mrs Blewitt, the farmer's wife who rented out a few properties to summer visitors, had prepared the tiny cottage beautifully. The small front room smelt of polish and flowers, the kitchen that led off it was shining with a new coat of blue paint and sweet with the appetizing aroma of apple pie.

The rosy-faced countrywoman led the way upstairs, pointing out the advantages of the back bedroom over the front. The front, said Mrs Blewitt in her strong Cornish accent, was a lovely room that got the morning sun, but the road outside was used by the fishermen and that meant Her Ladyship might be disturbed at any hour of day or night, depending on the tide.

Isabella had smiled on meeting her landlady, smiled at the cheerful warmth of the woman and at the excitement obviously fluttering in the ample bosom at the prospect of having a lord and lady staying in her cottage. Mrs Blewitt had taken it upon herself to organize a girl to clean, and meals would come from her own kitchen. Isabella was efficiently silenced when she ventured to suggest that she was quite happy to prepare her own meals; clearly she was going to have a lot of time on her hands.

She slept soundly on the goose-feather mattress, not waking until noises below her proved the presence of 'the girl'. She lay in bed, putting off the moment of getting up, like a child saving the best morsel on the plate until last. She was so excited to see it all, eager to get out and explore her surroundings; to begin was almost more than she could bear.

* * *

Isabella was allowed three days of perfect freedom until Mrs Blewitt arrived shortly after breakfast, flustered to be the bearer of an important telephone message that announced the imminent arrival of Victoria. 'She's being put on the Truro train, arrivin' three o'clock this afternoon,' the farmer's wife announced with obvious total belief in the timekeeping abilities of the Great Western Railway.

Victoria! Of all people to visit her, Isabella could think of no one less likely to enjoy the isolation of the rugged coast walks and the delicious simplicity of Mrs Blewitt's cooking. Still, there was no point in allowing the flood of irritation to engulf her and ruin the few hours she had left. Isabella issued instructions for the front bedroom to be made ready for the visitor, and then changed her mind quickly. Victoria would not take kindly to being woken by the fishermen using the road; Isabella would have to move into it herself, and Victoria could sleep on blissfully undisturbed in the back room. In fact, and Isabella smiled at herself for thinking it, Victoria might well sleep on into the mornings and give her aunt some peace.

Isabella still had time for one last solitary walk up on to the headland that she had come to love, and she pulled a thick shawl around her shoulders. The light wool dress she was wearing was warm enough for the village in the sunlight, but up on the headland the wind tore at mere mortals.

She had villagers to acknowledge on her walk through the village – she was now known and identified. Further on, as she reached the great rounded boulders that made the sturdy harbour, she nodded to the fishermen busy at their nets. The tide was nearly full and several of the boats were already out at the lobster pots. She climbed the steep steps leading up on to the high back wall of the breakwater and gained the view of the open sea, which was briskly choppy. She stood, as had become her habit, for several minutes watching the run of the waves along the base of the mustard lichen-splashed rocks that stretched down into the sea itself. Opposite her the high bluff rose, rough granite breaking out amongst the short sparse grass that was littered with grey-green cushions of thrift. There were similar plants around her feet, their once pink flower heads dry and brittle, cream-coloured, bleached by the sun and wind. The bore was not sounding yet, it needed a little more height in the tide for the spout of water to emerge from the rock face like a sounding whale. Then it would erupt with the grumbling roar of a sleeping giant that always stirred a deep primitive fear in Isabella that was followed swiftly by amusement at her own stupidity.

She turned her back on the water to face the rough-cut steps in the flaking rock. She was careful where she put her feet. A slip would be dangerous, and there had been accidents on the heights that guarded the entrance to the harbour. She breathed steadily as she climbed. Each day she became more agile. She put a hand down to steady herself as she crossed a loose piece of the path, revelling in the touch of the raw, elemental earth. She would not think of Victoria, would not think of any of them, this was a place to recharge herself and herself alone. It took nearly half an hour to reach the spot she'd been aiming for, where the path sunk back into the hillside and considerate hands had positioned a rough bench. She sat on it gratefully, her knees trembling as always at the sudden realization of height. The sky above was a vast blue cavern dotted with careering fluffy white clouds that trailed brief black shadows on the hillside around her. A gull swooped swiftly in front of her, on her exact level and only some twenty feet in front of her. It hung, suspended on the wind while far below it the sea pounded mercilessly on the rocks. This was the essence of the wildness of the place. The bird was so close that she could see every detail, the yellow merging to orange of its bill, the quivering flight feathers, stretched wide and turning to maintain the bird's position. A few short feet away and yet, by the power of flight the bird touched a space that Isabella could never enter.

Flight: the word made Isabella think of Timmy. She was convinced that Lucinda must be imagining things. How could Victoria be in love with him? Her brow wrinkled in concern. Timmy had no blood ties with the Cade family, that much was true, and Victoria was insecure, confused. Lucinda should have sorted this out long ago. It was just like her to send the girl on to Isabella. Out of sight of her adopted brother was presumably meant to be out of mind; well, they would see about that. Isabella stood, the wind jerking at her shawl, making her feel suddenly precarious and she leaned back towards the hillside for its comfort. She would talk to Victoria, she decided, as she made her careful way back down to the harbour. She would bring the problem out into the daylight, and that would solve it. That was exactly the opposite to what she was doing about Lucinda's allegation about Michael. Not once, since she had heard how her sister had seen Michael with another woman had she allowed herself to consider that what Lucinda said might be true. She repelled any thoughts of his possible infidelity. That way, she convinced herself, neither the allegation, nor the possible affair, had any substance.

Victoria squeezed herself as tightly as she could into the corner of the seat beside the window. She loathed being on the train alone. Her mother had told her to have lunch in the dining car, but that would mean walking into the restaurant on her own and then sitting by herself. She couldn't bear the thought. Why was she being sent down to Aunt Isabella? Why, why? She knew perfectly well why, of course, the voice in her head answered her. It was to keep her apart from Timmy. She was talking to herself again, acting like two different people and she became locked into it as always, one half of her thoughts working against the other. The only time they were in accord was when she thought of Timmy.

She pressed her forehead against the chill of the window, oblivious to the countryside rushing past. It couldn't really be wrong to love Timmy as she did. Whatever anyone said, he wasn't her brother. She had real brothers, three of them, and she knew what loving them was like. She loved them because they were part of her, irritating, annoying, but like her and made from the same mould. It wasn't the same with Timmy at all. It wasn't unnatural what she felt for him, however much her mother threw out hints. Hints that were like great clods of earth. If the law said that it was wrong for her to love Timmy then the law was wrong, the law was an ass. There were a lot of things people did that were against the law and they weren't wicked people. She had seen men on the London social round who took other men as lovers, she'd seen them holding hands, even kissing at one of the more risqué soirées, and what was wrong in it, she queried, pressing her hot head even harder against the chill glass. Not that she'd want any of her brothers to be like that – it would be a shame not to get married, not to have children. She wanted that for them, and for herself. Something must happen about Timmy, something. She squeezed her eyes tightly shut, it was all so confusing; she forced herself to relax, dropping her shoulders, unclenching her hands. She would make Timmy run away with her, that had to be the answer. They could go far, far away where no one would ever know that once upon a time in a far too complex world she'd had to be brave enough to tell the man she loved how she truly felt. Because she would have to tell him, she saw that now.

Now that there was no Lucinda to go on at her, now that she had these hours alone on the train to think, Timmy would never be the one to make the first move, he'd be too frightened he might hurt her. But he would feel the same, she was sure he would, when he was set free, when he saw it really could happen. She remembered vividly how desperate she'd felt when they'd told her he'd married a nurse out in France. She'd wanted to die then, wanted to just stop living because it seemed he'd betrayed her. Then the news that that awful girl, the interloper, had been killed, it just proved even God had known she wasn't right for Timmy.

She jumped suddenly at the loud voice so close to her. 'First sitting, first sitting!' cried the red-faced, blue-uniformed guard, and having stared at her for what felt like for ever he went away. She was hungry, she realized. It was making up her mind to tell Timmy that had made her ravenous. She looked surreptitiously at the couple opposite her, middle-aged and middle-class. They were organizing their parcels on the luggage shelf, obviously about to go to lunch.

The woman turned suddenly to face Victoria. 'Would you like to come in with us, dear?' she asked. 'It's not always very nice being on your own on the train, is it? We've got two daughters about your age and I know neither of them would like it, so I just thought . . .' She paused, smiling encouragingly.

Victoria was taken by surprise and her voice answered before she'd had time to think. 'Yes, I will if you don't mind. That's very kind of you.' She stood to look in the mirror above her seat and check that her pill-box hat was still perched jauntily to one side.

She really hated being alone, she thought, as she walked along the corridor, nicely chaperoned by the older couple, one in front and one behind. She had the sudden realization of how different life would have been for her if she had had a sister. At home the boys had each other to share their secrets, and her mother's life was totally immersed in her husband. Victoria was the odd one out. The fact flashed past her, come and gone as fleetingly as the red-brick bridge that the train shot swiftly under. She and Timmy were two people alone living in the same house and it had never occurred to anybody how inevitable an alliance would be.

'How will you come down to Falmouth?' Michael shouted into the telephone. The connection to Kent was very bad.

'By train, there's no point in my bringing a car. After all, with any luck, I'll be up in the air most of the time.' Timmy was also shouting to be heard above the crackle.

'Don't get your hopes up too much, Timmy, I'm trying my best, but nothing's definite yet. See you next Monday.' It was a relief for Michael to put the receiver back on to its cradle. Timmy's call from Reason Hill had been the last of several and the connections had all been poor. He looked down at the heap of papers on the desk in front of him and then over at Bill who was working at the other desk, jacket off and shirt sleeves rolled up, despite the chill in the room.

'Sometimes,' Michael said, 'I regret that the telephone was ever invented.'

Bill laughed. 'Oh, yeah, and the typewriter and the car and everything else that we'd grind to a halt without. However, if I was to suggest that the same lack of invention meant there'd be no submarines, I guess it would be another story.'

Michael smiled. It was true, the submarine was quite different, that was a part of progress that he was happy to go along with. He stood up and went over to the window, drawing back the tattered black-out screen that was a legacy of the war. It was dark outside, and rain was splashing up against the window of the Nissen hut that they used as offices. Out there in the black, gusty night moored securely to the wooden jetty was the vessel that was the centre of their lives. He let the screen fall back and looked down at his watch. It was only nine o'clock, still time to get through some more of the mountain of paperwork that threatened to engulf him. He walked back towards his desk. The soft sports jacket that he wore over a checked Viyella shirt was as close to a uniform as any of them wore. He sat down, hitching the twill trousers up at the knees. It would have been easier in many ways if their group had been more regimented. At first it had seemed a good idea to pull together half a dozen experts and enthusiasts to pit their wits against the problematical air system that threatened to keep underwater boats as little more than short-term vessels. There had to be a way to keep the air fresh for several days underwater. A peaceful future depended on Britain having superiority on the sea – and under it – that was the concept that ruled Michael's life. But the reality of their research team was that the individuals were too casual in their approach, and without a strict hierarchy of command it was inevitable that Michael would have to deal with the boring, routine office work that the others simply ignored. If Bill hadn't pitched in he didn't think he would have managed at all. The reason for the American's enthusiasm could be heard over the sound of the rain drumming on the tin roof as Arabella typed in the small office next to them. Michael settled down to work again. He would try to do something for Timmy. It was a waste to keep such a talented pilot on the ground.

* * *

Timmy put the phone down and went back to the kitchen. The house was very quiet: Thomas and Lucinda were out for the evening, and Tom was outside in the workshop with Jonathan, working on his motorbike. Albert was alone in the kitchen, or at least he had been when Timmy had left to make his call, but now as Timmy opened the door quietly he found the seventeen-year-old very much not alone. He and Maggy were locked in a passionate embrace. Timmy was so surprised that he didn't say anything for a moment, then finding himself watching the boy's hand go to the girl's breast he coughed loudly. They were apart in seconds, Albert putting a hand to the wall beside him to steady himself while Maggy took a swift step away from him. Two flaming faces looked at Timmy who had absolutely no idea what to say. The silence seemed to go on and on, only broken by the sound of the coal burning in the range. It was Maggy who recovered first, turning from Timmy to look quickly at Albert, then darting out of the room through the scullery door. Her movement seemed to give Albert back his power of speech.

'You might knock when you come in, Timmy,' he said plaintively.

'Knock when I come in? To the kitchen?' Timmy could feel a grin spreading over his face, however much he tried to stop it. 'That's a good one, I'll tell the others, shall I? I'll say, right, now everyone's got to knock before they enter the kitchen, it's a new rule made by Albert because he's . . .'

Albert looked hard at Timmy, waiting to hear how his bit of fun would be referred to. But Timmy wasn't going to give him the chance to throw a temper. Instead he walked over towards the range and stood beside it, warming himself after the comparative chill of the hall, his smile faded.

'You know,' he said after a while, 'you want to be

careful. You make that girl pregnant and you'll have all sorts of trouble.'

Albert snorted. What did Timmy think, that he was some kind of idiot or something?

'I'm not going to lecture, or anything like that, but I'll tell you, man to man.'

Albert paid attention, attracted by the man-to-man concept.

'Sometimes you get started on something like that, a bit of kissing, cuddling, then suddenly it's impossible to stop. It can happen to any man, it's not a sign of immaturity or stupidity, it's human nature, Albert, and the only way not to get trapped by it is to keep out of dangerous situations. If the two of you get on your own then Maggy is dangerous, remember that.'

They were facing each other now, Albert still flushed with passion, Timmy very pale. It was a long time since he'd had a woman.

'I'm going down to Falmouth,' Timmy said, making his mind up suddenly. 'I'll go first thing in the morning. Michael says he might be able to get me a job.'

He would go to Isabella. She was at Boscastle and that was on the way. He would stay a few days with her and then continue on down to Falmouth. He was restless, he needed to get away from Reason Hill.

Victoria lay in bed, listening to the sounds of the girl washing the dishes in the kitchen beneath her. The prospect of another boring day loomed ahead. The carriage clock on her bedside table showed just past nine o'clock, and she was irritated by how slowly it ticked. She was sure time passed more slowly here than at home. Certainly it was slower than in London, where the hours just raced by. She wished she was in town now. It would be lovely to just wander round the shops, have a light lunch with a friend, then perhaps shop a little more before going back to Cadogan Gardens for tea to see who was visiting. But best of all would be the evening, she could go to a show with a boyfriend, then on to a party – a beautiful, wonderful party with lots of lovely people, and martinis, oodles of them, perhaps one of those special cigarettes that Eli got for her, super. She closed her eyes; it was easier to imagine she was there with her eyes closed.

She must have drifted back to sleep, for she woke suddenly at the knocking on the door. The cottage was so small that it resounded throughout it; it had been a very forceful knock, definitely a man's. Now who would it be? Victoria pulled a face. Would it be the dreadfully earnest curate? The man of the cloth with a neck like wrinkled crepe, or perhaps, even worse, the young doctor? She pulled another face, picturing the unutterably boring man of medicine with that awful mole on his face. It seemed that there were only two eligible young men in this God-forsaken hole that Isabella deemed it suitable for her niece to meet. Which one would it be? Victoria sat up so that she could hear better. The voice came to her, barely altered by its passage up the small twisting stair.

'Good morning. Is my aunt, Lady Montford, at home? I'm Timothy Cade, it's a surprise visit. She isn't expecting me.'

Victoria's heart stopped – she felt it, her hand went up to her chest. She was breathless, her head was pounding. Timmy, it was Timmy. She threw back the bedclothes and grabbed the embroidered silk wrap that lay on the chair.

'Timmy, Timmy!' she cried, running down the stairs in her bare feet, rejoicing in the chill of the air coming in at the open door. 'Timmy!' she threw herself into his arms, beside the surprised girl trying to explain where Her Ladyship could be found out on the headland. The girl had never seen a sister so happy to see her brother. She beamed her approval at them as Timmy, startled by the soft, pliant body pressing up against him, stuttered his surprise at finding Victoria there.

Isabella returned, as was usual, at a quarter to twelve. She was carrying a small basket containing several fresh mackerel that she had bought off one of the boats. She couldn't be bothered fumbling for the key in her bag so she knocked happily on the door, humming softly to herself. She turned, a smile ready on her face for Victoria, whom she expected to open it. Timmy stood there, stooping slightly in the low doorway, his handsome face smiling tentatively, suddenly unsure of his welcome. He should have warned Aunt Isabella he was coming, he realized that now as he watched the colour drain slowly from her cheeks.

Chicago

'But I assure you, Mr Montford, I do take it seriously. Killing is always serious. No one can be responsible for taking another life without feeling something. It doesn't have to be guilt but it has to be something, take my word for it, I know.'

'And you think I don't?' Johnnie sat very upright on the chair. He was concentrating very hard in the opulent office belonging to Tony Bertiolie who sat impassive behind his massive desk. Bertiolie was a dark, thick-set young man in his early twenties. He was young to be a managing director in any business, particularly young to be the head of a family liquor company that had been threatened with collapse under the strictures of prohibition. Tony's father had succumbed to the pressure several months ago when a chronic liver infection had forced him to retire, but Tony's uncle was still standing the strain, and he ran the property side of their enterprise, the blocks of squalid tenements with the crummy stores at street level.

Johnnie had made Uncle Bertiolie's acquaintance through a property deal when he had bought up a whole street ready for redevelopment, apart from one Bertiolie-managed block, and the tatty red-brick church of St Saviour's. The site was ripe and the Bertiolies had been willing to sell for a good price. They didn't like it when the Church hierarchy refused to sell their few hundred square feet and that compromised the whole deal. The church stood in their way, so they'd removed it. It had been simple, a few fire bombs blitzed the building itself and local pressure was applied so that the town councillors began talking of a new, far-seeing urban development a few blocks away that had, as they pointed out, the logical site for a new St Saviour's. A deal had been concluded that suited both parties. Johnnie and the Bertiolies; it was good business. The only blot had been the unfortunate demise of a vagrant sheltering for the night in the church doorway.

Now Johnnie wanted another Bertiolie-type deal, but he didn't want another killing. Tony Bertiolie chewed contemplatively on his six-inch cigar. He couldn't quite make the guy out. He appreciated that the Englishman was a dealer, a buyer and seller, putting together marketable parcels that he sold on the open marketplace through a nominee company. Sure, at times there had to be a little pressure, but that was only business. But the guy really didn't come over as the squeamish type, so why the hassle?

'Look, Mr Montford – ' Tony applied a beaming smile to his thick red lips ' – like I'm telling you, I suffered when I found out, not that I personally had anything to do with it, of course. You arranged your business with my uncle, he just put the job out to a few of the boys. Low-key stuff, but still the organization you approached was mine and I'm a responsible type of guy. We'll do more business together, I'm sure, but this . . .' He waved the letter that Johnnie had sent him, demanding that the Bertiolie company provided proof of double indemnity life insurance for any occupants, legal or otherwise, of properties they were involved with disposing of. 'This is just so much aggravation. You don't really expect me to do business on these terms, do you?'

'No,' said Johnnie, 'since you ask, I don't. But I wanted your attention, and now I've got it. You can give me the letter back if you like. Now we're face to face it's done its job.'

The Italian's eyes narrowed. 'I don't like being suckered,' he said.

'Then you should lean on your "boys" who did the job at St Saviour's. They suckered you, not me. The police put a lot more effort into investigating that fire than they would have done if only the building had gone up in smoke.'

'The police we can handle.'

There was silence in the room. Johnnie felt he had to get alongside the man opposite him. He needed a close ally on the other side of the fence, otherwise he would always be at risk. 'Let me put my cards on the table.' He adjusted his position on the chair; sitting still for long periods made his leg ache. 'My business is property, speculative property. I have a big stake and I'm prepared to take risks because it won't crucify me if I lose it. That's why I'm making a fortune, I can go for deals that a lot of others can't. What I do need is some coverage on the ground, I need to know if the area I'm interested in is too hot, the wrong person's patch, that sort of thing. Also, as you put it so succinctly, when it comes to the police, you can handle them. I need that.'

'So what do you offer?'

'Ten per cent of the action and, don't forget, I deal in hundreds of thousands, it's ten per cent of a lot, for what could be very little effort on your part.'

'You hit the wrong crowd to hustle and it could mean very much effort on our part.'

'That's the point. With you keeping me right I won't hit the wrong crowd.' It was silent again, but this was a companionable silence.

'Fifteen per cent.' Tony gave himself away by leaning forwards in his seat as he spoke, Johnnie could see he was expected to barter.

'Twelve and a half.'

'Done.'

Johnnie felt a surge of excitement. He'd been prepared

71

to go up to twenty. With his end protected he would make millions: the city was wide open.

'Let's have a drink.' Tony got up. Behind the desk he had looked a big man: on his feet he was squat, a broad muscled torso on short thick legs. He walked around his desk and over to the opulent sideboard laden with bottled mineral waters with the brand name 'Fountain', the legitimate cover for their illegitimate profits. He picked up a bottle labelled lemonade. 'Gin?' he asked, then held up one labelled ginger ale. 'Bourbon?'

An hour later Johnnie was at home. He stood in front of the framed map of Chicago city that hung on the wall and raised the glass in his hand in a private toast to success. His drink was a double measure of 'ginger ale' from the case that Tony Bertiolie had thoughtfully given him. The Italian had been considerate and attentive after the deal was agreed, considerate enough of his own affairs to tell Johnnie that the twelve and a half per cent would be split ten per cent to Bertiolie Beverages and two and a half to him privately. Attentive enough to offer Johnnie the services of the petite curvaceous blonde who was over-generously paid as a receptionist for the time she spent in the outer office painting her pretty pink nails. Johnnie had declined the offer and Tony had smiled in sympathy. 'So it's true what they say,' he'd said. 'You lost more than your face in the accident. It's as well,' he'd continued, the smile never slipping, 'that you'd already fathered your son. A nice-looking boy, a kid to be proud of.'

Johnnie had felt the lurch inside, and had only managed to whisper his question, 'How do you know?'

'We know everything, Johnnie, but then that's what you're paying us for, isn't it, because we know all there is to know. And don't look so worried, it's good that we have a reason to trust you. You don't want anything nasty

72

to happen to your son, and since we're friends and business partners neither do we.'

It was a hard world, a dangerous world, that Johnnie was moving in. He wanted to talk to Mary, to tell her how well he'd done, but he wouldn't say they knew about the boy. His face twisted as he looked at his distorted reflection in the glass. One day, he promised himself, one day he'd have an empire to give to his son, then the world could know of the boy's existence. But until then . . . He tightened his grip on the glass, the bitterness flooding through him. He had to have the world to give the boy, to make his son love him, despite his face, despite the fact that he was no longer a man. He squeezed tighter and tears began to run down his face. He didn't hear the knock on the door over the thundering in his head. It was over, never to love again, over . . . the glass shattered into slivers, cutting his fingers.

Johnnie stared down at the pain of it as Betsy came in. His mother-in-law was an old woman, but still capable. 'Jasper!' she called, standing back to let the hired help deal with the man who'd married her daughter. If she'd been younger she might have hated Johnnie for the wreck he'd made of the marriage but she was beyond such emotion, so she tolerated him as she tolerated the irritations of the decay of her own body. Besides, she smiled vaguely at Johnnie as he was helped out of the room, having him in the house was an interest, an entertainment for her. That reminded her, she would go and see Mary, tell her of the accident with the glass. She would enjoy seeing Mary panic at not being able to run to her lover, for Betsy knew that that was what they had been, lovers.

Bill pushed the tiller a fraction away from him. He was working to keep the little boat scudding along with the wind, revelling in the freedom of their speed on the water, rejoicing in the sight of Arabella, her face tipped back to catch the sun. Dark wisps of her hair were blowing madly where they had escaped from the scarlet scarf tied around her head. She was wearing a blue-and-white-striped jumper and blue slacks and loafers. Bill thought she was beautiful. He breathed in the salt air, tasting it, savouring freedom in every lungful. He closed his eyes to fix the picture of her in his mind. They had driven over to Helston, getting away from Falmouth and the others. They'd planned to tour the great house at Menabilly and then to take their picnic into the country and spend the afternoon lazing, but the day was too fine to stay on the land when the water beckoned so brilliantly.

It had been easy to hire the boat at a ramshackle jetty on the water. At first they'd sailed up and down Frenchman's Creek, looking at the herons roosting on the low branches of the multitude of trees that swept down to the water, but the wind had been fitful there so now they were out on the wider stretch of the Helford itself, close to the river mouth. Suddenly the wind changed and the sail cracked loudly, almost a gunshot, startling Bill who jerked the tiller too hard so that the boat dipped over alarmingly. Arabella's laugh rang in his ears as he struggled to right the vessel. They came almost to a standstill out in the water, far off from either bank. Then the sail filled, they were under way once more, and he realized what was missing from Arabella's outfit.

'Arabella, put your lifejacket on,' he said.

'I will not.' She turned to face him, her teeth flashing as she laughed again. 'I refuse to be hampered by it. Anyway it's a horrible, beastly thing. I don't want to look ugly.'

'You couldn't ever look ugly, Arabella, whatever you wear. Come on, put it on again, please.'

'No, I won't. But I'll tell you what, if you steer for that

dear little beach over there and don't drown us en route I'll give you the most delicious picnic you could ever imagine.'

Bill aimed as she directed him towards a small beach made of smooth grey stones leading back towards a wooded valley. He was annoyed with himself for the near capsize and concentrated to beach the boat efficiently and haul it up out of the water. His annoyance faded as they ate their picnic of cold duck and salad followed by apple pie.

The weather was generous to them: there was a real warmth in the air, and although the colours were of late autumn, it was easy to imagine, lying back on a rug with his eyes closed, that it was summer.

'Are you happy, darling?' Arabella snuggled close to him.

'I've never been happier in my life.'

'That's a very serious thing to say you know.'

'Yes.' There were more words he wanted to say, he was almost urged into them. He wanted to share his life with her, couldn't bear the idea of living without her, but the thought of Mary was there, stopping him.

'You know, Bill, you're looking very serious for someone who's never been happier.'

He turned over on his side to look at her, and their faces were very close. 'You're very young,' he said. 'Too young to get tied into a situation like this. You should be in love with someone your own age, someone who can ask you to marry them.'

'Ah, but then I'm not in love with someone else, I'm in love with you.'

It made his head swim when she said it, but he still felt he had to make her see that the road they were travelling could be the road to nowhere.

'It's dangerous to commit yourself, Arabella, you must

think very hard. I want you to be sure.' He had his hand on her waist, he could feel her breathing.

'I am sure, darling,' she whispered. 'I don't need to think any more, I love you and I want to be everything for you.' She rolled towards him, lifting her face to be kissed. He tasted the salt on her lips as she pressed her body towards him.

Almost unheard above the rush of the waves on the beach, cutting through the rustle of the wind in the trees, came the sound, soulful, willing on their passion, of the peacocks of Menabilly crying on the wind.

Victoria slammed the door of the cottage behind her. How dare Isabella, how dare she? A small chill wind blown down from the hills tugged at her hair and she pushed it back irritably. It was one thing her mother lecturing her, but an aunt had no rights at all, none. It was cold standing outside, Victoria would have liked to go back indoors and up to her bedroom, to throw herself down on her bed and howl in fury. But Isabella would set on her again, she was sure of it. She began to walk slowly away from the cottage, uncertain where to go, then an idea struck her and she began to walk with a purpose.

Isabella heard Victoria's footsteps going away down the road and sat down hurriedly. She could feel her heart hammering. She had never shouted at her own children, to lose her temper with Victoria had been ridiculous, childish, but she couldn't help it. It was quite obvious that the girl had not been listening to her. She had stood passive in the kitchen as Isabella began her attempt at righting the situation, and then obediently followed Isabella as she had gone through into the sitting room. But the girl's eyes had been vacant, not a word had sunk in, Isabella was quite certain of that. At least Timmy was away for the day. He had driven over to Exeter to collect a tractor part for the farmer, Blewitt, happy to have something to do. Thank heavens, thought Isabella, he'd had the sense not to ask Victoria to go with him to keep him company. For a moment Isabella considered going out after Victoria and calling her back – the girl had obviously been upset – but what was the point in apologizing to her? Victoria must accept what she was being told. This whole business of mooning around after Timmy was nonsense.

At exactly the same time as Isabella decided to wait for Victoria to come back to the cottage of her own accord, Victoria was boarding the bus to Launceston. She was smiling as she stepped up off the pavement. The postmistress had been so understanding about Lady Montford's niece forgetting her purse, and had quite agreed what a shame it would be for her to miss the bus, after all there wasn't another for two hours. The two pounds that Victoria had been offered as a temporary loan were more than enough for her needs, and she took her seat beside a young mother with a toddler on her lap and several parcels that hung from her arms. Victoria smiled to herself. The woman was decked like a Christmas tree, but the little girl she clutched was sweet. The child had fair hair, bright blue eyes and pink cheeks. She wore a neat blue coat with a velvet collar, long white socks that ended just below her chubby knees and smart black boots. She would have looked quite at home in London. The mother, Victoria decided, was quite different. With her voluminous rough tweed coat, handknitted gloves and hat and a nose reddened from a streaming cold, she could have existed nowhere but in this Godforsaken spot.

Victoria peered out of the window beside her; she had to rub a clear patch in the condensation. It was so crowded on the bus, she would catch that beastly woman's cold, and she listened in irritation to the vigorous nose-blowing going on beside her. The trip was endless; at each hamlet and village the bus lumbered to a halt, and then equally slowly pulled off again. The only good thing about the journey was that it took her further away from Isabella.

At last they pulled into Launceston. The bus disgorged its occupants and Victoria could see why it had been so crowded – it was market day. Her spirits rose, there was life all about her. Filling the greystone town came the cries of the marketholders, the chatter of the women and the earnest low voices of the multitude of old men who thronged the crowded square. It might not be London, but at least it was life.

She thrust her hands deep down into the pockets of her jacket and began to walk around the perimeter of the market. There were shops fronting the pavement, a shoe shop and a butcher's with a queue stretching out past the door. She walked on further, until she was amongst the vegetable stalls. There were piles of dark green cabbages and mountains of cauliflowers with perfect cream curds peeping shyly from their overcoat of leaves. Next came the turnips, terracotta-coloured from the soil they grew in. She paused to look at them, their bulbous redness making her think of the pottery flasks she'd seen heaped on a market stall in Italy. It had been warm in Italy, she remembered. Then she saw a stall laden with pasties, the golden pastry crescents immaculately laid out on flat wicker baskets. The table beneath them was covered with a red-and-white cloth, and the stall was presided over by a handsome woman who slowly wiped her hands on a bright white cloth that was as pristine as the apron she wore. The smell of the pasties hung on the air. Victoria sniffed at it and remembered she hadn't had any breakfast. She hadn't thought of it till now. There must be a café somewhere. She'd like a coffee and a bun, not a pasty though; however delicious they smelt they were much too big to eat. She looked around, trying to see through the throng and then she saw an awning hanging out over the pavement further up the street. It looked prosperous with its scarlet scalloped edging and smart black and white paint. Most attractive of all was the sign swinging in the wind declaring the presence of the Tudor Coffee Shop. She made her way towards it.

It was a prestigious double-fronted building with two wide plate glass windows. Behind the first window was an arrangement of mouthwatering cakes and pastries to tempt the passer-by, behind the second were damask-clothed tables busy with customers. There was a steady stream of people going into the shop and Victoria followed them. Inside it was unbelievably crowded. A bustling waitress shouted out above the hubbub as she laid tea and scones in front of a family of seven. 'Full up, no waitin' inside.' There was a general confusion as those who'd ventured far into the shop tried to make their way back to the door, but more would-be partakers of refreshment were still trying to come in, jostling Victoria who was tired, exhaustion sweeping over her; she hadn't slept well and she needed a cup of tea.

'Victoria! Hey, Victoria!' She looked around startled, but of course it couldn't be, then he called again, 'Victoria!' Her face broke into a smile. It was Timmy, he was here. Like a miracle he reached into the scrum and pulled her out. He had a tiny table to himself, wedged in beside the till and within minutes she was sitting down, clutching a precious cup of tea and smiling at him.

'What on earth are you doing in Launceston?' he asked. 'I couldn't believe it when I saw you jammed in with all that crowd. It's busier here than in London – incredible isn't it?'

Victoria nodded her agreement happily. 'I was just beginning to feel desperate when you found me.' She paused, then continued, 'I . . . I'm here because I had a tiff with Aunt Isabella. I thought it would be a good idea if I cleared off, got out of her way for a bit, you know.' She felt uncomfortable. Probably Aunt Isabella would be worrying by now and that wasn't very nice, but still . . . She looked down into her cup, trying to hide her blushing cheeks, they always went pink when she felt guilty. Still, Isabella should mind her own business. 'Anyway, what are you doing here? I thought you'd be miles away by now.'

'So did I, and it's a pity you chose today to come to blows with Isabella because, well, not to put too fine a point on it, I've dented her car.'

'Oh, no!'

'Oh, yes! And I feel a complete fool about it, but I don't suppose that's going to make her feel any happier. It's the offside front wing and although it isn't affecting the driving it looks a hell of a mess. The stupid thing is that it was absolutely my fault. I pulled up behind a lorry that I didn't realize was parked, so the driver beckoned me round.'

'And you hit something coming towards you?'

'Don't interrupt, Viccy, I want to get it quite straight to tell Isabella, so just shut up and listen.' He grinned at her as he said it, and she grinned back. She felt deliciously warm and cosy chatting away in their corner as the whole world went about their business around them.

'What happened next was quite simple. I looked back over my shoulder to check there was nothing behind me, and,' he began to laugh, remembering it all, 'I put my hand on the brake to let it off, and I put my foot on the reverse pedal – at least that's what I thought I did. Now, I'll admit to you, but no one else, that I wasn't exactly concentrating at that point. I was feeling rather good, out in the car on my own, it's really very nippy and I was driving along with the hood down, feeling distinctly chipper. So as I said, I looked back over my shoulder, did my bit with my hand

and foot, and – ' he paused for effect ' – drove smack into the back of the lorry in front of me.'

'What?'

'Yes, I did, you should have seen the bloke's face. He was livid. He came hurtling round, swearing something rotten. At least I think he was swearing, his accent was so thick I could hardly understand a word.'

'Sssh!' Victoria put a finger up to her lips, she was shaking with laughter.

'Oh, yes, well, where was I?'

Victoria couldn't believe the change in Timmy. He was so happy, bright, being a bit of an ass, she hadn't seen him like this for years, no, that wasn't right, she hadn't seen him like this ever.

'Anyway, the thing is, the wing's dented, and it's going to send our auntie into a tizzy and cost me a packet. I'm so glad you're here, Victoria.' He leaned over the table towards her, covering her small hand with his own, 'It's so much better to have company, isn't it?'

'Yes it is, isn't it?' And Victoria sang inside; she had never been happier, never.

They worked out their tactics on the way home. Timmy had a very healthy respect for his aunt and, as he pointed out, there was the fact that Isabella and Victoria had already had a set-to. Eventually they decided that discretion was the better part of valour. Victoria would go straight back to the cottage and Timmy would stay out until later. Then he wouldn't have too long to face Isabella's temper.

Isabella sipped at the cup of tea she had made to give herself something to do. Her fingers were drumming on the kitchen table as she tried to keep her temper from boiling over. Victoria had been away for over five hours now. By sheer good fortune the postmistress had been almost the first person Isabella had talked to when she had gone out to look for the girl hours ago.

So, Victoria had taken herself off to the market. If Isabella had not found out where she'd gone then it was quite conceivable, after several hours, that there would have been search parties out on the cliffs. The weather was closing in and Isabella could imagine it all. She would have been convinced the girl had done something dreadfully foolish, and there would have been men out on the sea in a gale, trying vainly to find a silly girl who'd gone off in a huff. Isabella put her cup back on its saucer, rattling it sharply. She was quite, quite furious and the bus that brought the villagers back from market would be another hour yet. By then she would be livid.

Earlier than she had expected there came a timid knock at the door. Isabella rose to answer it and looked out of the window as she went through the sitting room. It was almost dark outside. What a stupid, stupid girl.

'Aunt Isabella.' The girl stood in front of her, smiling tentatively. 'I bought you these.' She held out the bunch of chrysanthemums that Timothy had suggested as a peace offering. Victoria's smiled faltered at the anger visible on Isabella's face.

'May I come in, please?'

Isabella stood back from the door to let the girl pass and then slowly closed it. She turned and followed her niece into the room.

'Where have you been?' she asked.

'I went to Launceston, to the market.'

'How did you go?'

'On the bus, I . . .' Victoria was about to say she'd had money with her when she left the cottage, but then thought better of it. 'I borrowed the fare from the postmistress.'

'And what did you do in Launceston?'

'Oh, this and that, I had a cup of tea first and then I

wandered round, eventually I had something to eat, then I came home.' I had the most glorious day of my life, she thought, I was with Timmy, all alone, he and I, and we laughed and laughed.

'And what did you think I would do all this time? Did you bother to think if I would be worried about you?' Isabella's voice was on the point of trembling with the fury inside her.

'I hoped you wouldn't. At first I didn't think, I was just too cross, you see. Then on the way home I wondered, but I hoped you'd have the sense to realize I'd just got away, out of Boscastle, just gone away for the day.'

'Have the sense? You hoped I'd have the sense? I despair of you, Victoria, I honestly do. I had hoped that beneath that veneer of sophistication you insist on assuming there was a real person. Someone who considered the feelings of others, who had a decent sense of responsibility. But you haven't and I'm very sorry, but I'm going to give up on you. At the end of the week you must go home to Kent. I shall telephone your mother and insist on it. Tomorrow I shall be out all day and Timmy will be with me. You shall have a whole day to think what a very silly girl you have been, how many poor souls might have risked their lives in this horrible weather.' Isabella gesticulated with her hands up towards the wind that was tearing around the roof. Her aunt really was extremely angry, Victoria realized, though what she was talking about it was impossible to guess. A sharp knock at the door interrupted them. Victoria took a quick step towards the stairs. She had no intention of being there when Timmy told his tale of woe.

'I'll go up to bed, Aunty, if you don't mind. I have the most awful headache, and I think, all things considered, it would be better if I went.' She went quickly from the room, dashing upstairs as Isabella let Timmy in. She locked her bedroom door and pulled her clothes off as quickly as she could. She hummed tunelessly to herself, determined to drown the voices below her. She didn't want to hear the row about the car. It was cold in between the sheets so she wriggled, trying to warm herself. She quickly pulled a pillow over her head. There! She couldn't hear a thing now, they could argue all night if they wanted. But it wasn't very long before she heard the door slam which must mean that Timmy had gone off to his lodgings. She snuggled down into the bed. It was warm now, she really was tired and she did have the faintest headache. It would be better in the morning.

Thomas closed the ledger on his desk with a slam. There was no getting away from it. Whilst his fixed capital position was sound, he was dangerously low on his working facility. He could remember when Lucinda's father, Eli, had come perilously close to financial collapse and, although the Cade empire was in no way as exposed as his father-in-law's had been, there was certainly a similarity. Several years ago Thomas had moved his bank accounts to London. It would probably be quite easy to enlarge his borrowings; he found his new bankers approachable and easy to talk to although that was what was bothering him. Now the only limits put on his enterprise had to be imposed by himself. There had been many years when outside influence had restricted him and he'd chafed at that, but he could see in retrospect that opposition had sharpened him, made his decisions more finely thought out. Now it would be too easy a matter to go astray.

He stood up, feeling claustrophobic in the farm office, although he could see out through the window in front of him to the vista of rolling orchards that was all his property. His sense of niggling unease was heightened by the fact that he knew what was causing it. For several days he had been putting off dealing with correspondence concerning Albert's farm. He always thought of the block of land around the weaver's house at Tenterden as Albert's even though it was still his by title. The over-generous offer that had been made for the property was the ideal answer to his present financial predicament. The amusement that he had felt when he received it had swiftly changed to interest that had then been tempered by annoyance at himself for even considering disposing of the acres that Albert thought of as his own. It was an American who had made an offer for the property. He was the descendent of a family of weavers who had long ago lived and died in the black-and-white timber-framed house. Now he was a self-made man of wealth and he wanted to preserve what he thought of as the family home as a kind of shrine to their memory. What with that American and Luke it seemed that the New World was intent on intruding on Thomas's peace of mind. And it was his peace of mind that was disturbed. The fact that Reason Hill would pass to Timmy was long-established, it had been a decision taken many years ago and one that Thomas had never regretted. But in accumulating farms for his other sons Thomas could see that now he should never have designated the blocks of land to the boys until they had come of age. He needed to be free to buy and sell to keep ahead. As it was, he was chained with too many static acres. He walked thoughtfully out of the room, closing the door on the ledgers and letters, but carrying them in his head. He would have to decide something, and it would have to be soon.

Lucinda heard Thomas's footsteps in the passage. She was trying to read as she waited for him in the kitchen, but the words on the page in front of her were little more than a blur. Her mind kept skipping away from the novel, so shocked had she been at seeing Michael with that woman. It was unbelievable that he of all men would be unfaithful to his wife. Isabella had dismissed Lucinda's allegations. It seemed she was prepared to discount the evidence of her sister's eyes. But the memory of Michael, so intent, was preying on Lucinda's mind. If Michael could stray then what about Thomas? With her overwhelming love for her husband Lucinda saw him as eminently more desirable to other women than her brother-in-law would be. Thomas was charming to the wives of his friends, she knew that, and she had always been pleased at the way he was fêted by the opposite sex. Especially now that they were becoming so heavily involved in charitable functions, they were mixing more and more with other wealthy members of the county. Amongst that set there were beautiful wives and beautiful eligible daughters all of whom might set their caps at her Thomas. That morning Lucinda had dressed more slowly than usual. After she had put on her stays she had surveyed the effect in the mirror. She was up in London often enough to know the modern, ideal shape, the slender, almost bustless outline that in no way resembled the generous figure reflected in front of her. Her skin was still good. She looked critically at her arms and legs. Their softness had hardly changed from when she was a young woman, but the outline most certainly had. She had put on her day dress with an air of abstraction; she had always been so secure in her self-belief that she had not noticed the extra inches, but had Thomas?

'Thomas, dear, would you like some tea?' Lucinda stood up quickly, smiling brightly as he came into the room.

'No, no, I don't think so. I'm going out. Don't expect me back before supper.'

Lucinda showed her dismay, 'Not before supper? But that's hours. Where are you going? We always have tea together on Wednesday afternoons.'

'Just out.' Thomas was irritated at himself. He had decided to go and talk to the resident manager at Albert's farm to see for himself if it was making any headway, or if the acres were going to waste.

'Can I come with you?'

'No, it's something I have to do on my own.' Thomas scowled at his feet. He hated deceiving Lucinda, but neither did he want her worried. This was something he'd have to decide for himself. He heard her sniff and looked at her, amazed to see her crying. 'What on earth's the matter?' He took her in his arms, holding her to him; he hated her to cry.

'It's nothing, I'm just being silly, but I look forward to Wednesday afternoons so much. Everyone's still at the market, even the boys don't come home till late, it's the only time we have alone together.' That wasn't strictly true, but it was how she felt at that moment. She felt that if he left her now, it was an omen, an omen that he would be led astray by a pair of younger eyes.

'You're sure you're not sickening for something?' Thomas ran his hand over her forehead to see if it was hot. 'You hardly ate a thing at lunch.'

'Yes, well, I tried not to. I'm trying to lose a little weight.'

Thomas let go of her in his surprise, 'Lose weight, what on earth are you doing that for?'

'I thought you might like it, I thought I should try and look slim, you know, like the models.' Lucinda's cheeks were flushed. She was all set to cry again if Thomas made the wrong answer.

'What an imbecile you are!' He walked swiftly to the range and banged the kettle down on the boiling-ring. 'Come on, you can help too,' he said. 'Get some bread out, and some jam, and we'll have fruitcake, or would you like an egg? I could boil you an egg. I can still do that, you know.'

Lucinda laughed happily; Thomas's concern was wonderful.

'I would love an egg,' she said, 'with bread soldiers, like the children used to have.'

'Then that's just what you shall have, and always remind me,' Thomas said, 'if I ever think of abandoning you on a Wednesday again that this is the "only time we have on our own together",' and he laughed, happily, throatily, and Lucinda realized how silly she'd been and how lucky she was. Not like poor Isabella, she thought, and her self-satisfaction made her bloom, to look ever lovelier in her husband's eyes.

Timmy had been adamant with Isabella. He had made his apologies for damaging the car and promised to pay for its repair, but he did not want to drive down to Falmouth with her. He would be going there on Saturday and, as he pointed out, with luck these last few days would be the only holiday he would get for months. Isabella would have to go on her own, or not at all. Of course, she had to go to see Michael, and Timmy was the last person she could tell why. Michael was the only person who could talk to Timmy, and first she must explain the situation to her husband face to face. Thinking out what she must do had made Isabella realize how close Victoria came to being reasonable. Timmy was not a child of the Cades, whatever the law had made him when Thomas had insisted on a formal adoption. Blood will out and there was no blood tie between Victoria and Timmy. They were less joined by nature than if they were cousins and cousins, after all, could marry. It was all desperately difficult. Isabella was convinced that someone must speak to the boy and it couldn't be his father, Thomas, or it could cause a rift that would make it impossible for Timmy to live normally at Reason Hill, as was his right. She hurried through her preparations for the journey. She should not be thinking in terms of blood ties: that was where Victoria had become confused. Timmy was a Cade as much as Tom and Albert were, but . . .

As Isabella pulled hard on the steering wheel to negotiate the hairpin bend she glanced down at the village she was leaving behind. She could give the jumble of grey roofs no more than a quick look because the turn was dangerous with a granite rock face rearing up to one side of the road and an almost sheer drop on the other. As the road wound higher she breathed a sigh of relief. Perversely, she was looking forward to the journey, to the drive itself. Fortunately the damage Timmy had done to the car was only superficial. The front wing would have to be repaired, it looked a mess, but it didn't affect the driving. She had a map handy on the passenger seat, as well as a packet of sandwiches and a Thermos flask of tea. At last she was on her own. Since Victoria had arrived it had seemed that even the cliff walks were haunted by her presence. No, that was unfair, Isabella smiled to herself, she was becoming paranoid about the poor child. And Victoria was a child, that was part of the problem. She might be a young woman in years, but her emotions were still unformed. It was such a difficult age to grow up in. Inevitably Isabella had come across the flappers, the gaunt little creatures who pursued their pleasures with squeals of delight, showing off their long thin legs, and gawky charms. It was all so mad. London had changed beyond all recognition, at least the social life there had. Once, long ago, Isabella had sought refuge in London, she'd gone into the heart of it, becoming absorbed in its crowds and noise. In those days she hadn't felt a stranger, hadn't seen Londoners as a breed apart, but today she felt an alien in her own city. That was quite ridiculous: she and Michael had a house there, of all people to belong it should be them.

The road stretched out ahead of her. Her thoughts of Victoria had taken her through the winding narrow lanes that led away from the Atlantic coast; now the countryside was open around her with the dark hills on the skyline that were the heartland of Cornwall. On either side of her, stone-walled green fields dotted with sheep and scrubby cows sped by. It was Michael she was going to see and she must summon her thoughts. Michael. They had grown apart, she knew that. The physical separation of the war years had begun the process, but what had continued it? She tried to picture him in her mind, but it was a hazy representation. He was too familiar to her, and yet a stranger. She no longer knew what he thought, how he felt. But had she ever known? It was so hard to remember. The years they'd shared had been crowded. There had been Michael's rise in politics, always tempered by his strong beliefs, the standards he lived by. He never swayed to fashion, yet he'd done well, perhaps because he'd been lucky, for many of the views he'd held had been those that suited the Government. No, he would never have compromised, and Isabella would not have loved him so passionately if he had. Perhaps that was the problem. Had she loved him with too much passion? Would a more controlled, reasoned loving have been easier on them both? She still refused to believe Lucinda's nonsense. So what if Michael had seemed captivated by his beautiful companion; there were a thousand and one reasons why he should be in the company of a woman they didn't know, particularly one in uniform. Lucinda always overreacted. Isabella pushed the doubt away, submerged it in thoughts of what she must remember to say to Michael when they met. She was quite sure now that she was doing the right thing in going to see him unannounced. After all, each time he made plans to visit her at the cottage they had had to be cancelled due to the pressure of his work. This way he would have to stop whatever he was doing and they could have a little time together. She wondered, briefly, if they would have seen more of each other if she had stayed closer to Falmouth, but Michael had been so convinced that she would love Boscastle, as he had when he had been a child. In any case, it was too late to change things now. He would be delighted at the surprise and it would be like old times.

The moment Isabella walked into the office Arabella realized who she was. Michael's wife was all she had expected: quietly beautiful, elegantly but understatedly dressed and faintly aloof. The clear blue eyes that appraised Arabella showed acknowledgement but that was all. It would be difficult to be close to a woman like Lady Montford, Arabella thought in the instant before she spoke.

'Good morning, can I help you?'

'Yes.' Isabella smiled slightly, she must make a determined effort, although her face felt frozen into immobility. This was the girl that Lucinda had described, the one with Michael. It had to be. 'Yes, I'd like to see Lord Montford, I'm his wife.'

'Oh, Lady Montford! Please, sit down, won't you.' Arabella came quickly round her desk, acting as if she was surprised by Isabella's identity. 'I'm so sorry, I didn't know you were expected.'

'No, I'm not expected. I didn't tell my husband that I was coming.' Isabella took the proffered chair. She was feeling lightheaded. It was rather unreal, the girl was quite beautiful and very, very young. Isabella drew her gloves off slowly, her eyes dropping to her hands. She was quite proud of them, with her long, slender fingers, but she saw suddenly that they were not the hands of youth. She looked up at the girl who was still fussing around, making, it seemed, an unnecessary performance of settling Isabella comfortably, as if – and the thought would not be dismissed – as if she felt guilty.

'Oh dear, I do hope your journey hasn't been in vain, Lady Montford. That is,' she paused, then walked towards the telephone on her desk, 'how long are you staying?'

'No, I'm not staying at all, I came to see my husband today and then I'm driving straight back. I'm staying at Boscastle. It's a few hours' drive away and I want to get there tonight.'

'Yes, yes, I knew you were there.' Arabella spoke distractedly, she was busy dialling a number. Isabella sat rigid in her chair. Of course the girl knew she was there. The jealousy she'd smothered flamed suddenly. How very cosy for the two of them to be closeted down here together. She looked around the office, cutting off in her mind Arabella's voice on the telephone. It was bleak enough outside, the water flat and grey today, the myriad boats bobbing on a windswept bay, but no doubt when the sun shone it was splendid. The door opened behind her and she turned quickly. But it was not Michael, it was Bill.

'Good grief, Isabella!' He came forwards to her. 'What on earth are you doing here? No problems, nothing wrong is there? I mean everyone's all right at home, are they?'

'Yes, yes, everyone's all right. I came to see Michael, that's all.' She didn't miss the quick look that Bill shot at Arabella.

'But he's not here, Isabella, not today. We don't expect him back until Saturday at the earliest.'

'Won't be back? Where is he? I didn't expect him to be away. He didn't tell me.' Her voice hung on the air, querulous, irritating, she could hear the unpleasantness in it herself.

Arabella looked up from the telephone, raising her voice to attract Bill's attention. 'I thought I might catch Michael at Gweek, then he could have been driven back, but I don't think there's any luck.' Arabella stared back into the mouthpiece of the phone, concentrating on the voice on the line.

Michael, the girl had called him Michael. Isabella was stunned; she felt as though she had been physically struck.

'Hey, Isabella, you should have let us know you were coming.' Bill looked awkward, embarrassed, as well he might, Isabella thought, as well he might.

'I shall go back.' She stood stiffly.

'Won't you leave him a note?' Bill asked. He was concentrating on not letting Isabella see the relationship between him and Arabella. He'd been unprepared for her visit and she was the first of the family to see them together, except Michael, of course, who knew everything. Good old Michael, thought Bill, he's a great guy, must help him out. 'Look, Isabella, why don't I see if I can ease old Michael away from his desk this weekend. Get him up to Boscastle to pay you a visit, what do you say?'

Isabella's face was like stone. 'No, please don't bother, Bill. I shall be leaving for Kent in the next few days. That was what I came to tell him.' She drew in a deep, shuddering breath at the lie. 'Perhaps you would be kind enough to tell him that I shall be going back home.' She walked quickly from the office, not looking at Arabella. She didn't want to see the girl ever again.

Timmy knocked on the cottage door shortly after eleven o'clock. The girl opened the door to him. Yes, Lady Montford had left, and yes, Miss Victoria was at home, she said. He stepped into the small sitting room that was so different from Pencombe to find a Victoria who looked different too. She had got up from her chair to greet him

93

and was standing by the fire looking vibrant in a scarlet woollen dress that clung to her narrow hips and swirled round her knees. It had a mandarin collar and long sleeves, she was comfortable wearing it and relaxed, her smile was warm, she was quite unlike the strained, wraith-like creature she sometimes appeared at home.

'How about a picnic on the cliffs?' Timmy asked. He had been inspired by the sunlight that kept breaking through the grey clouds.

'That sounds lovely,' Victoria said. She was bursting with energy. Now that Isabella had left she felt the atmosphere had lightened miraculously. 'I don't know that there's anything we can take to eat, though.' She turned to go towards the kitchen, but Timmy stopped her.

'No, you don't have to bother,' he said. 'I ordered a hamper from the hotel. It should be ready to collect.'

'Oh, so you assumed I'd say yes, did you?' She laughed.

'But of course. I'm your favourite brother, aren't I?'

Victoria felt a sickening lurch. She didn't want to be reminded of the problems that would face them. She shook her head, making her short hair swing and then laughed. 'You take too much for granted, young man.' She meant his assumption that she would go out walking with him, ignoring his remark about brothers.

Timmy picked a plaid travelling rug off a chair and threw it over his shoulder. 'Now we'll have something to sit on. Come on, the sun will be warm by midday. Let's get up on to the cliffs.'

They walked down through the village to the hotel, where as Timmy had promised the picnic awaited them. It was packed into a small wickerwork pannier with a leather strap that he put over his shoulder. The sun was shining almost continually now, although a cold wind was still blowing off the sea. They walked back past the few shops towards the harbour, and almost everyone they saw offered a greeting. They were becoming part of the community now and Timmy realized how sorry he would be to leave.

The river was rushing its way to the sea, gurgling over the stony bottom. There were ducks on the water, frantically paddling against the current to stay at the edge where two small children were feeding them bread. Victoria walked on the springy turf that formed the narrow bank, while Timmy walked on the track beside her. Soon he began to whistle, tilting his head back to squint up at the sky and the seagulls wheeling high above them. He laughed out loud for the joy of the day. It was idyllic here and soon, with any luck, he'd be up there, flying like the birds. He laughed again and turned to look at Victoria. She was striding out, almost matching his long paces. The air had made her cheeks pink and it suited her. He didn't like the white stuff she normally put on her face, he liked girls to look pretty. He realized suddenly that she was pretty — more than that, she was beautiful.

They crossed the stone bridge, pausing for a moment to look down at the water beneath them, then walked on. After a while they turned off the track to take the path that led up towards the coastguard cottages overlooking the harbour. As they passed the first cottage a small dog rushed out into the front garden. It barked furiously and its feet scrabbled noisily for a grip on the rough stone wall that fenced the garden. A voice from inside the house called out and the barking stopped. When they looked back the dog had gained the top of the wall and it stood looking after them, head up to sniff the air for their alien scent.

The path became steeper as they left the wood smoke of the cottagers' fires behind them, and in places it had crumbled. Victoria's shoes were too flimsy for the rough ground and she slipped. Timmy put out a hand to help her up, and then it seemed only natural for him to keep hold of it, in case she fell. Around them the wind pulled hard at the low-grown heather. The purple was dull now, dried blooms of the summer past, but against the brilliance of the blue sky it made a natural tartan. The path curled down for a way and a panorama of the harbour spread out beneath them. It was Lilliputian, populated by tiny people who moved from miniature boat to cart, unloading fish that had come in on the high tide. The water sparkled blue-green against the grey of the harbour wall and a thin line of white showed where the waves broke on the seaward. Up on the hill they were high above the gulls swooping for fish offal thrown from the boats. It was as if they were above the world.

Victoria's skirt blew tight against her, the wool moulding to her figure. She breathed in the freedom of it all, closing her eyes, feeling safe with her hand in Timmy's. She leaned close to him for balance and he let go of her hand to put his arm around her; it was warmer like that. Timmy felt restored. He didn't give it conscious thought, but his body was relaxing, the lines in his cheeks softening. After a while they turned and walked on up the hillside, apart now but companionable, supported by each other's company. Neither of them would have rather been anywhere else in the world but there, with the sea wind blowing, the gulls crying and the vast magnificent view of bay after bay stretching to infinity, suddenly theirs as they reached the headland.

They stood for what felt like hours. Not thinking, but feeling, absorbing it all, the immenseness of the sea, the land that fell away in giant stepping stones.

It was almost noon, and the sun as warm as it would get all day. Timmy led the way along the cliff path, then verged off back towards the land where a hollow in the hillside offered shelter from the wind. He spread the blanket out on the short springy grass, and Victoria knelt and reached up towards him for the picnic basket. It was the first time they'd looked at each other since they'd left the headland. Slowly, Timmy got to his knees in front of her, laying the basket down beside him. He reached out his hands to her face, cupping it. She was truly beautiful he realized, her face a perfect oval, her eyes like almonds, her lips . . . and he bent to kiss her. There was a sweetness in their kiss that neither had ever known, a questing innocence. Timmy's eyes closed, sinking into the remembered warmth, it was so short a time – and yet so long – since he had felt this way. It was as if the wind around them stopped blowing, as if time was still. Timmy felt the heat building inside him, he pulled her closer and her mouth opened for him. Victoria, the name sang in his head, Victoria, then with a sudden cry he pushed her away. 'Christ!' he was up on his feet, 'Christ All Bloody Mighty, Christ!'

Victoria was shivering, cowering with the shock of the conflicting emotions. She looked up at him in fear, not knowing what he meant, how he felt, she was dumb, unable to talk, because she didn't know the words.

'We've got to go,' he said, pulling her up roughly to her feet, 'we've got to get away, out of this place.' He looked around him, as if suddenly hating the beauty of it all. 'Come on, quick, quick.' He grabbed at her hand, squeezing it painfully as he hurried her along.

She couldn't think, he was making her go too fast. The rough stalks of heather caught at her skirt, tugging at her. What did he mean, 'get away', what was he feeling? She couldn't see his face, only his back as he hurried on down the path. 'Get away,' he'd said, did it mean that he understood at last, they had to go far, far away to live their love? The cottages were a blur; the dog hardly had time to rush out of the door before they were gone. They almost ran along the riverside track. By the time they reached the edge of the village she was gasping painfully for breath. The few villagers they passed looked startled as they careered on, ignoring the greetings, Timmy's face set and pale, Victoria wild-eyed and windblown.

'Pack your things. Go on, hurry up.' Timmy almost pushed her down the path to Isabella's cottage, then he was running on, up the hill towards his lodgings. Victoria fumbled for the latch key under the flowerpot by the door. Her breathing was loud, her chest hurt. She hurried inside, running upstairs, throwing open the wardrobe doors, pulling out the drawers. She had to pack everything and she must hurry, hurry. She heard a car pull up outside in the road. No, no, it couldn't be Isabella, not yet. She looked desperately at her watch as she ran into the front bedroom to look out of the window, but it wasn't Isabella, it was Timmy, in a car she didn't recognize. He banged his hand on the horn and then clambered out as she was running down the stairs to meet him.

'Is this all?' He pulled the suitcase from her hand.

'No, there's another upstairs, I'll go back . . .'

'No, get in the car. Go on, hurry up.' He ran upstairs, taking them two at a time. She paused for a moment watching him and then turned and ran up the path and out into the car. Panic was making her tremble. They must get away before Isabella came back, they must. Timmy was back in the car while the crash of the cottage door slamming behind him still rang in her ears. He'd left the engine running and immediately they were off, picking up speed as they swooped down into the village, then labouring up the incline to get away.

'We've made it, we've made it,' she whispered.

'Don't say anything, don't say a word, just let me drive, God, just let me drive.' There'd been a catch in his voice, almost as if he was crying. Victoria sank down into her seat. They were leaving, leaving it all behind them at last. She felt as if a vast weight had been lifted from her shoulders. She didn't notice the hedges flashing past or the change in the countryside as they left the windswept fields of Cornwall for the somnolence of Devon. By the time they reached Wiltshire she was asleep, and she didn't wake until Timmy shook her shoulder and she realized they'd reached the end of their journey.

Isabella did not look back at Bill standing in the hut doorway, she just got into the car and slammed the door. It was as if she was returning to her shell. Back there in the office she'd been naked, defenceless and she'd been hurt, so terribly hurt. She drove away from the port, hardly seeing the other vehicles on the road, driving by instinct rather than thought. Tears were streaming down her face. She wiped her cheek with the back of her hand. She would never have believed it of Michael; her whole world was collapsing. Fragments of memories kept rushing into her mind, Michael going to war, his father breaking down in tears after they'd gone. Michael coming home, changed, old before his time, as it seemed they all were . . . Back to the early days, Michael such a young man, so handsome, risking everything for her love, winning and making her so proud. Michael, how could you do this to me? she thought; Michael, how could you?

The miles passed and she still felt frantic. What should she do, where could she go? She felt homeless, abandoned. Michael no longer loved her. Her eyes were drawn to her hands on the steering wheel. They were old, she thought, old. She clenched the wheel tightly and blue veins showed, so old. With a screech of their horn another car shot past her. She must concentrate, she might kill someone. She could kill that woman, she thought, pure venom making her face burn. How could anyone be so brazen?

As she reached the moors the rain began, lashing down and deluging the road that swam in front of her through the water-laden windscreen. The wipers slowed, ineffective in such a downpour. She would have to stop, she couldn't see. The car rolled to a standstill. She had just come down a small incline and the ground rose again in front of her. The rain hammered on the fabric of the roof. She dropped her head down on to her hands that were still convulsively gripping the wheel. How could he do it? Michael, Michael. She couldn't sit still for another moment. She pushed the door open and the wind blowing off the moor grabbed at it, almost wrenching it from her grip. She stepped out onto the road and the ice-cold rain pounded her. She leaned against the car for support, then let her head drop back, letting the rain wash the tears away, cooling her anguish.

She got back to Boscastle as the first lights went on in the village. She felt calm now, she had come to terms with the situation. She would stick by what she had said to Bill and go home to Kent. There was nothing she could say yet to Michael. She had no proof of his infidelity, none that would sound reasonable spoken out loud. The boys would be home from school for the half-term soon, and she had plenty to do getting ready for them. And now there was her own future to plan. The last hour of her journey had been devoted to that.

Once before she had mapped out a future for herself, she had planned a life of involvement with others less fortunate than herself, but she had never followed it. Now she could take the same path, but this time she had already taken some steps along it. Her activities with the Red Cross during the war had shown her how much the organization could do. At recent meetings she had called for more activity in peacetime. There were still British men, women and children living out their lives in poverty and squalor, such a cause could give a woman a reason for living. That was what she needed.

There was no point in her hurting herself, bemoaning the fact she was growing older. That was a fact and nothing would change it; she must come to terms with her new status in life. To remain immured at Pencombe when she had so much to give to life was a sin. Now she knew that there was no one who depended on her being there. Self-pity pulled her mouth down in new lines. The boys were so nearly grown and they didn't need her. Michael had made his choice.

She stopped the car in the road outside the cottage. She ran her hands up over her forehead, pushing up the hair that was still damp from the rain. She was uncomfortable in her crumpled suit and the car smelt unpleasantly of wet leather. But at least the rain had stopped. She got out of the car and looked at the cottage. She was surprised that there were no lights on in the windows. Perhaps Victoria was dozing by the fire. To her surprise the key was in the latch; Victoria was quite careless, she would have to be told to pay more attention. Inside the cottage all was quiet and still. Isabella called out once and then again. Then she went upstairs. Victoria's room told its own story, with the drawers pulled out and the wardrobe doors hanging open. All the girl's clothes were gone, none of her belongings remained. Isabella stood quite still, then she realized she must see where Timmy was. She ran down the stairs, clutching at the banister as she nearly fell. In front of her on the doormat lay an envelope that she must have missed when she came in. She picked it up. It was addressed to her and she ripped it open.

'Dear Lady Montford,' the note began, 'This is to confirm that the car hired by your nephew from us this afternoon will be collected by our associates in London. As the transaction was perforce hurried we were unable to ascertain earlier which of our agents would perform the collection. We are now able to inform you that it will be one Saul Firkettle of Briggs Garages. He will carry a card with him to that effect and I would much appreciate your informing your nephew of the arrangement. We understand the car will be at the Cadogan Gardens residence from tomorrow morning. Yours,' and it trailed off into the salutations of a tradesman.

Isabella stared down blankly at the flimsy piece of paper. It told everything, Victoria gone, Timmy gone. She must follow them, must. Her tiredness seemed to fall away in a surge of adrenalin, but she got no further than the gate before realizing that she would never manage the drive, not overnight. She would go to Barnstaple, there must be a night train. She paused, trying to collect her thoughts. Should she telephone Lucinda? What should she do first?

Young Eli recognized the handwriting on the envelope lying on his breakfast tray and his high spirits faded: part of his country upbringing had followed him to London. He stared down at the rounded characters that were so clearly Jenny's. He had never known his own mother who had died giving him birth, and it had been Jenny, the wife of Thomas Cade's farm manager, who had fulfilled, more than anyone could ever have anticipated, the maternal role for him. That was why he felt guilty just looking at her writing. She had given him all her love and care and he had discarded her the moment he'd come into his inheritance at eighteen. But she never seemed to mind. On the rare occasions he now saw her she was always the same, always caring, always eager to hear what he was doing. She'd had children of her own and she'd been strict with them, curtailing any tendencies they had to look further afield for their future than the local fields of Kent. With Young Eli she was always different, she foresaw great things for him, could envisage him a man of power, of influence. His face was almost a sneer as he opened the envelope, but it wasn't a sneer directed at Jenny, it was directed at himself.

The letter was chatty, homely, full of life in the country, the doings of the family he'd grown up amongst. He skipped through it quickly, then slowed. There was something in it that interested him after all. There was another man in Jenny's life who she imagined great things for, and that was her brother Luke. Young Eli had never tired of hearing of Luke's adventures. He'd seemed to live a life of danger and romance. The story of how he'd rescued Eli's half-sister Lucinda out on the flood waters was more exciting than any fiction. Then there was Luke's life in America that Jenny painted as larger than life, all Luke's doings were that. And now Luke was in London, not only that, but he was asking to meet Eli. Jenny wrote that her brother was staying at the Dorchester for a few weeks. Eli thought that boded well. At least Luke had money; sometimes Jenny's tales had been so elaborate that he'd wondered if it wasn't all invention.

Luke took the call himself. His secretary was confined to bed with a cold. Luke couldn't stand being sick, so he'd told her to stay away until she'd stopped coughing and wasn't infectious. Eli's voice on the telephone was very London and Luke smiled into the mouthpiece; Jenny had looked after the boy like a broody hen but to listen to him he certainly hadn't turned out as if he were one of her chicks. They arranged to meet in the hotel bar at twelve o'clock. There was no commitment to lunch in the invitation. Luke would give Eli his time if it were worth it, but otherwise it would be a quick drink, just to please Jenny.

The bar was crowded and for a moment Eli thought he wouldn't recognize Luke but then he saw him sitting

103

reading a newspaper. The man wearing the steel-grey American-cut suit had to be Jenny's brother. He had the same high forehead, the same straight nose and then he looked up and Eli saw he had the same brown eyes. Eli suddenly realized that he did after all miss the woman who'd brought him up. With an empty ache inside he walked forwards to introduce himself.

It didn't take long for the two men to discover common ground. It was Thomas Cade, and of course the old, old story of Luke saving Lucinda from the flood. But what interested Luke today was Thomas's financial standing. Eli didn't know much about that, but, as he pointed out, he could always find out. Luke smiled, revealing perfect white teeth. 'I think we could get along very well,' he said. 'We speak the same language, and in this day and age it's a rare thing between different generations.'

'Why don't you come out with us this evening, Luke?' Eli asked. 'I'm taking Thomas's daughter and some friends to a new club, giving it the once-over, so to speak. You might enjoy it.'

'I'd like to do that, but not tonight, I'm already committed. Tomorrow perhaps.'

They went in to lunch together and discovered that they enjoyed the same foods, the same kind of wine. Each of them was making an effort to please, but it was an effort they enjoyed. They made a handsome and saturnine pair. It was a pity, Eli thought as he began his dessert, that Luke hadn't lived in England while he had been in Jenny's care. And Luke was thinking it was a pity too, a pity he'd never had a son.

Eli let the curtain fall back into place. There was nothing in the dark night street outside the house in Cadogan Gardens to hold his attention. He was the only member of the family staying more or less permanently in the house.

To the others it was no more than a *pied à terre*. A useful place to stay when they were in town. Even Michael and Isabella seemed half-hearted in their affection for the property. The cigarette between his fingers tasted flat, but he couldn't be bothered to stub it out, so he continued to smoke it, perfuming the bedroom with staleness. The girl in his bed was sleeping soundly, the even rhythm of her breathing almost soporific, almost but not quite. There was no point in his staying out of bed, but then neither was there any point in him getting back into it. He was sexually satiated but emotionally bored. He wanted someone to talk to, he wanted someone to laugh with. He wanted Herbert. It was ridiculous but true: he missed the whipper-in as he would miss a brother. Herbert had been a simple soul, but a loyal admirer and as such he was unique in Eli's life.

The sound of a car stopping in the street made him pull the curtain back again. A black tourer had parked beneath the streetlamp. It was dusty from travel and there were two people in it, a man in the driving seat and a woman passenger. The door opened and Eli smiled. He was rescued from his boredom, because it was Timmy down there on the pavement. In Eli's present mood even he would be a welcome visitor. When Eli opened the front door for his visitors he got more than he expected, for Victoria came stumbling through the doorway into his arms. She was desperately pale, clutching a light coat around her, her eyes frantic.

'I don't understand!' she cried out. 'Timmy, where are you going?' She struggled in Eli's grip, twisting to face Timmy.

'Hold on to her,' Timmy said. His voice was short, breathy, his eyes streaked with tiredness. The muscles in his cheeks stood out like whipcord. 'You'll have to look after her, calm her down, for Christ's sake.'

Eli had never heard him swear before.

'You'd better get her mother up here. Yes, that's it, her mother. She's not my mother, of course,' he laughed too loudly, 'whatever Thomas wanted to make of it. Christ, it's a mess.' He was walking away from them now, back towards the car in the pool of light. 'Take care of her, Eli,' he shouted back, 'tell her, tell her ... Christ, I don't know.'

They stood quite still in the open doorway as the car engine burst into life. They didn't move as it pulled away, leaving a smudge of exhaust fumes heavy on the night air. Then Eli reached out and slowly pushed the door closed. He still held Victoria tightly. She was slumped against him, and he had the feeling that if he let her go she would fall to the floor. He took her through to the study. There was still a low fire in the grate, and there was brandy in the tantalus. That was what she needed – spirit for shock. What he really wanted to know was just what her shock had been. She was shivering uncontrollably, hugging her arms around herself and she wouldn't look at him, not at all.

'Here,' he handed her a glass of brandy. 'You'd better drink that quickly, then I'll give you another to sip and you can tell your Uncle Eli everything.' He poured himself a drink, too, and then bent to stir the fire into life. He was beginning to feel quite good.

'I thought,' Victoria's voice was shaking, 'all the way, I kept thinking how it would be. I thought we would go away together. I never dreamed he was going to leave me here.' She looked up at Eli now, and he saw the hurt in her eyes, but something more as well. She tipped the brandy balloon up in her hands, tilting it to drain the last drop. 'I'll have the second one now, thank you.' Her voice was steadying. 'Then I'll probably have a third.'

'You know it's a pity we're related, Viccy,' Eli said. He

could see she was working hard at retrieving her composure; he admired a woman who could take it on the chin.

'Oh, no please,' Victoria laughed bitterly, 'I don't want any more complications like that in my life, not now, not ever. In fact – ' her eyes narrowed ' – I don't want Timmy in my life ever again.'

'He's your brother – you can't change that.' It was very quiet in the study, the fire crackled busily but that was all, London was very still at three o'clock in the morning.

'Don't tell my mother I'm here, not yet anyway. I want some time just to be myself. You see, the most difficult thing is to know who I am. I need time to find out. Time doing the kind of things I like, mixing with the people I like. I can't have my mother going on at me, she doesn't understand anything. She's completely out of touch. It's that dreadful farm. God, I hate it down there. It's muddy and foul. And boring, so dreadfully, awfully boring.'

'Nothing worse than being bored,' Young Eli said complacently, forgetting that before Victoria had arrived he, with all London at his beck and call, had been suffering from the same complaint.

'What shall we do tomorrow?' Victoria asked. The brandy was soothing her tiredness, taking the stiffness from her. Cornwall seemed a lifetime away.

'There's a new club you might enjoy. Run by an incredibly beautiful young Turk, he'll probably take a fancy to you.'

'How lovely.' Victoria stretched back in her chair. A foreigner would be something special. A Turk, how romantic, she thought. The door to the study opened and made her jump. Eli's companion stood framed in the doorway. She was wearing nothing but a linen sheet twined round her slim body. Her short cropped dark hair exaggerated the size of her eyes; she looked almost more like a boy than a girl.

107

'I wondered where you were.' Her voice was fashionably thin and high. 'I'm absolutely ravenous.' She was staring at Victoria, but without animosity, and only the requisite amount of curiosity. 'You must introduce me to your friend, darling,' she continued. 'After I've had something to eat that is, I'm . . .' As her voice trailed off Eli jumped up from his chair. He was full of go, raring for the off.

'Yes, yes I know, you're absolutely starving, and so am I, and so I expect is Viccy. Come on, my sweets,' he put an arm around each of the girls, 'let's go and scandalize the staff by playing about in the kitchen. Personally I fancy some eggs, loads and loads of them, cooked with cream and perhaps a little ham. Can either of you sweeties cook?'

They careered down to the kitchen and it was Victoria who began breaking the eggs into a bowl: 'Six, seven, eight,' she counted out loud. She was starving. There was a phrase that kept running through her mind, 'Hell hath no fury like a woman scorned'. Well, Timmy would find out all right. She had nothing but scorn for him now. He was a coward who'd run away from what he wanted. She beat the eggs vigorously, frothing them up in the bowl as Eli spooned in dollops of cream. The girl in the sheet was posing decorously in front of the range. 'You know,' she said, 'when we've had our eggs it would be quite fun to go back to bed, all of us, you know.'

Victoria stopped beating the eggs, then she smiled. 'No, thank you, I think I'll give that a miss. You see the thing is – ' she looked up at Eli ' – I'm saving myself for a dark handsome stranger, a very dark handsome stranger.' And then she laughed.

It wasn't until he stepped down from the train and on to the platform that Timmy felt safe. He felt the soothing atmosphere of Brighton all around him. Even in the middle of the night the station had life; there was a subdued bustle of porters and the smell of the sea had reached into its cavernous interior.

Timmy swung his kitbag up on his shoulder and began to walk slowly towards the ticket barrier. He was drained of emotion, unclean. It was impossible now to believe how he'd felt up on the cliffs above Boscastle. It was all a nightmare. He swallowed convulsively, his skin felt clammy and he began to hasten his steps. He needed to get back to normality. The inspiration to come down to Brighton to stay with Margaret Smith had seemed God-given. She was far enough removed from his family, being the sister-in-law of Thomas's farm manager. Timmy had stayed with her and her husband every summer of his youth. Margaret was a widow now, but always welcoming, always happy to see him. He was uncertain how to announce his arrival in the middle of the night. To arrive in his present confused state would require him launching at once into some kind of explanation, and he wasn't able to do that. He didn't want to talk about Victoria, didn't want to think about her.

Timmy made his way down to the promenade. He leaned for a moment against the wrought-iron railings that divided him from the beach. Ahead of him a dim line of phosphorescence marked the edge of the waves and a soft swishing sound of pebbles in the surf told of a calm sea. It was very different from the waters at Boscastle. This sea was tamed, it was a background to the amusements of the town. He began to walk, letting the sound of the waves fill his head, breathing deeply to draw the ozone into his lungs. The streetlamps made bright pools of light that he avoided. The blocks of flats that overlooked the beach were closed, their windows lifeless, and that suited him. He wanted nothing but solitude.

Timmy walked until the dawn had coloured the waters salmon pink, a pink that turned to purple and finally to blue. Life had begun once more, tradesmen were beginning their day, pre-breakfast walkers were out. He remembered suddenly that he hadn't eaten since yesterday's breakfast; Margaret would take that as a challenge. He smiled as he thought of her. She was always cheerful, jokingly calling herself the Merry Widow. And Meg, her daughter, would be there too. She was a young woman now, but he still thought of her as the little girl who used to cling on to his hand while she watched the Punch and Judy show on the beach. They were days that had been full of fun, full of laughter, the days before the war.

He'd been wrong in thinking he'd find Meg at the yellow-painted terraced house. She'd been staying the night with a girlfriend after they'd been out dancing. Margaret was amused at Timmy's astonishment that her daughter was not at home. He'd not noticed her growing up – but then that wasn't surprising as they didn't see him that often any more.

'So how long can you stay, Timmy?' Margaret asked. She was drinking tea with him after he'd eaten an enormous helping of bacon and eggs. It was nice for her to have a man's company about the place – not that she couldn't have remarried any time she wanted. She was only just forty, short and jolly, her dark hair was hardly touched with grey and her smile was as bright as ever. All that apart, she'd been left very well provided for and that made her an attraction on the marriage market, but she wasn't going to marry again, not while Meg was still living at home.

'I don't know,' Timmy stared down at his tea cup. 'There was the chance of a job down at Falmouth, a flying job. But I don't want to take it now. It's too . . .' He paused, uncertain of the words to use, but he knew inside that it wouldn't work. He had to get away from the family, away from all of them.

Margaret didn't hurry him. He'd be able to talk about whatever had happened when the time was ready. But it must have been something bad, because he looked dreadful. The strain had all come back, and the pallor, the sheen on his skin that looked like illness and had worried her so much when he'd first come back from the war.

'You might like to come out with me this evening, Timmy,' she said, talking to fill the silence. 'I thought I'd go and see the moving picture show. It's all about Australia, and I'd like to see it. They've got kangeroos and things. Meg said she wouldn't come. Mind you – ' she smiled, aware that Timmy wouldn't understand the implications of her words – men never saw what was under their noses ' – she might come now that you're here.'

Perhaps he should go into the moving-picture business, Timmy thought. After all, it was the way of the future, just like flying. Maybe he should go to Australia: that was far enough away to make sure he wouldn't stumble over any more of the family. His thoughts stuck on Australia. Where he'd been rambling in his mind, suddenly his thoughts narrowed. Why not Australia? He'd heard about the vast, wide-open spaces, heard that there were isolated settlements. A man with an aeroplane running supplies might make a living in a country like that. He looked up at Margaret and smiled properly for the first time since he'd arrived.

'Yes, I'll come with you. It might be quite interesting; in fact it might be very interesting. Did you say there was more toast? I could do with another bit, and another cup of tea perhaps.' Margaret smiled as she got up from the table. Busy in the kitchen she listened as Meg came in through the front door and heard the surprise in her daughter's voice as she saw Timmy, the surprise and delight. Yes, Meg would definitely change her mind and come to the picture show. Margaret put two pieces of toast in the grill. Her daughter could have a little extra breakfast with Timmy. If only the silly boy would see how perfect a wife Meg would make him, then Margaret could be free to put some thought to her own future.

Isabella was utterly exhausted. The journey up to town had taken her far longer than she'd expected. It was early evening when she at last reached Cadogan Gardens and she'd hoped to have arrived shortly after lunch. But it didn't do to worry about it now. She rang the doorbell for a second time. Where on earth were the staff, she wondered as she slowly took off her gloves. When the door did eventually open it was to reveal a very timid young maid, obviously newly appointed and unused to the duty she was performing.

'I'm Lady Montford,' Isabella announced as she stepped through the door past the girl. 'Where on earth is everybody?'

'Everybody, your Ladyship?'

'Yes, everybody. The butler will do to begin with. Where is he?'

'Oh, he left this morning, your Ladyship.' The girl's eyes were enormous, her voice almost a whisper.

Isabella walked towards the kitchen with the girl hovering behind her. What on earth was going on here? 'Where's my niece Victoria?' she asked as she began to descend the stairs.

'She's out with Master Eli, they're out for the evening.'

Isabella paused. If Eli was here, then perhaps he was involved with the Victoria and Timmy débâcle.

The chaos amongst the staff was quickly resolved. There had been an argument over the liberties Eli had taken in the kitchen. The cook made it sound bacchanalian at first but then it transpired to be little more than a storm in a tea cup. The butler had left in umbrage and so had the housekeeper. After a little judicious questioning it appeared that Eli's advances towards the housekeeper had trespassed on ground the butler assumed was his. Isabella struggled to control her temper. She had not yet telephoned Lucinda and she wanted to find out what was happening with Victoria and Timmy before she did.

Eventually it seemed that Timmy had not been seen by any of the staff, that Victoria was out on the town with Eli and his friends and that they were not expected back until late. What Isabella wanted most of all before she spoke to her sister was a bath. She was tired, grubby and desperate to change her clothes. She went upstairs slowly, feeling horribly stiff. She pushed the door to her room open gratefully and then stood very still. The room was in chaos, the bed had clearly been slept in, the dressing table was littered with jars of make-up, there were strange clothes flung over a chair. It was a disgusting mess. Isabella's tiredness disappeared as her temper took its place. Eli was the end, the absolute end. She ran downstairs to the hall, where she picked up the telephone and savagely dialled her sister's number. After the fourth digit she broke a fingernail. She was still swearing under her breath when she heard Thomas's voice on the line. If Lucinda hadn't tried to discharge her responsibility by sending Victoria down to Cornwall, then none of this would have happened, none of it.

'Thomas!' Isabella shouted into the phone. 'Thomas, I must speak to Lucinda.'

Thomas made a face as he passed his wife the telephone. Something had got Isabella's goat and no mistake.

Victoria relaxed in the arms of her dance partner. She was still hot from the Charleston, and the slow waltz that had followed it was delightful, like a cool shower. She tipped her head back to look up at the multi-faceted crystal globe revolving above her. She just adored the decor of the club, felt cocooned by the deep red opulence of it. She didn't want the evening to end.

'Victoria!'

She jumped. She'd been drifting away on the music when Eli tapped her on the shoulder.

'Come on, I want you to meet someone.'

She abandoned her partner without an apology – it was that kind of evening, everyone swopping escorts, dashing after a new sensation, everyone out for themselves.

'Dimitrou, this is Viccy. Viccy, Dimitrou.' Eli performed the perfunctory introduction with his inimitable nonchalance, but he was really quite interested to see how it developed. Dimitrou was the newest available man on the scene, and novelty was the thing these days. He was also extremely handsome, dark and dashing with soulful eyes. Eli's lips formed a twisted smile. He always did well with the girls himself, but he had a feeling that the young Turk would break hearts where he himself only broke reputations.

'I am charmed to meet you, Miss Viccy.' Dimitrou raised the proffered hand to his lips, scarcely touching it, but sending delicious shivers down Victoria's spine. She scented delectable danger: he was devouring her with his eyes. She smiled slowly, keeping her eyelids lowered and tipping her head forwards so that when she eventually looked up into his eyes he had the full benefit of her allure. Victoria had worked out her stratagems as had all the flappers on the circuit. Dimitrou had come across dozens of them in the few weeks he'd been hosting the club. He didn't find this one anything special, but it made no difference to his tactics. He acted as if she was the most beautiful creature to enter his life, and Victoria believed it. She deliberately pushed any lingering thoughts of Timmy to the back of her mind, and was captivated with the desperate fervour of being on the rebound.

114

'If you can stay until the crowd has gone, we could dance.' The softness of Dimitrou's consonants had her spellbound. She glanced at Eli and said, 'Please, please can I stay?' at the refusal she saw in his expression.

'There's always tomorrow, Viccy,' he said, which she knew was untrue, because tomorrow her mother would catch up with her and all of this would slip away.

Dimitrou shrugged, the complete Continental. 'As Eli says, there is always tomorrow.' He knew Eli would be frequenting the club night after night until his credit ran out. Eli was hooked, he was a gambler, a compulsive player of the tables who had no luck whatsoever. He was the kind of club member that suited Dimitrou and the men who had put him into prominence, the men who would never be seen by the London socialites whose innocent prattle was establishing the club as a place to be seen in. Amongst the youth of society patronizing the club was an ever-increasing number of the senior members of the establishment: politicians, generals and leaders of industry, as well as their women, their fancy women. It wasn't the kind of place to bring their wives but to bring mistresses to it was perfect, and they all treated Dimitrou as a pal, a chum, because he created the ambiance.

Victoria was unhappy when Eli took her off to dance. She understood the unwritten rules, that Dimitrou couldn't be seen to squire her while there were other guests to entertain, but she was eager to feel his arms around her. She could imagine how it could be, would be, if it wasn't for spoilsport Eli. She trod viciously on his toe.

'Ouch! You did that on purpose!'

'Yes, I did. And I'll do it again if you don't say I can stay. God, you're the limit, if it was some girl you wanted to be with you'd stop out all night. What business is it of yours what time I get home?'

'Now, now, Viccy.' He sidestepped neatly to avoid her

kick. 'There will be another time. Dimitrou's not going to go anywhere, and it would be most unladylike to succumb too obviously after just one kiss on the hand. Let him at least wait a few days for what you're so obviously desperate to give him.'

Victoria stopped dancing instantly. She looked livid. 'You make me sound like a tart!'

'And he makes you feel like one, a willing one, and I don't see you complaining. Just take a tip from an expert, Viccy, and let him do a bit of the chasing, otherwise you won't last long.'

She stood for a moment more, undecided, then held her arms out to dance again.

'Perhaps you're right,' she said. 'But it would have been nice.'

'And it will be, just don't throw yourself at him, there's a good girl.' He dropped his hand to pat her bottom and she giggled. He was probably right.

Isabella and Lucinda had long ago run out of things to say to each other. The fire in the drawing room was burning low, but neither of them made an effort to resurrect it. It would have been an admission that they may well still have hours to wait. Two o'clock. Isabella looked for what felt like the hundredth time at the clock on the mantelshelf. Physically she was very, very tired but emotionally she was charged with energy. She had had to work very hard at not losing her temper with her sister who was every minute looking more like the Lucinda of old, and less like Thomas's pliant wife.

'I do think it must have been something you did, Isabella,' Lucinda snapped. 'Victoria is not the sort of girl to go off the rails. You've stirred up something, and I only wish I knew what.' She was fidgeting with a needlework cushion, pulling on its tasselled corners.

116

'It's nothing to do with me,' Isabella replied. 'All I've had to do is become involved when I shouldn't. You should never have sent her down to Cornwall. You can't cure things just by pushing them out of sight.'

Lucinda snorted. She was completely furious with Isabella. Victoria had needed a change of scene, that was all, and now look what had happened. They both sat up as they heard the key turn in the door. Now at least they would find out what was going on.

They heard Eli's voice, then Victoria's, suddenly high: 'It's Aunt Isabella's car! Oh, no, quick, look . . .' then it tailed off because Isabella and Lucinda were in the hall and Victoria stood framed in the doorway, panic touching her painted cheeks. She laughed nervously. 'Hello, Mummy,' she said, then looked imploringly at Eli, who raised his evening hat deferentially to his half-sisters, and walked past them and up the stairs. He was humming to himself as he went. Victoria watched his back until he went out of sight. Then she was alone to face them. She hesitated a moment more, seeing the fury in her mother's face, the implacable righteousness in Isabella's and then she turned and fled back out into the night.

Part Two

Tell me, my heart, if this be love.
George Lyttelton (1709–73)

Victoria turned over in her sleep. She flung out an arm, searching subconsciously for companionship, but the pillow beside her was empty. Slowly she began to wake up.

'Dimitrou,' she murmured drowsily. 'Dimitrou, come back. Where are you?' Her thoughts were jumbled, memories of the night's passion seemed almost dreamlike. She sat up abruptly in bed, aware now that she was alone in the room. She shivered at the early morning air on her body and pulled the bedclothes up to her neck. She was quite naked, and she smiled slowly at the returning memory of how she had been undressed, slowly, tantalizingly, she had never felt like that in her life before, never. And then to lose her virginity at last, to a man like Dimitrou, a beautiful, wonderful man like that. She closed her eyes to picture more perfectly the comparison their entwined bodies had made, the olive brown of his skin against her porcelain white. She shivered again, but this time it was not with cold.

She raised her voice. 'Dimitrou!' she called again, but there was no sound. The room on the top floor of the club that Dimitrou had brought her to was as characterless as a hotel bedroom, and it offered no clues as to her lover's whereabouts except for his dinner jacket lying casually abandoned on a gilt-backed chair. He couldn't be far away.

Victoria lay down again and wriggled her toes luxuriously. She was aware of every inch of skin on her body; it glowed. She thought back to the first time he had made love to her: it had hurt, but only fleetingly, and then she had felt warm, alive, more alive than she'd ever been. Later, it had been ... she could not even think of the words to describe the sensation when he had loved her for the second time. She concentrated desperately hard trying to remember the engulfing surge of pleasure. After a while she fell asleep again.

Dawn was streaking the sky as Eli walked out on to the street. He bit savagely into the cigar that was clamped between his teeth. He hadn't even paused to light it as he had been pursued down the hall by his half-sister Lucinda. She'd screamed at him like a harridan. Her face was blotched with crying, puffy with desperation. Eli had been up all night like the rest of them, they'd spent the first few hours scouring the streets for Victoria. Stupid, stupid girl to run off like that. He could understand her fleeing from her mother's anger, but she should have had the sense to run upstairs and lock herself in her bedroom. No one but an idiot ran out into the night.

After admitting that they couldn't find her they'd rung every one of her friends they could think of. The search had been a public affair conducted from the telephone in the drawing room with Isabella listening as Lucinda telephoned, and then Lucinda watching Thomas, who'd arrived after a frantic drive up to town from Kent. Eli hadn't had a chance to get to the phone unobserved, and he certainly wasn't going to tip them off as to where he thought she might be. 'Might be', that wasn't right, it was more a matter of where she was bound to be. If they found her with Dimitrou there would be hell to pay and Eli would be the one to have to pay it because he'd taken her to the club in the first place. The moment Lucinda had found him putting on his coat she'd guessed that he must have been hiding something from them. She'd screamed at him, and then Thomas had threatened him physically to try and get an answer from him, to find out where Victoria might be. The only way he'd got out on his own was by vowing that if they didn't leave him alone he wouldn't try what he'd said was a 'long shot' and neither would he tell them what the 'long shot' was. There were only a few hours left before they were going to the police. It would ruin her daughter's reputation, Lucinda sobbed, but if she hadn't come home by mid-morning then they had no choice.

It took him a while to find a cab, they were hard to come by at this Godforsaken hour. When he arrived at the club it was closed, locked and shuttered. It was a night place and as Eli went up to the door he disturbed a stray cat that had been scavenging amongst a heap of rubbish awaiting collection. The cat darted away with a screech and an empty champagne bottle rolled towards him, sounding hollow on the tiled path. Eli grimaced; it was quite revoltingly tawdry by the light of day, he decided, as he pulled the brass doorbell for the second time. The door opened eventually, but only a crack, and a man's voice called out, a cross voice, one disturbed from sleep. It wasn't Dimitrou.

'We're closed, go away, stop ringing the bell.'

Eli pushed the toe of his shoe into the closing gap, 'I want to see Dimitrou,' he said. 'Tell him it's Eli Bradbury. He'll see me, go on, tell him.'

'Dimitrou's not here, he doesn't sleep here. Anyway – ' the pressure increased on Eli's foot ' – he's on holiday, he went away last night. He won't be back for weeks. Go away.'

Eli stumbled back as the door closed at last. He stood undecided on the doorstep. He didn't believe the faceless voice: Dimitrou had quite obviously not been planning to go away when they'd spoken last night and Young Eli did not believe for a moment that the ultra-sophisticated Turk had fallen so wholeheartedly for Victoria that he'd chucked up his job at the club. What the hell should he do now?

A taxi stopped further up the street to drop off a fare and Eli hurried towards it. He needed time to think, and he was hungry. After all, he'd been up all night. 'The Dorchester,' he instructed the driver; that was the nearest decent hotel.

Young Eli walked slowly into the dining room and looked around for some service. The first person who attracted his attention was Luke, who was standing up and beaming his delight at the prospect of some convivial company at breakfast. Luke fussed around his visitor, making sure he was comfortably seated, advising him to try some braised kidneys that he had found particularly good that morning. Not once did he show how interested he was in the reason why Eli would leave his comforts at Cadogan Gardens to take his breakfast in a hotel. Neither did he show any surprise at the less than immaculate turn-out of his guest that hinted at a night not spent in bed.

Young Eli relaxed with the warmth of the coffee, the aroma of the kidneys and the calm atmosphere of luxury. He was soon telling Luke what he had refused to tell Lucinda, and it was a relief to be able to unburden himself. So, Luke mused, it seemed he might have Lucinda's daughter to rescue, as once he had rescued Lucinda herself. But he was a very different man now. In those days he hadn't looked for reward. This time he knew better. He spread his toast thickly with butter and then sparingly with bitter marmalade. He was an epicure where pleasure was concerned and he would find manipulating Thomas very pleasurable indeed. His eyes were distant as he beckoned to a waiter to bring some more hot coffee. Often, over the years, he had remembered how Lucinda's

124

body had felt when she had thrown herself into his arms. Then there had been chaos and fear and desperation, but he could differentiate something else, an animal passion that could have been his to fulfil. But Thomas had reaped the reward; he had enjoyed the fruits of Luke's labour. Yes, it would be a pleasure to save poor, sweet Victoria from her young Turk, and then he would see what should be done with her. He poured more coffee for Eli without asking if he wanted it. Their relationship might have been forged years ago, they were from a similar mould, and together they would be very powerful.

'Wake up, wake up, Victoria. Come on, it's time for you to go home.'

Victoria opened her eyes and stared up at Dimitrou in disbelief. 'But I'm not going home,' she said. 'I'm going to stay here with you. You said you loved me, last night . . .' She tailed off as Dimitrou turned his head away from her.

He was sitting on the edge of the bed holding a cup of coffee that he'd brought for her. It smelt bitter, strange and enticing. Perhaps he was teasing, she thought. Dimitrou didn't move, he hadn't turned his face away to hide the fact that he was playing a joke on her, he'd turned it away to hide a smile. A smile at the simplicity of a girl who believed what a man said in bed. Still, he'd had her virginity, he owed her something for that.

'Come, drink the coffee,' he said, 'it will help you to wake up properly, then you must leave right away. Everything is organized. I have a friend in a hotel near here who has arranged that your name appears in their bookings for last night. You must tell your parents that you went to the hotel when you left home, and that you breakfasted there this morning. The last part at least we can make true. Can't you see?' He looked deep into her eyes and she felt her stomach turn over; she loved him, she really did. 'You can't stay here with me. After all, a London gaming club – it's not a place for a lady, is it? Come,' he said again, 'drink the coffee and get dressed. I'll get you a taxi. Your family won't be cross, they'll be too glad to get you back. We can meet again soon. Be a good girl now.' He stood up abruptly; he'd spent his quota of pleasantries for the morning. Eli Bradbury had worked out where the girl had run to, and he hadn't been taken for nearly enough on the gaming tables yet. Dimitrou's good deed in sending back his niece would help in the final act of fleecing the Bradbury inheritance.

Dimitrou didn't look back as he left the room. Victoria sat very still. She was poised, trying to decide if she should react with rage and take Dimitrou's actions as a thinly disguised dismissal, or accept what he said at face value. She raised the cup to her lips and sipped the coffee. It was strong and sweet, like Dimitrou, she thought, and let herself be lulled into the security of believing the words he had murmured during the night. She dressed quickly. Leaving off her jewellery and make-up, her evening dress would look less obvious by the light of day. When Dimitrou saw her coming down the stairs he smiled genuinely. He had thought she might be difficult and he disliked having to be heavy-handed with women. They kissed goodbye before opening the door. There was a taxi waiting outside and Victoria stepped into it happily. She looked back to wave, but Dimitrou wasn't there. The door of the club was closed, and she felt comforted to see how considerate he was being of her reputation.

'There she is!' Eli jumped up from the table, almost overturning it. 'Victoria!'

The other breakfasters watched in amusement as a young woman wearing a sequined evening dress that looked most incongruous at nine in the morning made an embarrassed entrance into the Dorchester's dining room.

'Victoria, where the hell have you been?' As soon as Victoria was seated, Eli's relief turned swiftly to anger. He had been worried half out of his mind.

Victoria darted a look at him that was defiant and yet vulnerable, and it told him everything. He'd been right, she'd been with that bloody Turk.

'Eli, remember your manners.' Luke's voice was lightly amused, he was working at hiding the annoyance he'd felt at realizing he wasn't going to get the chance to use Victoria's disappearance in his negotiations with her father.

'I'm sorry.' Eli's voice was tight with anger. He'd actually been worrying about the girl, and here she was brazenly coming back after throwing herself at Dimitrou. 'Luke, this is my niece Victoria. Victoria this is Luke Jones, Jenny's brother.'

Victoria hardly spared Luke a glance. She was too concerned with trying to decide how to deal with Eli. She needed him as a friend, she would need his help in seeing Dimitrou, but she couldn't decide how much to tell him.

'Are you hungry, Victoria?' Luke asked.

'No, yes, I don't know.' She flushed. She couldn't decide how she felt. It was all too much having to face the world again, so soon after last night.

'Let me order for you.' Luke was most supportive. He dealt smoothly with the hovering waiter and began to chat amicably about the weather, the theatre, anything except the reason why Victoria obviously hadn't been home all night.

Victoria began to pick at the aromatic kedgeree that was placed in front of her. After a few mouthfuls she began to eat in earnest, it was delicious. The coffee was good too, only not as stimulating as the coffee that Dimitrou had brought her. Perhaps Dimitrou had been right and it was the best way after all for her family to think that she had spent the night on her own in a hotel.

'How funny to find you here, Eli,' she said. 'You didn't spend the night here too, did you?' She looked at him with her eyes wide open and innocent.

'Spend the night here? No, I most certainly didn't. I spent the night searching the streets for you, as we all did. You're going to have to do more than try and pretend you stayed here last night to placate your parents, my girl.'

'But I did spend the night here. You can check with the desk, you'll find my booking.'

'And of course,' Luke added, 'I can confirm that Victoria was here last night, Eli. I have to admit that I did not at the time know who the beautiful young woman was that I admired from across the foyer, but I could not possibly make the mistake of not recognizing her again.'

'Across the foyer?' Eli's face clearly showed the fury he felt. 'At what time would you say you saw this apparition of loveliness that was apparently Victoria?'

Luke's expression of studied charm didn't change. He turned to Victoria and asked, 'What time would you say it was, my dear? I never bother much about small details like time, after all the night is very long.'

'It must have been about two-thirty, I would think. That was when I came into the hotel.' Victoria had found an ally at the exact moment that she most needed one. She gave Luke her best smile, the one that made her look so like the young Lucinda that Luke felt a sudden lurch inside.

Eli pushed his chair back and coughed into his fist. He disliked feeling the odd man out. He leaned back and looked up, unseeing, at the ceiling, letting the pounding in his chest subside. It was simple when he considered the situation dispassionately. He must side with Victoria; that also meant siding with Luke, and he had already decided to do that. Luke wanted to find out more about Thomas, well, he could start this morning.

'When you've finished your breakfast, Victoria,' Eli said, 'I'll take you back to the others. I think it would be a good idea if Luke came too. It was very convenient his seeing you last night, and it would be stupid not to use the fact that he did.'

Victoria could feel the last of her tension flying away. She would go back to Cadogan Gardens protected by two stalwart men. She had forgiven Eli for abandoning her last night when Lucinda had confronted them. After all, if he'd stood his ground Victoria would never have run away, never have gone to Dimitrou, never have learned that loving was everything. She wiped her lips carefully with her napkin. They would go now; she was quite looking forward to confronting Mama.

Michael arrived at Cadogan Gardens ten minutes after Victoria had returned with her entourage. He walked unannounced into the bedroom where Isabella was studying her face intently in the dressing-table mirror.

'I gather Victoria's downstairs.' He was shrugging off his driving coat as he walked towards her. 'Is she all right?' He came up to Isabella and put his hands round her waist. She had her back to him, watching him in the mirror. He leaned forwards to kiss her cheek and still she didn't move; her face was blank, expressionless.

'Yes, she's fine,' she said flatly. 'At least, she looked fine when she came in. Lucinda and Thomas have her closeted up in the drawing room, and I thought it was best to leave them to it.' Isabella had been upset when Victoria had returned with Eli and Luke in tow. The girl had swept into Isabella's drawing room and Lucinda and Thomas had followed, then the door had closed. Isabella had stood for what had felt a long time in the hall before making her way upstairs. She seemed always to be the odd one out. Unwanted downstairs, unneeded by her sons, unloved by Michael.

'What a drive!' Michael sat down on the bed then lay back and closed his eyes. He was exhausted after the journey and walking in to Isabella's less than enthusiastic greeting didn't help.

'Shall I ring for some coffee?' she asked.

'No, not just yet. Come and sit here.' He patted the space on the bed beside him. He listened for her footsteps, but there was no sound in the room except the light ticking of the bedside clock that emphasized the silence. 'Did you have a bad time last night? It must have been very worrying.'

'Yes, we were all worried.' Isabella's voice was flat, lifeless. 'It was typical of Victoria, frightening us half to death, then waltzing back into the house as if she hadn't a care in the world.'

Michael heard the bitterness in his wife's voice. He didn't think it was really aimed at Victoria. There was something else, something that had changed Isabella. He opened his eyes and sat up to look at her. Her face was cold, expressionless and she looked somehow older.

'I'll let Cook know you'll be here for dinner, shall I?' she asked. 'Or are you going straight back to Falmouth since you're not needed here any more?'

'Not needed?'

'Victoria's been found, hasn't she? That's what you came back for, because Lucinda was so desperate for everyone in the family to help search for the girl, now you've no reason to stay.'

'What on earth is the matter, Isabella?' He got up off the bed and walked towards her, putting his hands out to take her by the shoulders.

130

'Don't touch me!' Isabella took a swift step back, and Michael slowly lowered his arms.

'What on earth is it? You've never not wanted me to touch you before, Isabella, never.' He looked down, puzzled, at his hands; she'd never spoken to him like that before.

'Nothing, it's nothing,' she said, her voice too high. 'I'm on edge, that's all. Lucinda's been crying all night, Thomas has been frantic, and all of that after my having to rush back from Boscastle, it's been too much, that's all.' Isabella was hugging her arms around her body. She felt cold and alone, and very tired. 'I'd like to sleep now,' she said.

'Would you like me to leave?'

'Yes, yes I would.'

Michael picked up his coat from where it lay on the bed. He was confused, his head was still aching from the hours of hard driving and he was shaken by Isabella's attitude towards him. He felt that he had been talking to a stranger. He walked slowly towards the door and paused. There ought to be something he could say that could put it all right. He heard Isabella moving across the room behind him. When he looked at her she was standing by the bed, obviously waiting for him to leave before she lay down.

'I'll see you later, Isabella,' he said and went out, closing the door quietly behind him. He paused on the landing, undecided where to go, then he walked over to William's bedroom and opened the door into the room that was so particularly his elder son's. There were boxes of birds' eggs, a jumble of old cricket bats, several models of ships. He sat down on the bed which was low, close to the floor. William had refused a more grown-up one, he'd slept on what was little more than a truckle bed since he'd been four years old. Michael stretched out carefully: the bed didn't feel all that secure beneath him. He lay with his eyes closed, trying to picture Isabella as he'd just seen her, but it was impossible; he couldn't remember the new face that was like a stranger's.

The house was solidly built, so that Michael wasn't disturbed by the voices in the drawing room or Isabella crying in their bedroom. She had her face pressed into the pillow to stifle the sound. Seeing Michael had made her realize how much she still loved him. She'd convinced herself on the journey from Boscastle that she could live without him, created in her mind a Michael who she could hate, but it was an image that didn't exist; he'd only had to walk into the room and she'd longed to run into his arms. She'd wanted the years to sweep away, she wanted it to be as it had been when they were young together, when just being in his arms was the most secure feeling in the whole world. When she ran out of tears she got up and washed her face, then she wrote a short note to Michael, saying that she had gone back to Pencombe. She signed it simply 'Isabella'. She couldn't bring herself to write the word 'love'. She left the house eagerly, she couldn't wait now to get home. She could picture it all in her mind, the greenness, the fresh air after the dust of the town. And it would be far away from the sea. She didn't care if she never saw the sea again, she felt betrayed by her visit to Boscastle. She would go home to Kent, where the fertile land had never betrayed her trust.

Meg walked swiftly along the promenade, her head held high. She was only just over five feet tall and lightly built, but the determination in her face made the other pedestrians step aside for her. It was as well that they did, because she could hardly see for the tears that she was fighting back. Timmy's letter was crumpled in her handbag. She'd read it twice before giving in to her rising rage and squeezing it into a ball to throw into the fireplace.

Fortunately the day was mild, the fire had not been lit and she'd been able to retrieve it.

She kept thinking that it had been her own mother who had put the idea of going to Australia into Timmy's head. She seethed at the unreasonableness of fate. For years she'd felt condemned by her youth. Timmy had been unattainably older than her, but she'd still loved him, loved him for as long as she could remember. When the girls at school had played out their fantasies of marriage it had always been Timmy she'd imagined as the groom to her bride. She stopped suddenly and was cannoned into by a couple who'd been walking behind her. In the confusion of apologies her bag fell to the pavement. She stooped quickly to pick it up. Timmy's letter was in there, making it doubly precious. When she started to walk again it was more slowly. She no longer seemed apart from the crowd taking the air. She was remembering what Timmy had said to her in the few days he'd spent staying with her mother. She hadn't given consideration until now to the fact that he had confided in her. He'd explained that Victoria thought that his being her adopted brother made no barrier to her love for him; it was the first time he'd treated her as an adult.

Meg hadn't seen Victoria since they'd been very small children. Long ago the Smith family had stayed at Aunt Jenny's house. It was a cottage really, surrounded by orchards that were owned by Thomas Cade, Victoria's father. There was a pond with ducks, and a goat that was tied up to a stake in the ground. To Meg it had seemed like life out of a fairy tale. Until then the streets of Brighton and its orderly beach had been her whole world. The land at Reason Hill was so green, and so full of strange smells. She remembered that she'd thought Victoria smelt strange too: she smelt of camomile face cream and dresses washed in lavender water. She was a very pampered little girl.

Meg's mother and Aunt Jenny had talked together about Victoria while Meg, as was natural, had sat on her mother's knee and listened to every word. Victoria's mother spoilt her only daughter, that had been said, as had the fact that little Miss Victoria would be greatly improved by a roll in the muck heap. Aunt Jenny had laughed when she'd said that, to show that she didn't really mean it. But Meg had met the vision of perfection that was Victoria and she had silently agreed with her aunt.

Timmy had not told Meg everything that had happened at Boscastle, she realized that, but he had told her enough for her to understand that Victoria was in love with him and not with a sisterly love. It had compromised all of Timmy's feelings for his father Thomas, because, whatever Victoria felt about Timmy not being her brother, Timmy loved Thomas, and that love had always been securely based on the fact that the farmer was his adoptive father. Meg shook her head to try and clear it; the confusion in Timmy's thoughts had spread to hers. Suddenly, like the shaft of light that broke through the clouds over the sea, bathing a small sailboat in yellow, she saw what Timmy needed. He needed her. Timmy would never be happy until he had a family of his own. He had outgrown the tangled affections of the Cade household. He had to have his own home. Meg began to walk more quickly, she had to begin at once, Timmy was never going to see his way out of the mess he was in on his own; he needed someone to show him the way, and that someone should be Meg. She gave no thought, as she crossed the busy road running parallel to the beach, to the thousands of miles that would separate her from her intended. For that was what Timmy had become, 'her intended', because she intended to show him the error of his ways. He should stop looking backwards for love, he should look forwards, and Meg was just the person to provide him with a whole lifetime of love. She had to get home to get started, she needed to enlist the help of her mother who was very good indeed at sorting things out. Timmy had to come home to England and to Meg.

Thomas sat very still. Timmy's letter lay on his desk in front of him. He was trying to soothe the hurt he felt by fathoming out the reasons why Timmy had gone away, without a goodbye. That was what was hurting Thomas, the boy had gone without a goodbye. Thomas felt guilt mixed with his hurt. He worked so hard at showing no preference to any of his sons that he realized he showed them all less affection than he felt. He was a warm-hearted man. He wanted to hold his children to him, to protect them from the world, but he believed he must encourage them to stand on their own two feet. He let them make their own decisions about their lives, ones that he was desperate to influence, but determined not to, because he believed that for him to do so would be weakening for them. Thomas didn't see that his natural sons stayed tied to the farms as part of an expression of their love for him. And he couldn't see that in choosing to become a pilot Timmy had tried to prove that he wasn't a burden to his adoptive father; he wanted to show he could exist on his own. There was an excess of guilt in their relationship, for each of them felt that too much affection would compromise the other. So Thomas stared blankly out of the window ahead of him, steeling himself not to show his hurt when he told the rest of the family that Timmy had gone to Australia. The short letter made no mention of when he was coming back or, in fact, if he was ever coming back.

The knock on the office door interrupted his thoughts. 'Come in,' he called.

It was a red-faced Albert, and also, much to Thomas's

surprise, Maggy, the scullery girl, whose face was as pale as his son's was puce.

'I'd like a few minutes of your time, Father.' Albert almost choked over the words. Thomas dropped his scrutiny from his son's face and saw with shock that Maggy was clutching the boy's hand.

Thomas stood up slowly, his dignity making Albert feel sick with apprehension. 'I think,' he said, 'that whatever you have to say, Albert, it would be better without Maggy being in here. You can wait in the hall,' he finished, offering the consolation of a seat in a family part of the house, to soften the effect of the girl's banishment. But Albert was not going to have that.

'I want Maggy to stay, Father. What I have to say affects her as much as me.'

Thomas could feel the rush of blood to his face. To be crossed in front of a servant was intolerable.

'Well, what is it?' He snapped the words out, short and cold.

'Maggy and I want to get married. We want to get married right away, and we'll go and live at Weaver's, I've a plan worked out for the next few years. I've been busy on it during the evenings.'

The pounding in Thomas's temples was almost deafening him. 'It looks to me,' he roared, 'as if you've been busy at something else in the evenings, too.' He dropped his gaze to Maggy's belly and the girl flushed suddenly, pulling the shawl she'd put over her work dress more tightly around her.

Albert's face changed. He became very like Thomas: they were bull-like in their aggression.

'I shall ignore that,' Albert said. 'I think it's better we all pretend you never said that, Father. I want your blessing, that's all. With or without it, I shall marry Maggy.' He held his head high and clutched Maggy's hand more tightly.

'You need more than my blessing, boy, you need my permission.' Thomas felt sweat break out on his forehead. This couldn't have been worse timed. The contract for the sale of Weaver's Farm was in the drawer of the desk behind him. He must sign it and effect the sale: he needed the money.

'You can't not give it, Pa,' Albert almost wailed. He looked very young. 'Maggy and I, that is we . . . well, you and Mother had to marry because of a baby and no one stood in your way.' The silence in the room was thunderous. Albert could feel the trembling in Maggy's hand, and the colour of his father's face was terrible, but what else could he do? Babies didn't wait: he had to marry Maggy and get settled in at Weaver's before it was too late. They couldn't stay on at Reason Hill, surely his father could understand that.

'Anything I can do?' Bill looked over at Michael, who for the third time that morning had slammed the telephone receiver back on to its rest after getting involved in an argument with a caller.

'What? About that?' Michael's voice was curt. 'No, there's nothing you can do, that was just another paper-pushing idiot making my work as difficult as possible.'

'No, I didn't mean about work. I mean about whatever is wrong between you and Isabella.'

Michael's face became – if it was possible – even more forbidding. He had returned from London a changed man.

'It's none of your business,' he said.

'Not yet it isn't, I agree, but a few more shouting matches like the one you had on the phone just now and it will become my business. You've been concerned enough about pointing out how my relationship with Arabella

137

mustn't interfere with the project and now it's my turn, Michael. No one can talk to you, and it's making our job impossible. If you don't want my help, then fine, but you've got to sort yourself out.'

Michael stood up abruptly. He knew he was on a short fuse. It would be the easiest thing in the world for him to rant and rave at Bill, but it wasn't the answer. 'I'll go out for a bit,' he said. 'Mind the shop will you?' He made a small attempt at a smile, then went out of the office.

Arabella kept her eyes fixed firmly on her typing. She'd learned not to volunteer to communicate with Michael over the last few days.

The day was chill, the water windswept. Grey water, grey clouds, the waves were short, vicious. Michael shivered abruptly. He was only wearing a jacket, but he wasn't going back inside for his coat: he felt he needed to be buffeted by the wind to clear his head. He stood still for a while, breathing in the salt-laden air, but it didn't seem to help so he turned and walked out of the camp. He took the road that led up and away from the harbour. Once out of the perimeter gates it became narrow and twisting; it was sunk between high verges and topped with hawthorn. There was shelter here and the sound of the wind no longer made thought difficult. He began to stride out, he needed to stretch his legs. He'd been cramped up in the office for too long after being confined in the car for all those hours driving. How many hours had it been? He couldn't really remember, but he'd left London as soon as he'd found Isabella had gone back to Pencombe. He couldn't understand her any more.

Michael kicked savagely at a stone lying in the road. It skittered along, and when it stopped he kicked it again. He was being like a boy, a child, like one of his sons. He missed them. He'd hardly seen them growing up. They'd soon be men and he wondered if they thought that they knew their father. Were they proud of him?

Michael had been proud of his father, but he hadn't realized it until the end. Then, when it had been too late to tell the old man, he'd understood how proud he was of the stubbornness, perhaps even of the selfishness. His father had been one of a generation of spectacular achievers. In retrospect the late Lord Montford had achieved less than most, but he'd gone by his own lights, followed his own path, been unswayed by others. Would Michael's sons feel the same about him? He thought of Pencombe. The lane he was in could never have been in Kent. The plants were different and even in late autumn there was a strange foreign richness, but it was still England. It was like meeting a woman you knew well who had subtly changed, wearing a new style of dress, a different perfume. A woman, he thought again, bringing his thoughts back to Isabella. She would be at Pencombe now. It was his home, his responsibility. He should want to be there – but he didn't. He kicked the stone for a last time, sending it skidding far up the road, then turned to walk back. He would have to do something about Isabella, but he hadn't got the energy to do it today, he would wait a few days, until he'd cooled down, until he was less likely to say the wrong thing.

Bill had a message for him on his return. Lucinda had telephoned and she would like Michael to return her call. He dialled her number hurriedly. He had been disloyal to his wife in his thoughts, it was like invoking fate to do something unpleasant.

'Hello, Lucinda.' His voice was high, questioning, but he relaxed at the calm, unhurried tone of her reply.

'Hello, Michael, thanks for calling back. How are you? How's Bill?' She wasn't listening for his reply, he could feel that, and she went on. 'You know I'm concerned about Isabella. She's hidden herself away at Pencombe. She's not getting out and about, and after all there's no excuse, she's got that car.' Lucinda envied Isabella the car. 'I've asked her over here to Reason Hill, but she won't come and when I suggested that Thomas should take us all over to Pencombe she made an excuse. It's not natural. After all, we are family.'

Michael felt himself smile. Isabella had said she was sure they'd see more of Lucinda when they inherited the title. 'I don't see what you can expect me to do about Isabella being a bit difficult to get hold of. I'm a lot further away from her than you are,' he said.

'Yes, you certainly are.' Lucinda's voice was heavy with sarcasm and Michael flushed with embarrassment.

'Well, what do you want me to do, Lucinda?'

'I want you to start looking after your wife! And don't splutter at me, Michael. You should be at Pencombe with her. The estate is in the most terrible mess. Thomas has heard all sorts of things about the state of the tenancies there. It's a scandal. You should be dealing with all of it, not leaving it to a woman. And your sons are your responsibility, too. They need their father; I would have thought even you realized that.'

'What exactly do you mean by that?'

'Oh my goodness.' There was a muffled sound of voices on the line and Michael realized Lucinda must be conferring with Thomas. After a while her voice came back clearly.

'William and Edward are at Pencombe,' she said. 'They've not actually been expelled – ' she emphasized the word 'actually' ' – but it was pretty close, I gather. They've been found out gambling, it's the most tremendous fuss. You know, Michael, you really do have a lot to answer for.' Lucinda stopped talking, her smugness hung on the line.

'Thank you for telling me, Lucinda,' Michael said. His voice was very calm, quite correct. 'I'll tell Isabella that you're concerned about her.' He put the telephone receiver gently on to its cradle and sat back in his chair. He'd never been in trouble at school and neither had Johnnie, but they'd seen plenty of others who had been. The verdict on most of those boys was that it had to do with trouble at home. Unbelievably that was how it must be for William and Edward. Michael closed his eyes and breathed in slowly. He had to face up to it. He would have to go to Isabella, and they would have to sort things out, for the sake of the boys, as well as for the sake of themselves.

A light sleet blew on the wind and stung Isabella's face. It was early November, but it felt more like January. She screwed up her eyes and pulled her headscarf further forward.

'Patch! Patch!' she called. She had lost sight of the terrier for a moment and now he seemed to have disappeared completely. She was walking over some rough plough at the edge of a small plantation of pines; they were nearly home. It was typical of Patch to go off exploring on his own.

'Where are you?' Isabella poked the walking stick she carried into some dead bracken and rustled it encouragingly. Terriers were the end, they were always getting into mischief, and the black ring around the little dog's eye that had given him his name seemed to add to the little chap's naughtiness. She was getting wet, she could feel the damp soaking through her coat. It hadn't looked like rain when they'd set out so she hadn't bothered with a waterproof. Her feet were freezing and she jumped up and down on the spot, trying to warm herself. 'Patch!' she shouted again. 'Where the hell are you?'

'Afternoon, your Ladyship.' The greeting made her spin round in surprise. She hadn't heard anyone come up behind her.

'Good afternoon, Mathew.' It was the farmer who tenanted the Home Farm. His weatherbeaten face looked older than the fifty-five years she knew him to be: she'd seen his age on the tenancy papers when she'd gone through them with the factor only that morning. 'I don't suppose you've seen my dog, have you? It's the fox terrier, the one with the black eye.'

'No, I've seen no terrier,' he said. 'How long's he been gone then?' The farmer's defences were aroused. Her Ladyship might own the acres she walked on, but he farmed them. The stock that ran on the land was his and a loose dog was a menace.

'Ten minutes, a quarter of an hour perhaps. I think he's in these woods. He was sniffing along the edge when I saw him last.'

'As long as he's not in with my chickens.'

'No, no, I'm sure he's not.' Isabella felt suddenly concerned for the little dog; he did get into scrapes.

They walked a short way into the wood. The wind moaned in the swaying tree tops above them, it felt very bleak.

'Years ago I shot a dog belonging to your husband,' the farmer said. 'I found it worrying my sheep. I won't have people's dogs savaging my livestock.' He stared implacably ahead and Isabella shivered. Poor little Patch, she thought. Where are you?

'There!' The man beside her moved forwards suddenly and she followed. He pointed at the base of a pine, where tangled bramble had been left to grow by a careless forester. 'That's where he'll be.' The ground the brambles grew in was pitted with several burrows. It was small for a warren, but fresh earth showed that it was occupied. 'He'll be down there. He'll gorge himself on a rabbit, then get too fat himself to come out, he'll probably smother. I've seen it often enough.' He rocked back on his heels in satisfaction at the usual way of things.

'Smother? What a horrible thought. We can't let him die down there. Patch! Patch!' Isabella knelt by the nearest rabbit hole and pushed her face close to it so that she could shout down into the inky blackness. She had to be careful of the thorns. 'Patch!' she called again, then she twisted her head to look at the man standing so complacent. 'If he's here we'll need help, we'll need spades, and a blanket in case he's hurt. Patch!' she shouted again and then stood up quickly; a tiny muffled bark had answered her. 'That's him, go on, please, and get some help,' she said. 'I'll stay here, only do hurry, I can't stand the thought of him suffocating – it would be dreadful, poor little thing.' She looked distractedly back at the warren and the farmer went slowly away. She could hear him muttering. She closed her eyes, she'd seen just this morning what a pitiful rent he was contributing to the estate. Then, in his absence she had sympathized with him. She had ignored the factor's rumbling discontentedly at the man's refusal to modernize, to do something to improve the pittance he made on what could be fertile acres. Now she wanted to shout after the farmer, to tell him to hurry up, get a move on or she'd make him, she'd make him all right. She opened her eyes, she realized how ridiculous she was being. But it was so difficult trying to put the estate on some kind of even footing; without selling off some of the land it was going to be impossible. She bent to call again for Patch, thinking that the sound of her voice might keep him going. The answering bark was cross. The little dog was beginning to resent his captivity. She listened carefully

143

and she could just hear him scrabbling. 'Patch!' she called again. She put her ear right by the hole, she could hear him trying to dig his way out. She put her hands to the earth. It was cold, clinging to her fingers, she began pulling it back, it was surprisingly easy to move. She knelt to work more efficiently and soon she had moved enough earth to see further into the rabbit hole. It went right under the tree. She looked in dismay at the thick roots barring her way, no one could dig down in amongst those. 'Patch! Patch!' she called again, but this time there was no answer.

The farmer brought his son with him, a broad, cheerful young man in his mid-twenties. He grinned at Isabella, obviously amused to see the lady from the big house with mud on her hands. Isabella stood and brushed some of the sticky clay from her skirt.

'Are you going to try and dig him out?' She didn't believe that would work, not now that she'd seen the tree roots.

'We might have to, then again, we might not.'

She watched as the younger man laid down a haversack beside the small pile of earth that she'd moved with her hands. He fumbled inside the bag for a moment and then with a flourish brought out a handful of something dark, reddish brown. Whatever it was it stuck to his fingers, and Isabella leaned forwards to see it more clearly. The smell struck her like a blow; it was putrid.

'Ox melt, 'bout a week old,' the farmer's son said, happily oblivious to the stench. 'Pull a ferret out of a hole at twenty feet, reckon it should work on your little blighter.' He smeared the decomposing meat around his fist and then knelt down to shove his hand as far as it would go into the hole. 'Come on out, you little bugger,' he shouted cheerfully. Then he remembered Isabella, 'Beggin' your pardon, your Ladyship,' he said, but the grin didn't falter.

* * *

Isabella carried a chastened Patch home wrapped up in the tattered blanket that the farmer had provided. Now the blanket, the dog, and she reeked of that dreadful meat. She was furious with the little dog now that it was safe, and furious with herself for having been so silly as to have let him go down the hole in the first place. She went round by the stables to shut Patch up and change her clothes before returning to give him a bath. A thorough bath he could have. He hated them; perhaps it would make him think twice before going down another rabbit hole. She had just closed the stable door on the dog when Michael called out.

'Isabella!'

She turned as he walked towards her. For the first time in their lives neither of them smiled in greeting; the kiss he gave her on the cheek was perfunctory. He fell into step beside her as she walked back towards the house.

'I've heard about the boys,' he said. 'I've taken a week's leave, it should be long enough to sort something out.' The coldness in his voice was matched by the chill she felt inside.

Michael and Isabella faced each other across the desk. The tenancy documents made a formidable pile between them, but the précis of relevant facts that Isabella held in her hand was only a few foolscap sheets.

'This might have been easier with Smaile to help,' Isabella said. She had been annoyed when Michael had refused to have the factor present.

'I don't need an outsider to tell me things I know already.'

'Does that mean you don't want to see this?' Isabella held up the pages she and the factor had prepared.

'Don't be silly, Isabella. Pass it to me, will you?'

Isabella handed over the sheets of paper that told Pencombe's story. It wasn't one with a happy ending.

145

'We'll have to sell a lot of the land I'm afraid,' she said. 'The tenanted farms won't fetch a great deal, but they're too much of a drain on the estate.' Isabella tailed off as Michael looked up from the papers. She couldn't judge what he was thinking from his face, the expression on it was closed, defensive. But the situation had to be resolved and she began to talk again. 'If you're only here for a week then you'll have to rely on me for help, Michael. You won't have time to go through everything from scratch.' She was controlling her temper, what happened to Pencombe was too important for too many people; she couldn't allow her own problems to get in the way. And there were still the boys to sort out. They were keeping out of their father's way, but they couldn't stay away from school indefinitely.

'Very well,' Michael tossed the papers down on to the desk. 'What do we do?'

'You must approve the plan that's been drawn up. With luck we'll be left with the Home Farm, a couple of hundred acres of woodland, and the house and gardens. I've worked on a scheme to increase the money we get from day visitors who come to look round the house. We're not too far from London now that more people have cars, and what we really need to do is encourage the trippers, make a car park for their charabancs, open a tea shop, things like that. Pencombe could be very popular, after all it's very historic, there are still some lovely pieces of furniture and the countryside itself is so beautiful here.' She looked defiantly at her husband who was leaning back in his chair, clearly scandalized at her suggestions. 'Then I think we can hold on, as long as nothing too awful happens, like the roof falling in.' She smiled nervously, feeling tempted for a moment to touch wood. 'Or, God forbid, there's another war. I know you'll hate it, Michael, but it's this or nothing. The easy way out would be to sell up everything and move up to London. We'd have a better standard of living that way, but I thought you would want to keep Pencombe for William.' Poor William, Isabella thought, he'd inherit a millstone round his neck and she only hoped he'd be happy with it.

'Yes, William must have Pencombe.' Michael could hardly believe it, he really was going to have to sell up. What a stigma to be the Montford to break up the estate.

'Can I tell Smaile to set things in motion then?'

'Yes, yes, do that.' Michael would have liked to say to wait until he'd gone back to Falmouth. He couldn't bear the thought of having to face the worried farmers who, he knew, would come, cap in hand, to see him, to try and get him to change his mind. God, he thought, what an awful mess. He stared unseeingly ahead. 'And now that's decided I suppose we'd better talk about the boys.'

'I think,' Isabella breathed in deeply, 'it would be better if we began by talking about us. We can't go on like this, Michael, or at least I can't go on this way. I'm sure that our relationship is what's affected the boys.'

'Yes, I'd thought that, too.'

'Then, we can't allow it to. I don't know what you feel, Michael.' Isabella suddenly felt desolate. 'What an awful thing to say, after all these years, I don't have any idea what your feelings are about me any more.'

Michael stood up. He felt claustrophobic, trapped into investigating his emotions, and that was something he didn't want to do. 'I love you,' he said, but it was a defence rather than a statement of fact.

'What is love?' Isabella almost whispered the words. What, after all, was love? Was it the passion that seemed to have faded over the years, was it loyalty, faithfulness, or was it, in the end, staying together for the sake of the children?

'I was very hurt when you left London without a word,' Michael said. 'Why on earth did you go off like that?'

'I don't know really, I just couldn't face you, couldn't face up to the fact that we seem to be two strangers. Michael, what on earth is happening to us?' It hurt her, almost more than she could bear, the realization that something really was happening, they were going to part — they had already in a sense.

'I'm going to talk to the boys. This isn't getting us anywhere. Do you want to come with me?'

Isabella shook her head. 'I think you should see them on their own. They know something's wrong.'

'I'm not bloody well surprised.' Michael's temper snapped suddenly. 'Anyone with half an eye could see something's very wrong indeed. You look as if you're in mourning. Good God, why on earth are you wearing that ghastly dress? And couldn't you put on some make-up or something? You act as miserable as sin, and you look it too.'

'How dare you!' Isabella's cheeks were flaming. 'What right have you got to speak to me like that? How dare you, Michael, after all I've put up with . . .' She was so angry that she was almost lost for words.

'Put up with? That's a good one.' Michael looked very autocratic, he was holding his head high, looking down on her from the superiority of his height, and suddenly from what he felt as the superiority of his lineage as well. 'I seem to remember that your father was more than delighted with what I brought you, and you can't say you've ever gone without. Many women — no, I'll change that — most other women would envy you your life, Isabella. I expect a wife of mine to act like a lady and to look like one. That means that I don't want to hear suggestions of charabancs or tea shops; no one in my family has ever considered that kind of thing.'

'No one in your family ever inherited an estate on the verge of bankruptcy. And there's nothing else you can do about it, because you can't do the traditional thing and marry an heiress – or is that what this is all about? Do you want a divorce? Because if you do, Michael, you can damn well have one.'

They were standing facing each other in their fury, Isabella's final words had shocked them both into silence, as William came bursting into the room.

'Mum!' He looked excited. 'I was on the phone to Eli. He said that Viccy's done a bunk again. Apparently there's hell to pay up there.'

'Oh no, that silly girl . . .' Isabella was exhausted by her own emotions, the thought of Victoria throwing life into further chaos was almost unbearable. She was too tired to tell William to mind his language. 'I'll have to go to Lucinda.' She looked at Michael, willing all their differences to be over, wanting him to say he would go with her.

'Yes, you'd better go,' Michael said. 'And while you're gone I'll sort this problem out with the boys. To begin with, William – ' he looked sternly at his son ' – what precisely were you doing on the telephone to Eli? You know perfectly well I do not consider him a good influence for you.'

Isabella walked slowly from the room. Perhaps it was just as well that she had to leave. It seemed that she and Michael found it impossible to communicate any more. Was this how it happened, was this why people began dealing through solicitors, why divorce was bitter, painful? She would change her clothes before going up to town. She knew she looked dowdy, but it hadn't seemed to matter.

With a flare of defiance at the hurt that Michael had inflicted with his words, Isabella dressed in her most elegant suit, then she put on a maroon felt cloche hat that she had bought for a country wedding they were to go to soon, and finally she put on lipstick and a little rouge. She looked at the finished result in the mirror and was pleased with it. When she walked out and closed the bedroom door behind her it felt as if she was closing the door on a part of her life.

Arabella kept on waving until Bill drove out of sight. She stood for several minutes more, looking up the now deserted lane, knowing that the car wouldn't come into view again but loath to admit that she had the next few weeks to face alone.

It was the first time that she had felt isolated, too far from London. The prospect of the hours of typing that awaited her attention was definitely not appealing. She turned and walked slowly back towards the hut. It was such a pleasant day that it was a pity to have to be indoors. That was one advantage of being in the south, the weather was generally better. The sound of a bicycle on the gravel behind her made her look round. It was Sally, at least she didn't have to start her lone vigil at the typewriter right away.

'Arabella, just the person I wanted to see.' Sally was bright, cheerful. Pretty in a freckly sort of way, she was very typical of the girls who did well in the forces. She was a stenographer like Arabella. 'Look, it's such a lovely day today that it's inspired me. I've got next Saturday off, so how about a sail in the bay? Your beloved's got a boat, hasn't he? I thought just a potter, nothing too strenuous. I'm desperate to get away from the office for a bit. David's throwing a moodie, you know how awful he can be.' She pulled a long face that was a reasonable enough imitation of Sally's boss to make Arabella laugh.

'That's a lovely idea,' Arabella smiled. It would be much

better facing the next few days' official chores with the prospect of some fun at the weekend. 'I'll have to be on duty in the morning, but how about two o'clock down on the jetty?'

'Done!' Sally cycled off with a wave and Arabella hurried back into the hut. She would get through mountains of work with Bill away. That would show him that she could survive without him – not that she wanted to.

There were two lifejackets belonging to the sailing dinghy *Kittiwake* and they were much lighter to wear than the regulation issue that they all tried to avoid, so Arabella went all the way back to her lodgings to fetch them before going down to the jetty. She smiled to herself, Bill would be delighted at how conscientious she was being. He still kept reminding her about the time she hadn't been wearing her lifejacket and they'd nearly capsized. Dear Bill! He'd only been away a few days and already she was missing him madly.

Kittiwake was bobbing merrily on the water. The dark varnish shone like chestnut on the clinker-built hull. The boat's name was painted in flowing script in a sky-blue paint. Bill had fallen in love with the boat the minute he'd seen it, just as he'd fallen in love with Arabella, he'd said. She tugged on the painter that tied *Kittiwake* to the jetty and looked down into the boat. There was no water slopping around in the bilge to need baling out so she had nothing to do but wait. She sat down on the jetty, her feet dangling over the edge, only inches from the water. It was a splendid afternoon: the sun kept breaking through the dove-coloured clouds sailing majestically high above. The water was choppy but inviting, blue rather than grey, friend rather than foe. She tilted her face back to catch the sun and closed her eyes.

The rumble of Sally's bicycle on the wooden jetty

interrupted her day-dreaming. She turned to smile a greeting and then got to her feet. Inexplicably Sally was still in uniform.

'Arabella, I'm so sorry.' She sounded angry. 'I told you the old so-and-so was in a mood. He's ordered me to turn out with him this afternoon at some awful reception, miles away. I've taken a chance dashing down here to tell you – he'll be furious if he finds out I've left the office. Look – ' she paused, seeing Arabella's disappointment ' – I am sorry, let's do it another day, soon?' She was cycling away before Arabella had even replied.

Damn and blast! Arabella stared at the cheerful yellow of the lifejackets mocking her from the boat. She'd never sailed *Kittiwake* on her own, Bill had said he thought it would be too much for her to handle. She looked out across the water. A sprinkling of other boats were enjoying what may well be the last good sailing day of the year. 'Nonsense,' she muttered as she pulled hard on the painter and then stepped down easily into the boat. Of course she could manage it on her own. She put on her lifejacket and began to unfurl the sails. As she performed the familiar tasks she began to relax. There had been no need for her to have company, and Sally's prattling sometimes got on her nerves. This was a much better idea.

She was doing famously! *Kittiwake* responded well to single-handed sailing, communicating through the vibrating tiller and a friendly whistling in the rigging. Arabella had tacked across the open water of the harbour, changing course with the demands of the wind. When the sun shone she was warm, almost hot, but when it went behind a cloud she was cold and the grey light reminded her how close they were to winter. It made her afternoon's sailing doubly precious. She glanced at her watch: half past three, there wasn't much more time. She should aim to be back at the jetty by four-thirty at the latest. Evening came surprisingly quickly and she didn't want it to be dark for the bike ride back to her lodgings as the battery in her front lamp was almost dead. But she had a little while longer.

It wasn't until she looked back towards the shore that she realized how quickly the mist had come up, or was it down? She couldn't tell if the grey, fluffy fog that hung on the water had rolled down off the hills or blown in from the sea. Not that it mattered, but she would have to be careful. She didn't want to collide with another boat coming back late. Not that she could see any other boats out on the water; they must have got in before her.

The sun had stopped its struggle with the clouds and it was uniformly grey now. Rain scudded suddenly across the water, drumming against the tight drawn sail. She had to tack again and again. The wind kept changing direction, and although there was plenty of breeze to sail by, it wasn't blowing away the mist that was getting denser, rolling towards her. She had to tack again. She wished that Sally had been with her; it was awkward keeping her sense of direction with the wind changing so often, and her having to work to keep the boat heading into it. She looked again at her watch. Four-thirty. It was taking much longer than she'd realized to get back. Of course, the tide was against her, it was going out now and she hadn't bothered too much about that as they could always get up to their jetty, even at low tide. She realized that she'd been a bit too casual about coming out. She shook her head irritably. There wasn't any point in lecturing herself, first she had to get back on shore and with the mist that was now, finally, all around her, she had to concentrate.

'I'm disappointed in you, Eli.' Dimitrou's handsome face was most expressive in its displeasure. 'You know I wouldn't let Victoria stay here, and yet you start throwing accusations around.' He paused for a moment as, with an elegant flick of his wrist, he swirled the inch of cognac in the bulbous glass he was holding. He was beginning to relax now that the club had closed and he was secure in the knowledge that Victoria was safely hidden away. 'Of course,' he continued, 'if I was a cynic, I would say that the little business of Victoria is simply a smoke screen. But whether it is or is not true that she has run away from home again, is not a matter that concerns me. The position of debt that you have got yourself into here is quite another matter. When do we get our money?' His voice was soft as silk, and as strong.

'I've told you, you'll get it when I can squeeze some out of my trustees. You've no idea how difficult they are. My old man was an idiot to leave my inheritance tied up like that.'

Dimitrou didn't smile back at Eli who was trying to appear nonchalant while his stomach was contracting in knots of fear. He had the feeling that he had got into debt with the wrong people. Dimitrou looked suddenly very foreign indeed.

'We understand that another member of your family was left a great deal of money by your father. And his inheritance was not tied up in a trust. We also understand that that man's daughter happens – ' he paused, under-lining his point ' – happens to be Victoria.'

Eli suddenly understood all of it: Victoria had stepped, or rather run, straight into the spider's web.

'Fifty thousand pounds,' Dimitrou said. 'Fifty thousand pounds you owe us Eli, and you're overdue. I suggest you ask your family for help. I am sure in the circumstances that they will get you out of your difficulty.'

Eli left the club in a daze. He was in way over his head. There was no way he could raise that much money himself.

He'd been a fool to carry on gambling but he'd been so sure it would come out all right in the end. It had just needed his luck to change; he'd had a losing streak that was all. He was so agitated that he walked away from the club without even bothering to look for a taxi. He began to imagine the words he'd have to use to tell Thomas what had happened. How on earth could he tell the man that they'd got Viccy? The more he thought about what to say to Thomas the more he realized that he couldn't bring himself to do it. Perhaps flight was the answer. But to hide from people like Dimitrou you needed a lot of money, and he didn't have access to it. He stood still. There had to be a way out of the hole he'd got himself into, he just couldn't see it. He needed help. He stepped towards the edge of the pavement and scanned the road. He wanted a taxi, he was in a hurry.

Luke listened to Eli's story and then sat silently thinking. Eli found the silence unnerving, but he didn't break it. He was depending on Luke to come up with an answer.

Eventually Luke spoke. 'Go back to Cadogan Gardens now, and talk to Thomas,' he said, 'but don't tell him you believe they have Victoria.' Luke was staring down at his hands, concentrating hard. 'Tell him about your own situation, and make sure you appear very, very worried.' He looked up, enforcing his words with the seriousness of his expression. 'You are to go to any extent, beg if you must, to get Thomas to pay that debt. Say that you believe they will harm you, seriously harm you if you do not repay now.'

'I won't have to fake that,' Eli laughed nervously. 'I think they'll murder me if they don't get paid.'

'No, they won't kill you.'

To Eli's horror, Luke had taken the remark seriously.

'At least not right away,' he continued. 'The thing to

remember is that they want their money and dead men don't pay debts, but they'll certainly make you wish, very much, that you had paid them off. Violence is one of the results of gambling debts not being enforceable by law. The only recourse these people have is to pain, which, I must agree is very effective.' He smiled. 'You've been foolish, Eli, but it's done me a favour, so you'll come out all right in the end. Tell me as soon as Thomas has handed over the money.' He stood up, wanting Eli to get going with the business in hand.

'But you'll want to know before he hands over the fifty thousand, won't you? I mean that's how we'll get Victoria back isn't it?'

Luke smiled at his naïvety. 'I'll get Victoria back long before you and Thomas pay your Mr Dimitrou a visit, but she won't be going straight home. No, we'll make Thomas wait a little longer to have his daughter back.'

Eli realized then how much of a pawn he was – as was Victoria. He wished very much that he'd never discovered the seductive delights of the gaming tables.

'No, I can't do anything to help you now, can't you understand?' Thomas was distraught. Eli's admission that he was in urgent need of financial help had pushed Thomas's emotions to the edge of despair. 'We've no idea where Viccy is, nobody has. You swear you don't know, Eli, but by God I'd kill you if I thought . . .'

'No, no.' Eli put out a hand to fend off the attack he thought his brother-in-law was about to make. 'I've told you, I've no idea where she's gone. But she just went to a hotel last time, I don't see why you're so worried, she's probably done the same thing again.' He looked uncomfortable, but fortunately Thomas was too overwrought to see it. Victoria had certainly done the same as last time, only now she wasn't going to get home so easily. Eli let the fear he felt touch his voice. 'Anyway, Thomas, you're not the only one threatening to kill me.'

'What on earth do you mean?'

'I said I couldn't wait for the money, and I meant it. If I don't give them the fifty thousand pounds before Thursday then, well . . .' His voice broke and he looked down at his feet. He didn't want Thomas looking in his eyes to recognize the Judas he felt inside. 'It's Thursday or I've had it.'

'My God, fifty thousand pounds? But that's ridiculous, you've to raise that kind of money in just two days – you can't be serious, Eli.' Young Eli's revelation had taken Thomas's thoughts from Victoria. He looked at his brother-in-law in open disbelief.

'I've never been more serious. If you want to know how bad it is, I've sold my car. Yes, go on, look amazed, but it's true, it's that serious, I've sold the Bugatti, for a pittance of what she's worth, but I don't have any option. And I phoned the chap renting Linstone to ask him if he wanted to buy, I've got to have the money, it doesn't matter how I get it.'

'Have you approached your trustees?'

'Oh, what, the marvellous lawyers? Yes, I've spoken to them, but it's no go, and in any case if they did cash it all in and hand it over there still wouldn't be enough. There's precious little value in my inheritance, you should know that.'

Thomas flushed brick red. When Eli Bradbury died he'd left a complex will. Lucinda and Isabella had been allocated comfortable incomes from the brewery-based business empire that their father had owned. To Thomas, as natural guardian of that business, had gone the largest portion of capital from the estate, to be injected into the companies, as was right and proper. Young Eli had been left Linstone Park, the Bradbury home; that had been a logical provision as both Isabella and Lucinda were married and had homes of their own. Young Eli's income was to come from a moderate trust fund, administered by his father's solicitors. It provided him with a reasonable income, but left room, his father had hoped, for inspiration to go out into the world and make his own fortune. The impetus had not worked.

'What was Wright's answer?' Thomas asked. Wright was the retired general who rented the lovely sandstone house called Linstone. It had struck Thomas forcibly that he would be very loath to let the property out of the family.

'He said he couldn't afford it, even though I told him it would be dirt cheap.' Eli's face twisted at the remembrance of the airs and graces that the military man affected, whilst in reality he was as poor as a church mouse.

'What do you want for it?'

'Why?' Eli was suddenly very alert; there was a new interest in Thomas's face.

'If I pay your debts off, will you give me the title to the property in exchange?'

Fifty thousand, Eli thought. It was a lot of money to get for the house, a lot more than it would make on the open market. 'In full and final settlement of the fifty?' he asked. 'You wouldn't turn round and want me to pay anything more back?'

'No, I reckon that would be reasonable,' Thomas said.

'Even though there's only twenty-five acres of land with it?' The twelve hundred or so acres that had once been Linstone's land were now owned by Michael and Isabella: it had been Isabella's marriage portion from her father, and now formed part of the Pencombe estate. Thomas had the tenancy of the land; it was an arrangement that suited them all.

'I know all there is to know about the property, Eli.

Now come on, do you want to do it? I'll pay your debt if you'll transfer the house to me.'

Eli stepped forwards, his hand outstretched. 'Done,' he said. Thomas felt a surge of pleasure. He was an experienced man of business; he would bargain with the club owners to buy out Eli's debts – they'd probably be more than happy to settle for ten shillings in the pound. The prospect of getting hold of Linstone for what would probably be only twenty-five thousand pounds was very pleasing. He would have to raise the money through his bank, but on such a security there would be no problem at all. Then, like a cold chill, the thought of Victoria came back. For a few minutes he'd forgotten she was missing. In his mental picture of his family at home at Linstone he'd seen her there. Now he had to face again the fact that they didn't know where she was. Eli watched the consternation on Thomas's face with alarm. 'You're not changing your mind?' he asked.

'No,' Thomas said, 'but I can't allow it to take up my time. We'll have to do this very quickly.' He looked down at his watch, it was past three o'clock in the morning. 'Well, at least that sort don't sleep at night,' he said grimly. 'Come on, get your hat and coat. We'll go at once. I'll leave a note for Lucinda. With luck we'll be back here before she wakes up.'

They went out of the front door very quietly. It was bitterly cold and the streets were glistening with frost. Thomas pulled his Crombie coat more tightly about him. He felt an unreasoning fear for his daughter. Where intelligent thought convinced him that she was indeed acting as she had before and simply staying away to upset him, irrationally he thought of her being out in the night. Memories of his Victorian childhood came unasked for into his thoughts, waifs and strays abandoned in the frozen dark. He gripped Eli's elbow firmly and hurried him along the pavement. They had to get this over and done with quickly. He was desperate to hurry towards the dawn.

Johnnie was walking across the hall towards Mary's room when the doorbell rang. The restrained hollow chimes were still echoing as he turned and went quickly back into his study. He slammed the door hard behind him. Visitors were not encouraged to call until after luncheon at the white-painted mansion. He liked his mornings private. He went straight to the window knowing that he would not be able to see the caller from the restricted angle of vision it gave him, but he was inspired to tell Mary how beautifully their plans were dovetailing together and he couldn't bring himself to sit down again at his desk. He strained to listen for voices in the hall, but could hear nothing. How long should he wait? He began to count slowly. When he reached twenty he turned back from the window; this was ridiculous.

'Mary!' He strode into the room, looking to where she was lying, as always, on the sofa. For once she was not looking towards him. Her attention was fixed on the man who stood by the fire.

'Hello, Johnnie,' Bill said. 'Don't you have a welcome for the returning hero?' The sarcasm of the tone was matched by the expression on his face. He looked from Mary to Johnnie, from his wife to his brother-in-law, and his face twisted in a grim smile, he could see now everything his mother had told him was true. 'I've gone through years of hell thanks to you two. I never knew, God, I never even guessed what was going on.' He walked quickly across the room to lean over Mary, wanting almost to hit her but when he looked down into her eyes, he felt it suddenly wasn't worth it. Why waste his emotion? He stood up again. 'Suddenly I'm free, and it's so good I can hardly bear it. You deserve each other, you two. I suppose you always did. I haven't told your wife, Johnie, and I don't think Mother did. You'll have to perform that chore yourself. And you'd better do it, because if you don't I shall and that won't look too good during the divorce proceedings. I reckon Adele will end up a very wealthy woman.'

Johnnie was standing very still, watching Bill. He was mesmerized, he had never thought this was how it would happen. It must have been Betsy, but why now, why after all this time?

'I've instructed my attorney already, so the legal proceedings are under way,' Bill continued, 'but I wanted the pleasure of telling you both face to face. And I also wanted to let you know the good news. The day I get my divorce I'm going to marry the most beautiful girl in the world. Now don't turn your lips down like that, Mary, or Johnnie won't like you any more, and no one else is going to take over his role. You know, I never thought I was the vindictive type, but I think I've discovered a flaw in my character. I'm glad you two will be left with each other; it won't be such fun when it's all out in the open. After all, what's the expression? Forbidden fruit tastes sweetest and all that. You can wish me *bon voyage*, if you want. I'm going straight back to England to start the rest of my life, my wonderful, happy life.' He walked towards the door, with a spring in his step that Mary had never seen before. 'Oh, and I nearly forgot.' He turned and smiled at them both, the smile of a man delighted with his lot. 'There's no point in your getting excited about my revelations that I already have plans to remarry. If you try to make me the guilty party in our divorce, Mary, I will enlighten the police as to you and your boyfriend's business relationship with some of the most vicious bootleggers around. Don't look so surprised, Johnnie, nothing goes on in this house that Betsy doesn't know about.'

Johnnie hadn't moved since Bill had begun talking, and he didn't move for a long time after his brother-in-law had left. Mary stared at him. She was too frightened to speak, too terrified that she might say the wrong thing. Abruptly, Johnnie turned and walked out of the room, the door slammed behind him and Mary found herself looking at the empty space where he had been. She put her hands up to her face. She felt trapped, the walls seemed about to close in on her. She huddled down into the sofa, feeling the smoothness of the cool fabric through her thin dress. She could feel everything, the touch of her own hands on her face, her shoulders against the cushion, her heart beating too fast, she could feel everything except her legs that stretched out in front of her. They'd tied her to this house, to Johnnie, and now that was all that was left, Johnnie, and he had walked away. She dropped her head back, waiting for the tears to come. But she had changed from the fragile creature who used to run away from hurt. Her mind began sifting the facts, dismissing as irrelevant Bill's assertion that they would not dare use his own admitted infidelity. There was something to be gained from all of this, and that something was money.

When Johnnie came back to her, having reached his own conclusions in the privacy of his study, she was ready. She began at once telling Johnnie her ideas, tugging at his jacket for him to sit down beside her on the couch.

'I had a phone call,' he lied. He had made a call, not received one. 'I have to go out. We'll talk later, maybe tomorrow.' He left the room after kissing her perfunctorily and she lay back. Johnnie would see, given time, that Bill's knowing was for the best. Without having to spend their time on subterfuge, they could achieve even more. She closed her eyes because the morning's events had tired her. Poor Johnnie, she thought, he was like a child who hated to be crossed. Tomorrow he would be on his knees begging her to forgive him for his churlishness.

'Nice of you to change your mind and agree to do our business down here, Johnnie.' Tony Bertiolie sat back in his chair; they had achieved the objectives of their meeting in the hotel lounge. The setting, with its midnight blue velvet-covered empire style furniture and ornate chandeliers, was almost feminine, but the business conducted in it – during the day – was uniquely male. The deal had been hard, but reasonable, now he could relax, and be a little civilized.

'Not at all, it made very little difference to me,' Johnnie said, he had appeared relaxed throughout the transaction, 'I just tell the driver where to go, sit back and enjoy the scenery.'

'Not much scenery for you down here,' Tony laughed. 'Could never understand my old man, he used to love it in The Loop. Breathe in the rotten air like it was French perfume. He loved the noise, the chaos. Now, me, I'm second generation, I'm more refined. I think the area's a dump. Sure we need the railway but whoever stuck it up on stilts like that, shoulda been certified. And the traffic, they're gonna have to do something, one of these days.'

'Let's just hope we're in on it, there'll be a lot of money made when they start rebuilding this area.'

'Talking about a lot of money,' Tony flicked his fingers, summoning the bell boy to top up his cup. 'You ever met Tex Rickard?'

'The man who runs Madison Square Gardens? No, I've never met him. Why, is he a friend of yours?' Johnnie watched as the boy poured the brown liquid from the tea pot; the bourbon was almost identical in colour to the best Indian tea.

'Will be. I've arranged for a mutual acquaintance to

introduce us. After the Toledo fight. I'm impressed, more than impressed. You know, they grossed over a million dollars. Now, that's what I call money.'

Johnnie sipped his drink in silent agreement. It seemed suddenly that he may have been underplaying his hand. The word 'millions' had a definite appeal.

'I lost a pile backin' the champion, Jess Willard. Never thought the boy Dempsey could beat him. Six foot seven in his socks, weighs in at two hundred and fifty pounds, used to be a cowboy, that's Willard. And he sure packed a hell of a punch.'

'I seem to remember Dempsey decimated him.'

'Sure, knocked him over seven times in the first three minutes, and it was all over after three rounds. Jeez, what a fight.'

'One million dollars.' Johnnie savoured the phrase, then he stood abruptly. 'Well, we've finished what we had to do. I'll set my end of things in motion, you know what to listen out for.'

'Sure, and look — ' Tony stood up to shake hands, to perform the usual farewells ' — like I said, thanks for comin' down here, it's meant I can get a couple of extra meetings into the day.'

Johnnie nodded his head and walked out of the hotel, and into the sunshine. He pulled his felt hat well over his face and hurried across the pavement to his car. Pavement, the word had surfaced unasked for, he was in America, it should be the sidewalk; Bill had brought memories of England with him. Johnnie was smiling lightly as the driver opened the door for him.

On the slow drive away from his meeting he had plenty of time to think. The Loop was throbbing with life, chaotic with traffic. Above him he could see the sinuous raised railway that offended Tony Bertiolie. He kept the windows of the car wound up against the noise and the fumes as they crept towards the intersection of State and Madison. What was it they said? It was the busiest corner in the world.

Chicago. How lucky he was that Adele's family had come from here. It was the centre, the crossroads. For the past couple of years it had also been the home of the new Mercantile Exchange; if Thomas Cade were here, he'd be mesmerized by the daily trading in carloads of eggs and onions, potatoes and poultry. If he visited the Union Stockyards, he'd never go home again. And what if Johnnie's brother Michael ever visited the Macaul establishment? Along with his wife Isabella they could join Betsy and her circuit of culture, her patronage of the Chicago Symphony Orchestra. She could bore them to tears, instead of him, with her reminiscences of how involved she'd been when it was founded by Theodore Thomas, and the story of her continuing friendship with the great conductor until he died.

Johnnie slowly lit his cigar. It was amusing to think of the people he knew in England, and how they would react to the life of the city. He himself — he breathed in the perfumed smoke — rose to the challenge. The Loop would be redeveloped, it was screaming out for it, there would be millions of dollars for the bold. But the Bertiolies' percentage was too high a price to pay for their assistance. He would be judicious in what he allowed them to see, he would create a few shell companies, trade behind a few brass plaques.

He settled back comfortably into his seat. From now on Mary also would be privy to only a portion of his secrets. Her husband's impending divorce action meant that she might be a risk and nothing appalled Johnnie more than the thought of his money being siphoned away. At last they left the traffic jam. Soon they would be back at the mansion on the hill, soon he could begin.

* * *

Michael read and reread the Pencombe figures. Isabella had been right. They couldn't take the financial drain of the tenanted farms any more. Having faced up to that fact he felt calmer. He helped himself to a generous whisky and sipped at it. In his anger, he had been too hard on the boys this afternoon, he realized that now. He wouldn't apologize to them, he wouldn't go that far, but he would be easier on them tomorrow. He'd also been too hard on Isabella. She'd worked effectively on the problems of the estate and all he'd done was to act like an idiot. But she should understand how painful it was. He poured himself a second drink, knowing as he did that he was being foolish. There was no one to keep him company and to begin drinking alone this early in the evening meant he'd go on until the early hours. That was a negation of responsibility suited more to youth than maturity.

He reached down to pat the dog that lay beside him. He liked to have Blackie in the study when he was alone. She lifted her head to stare up at him and the brown softness of her eyes enveloped him. He stroked around her muzzle, fondled her ears. He would have liked to take her out for a walk, but for all he knew the first letters from the factor had been delivered and he didn't want to have to face up to the reality of it all yet. He went up to the window and looked out. It was dark, not much moon, but that wouldn't have stopped him, he knew the paths like the back of his hand and Blackie could have led even a stranger. The world of darkness that he looked out on would be inhabited, he knew that. If they went up the lane away from the river they would come across someone out after rabbits. It was early for lanterning, but if it wasn't the men out, it would be the boys. If he walked along the riverbank he was more than likely to disturb a courting couple. Michael stared out into the blackness, the last thing he wanted was a reminder of bodily pleasures.

But he couldn't stay cooped up like this. He put the glass down on his desk. The second whisky had tasted peaty, over-oily; he wasn't enjoying the alcohol so what was the point in suffering for it in the morning? 'Come on, Blackie,' he called. They would go out on to the public road. In the dark he'd be just an anonymous man and his dog, but at least he'd get some exercise, and perhaps that would help him to think. That was what he needed to do, to think clearly and concisely. He must be decisive; he'd wasted too much time already.

'But this is Eli's car!' Victoria tried to pause on the pavement, but Dimitrou had her firmly by the elbow and was propelling her forcibly towards the red Bugatti that she had recognized. 'He never lends it to anyone.'

It was dark, but the interior light of the car was switched on and she could see there was a stranger sitting behind the wheel of the car, a young man with dark hair who looked rather like Dimitrou. She had never seen him before.

'Go on, get in.' Dimitrou almost pushed her into the car. He looked up and down the road, but there was no one in sight. 'It doesn't belong to your uncle any more, he sold it to my brother.' The man in the driving seat turned round to look at Victoria. His face was handsome but expressionless, and Victoria realized with alarm that Dimitrou was not coming with her. 'You'll be safe with Alexi,' he said as he closed the door.

She didn't want to go on her own. Quickly she wound down the window. 'I thought you were coming with me.'

'How could I? The club doesn't run itself. Besides if we both disappear it will be much too obvious.' He smiled encouragingly at her.

'But I thought, tonight . . .' Her cheeks were burning. 'I thought.' I thought you would make love to me, the words were so loud in her head, but she couldn't speak them, not with the other man listening.

He put his finger under her chin, tipping it up, so that her face was raised to him, 'I shall be with you soon, we will be together.' He dropped his gaze to her lips, and her eyes began to close, he was going to kiss her.

'You must go now,' he said, his voice compellingly full of concern. 'I promise, we will be together.'

'When? When will we?' she asked.

'Soon, don't worry.' She had her hand on the edge of the window and he squeezed it briefly. 'Just trust Alexi, and it will be all right.'

She looked back as they drove off, Dimitrou was standing beneath a streetlamp looking after the car. He raised a hand briefly in farewell.

'Where are we going?' she asked.

'Please, I do not like to talk when I'm driving.' Alexi's accent was very strong. Victoria felt that he was not at all like his brother.

The passion she had felt for Dimitrou cooled swiftly, in its place came a chill doubt.

She didn't like being driven off like this at night when all around her the houses were dark, shuttered. The London streets were empty, everyone was asleep. She wanted to be in her own bed, she realized suddenly, at home with her family. What on earth had she done? It had seemed so natural for her to run to Dimitrou. She had argued with her mother yet again. Been driven to it by the awful boredom of her days. To go to the club was the only thing to do. Thinking back she had been almost a prisoner in the bedroom in the attic. Dimitrou had visited her only briefly there, never even kissing her, let alone making love. She nearly asked Alexi to let her out of the car, there and then, but with a sinking feeling she realized that what stopped her asking was the certain knowledge that he would refuse.

She closed her eyes, trying to shut out the reality of the speeding car. The sound of the engine was familiar to her, she'd ridden in the car so often with Eli driving her. But now, even the remembered rich smell of the leather seemed a threat. Dimitrou was too forceful for her. When he had said that she must leave London to go into hiding she hadn't thought to question his decision. He had seemed pleased to see her, but he had not been demonstrative towards her. She thought back to his greeting, it had been perfunctory, no more than the social kiss that he bestowed on many of the club's female guests. How many of them had he made love to? She felt cold. Was he in love with her or was she simply useful to him? Why would she be useful? A vision of Eli standing by the gambling tables at the club came to her. He'd been betting heavily, she knew that. And he didn't have all that much to bet with. He must have given them the car to settle a debt, that was it. But he must have been very desperate, because he'd often said that he loved the Bugatti more than any woman.

She opened her eyes again, they were out in the suburbs, hurrying along roads that she didn't recognize. For a while she stared forlornly out at the sky, it was beginning to lighten with the dawn. The neat terraced suburban villas began to give way to properties with bigger gardens. Then the houses stopped, and they were in the country. They hadn't come by a route she knew, but she realized suddenly that they had driven into Kent. As dawn became a reality she saw a thin silver line on the horizon that was the Thames in the distance. They were driving parallel to the river so they must be on their way towards Thanet. She screwed up her eyes, closing them tightly to help her concentrate. Why on earth would they be going towards the flat, deserted fields that were all she knew of the area?

Unless they had a hide-out there. She nearly laughed out loud as she thought the word, 'hide-out' – it made Dimitrou and his brother sound like crooks. A small chill ran up her spine. Here she was, being driven away from all she knew by someone she had never met before, whose only claim to recognition lay in his being a relative of Dimitrou's, and what did she know of the man she had supposed she loved? She could summon a picture of him in her mind; it was clear, too clear. His eyes were very cold. She concentrated again on the route they were taking. Now she recognized that they had joined the Dover road and they were making for the coast. She felt suddenly very young and afraid, they might be making for the Channel port. What on earth was going to happen to her?

Luke was pleased with the mansion. He had admired the elegant Georgian façade of the outside, and was now enjoying the opulence of the panelled walls, the Adam fireplaces and splendid furnishings. It had been available to rent immediately; that was most convenient. And there were resident staff to go with it – who could ask for more? Luke rang an embroidered bell pull hanging in the powder blue painted dining room. As he waited for a reply to his summons he surveyed the grandeur that was his, thanks to the payment in advance of six months' rent. A handsome Chippendale sideboard was laden with ornate silverware. Every salver and meat cover bore a family crest in the form of a dolphin. There were ten-branched silver candlesticks placed in a row of three down the centre of the massive dining table. Four side tables matched the suite of mahogany furniture that was finished by twenty dining chairs. Yes, he could entertain in this house and be proud of it. However, he looked down at his watch, it was several minutes since he had rung for service. He was not prepared to tolerate slackness and he rang the bell once more, this time keeping his hold on the bell pull for much longer. His eyelids lowered as the door opened, he would deliver a lecture that would leave none of the staff in doubt as to the requirements of their new overlord.

They were quite close to Dover when Alexi took a right-hand turning off the main road. They had driven into a narrow lane that led downhill, towards a small picture-book village that she remembered seeing once before from the Dover road. The timber-framed village shop was already open and a curious shopkeeper looked up as they passed, happy to relieve the tedium of sweeping the doorstep by the sight of a beautiful car. There was a row of pretty red-brick cottages, and then they were faced by a pair of massive wrought-iron gates flanked by cream-painted lodges. Alexi banged imperiously on the car horn and an old man came out to open the gates. Victoria felt a tremor of excitement. The opulence of the entrance impressed more than frightened her. At least she was entering a world she understood. The driveway was long and sweeping. Tall trees bordered it, and beyond them flat parkland stretched away as far as she could see. Fat sheep grazed contentedly, only those close to the fencing bothering to look up at the car's passing. There were crows out on the grass too, great fat inky black birds that poked their beaks savagely into the ground in search of their breakfast. Victoria was hungry too. She could see the house now. It was classically beautiful, with a central Georgian porch ornamented by a shell-topped portico, and a great many long windows. The house was smaller than Pencombe, probably not much bigger than Linstone, but the cream paint made it seem almost too perfect, unapproachable. Victoria began to flick at her hair with nervous fingers. She looked down anxiously at her dress. This was a house to visit at one's most elegant leisure. The car swept around to pull up with a flourish in front of the door. Alexi turned suddenly and smiled at her, showing strong white teeth, and obvious relief at their having arrived.

'You see,' he said, 'there was nothing to worry about.'

The door of the house opened and to her complete astonishment Luke was standing there. She fumbled with the door handle in her excitement.

'Luke!' she cried. 'How absolutely fantastic, oh, you've no idea . . .' He had come down to help her out of the car. She stepped out, and he held his arms out to greet her, comfortingly, charmingly. She allowed herself to step into his embrace, kissing his cheek with fervour as the relief she felt at finding someone she knew made her feel wonderful.

'Come into my kingdom,' he said, and she held on to his arm to walk into the beautiful house that surrounded her like a cocoon with care and affluence.

Isabella fumbled with her change as she paid off the cab in Regent Street. Michael had telephoned her from Pencombe, suggesting that they meet somewhere for lunch. He did not want to come to Cadogan Gardens, he'd said. They had matters to discuss that were not for the family's hearing.

Michael had offered her the choice of venue, and when she had suggested the Grill Room at the Café Royal he had made no comment. They had used the restaurant when they'd been newly married, revelling in the Bohemian atmosphere, enjoying the eccentric celebrities who frequented the mirror-decked room. At least it was only lunchtime: Isabella could never have faced the gaiety of an evening. It was so strange, meeting in public to discuss their problems so private.

She hurried across the marble foyer, there were two women chattering animatedly at the bottom of the great sweeping staircase. With dismay she recognized them as friends of Lucinda, and she kept her eyes lowered as she hurried past, hoping they wouldn't see her, she couldn't bear the thought of having to make small talk. With relief she stepped into the Grill Room, its familiar gilt opulence warming her. She glanced quickly at her reflection in one of the mirrors, she was pale, but her eyes were bright; she surreptitiously bit her lips, she needed a little colour.

The maître d' came quickly and Isabella was treated with all the deference that her title demanded. He personally ushered her to the table where Michael was already waiting and, having seated her to his satisfaction, removed himself to a discreet distance.

'How's Victoria?' Michael was clipping his words. Isabella realized her husband was nervous, however composed he appeared.

'I don't really know. Lucinda had her closeted up in her bedroom. I think she must be all right though, no one's sent for a doctor. Mind you I think it's her head that needs looking at, rather than her body. The child's obviously not stable.'

'She's not a child any more, Isabella, she's twenty, she's a woman.'

'Then she should act like one. I can't understand Lucinda's attitude either, she fusses around Victoria instead of ticking her off. My goodness, if one of the boys behaved like that I'd certainly have something to say.'

'It didn't sound to me as if you'd been all that heavy on the boys after their débâcle.'

'What, because of the fuss at school? I don't think that's the same sort of thing at all. Certainly I was furious with them. They shouldn't gamble and they know it, but it's not as if they did it deliberately to hurt us. Victoria has been running away to upset her parents, to frighten them. The boys were just being too high-spirited.'

Michael didn't reply. Instead he beckoned the waiter

173

over and issued his instructions for the lunch he wanted. He ordered consommé followed by lamb cutlets and to drink with it a half bottle of claret for himself and spring water for Isabella. It was a light meal; his stomach was unsettled, and Isabella never ate much at midday.

When they were alone again he reached across the table and took Isabella's hand. She was so surprised that she nearly pulled away, but he held her firmly.

'I think you're wrong about the boys, Isabella, and I think you're wrong about a lot of other things too. William and Edward set out to shock us. No, don't dismiss what I'm saying with a shake of your head, it's true. They're unhappy with the life they see being lived at Pencombe. I've talked to them now, and the truth took a lot of getting at, but that's what it's all about. They see their friends as having a high old time – their friends' parents, according to them, career around town socially, drive fast cars, live a continual life of pleasure. They see us as old fogies, Isabella, and, you know, the really sad thing is I think I agree with them.'

Isabella opened her mouth to speak and then shut it abruptly. Perhaps the boys were right. Before Michael had inherited the title they had been quite different people. Even the clothes she'd worn had been brighter, gayer, even through the war years there seemed to have been more fun. Now it was solely duty.

'We could fall in love again, Isabella.' Michael looked at her, and suddenly she wanted to kiss him. More than ever she wanted to be in his arms.

'Michael,' she whispered.

There was subdued commotion as the consommé was placed before them and they quickly dropped hands. Isabella could feel herself blushing, then she stiffened, there was something she had to ask. 'Michael, I have to know.' She was holding tightly onto her soup spoon and the amber liquid quivered in its bowl. 'Are you still in love with her?'

'I beg your pardon?' Michael looked up at her, he looked quizzical, he thought he must have misheard.

'I said, are you still in love with that girl?' Isabella put the spoon down with a clatter. 'However much I want to go on, to act as if nothing ever happened between you, I can't. And I have to know, please, Michael, please tell me the truth, are you still in love with Arabella?'

'Me? You think I'm in love with Arabella?' Michael sat back in his chair, astonished. 'But why on earth would you think that?'

'Lucinda saw the two of you together. It was in London, before you even went down to Falmouth. You see, I've known all along.'

'But there's nothing to know. I've never felt anything for the girl. Good grief, I can't believe you've been thinking that.' He looked at her in growing incredulity. 'Actually, it's utterly insulting that you'd imagine that of me. I've always been faithful to you, I've never even thought about another woman that way. Good grief.' He stared down at his plate, shaking his head at the injustice he was suffering, then he picked up his spoon and began, very energetically, to drink his soup.

'I didn't mean to be insulting. But Lucinda was so sure, she said the two of you were so obviously – ' she paused, she was close to tears ' – so obviously lovers.'

'That bloody woman – ' Michael's face was flushed with fury ' – she's always been a meddlesome creature.'

'But she thought she was helping me, after all, if it had been true . . .'

'If it had been true,' Michael looked up at her then, his face softening at the pain he saw in her face. 'Then I would have been the biggest idiot alive. How could I fall in love with anyone else, Isabella, when I'm still in love with you?'

They sat silently, the years they had spent together suddenly seeming very precious. They began to speak again, tentatively at first, but then with the well-remembered familiarity they went on to talk about the behaviour of their sons and the situation at Pencombe.

'Mike? It is Mike, isn't it?' The man addressing Michael was red-faced, white-haired, tall and wide. He had been lunching alone. He carried himself well, with a military bearing, the only thing about him that surprised Isabella, marking him out from any number of other similar-looking gentlemen who might have recognized her husband, was the use of the abbreviation of Michael's name, and the fact that he spoke in an Australian accent.

Michael stood up to shake the proffered hand. 'Mike was close enough for those days,' he smiled. 'I think Michael's more the mark now. How do you do, sir?'

'Very well, very well indeed, my boy. In fact couldn't be better. And all thanks to you. Well, are you going to introduce me to your wife, at least I assume the lady is your wife?' He laughed loudly at his own joke, and Isabella felt she had to smile. He was so loud that other diners were looking at them, and to achieve notoriety in the Grill Room you had to be something special.

Michael effected the introductions, and Major-General Benot established himself at their table. When he had got over the surprise at the fact that the man he knew simply as 'Mike' was an English lord, he ordered a magnum of champagne. This was despite the fact that Michael pointed out he already had wine to drink with his lunch, and that there were, after all, only three of them.

'When I drink the health of the man who saved my life, I'm certainly going to do it in style.'

'Saved your life? Michael saved your life?' Isabella felt

bemused. Michael was obviously embarrassed, as well as pleased at meeting the man.

'Let me tell you all about it, my dear.'

Isabella held out her glass to be filled to overflowing. The Major-General had dismissed the waiter, he wanted some privacy, he explained, and then proceeded to talk to them both at the top of his voice.

'Dardanelles,' he began. '1917, bloody death trap.' He stared into his glass for a moment, watching the bubbles rise madly to the rim.

Isabella felt intuitively that he was savouring this moment of time, that he would never have had except for Michael. The enormity of the man's claim that Michael had saved his life seemed suddenly very real.

'You can have no idea what the carnage was like, my dear. And you should thank God for that ignorance, I can tell you, it haunts my dreams. And suddenly there was your husband, rising from the waves like some bloody sea monster – no, don't look alarmed, I'm not mad. He'd come in that blasted submarine, commandered it, along with its crew. I was one of the first they took off the beach, I've never been more terrified in my life as we went under the sea. I'd read that book you know, Jules Verne, *Twenty Thousand Leagues Under the Sea* and all that nonsense, the reality is very different. Too bloody small, too bloody small for a man like me, couldn't even stand up straight. Come on, drink up, don't enjoy having to drink alone. Where was I?' He stared again into his glass. Isabella looked at Michael, his embarrassment seemed to be fading, and he was looking at the big bluff man beside them with sympathy.

'Well, anyway, he got us out, and then he went back for some more, couldn't get over it. I kept saying, "the man's a hero, a bloody hero" and a maniac, of course, but I didn't say that, kept that thought to myself. But he had to

177

be a bit touched, you know, to go under the sea in that miserable tin can. What did they give you for it then, a decent medal, I hope? Or a good promotion at the least?'

'I didn't need a medal,' Michael said. 'I was just the person in the right place at the right time. And I knew what was happening there all right. It was inevitable, right from the beginning, that it would be a death trap. When I was offered a run in that sub I just knew that's what we had to do — no, I wasn't the only one, I didn't need a medal.'

'Nobody ever needs a medal, Michael, but they're nice for the family. What recognition did you get?'

'It was all a bit hush-hush. It wouldn't have done to make a fuss about it.'

'That's absolutely bloody typical.' Major-General Benot paused on each and every syllable. 'That's you Britishers right down to a tee. Well,' he stood abruptly, 'I'm a man of action, Lady Montford, always have been and always will be. Legend has it I came into the world shouting and hopefully I'll go out doing just the same. I'm going to do a bit of shouting on your husband's behalf, my dear. Just see if I don't. It's been a pleasure talking to you.' He leaned over Isabella's hand and kissed it gently. She felt the tickle of his moustache. 'I don't get all that much chance to talk to a lady, not now that my dear wife has gone.' He straightened slowly, held out his hand to Michael and after a strong clasp, he was gone. Leaving the room much quieter, much emptier, by his going.

'Good God.' Michael slumped back in his chair. 'I feel utterly exhausted. He's got incredible energy, that man, it just radiates . . .'

'Michael, why on earth hadn't you told me?'

'It was all a long time ago, Isabella, and I wasn't really like Neptune rising up with his trident. It wasn't all that important really.'

'But it was. It was obviously important to that man, he wouldn't even be alive today if you hadn't rescued him, he said so himself. And it's important to me, and to the boys. None of us knew anything at all about you being in a submarine during the war. Is that why you were so set on going down to Falmouth? I had no idea.' Isabella clutched her glass firmly. She could easily become cross at Michael's reticence; she wanted to be proud of him, and to have a reason for him being set on the posting to Falmouth would make it all so different.

'I'd rather you didn't tell the boys.'

'Why on earth not? They have a right to know if their father was a hero.'

'A right? Is that what you think?'

'They heard all about their Uncle Johnnie. The other men from the regiment who came back to work on the estate brought all that home with them, they deserve to know what you were doing, Michael.'

'Then of course you must tell them. Only please, water it down a bit,' he laughed nervously, 'and cut out some of our Australian friend's adjectives.'

'Poor man, he obviously misses his wife.'

'Isabella.' Michael reached across the table and took the champagne glass from her hand. 'Let's get back to where we were.' He watched her face, saw the softness slowly returning as she remembered how they'd been before the Australian had joined them. She was too highly strung and that was his fault, Michael realized, he would work at making her happier.

He asked for their cutlets and after a while they came back to talking of themselves. Michael took another glass of champagne with his food. He was feeling very much better; they would take a more leisurely progress through the dessert and cheese. It was Isabella who suggested that what they really needed was a holiday. Somewhere warm, in the sun. Just the two of them, and ideally they should go for a month. They needed time to get to know each other again. This time when Michael took her hand he did it surreptitiously, under the table, and then he let go of it, to stroke her knee so that she laughed and pushed his hand away. They agreed that the expression on the waiter's face was quite remarkable. Isabella took some Stilton, which was unlike her at lunch, but she was surprisingly hungry.

'It's a pity that the others are at Cadogan Gardens,' she said, studying her plate intently.

Michael looked at his wife in surprise. 'Are you meaning what I think, Isabella?'

'Well yes, I suppose I am,' Isabella laughed, her eyes very bright. 'I suppose you think I'm a loose woman,' she added.

'Absolutely not,' Michael replied, 'I think you're splendid. How quickly do you think we could drive down to Pencombe? Or are you prepared to live dangerously? How about us going off to a hotel, booking in with no luggage, in the middle of the afternoon? How about it?' He looked round the dining room, apparently to find a waiter to chase up the bill, and as Isabella hid her face in her napkin the waiter did in fact come hurrying to the table, but not to Michael's summons.

'There's a telephone call for you, my Lord, from Cornwall. I believe it is a matter of some urgency.'

Michael stood up abruptly. He wasn't in the mood for dramas from Falmouth. He smiled down at Isabella as he left the table and she thought how handsome he was, distinguished and charming, and the bitterness that had haunted his mouth for the last few weeks had faded right away. How on earth had they become so immersed in the daily act of living that they'd lost each other? What a boring person she'd become — come to that so had

Michael. They had the rest of their lives together, beckoning like a great glorious adventure: how suddenly the world could change.

She was pouring herself a glass of water when Michael came back to the table, so she hadn't watched him walk across the room towards her. She hadn't seen the expression on his face so the pain in his voice came as a complete surprise.

'I've got to go,' he said, and Isabella looked up at him. He looked desolate. 'There's been the most awful accident. God, I don't know how to cope with this. Look, can you get yourself home? I'll have to go down right away.'

'What on earth is it, what's the matter, Michael?'

'It's Arabella, there's been an accident. She's dead, I can't believe it.' He leaned on the back of the chair, clearly needing its support. Bill, he was thinking, how on earth do I break this to Bill? He's gone to America to tell Mary he wants a divorce. How do I get hold of him – what if he's on the boat? Dozens of thoughts crowded into his mind.

Isabella watched her husband in disbelief. It had been true after all, all of the things she'd suspected. She stood up, pushing her chair back jerkily, and the waiter came to help her.

'I'll phone you.' Michael didn't look at her face as he kissed her quickly on the cheek. He turned to hurry from the restaurant. There were so many things he had to do. He had to write to the girl's parents who lived on a tea plantation in Ceylon. Somehow he had to get hold of Bill, but the first thing that he had to hurry back to Falmouth for was to identify the body. All his earlier queasiness returned as he stepped into the taxi. He leaned back against the seat and closed his eyes, fighting the nausea.

Isabella too felt sick, sick at being taken in by Michael's lies. She straightened her hat mechanically as she looked in the gilt-framed mirror, acknowledged the farewells of

181

the waiter, walked unseeingly through the marble foyer. She felt dazed, confused, she hailed a taxi to take her back to Cadogan Gardens, her mind in turmoil. She had no idea what she should do now, none at all.

Thomas had his eyes fixed firmly on the brow of the hill ahead of him as he made his way up through the orchard. For once he was not interested in the apple trees on either side. He wanted to look at Linstone. He had the feeling that until he was actually in front of the house he would not be able to make up his mind. He was very aware of the letter that was tucked into the inside pocket of his jacket. The strangeness of a communication relating to family-owned land being sent to him by the factor at Pencombe had been lessened by its coinciding with Victoria's return. But now, when they were all safely back at Reason Hill, he had time to consider why Michael had not broached the matter to him personally. There was a major problem between Isabella and her husband, that much was clear. Thomas thought back. How many years ago had it been when Isabella had run up the lane towards him, run into his arms? They would have been lovers that hot afternoon if fate hadn't intervened. Then perhaps he would never have married Lucinda. The thought brought him pain: he loved his wife with increasing, rather than diminishing fervour.

He had never been able to fathom Isabella, although over the years he had begun to think that marriage with Michael had been the ideal thing for her. Thomas had almost reached the summit of the hill and soon the house would come into view. He slowed his pace. He was almost frightened of facing up to how much he wanted. There was the property itself, then its thousand acres of land, the freehold of which was now on offer to him. With that around him, and his hard-earned image in the county, it would only be a matter of time until he was in line for a knighthood. He would have bought it in the same way as hundreds of other men had through the centuries. As Linstone came into view he wondered fleetingly if more knighthoods had been bought by money than by blood. The strangeness of the thought stayed with him as he looked towards the broad vista of the house with its welcoming honeyed stone, the shining diamond-patterned windows. The gardens were dull in their winter drabness, but come summer they would be a riot of colour. There were new fashions in houses, but Linstone was timelessly appealing.

He turned around to look out over the view the house enjoyed. It was subtly different from the outlook at Reason Hill. There was more of a feel of the presence of the far-off sea. He had signed the contract for the sale of Albert's farm and told the boy that he and Maggy would have to move into one of the cottages in the village. The memory of Albert's disappointment still upset him. The boy had been close to tears. Thomas began to walk parallel to the wall of the garden boundary. The sandstone blocks were beginning to crumble apart, the mortar between them needed repointing. Thomas wondered how many other routine maintenance tasks had been let slip since Eli had inherited the property. He stopped in irritation. On the orchard side of the wall there were several large mounds of semi-rotted grass clippings. Some slovenly gardener must have tipped them over the edge. He poked the nearest pile with the toe of his boot. It was greasy on top but inside there was the white of mildew. He looked at his trees, too close to such contagion, and a dull anger began to well inside him. He had to own Linstone. It was a long time since he'd had to take chances, he would have to sharpen up. The prospect of acquiring assets made him thoughtful. He had disposed of Weaver's Farm, but there were other things he could dispose of too. Luke was still waiting; he knew that because Eli had referred to him still being in town. Well, Luke could have what he wanted, but on Thomas's terms. With a final glare at the offending compost, Thomas turned to make his way back along the ridge, leaving behind the memory of a young Isabella running towards him. He walked purposefully towards a new challenge, excited by the prospect of it.

'So you've come to talk about Eli have you?' Luke looked at Thomas with amusement. He did not believe the reason the farmer had given for his visit to the hotel. Thomas was dressed too smartly just to want to talk about a wayward member of his family. Thomas was here on business.

'Yes, I have. We are very concerned that it's his influence that is unsettling our daughter. He's immature, won't settle to anything. He needs a change of scene, of inspiration.'

Luke said nothing, drawing Thomas on by his silence.

'I thought that the two of you seemed to have struck up a relationship. He admires you for your success. I thought that if you agreed to take him in hand, it could do him nothing but good.'

'Like to like, is that what you really thought, Thomas? I mean, you of all people know that my beginnings were not only humble, but shall we say precarious. Young Eli, I would say, has scant regard for authority.'

'I wouldn't go that far,' Thomas said, although in his head he would go further. He would say that he thought Eli had no morals at all, and morality and the law were one and the same thing. Except . . . Thomas had suddenly discovered that he would find things easier with a less rigid application of the law, albeit American law.

'So.' Luke paused, he wanted to make certain he had Thomas's full attention. 'You would like me to take Eli off your hands. And you must have in mind some form of exchange, that is only reasonable. What do you suggest?'

'I'll sell you my distilleries, lock, stock and barrel. For a more than fair price, I'm not a hard man.'

'But of course you are a hard man, or you would not be here. Tell me, what plans do you have for your daughter, Victoria?'

Thomas was disconcerted by the question. 'For Victoria? I have no plans at all for her, apart from keeping her closer to her mother, and getting Eli out of the country. Why? Why do you want to know?'

'I'm an old-fashioned man in some ways, Thomas. So I am approaching you first, as her father. I want to marry Victoria. I'm a wealthy man as you are no doubt aware, very wealthy. I have never married before, because, well because I have never wanted to. Now, I find myself captivated.'

Thomas could not believe what Luke was saying. It was unthinkable. He looked at the man standing so sure in front of him. Luke was handsome, strong, affluent, but he was also middle-aged: he must be nearly thirty years older than Victoria. Age put a bar to their union, let alone all the other considerations. Thomas felt his shock give way to fury.

'You're nothing but a jumped-up crook!' he said, controlling his voice as well as he could. 'How dare you make such a suggestion?'

'But it's not a suggestion, Thomas, it's a proposition. Of course I shall not buy your distilleries. What use would I have for companies tucked away up in Scotland? All I want is their produce, I want nothing to do with the production. But I will help you out of your predicament. Please – ' he held up an elegantly manicured hand to forestall Thomas's interruption ' – I am aware of the assistance you require. First there is Linstone, you want to buy that and the land around it, and then there is the fifty thousand pounds that you have paid over to Dimitrou. He was very cross that you tried to bargain with him, you know. He thought that was less than gentlemanly, Thomas. The sale of the farm that was to be your son's helped a little with your money problems, but it will not help you to do this. It's easy, Thomas. If I marry Victoria, I will fund the purchases you require, and you will sell the total output of your distilleries to my agents. We will make excellent business partners, you and I.'

'Over my dead body!'

'Now, now, Thomas, a wise man does not tempt fate. Think it over. Life could be very pleasant for you, you know. Lucinda would make a very beautiful lady of the manor at Linstone. Your son Albert, with his new family, could live at Reason Hill; I'm sure Timmy would be more than delighted to be let out of his inheritance. Not everyone loves the land as you do, you know. I'm making you an offer you can't refuse, Thomas, but take your time. Discuss it with Lucinda. She's a clever woman, she'll see things my way. For you, this will bring nothing but pleasure.' Luke smiled, invitingly, openly. He enjoyed getting what he wanted. And he wanted Victoria, she was so like Lucinda had been, there was the same fire running through her veins, he was convinced of it. Lucinda had haunted his dreams for years and now her daughter could fulfil them. Thomas stood for a moment, then walked out of the room, away from the temptations laid so plainly before him. It was as well, he thought as he strode back out into the street, that he remembered Luke Jones of old. He discarded the thoughts of the man having saved Lucinda, ignored the fleeting vision of the one-time waterman's beguiling smile. Years ago Luke had had to leave England because of a murder, not one that he had committed, or so it had seemed at the time, but one that was

186

bringing the authorities on to the trail of his smuggling activities. If Luke thought he could try financial blackmail, then Thomas would resort to the application of fear as well. He felt bitter as he went home to his wife, bitter and vindictive against a man who held too many high cards.

Timmy pushed a lock of lank hair up off his forehead with the back of his hand. His sweat-streaked skin was impregnated with grease from the wool, and the stink of the sheep had contaminated everything. There was a band of pain across the small of his back that made him wonder if he would ever be able to stand up straight again. He clamped his knees more firmly around the trembling ewe that would make the tenth animal he had shorn that morning. The muscles in his right arm were corded hard, the tendons running down the back of his hand stood out like iron-hausers, the fourteen-inch-long shears that he wielded would snip through the risen fleece like a hot knife through butter. Everything out here in the dust-dry pen constructed from wooden hurdles and twine with no protection from the merciless sun was hot, hot and stinking. A rivulet of salt-laden sweat ran down towards his eyes and he flicked his head quickly. He didn't have to think any more how to deal with irritations like sweat and the flies that hovered round his head, it was all a part of life. How many more days before the shearing was over? He couldn't spare the time to think. Instead he immersed himself in the noise, the incessant bleating, the whine of the insects. He heard Paul shouting somewhere close by. His friend and employer was picking up the accent of the travelling shearers, his vowels were hardening, but the quality of voice was still there, the purity of tone of a natural tenor.

Much later Paul slapped Timmy on the shoulders. 'Finish that one, old man, and we'll call it a day.'

Timmy could hardly lift his head. Pain now ran the length of his spine, but it would subside to a dull ache through the evening, he knew that now. He would be ready to start up again in the morning. They rode their horses slowly back towards the homestead together. It was only a few miles, but night came quickly after the brilliant day, and it was dusk when they kicked their boots off on the ramshackle wooden veranda. The corrugated iron building was no more than a hut, but it promised food and rest so it had become home. Timmy began to whistle as he started to cut thick slices of hard, coarse, country bread. Paul got the stove going, and within minutes there came the smell of hot lamb fat.

'Another two days should see us through,' Paul said as he stirred the collops of meat that were sizzling in the pan. 'And the first thing I'm going to do after that is ride into town and pick us up some onions. What I'd give right now for a real tear-jerker to throw in with this I can't tell you.'

Timmy laughed in agreement. He was ravenous for his supper of bread and meat, and now he could almost imagine the savoury smell of frying onions that would have changed the simple food into a feast.

'And I'll try and find some seed somewhere so that we can grow our own from now on. That is, I assume onions grow from seed.' Paul's red, freckled face creased for a moment as he considered the likelihood of his assumption being right. For a man who didn't know one end of a plough from another he was doing remarkably well in his guesswork as to how a man could live off the land. The men sat down to their supper in a companionable silence. It no longer seemed surprising to Timmy that he had exchanged a farming environment in England for one in Australia. He had met Paul Macneith on the boat out. They were much of an age, and much of a type. Paul had been a flyer too. It was a pity in a way that they hadn't met during the war because then they could have started earlier on what they both now believed to be a shared future. One flyer with a dream of developing a short-hop air taxi business in a new country was a man alone; two men sharing the same goal was the basis of a business. But first they had to sort out the sheep station that Paul had inherited. It had come out of the blue, he had explained. He had had no idea that a distant relative was beavering away acquiring land and stock in the far distant Antipodes. Not that it had done much for the old man's lifestyle, for the elderly Macneith, while being rich in land and sheep, was poor in heirs, having been too busy to take himself a wife. It was fortunate that some distant memory of having attended the infant Paul's christening had stuck in the old man's head to the extent that he had left all his worldly goods to a babe in arms who had grown into a man unaware of his potential inheritance.

Paul's plan was to work the farm for a few months while they got the feel of its value. It wouldn't do to sell up too quickly, the solicitor at Sydney had advised them, or the locals would inevitably get the best of the deal. Eventually, when they had their precious capital, they would begin the great adventure. Timmy felt that at last he could look forward to the future.

They were sitting back, feeling the inevitable onslaught of tiredness after much needed food when the sound of a wagon pulling up outside surprised them. It was totally dark now, and Timmy got up quickly and went to take the shotgun down off the wall, tucking it over his arm as he walked towards the door. Paul stood very still, concentrating on the sounds outside. His face relaxed when he heard a woman's voice quieting her horse and he went quickly past Timmy and out into the night.

In the white moonlight the old wooden wagon was touched with silver, as was the woman's hair, although when he got close enough Timmy could see she was young and her hair was really fair.

'Mr Macneith,' she said in a lilting Irish accent, and Timmy understood at once who she must be.

'Good evening, Miss Brodie, I must say . . .' Whatever Paul had been about to say was interrupted by a frantic bleating from the back of the wagon. What had looked at first like flour sacks crammed tightly together suddenly burst into life.

'Sheep?' Paul stopped still in his surprise. 'My sheep?'

'Well, yes. I think they must be, but it's a long story.' She paused, clearly feeling awkward. 'I'd really be very grateful if you didn't ask me where I found them.'

Timmy stood unregarded to one side of the couple. Paul had told him that he had met the school teacher on his last visit into town. What he hadn't mentioned was that he had also, quite obviously, fallen in love. And so, by the look of things, had Miss Brodie.

'Very well.' Paul had regained his composure. 'I won't ask. After all, it wouldn't be very gentlemanly of me to question why a lady of such propriety as yourself has gone into a little sheep rustling, and clearly repented of her crime.' They could hear the smile in his voice. He walked towards the tailgate of the wagon, and the teacher called out quickly to him. 'No, don't open it, at least not yet. I think you'd better look at this.' She was busily lighting a storm lantern that hung on the side of the wagon. When it showed a dim, orange light she took it down off its hook and walked round to the rear, holding it up as high as she could.

'I'm afraid you're not going to like this. There, see where the fleece on their backs looks dark and oily. Go on, look.' She gave a short sigh of exasperation. 'Goodness, it's easy to see that neither of the pair of you are farmers. They've been struck. Go on, have a look. They're swarming with the foul things.'

Timmy leaned over the back of the sheep nearest to him. There was a dark patch about the size of a hand just above the tail. He peered at it, in the half-light uncertain as to what he was looking for. The woman pushed him aside and thrust the lamp at him. 'Come on,' she said, 'you hold that and I'll show you.' Timmy lay the shotgun down on the ground and took the lantern she handed him.

'I hate this,' the teacher said as with a look of extreme distaste she put her hands down on to the sheep's back. The animal squirmed under her touch and then stood quiveringly still as she parted the tangled fleece. Looking down in the lamplight the men could see that there were hundreds of fat white maggots, pulsating, making a living wool. 'They're eating the poor creature alive,' Miss Brodie said authoritatively. 'You'll have to scrape them all off, then try and get the skin to heal. I don't know how it'll work in this heat, but at home we saved some, lost some. Eaten alive. Poor things, it's a horrible way for them to go.' She held her hands out in front of her. 'I'd like to wash before I go back,' she said, and turned to walk towards the shack. Timmy watched her go, and saw Paul fall into step beside her. Her brisk efficiency had made him think of Meg. She would make an excellent farmer's wife, just like Miss Brodie would. He had a vision of the future, Paul and his capable wife ruling the acres, creating a family, a future. He didn't hurry in, but busied himself unloading the sheep. When they were safely penned up he gave the pony in the shaft of the cart a handful of hay, then walked in slowly, coughing loudly as he crossed the veranda to announce his presence.

They were sitting either side of the small table and Paul turned towards Timmy. 'Maureen says she'll give us a hand to make life a bit more homely here,' he said.

Timmy knew that he was a man on his own again.

* * *

It wasn't possible to be so tired, or so cold. Arabella could no longer feel the pain of her lacerated hands and feet. She was shaking all over, vast, uncontrollable lurches of her body, that made her teeth chatter. She mustn't sleep, she knew that. She huddled closer into the thistle-infested hay around her, not feeling warmth from it, but knowing that she needed its protection to survive. She mustn't sleep, although a vast dark cavern of oblivion beckoned to her; inside it she would be comforted. She forced her eyes wide open. It was a dusty gloom around her, the grey morning light barely penetrating the hole she had torn in the side of the stack. The wind howled around her sanctuary.

Arabella had no idea where she was. There were rough, cliff-top fields stretching as far as the eye could see and no sign of life or habitation. The haystack was the only landmark on the wind-blasted landscape. At first, in the dark, she had thought it was a barn she was making for, but she'd been drugged by her exertion, too exhausted for disappointment when she found out the truth. She was still wearing the yellow lifejacket. To begin with, it had been like a talisman – after all, it had saved her life. When she'd realized that *Kittiwake* was going to be hurled up on to the rocks, she'd thrown herself over the side of the little boat and into the heaving sea. It had been a desperate decision to make, because she had been certain then that she too would be dashed to pieces against the rearing granite boulders. But some quirk of the current had swept her out a little way to sea, where she'd floated helplessly, struggling for air in the windblown waves. Then she'd been swept back, towards a small, steeply shelving beach. She'd laughed out loud when she'd felt the sand beneath her feet and realized that she'd cheated the sea. All because Bill had made her wear the lifejacket. He'd be so pleased, she thought, so delighted that she'd done as she was told. She was light-headed as she fought her way out of the clinging waves and struggled up on to the beach. It was very nearly dark and she couldn't make out a path leading up off the sand. Was the tide coming in or going out? How high up the beach would it go? The thoughts jumbled in her head, she felt so sick, nausea kept trying to engulf her, but she mustn't let it. She had fallen on to her knees, her head hanging down in her sickness, but she must get up, get above the high-water line. She struggled to her feet and the coarse-grained sand grazed her legs where her trousers had ripped. She must get help. She fell so many times, the soft, yielding sand tripping her tired steps. Then she reached the stones, plate-sized, round and smooth, they slipped over each other under her stumbling feet. Soon her knees were bleeding. It wasn't a high cliff ahead of her as cliffs went on that part of the coast, but rearing up in front of Arabella in the moonlight it looked endless.

'I must get away from the sea,' she whispered through cracked lips. She was convinced that the sea pursued her, jealous of her escape. She clutched frantically at the tussocks of rough sea grass and didn't feel the cuts it made in her soft palms. She leaned her body close to the crumbling earth, her desperation driving her. Time lost its meaning, there was no definition to her struggle that took forever and then suddenly there was nothing left to climb. She pulled herself up over the edge, clods of earth coming loose in her hands, the smell of it stronger than the salt taste of the sea. She buried her face into the ground and cried. But she must go forward, she must find Bill. She had a picture of him looking for her. She couldn't bear the thought of him searching, searching. The bulk of the haystack that loomed ahead of her seemed to reach out towards her. She pulled at the tightly packed stalks, burrowing like a lost creature into its centre, needing the shelter.

Dawn had come with a white light. She'd watched it,

forcing her stinging eyes to stay open. She'd tried to sing for a little while, nursery rhymes, silly nonsense things, but it hurt her mouth to move it, so she sang for a while in her head, but eventually she came back to thinking of Bill. He would make sure they found her. She had stopped feeling cold, her shaking was subsiding. She lay back against the softness she had made. Of course, she remembered, Bill wasn't here, but he would be soon, she would wait for him. She let her eyes close gently. It was such a relief after all the struggle. She was so pleased, she thought as she drifted into sleep, that he would see she'd done as he'd asked, and worn the lifejacket.

'Bill!' Michael stopped abruptly in the doorway of the Nissen hut. Bill was the last person he had expected to find in the office.

'Hello, old man,' Bill beamed his welcome. 'You're just in time to tell me where I can find my woman. Now, don't look so scandalized, Michael, I'm all set to make an "honest" woman of her. Come on, don't keep me in suspense, where's Arabella?'

Michael didn't answer. He was stunned. He could see Bill standing by Arabella's desk, hear his voice, but he couldn't believe in the reality of the moment. Bill had to be in America, all the thinking he'd done on the train journey down, all his preparation for who he must tell, and how, had been based on the fact that Bill wouldn't be here.

'When did you get back?' Michael's voice was little more than a whisper.

'Just now, of course, and I came right here to tell Arabella the great news. Didn't even stop to drop off my luggage.' He gestured with his hand at the pair of brown leather suitcases on the floor by the filing cabinets. His smile was starting to fade. He was beginning to feel that there was something wrong. 'What is it?' he asked. 'Arabella's all right, isn't she? I mean nothing's happened to her, has it?' He didn't really mean his words, he thought. After all, nothing could happen now to spoil their happiness.

'I think you'd better sit down.' Michael walked forwards into the room. 'You'd better prepare yourself for a shock.'

Bill stood very still. He didn't want to sit down, didn't want to prepare himself for anything. Suddenly he wished he hadn't rushed back to England. He wanted still to be far away, where it was safe to believe that he and Arabella had forever together.

'Arabella's missing,' Michael said. 'She went out in *Kittiwake* and the mist came down, it looks as if she lost her bearings.'

'How long ago did this happen?'

'The day before yesterday. She'd gone for a sail in the harbour. Quite a lot of boats went out, it was a fine day.' Not like today with a slate-grey sea and a lowering sky. 'She wasn't reported missing until after dark. Then her landlady got worried and they had a look around. Then someone noticed that *Kittiwake* wasn't back at its moorings.'

'God.' Bill's face was the colour of marble. He put his hand on the back of the chair beside him for support: it was Arabella's chair. 'She could be miles away by now, the current could have taken her almost anywhere. Is everything possible being done? Have they got an air search up, are they searching the cliffs?'

'No, no, there's no land and sea search. I'm afraid there's no point because *Kittiwake* was found yesterday, at least bits of it were. They found some wreckage smashed up on rocks on the edge of a small beach down the coast. The name board was washed up and they found a lifejacket

195

too. I'm so sorry, Bill, if it hadn't been for finding the lifejacket then there could have been some hope, but she wouldn't have stood a chance in the water without one.' Michael tried to help Bill into the chair, but he wouldn't move. He was stiff, rigid.

'She wouldn't wear one,' Bill stated flatly. 'She hated to. We've argued about it. What about – ' he swallowed hard, it was difficult to speak ' – what about Arabella, where do they think they'll find her?'

'They're watching the beaches further south. They think she must have been swept further on by the current.' They stood silently, Michael couldn't bear to look at the suffering in Bill's face. Instead he stared down at the desk at the neat piles of typing that had been done by the efficient Arabella.

'I don't know what to do.' Bill slumped down on to the chair. 'I mean, I had everything planned, and now . . .' He made a vague motion in the air with his hand. 'Who plans things now? I mean, we weren't even officially engaged, I suppose I don't have any right at all, any . . .' He tailed off.

'I was her commanding officer,' Michael said, 'so it's all down to me. I think the best thing you can do is to go back up to town. I'll contact Adele.'

'Yes, that's right, Adele. I've got a lot to tell her.' His voice was tremulous, there were tears brimming in his eyes. He stood up abruptly. 'If you can, make sure there are plenty of flowers, she liked flowers.' Then he slumped suddenly down into the chair, his head dropped on to his hands, his shoulders heaving. 'Arabella,' he cried, 'I told you to wear that bloody thing, Arabella.'

Victoria took a few steps back so that she could see the painting more effectively. Lucinda had stepped closer to the work by Reynolds that was part of the exhibition in progress at Burlington House. She turned around quickly when she realized that her daughter wasn't beside her. As she came up to Victoria she whispered, 'How about some tea? We're very near Fortnum's, you know.'

'Mama, you're a philistine.' Victoria hadn't lowered her voice to suit the academic hush around them and a uniformed attendant standing close to them smirked his appreciation of the remark.

'Then I'm a hungry philistine.' Lucinda firmly took hold of her daughter's arm. 'And my feet hurt. I don't think that culture is meant to be painful.'

Victoria was very pleased with herself. Her mother was mildly flustered, but not at all antagonistic. Most importantly she was away from her home ground. Victoria would never have dared face her mother at Reason Hill with the news that she was determined to marry her rich American.

The tea at Fortnum's was delicious and generous. They began with smoked salmon sandwiches, went on to assorted fancies that were iced in yellow and pink and white, and then finished with some excellent fruitcake. The Cade womenfolk had country appetites.

'Now.' Victoria dabbed at her lips with her napkin. 'I have something to say to you, Mama, and I would find it easier if you didn't interrupt.'

'You have a crumb on your lapel, Victoria.' Lucinda placidly sipped at her third cup of tea, unaware of the rising excitement that was making her daughter's hands tremble.

'I know I've been a problem for you at times, Mama. I've found growing up difficult. It was different for you, you had a sister.'

Lucinda raised her eyebrows in amusement; Isabella had certainly never been a help, more of a hindrance, to an easy girlhood.

'But I am grown-up now. And I've spent a lot of time thinking what should be the best thing for me to do with my life. I mean, of course, it would be really lovely if I could just live at Reason Hill with you and father, for ever.' Both women appreciated the falseness of that statement, but it had to be said, out of simple good manners. 'But I know that you both want me to get married and to have babies,' Victoria paused for a moment to look suitably misty-eyed at the prospect of a nursery full of chubby little darlings. 'I also appreciate how very important it is to make a good marriage, and by that I mean that I see how necessary it is for me to marry someone with money, lots of it.' She stopped then, and looked her mother full in the face. Lucinda understood the implications of the pause instantly.

'No. You shall not marry that man. Your father and I forbid it.' Lucinda's face had reddened, but her voice hadn't risen. Their surroundings were having the effect that Victoria had planned for.

'But I shall, because eventually you will see, as I have seen, how absolutely suitable he is.'

'Suitable?' Lucinda would have liked the freedom to shout her rage, but being constrained to speak in reasonable tones sharpened her perceptions. 'A girl in love would never refer to the object of her affections as "suitable". Yes, it would be ideal if you married wealth. In fact, knowing you as well as I do, Victoria, I would almost say that it would be an essential requirement for your future happiness. But money is not enough, I would have thought that you were intelligent enough to see that for yourself. There are lots of eligible, wealthy young men around. In another year or two I intend to contrive a few very special introductions. You're a lovely girl, and it won't be difficult to find you a husband. But not yet. You may think that you've grown up, but I don't. You've been through several dreadfully emotional experiences recently. Come to that, we all have. You just prove to us that you have grown up a bit, and we'll do the rest.'

Victoria was almost crying, she was so vexed. How could her mother dare to act as though she needed men brought to her on a plate. And what did they know about the kind of man she'd want to marry? She no longer enjoyed the company of younger men. She'd had enough experience of their ineffectiveness to last a lifetime.

'Now would you like another cup of tea, or shall we make our way back to the station?' Lucinda asked.

Victoria couldn't give up now. If she did she would never get her way. 'I'd like some more tea, please,' she said. While the waitress was attending to their needs Victoria was thinking quickly. She must be positive. At least her mother had accepted that money was important for her, and also that Luke was wealthy. If it was just the age difference then that could be surmounted, but was there something more? 'I'm just going to the powder room.' Victoria stood up. It was terribly funny how much tea she was having to drink in the pursuit of her true love, she thought. True love: the words stayed in her head as she made her way down the stairs leading to the ladies' room. She didn't feel the same surge of longing for Luke as she had for Timmy, or even for Dimitrou. But she did feel a desperate need to be able to call herself his wife. She wanted to own him, to be proud of his wealth, his charm. He was an attractive man to women, he was handsome, mature and yet debonair. But true love – she couldn't decide whether he fitted that role, but she must convince her mother that he did. She checked her hair in the mirror over the basin. Her eyes sparkled, Luke would think she looked pretty, and tell her so. She must persuade her family. She would persuade her family.

Lucinda watched her daughter walking across the room towards her. She was a very attractive girl, beautiful in a way that age would enhance. She was also vulnerable, and she looked it. That was probably part of her charm for Luke. But she was so young, younger than Lucinda had been when Luke had rescued her from the flood. He had fallen in love with her then, Thomas had joked about it. It wasn't right that he should marry her daughter – not having loved her once.

Lucinda stared at the new plate of cakes on the table before her. Was that it? Was it jealousy that was making her so adamantly against the marriage? She absently poured the tea for them both. Victoria saw that her mother was preoccupied with her own thoughts and kept silent. Around them the discreet bustle provided a suitable background for contemplation. Victoria studied her mother's face. It was clear that she was concentrating hard. There was a furrow between her eyebrows that never showed at home, and she was paler than usual.

Eventually Lucinda spoke, her cheeks reddening with guilt as she admitted the truth to herself. It was jealousy that had prompted her to be so much against Luke. He had wealth, he was an attractive man, she did not consider that the age gap was an impediment to their future happiness. 'Whatever I say, I don't think your father would ever agree. He's too set against it.'

'Mama!' Relief made Victoria smile widely. 'You know father always does as you tell him. Well, at least, about things like this he does.'

'Now, now, Victoria, that will do. Come on, we don't really want any more tea do we? Let's go and catch the train home, and on the journey you can try and convince me. Don't grin like that. I haven't promised anything, I just said you can try.'

By the time their taxi turned in at the drive of Reason Hill the mother and daughter were in agreement. Thomas's objections would never stand a chance.

* * *

'Good evening, Dimitrou.' Victoria coolly accepted the kiss that her former lover pressed lightly on her cheek.

'Good evening, Victoria. You look ravishing as usual.' In reality Victoria looked more than usually beautiful. The short black evening dress that she wore was hung with jet beads that glittered and danced, accentuating the slimness of her body, and the vibrancy of her mood. Luke's suit had been approved. Lucinda had positively encouraged him to take Victoria 'out on the town', on the loosely worded condition that she was brought back at a civilized hour to Cadogan Gardens.

'As usual? Oh, but I haven't been here for ages and ages, you must be confusing me with someone else.' Victoria smiled brightly. She was revelling in the sensation of release that seeing Dimitrou again had given her. She was free now, she no longer felt attracted by him.

'A few days since I last saw you, possibly a week – that isn't ages Victoria.' Dimitrou had kept hold of her arm. He was deliberately detaining her and she felt delighted. Perhaps, after all, he cared. She would be delighted to make him suffer.

'Ah, but then I suppose it depends what I did in those few days.' She fluttered her eyelashes, certain that she was annoying him. 'You see, Dimitrou, I've fallen hopelessly and madly in love and it makes every second of every day feel like hours. Hours and hours of bliss. Oh, Dimitrou, if only I could explain to you how wonderful it is to be in love.' She was aglow with pleasure, Dimitrou's eyes were flashing fury. He was actually looking like the wounded lover and his grip on her arm tightened.

'Who are you here with tonight?' he asked. 'Where is Eli?'

'My beloved Uncle Eli? Surely you don't want to see him again do you, Dimitrou? You know he really can't afford you as a friend. It's terribly sad, but I'm afraid that this place is too rich for his blood. No, I think a man has to be really monied to play here. Only someone who is seriously wealthy can enjoy such expensive pleasure. That reminds me. Have you met Luke Jones?' She put out her free hand to tap Luke on the shoulder. He was standing with his back to them, talking to an acquaintance. She wanted him to turn round so that Dimitrou would see how they were together.

'Dimitrou, how are you my friend?' Luke was at his most courteous. 'You really do have the most exciting club in London. Why, I think almost everybody that one ought to see and be seen with is here tonight.'

'We try to attract the right people.' Dimitrou's English was very stiff. He had let go of Victoria's arm and she stepped close to Luke.

'I'd love to play a little on the tables, darling,' she said, turning to smile up at Luke, hiding her disappointment at the fact that the two men knew each other already.

They walked away from Dimitrou, becoming engulfed in the crush of beautiful bodies. The club was very crowded, its popularity had reached a zenith. Victoria clung to Luke. She adored the power that he exuded, and tonight she could gamble without a care. It was unlike any sensation she had savoured before. She was totally captivated by the aura of wealth that surrounded Luke and her world was suddenly very secure. There was nothing to mar her happiness, except the memory of Dimitrou having made love to her. Not for the act itself, for that had brought her nothing but pleasure, but Luke was a strange man, who had declared his undying love and his more than honourable intentions towards her in the same breath as he had declared that he would never compromise her before their wedding night. It was clear that he assumed her to be a virgin. He had made that abundantly clear, accepting her word that her night spent at the club with

202

Dimitrou had meant nothing more than kisses. She must make him love her even more before their wedding night, when he would find out the truth.

It was nearly midnight, and Victoria was thinking she would ask Luke to take her home soon, when Dimitrou came up to her as she stood watching the play on the tables.

'I want to talk to you,' he said. His expression was very severe and she grimaced. She no longer intended to be dominated by him.

'No, I really can't talk to you now, Dimitrou. I want to go home soon, and besides Luke is playing, I want to watch him.' She went to take a step closer to the table, but Dimitrou moved quickly in front of her.

'You can't love a man like that. He's old enough to be your father.'

'Can't, can't? What do you mean by that? Please get out of my way. I don't like you talking to me like this.'

'You love me, you know you do, Victoria.' His voice was low, cajoling. He refused to accept that he had been dismissed, cast aside.

'Me, love you, Dimitrou?' She laughed as if she had heard a funny joke. 'Whatever made you think that?'

'You did, you told me.'

'In bed, you mean?' She was whispering, he had to lean forward to hear her. 'But you of all people must accept that no one means what they say in bed.' Her eyes glittered with victory. She felt powerful, seeing the damaged pride clearly in his handsome face. 'You see I know now what was going on. You used me to get at Eli, that was all I was to you, a tool, a device. But I'm no longer an idiot. So if you'll oblige me by getting out of my way, I want to go home.'

Dimitrou stood for a moment longer, staring perplexed at the strength he saw in Victoria's face. He had misread

203

her. He had thought her a shallow, insignificant female, but now he saw that she had a hidden fire, and in seeing it he was dangerously close to believing that he was, after all, in love with her. 'You haven't heard the last of this,' he said.

'Of what, of a one-night stand that meant nothing to the man involved until his pride got hurt? Why don't you grow up, Dimitrou? I have, and you can take my word for it, life's much more fun when you do.' She held her head high as she stepped around him to go and stand beside Luke. She was a woman now, and she felt like one. She would never again be taken advantage of by a man, however handsome, however skilful at making love.

Dimitrou walked around to the far side of the table. He stared down at the croupier's hands working swiftly above the green baize. He had no intention of allowing any man to get the better of him. He would not allow Luke the satisfaction of having bought Victoria without her knowing it. The money that the American had paid to get Victoria into his keeping was no more than a purchase fee. Victoria would see what the man was when Dimitrou revealed the truth. Luke should suffer, too: he should understand that the woman he wanted had already been enjoyed by a younger, more able lover. Yes, Dimitrou thought, as the croupier fanned out the cards, he would be skilful in his revelations. As Luke turned away from the table Victoria looked over at Dimitrou and the look they exchanged was a challenge.

'I'm sorry, Adele, but I don't think I quite understand what you're saying.' Isabella carefully balanced the glass of brandy that she held in her hand on the arm of the sofa.

'I'm trying to explain to you that Johnnie has been being unfaithful to me.' Adele turned away from where she had been standing staring into the fire and sat down quickly on the tapestry-covered stool in front of Isabella. All of her movements were sudden, staccato; she couldn't get over the shock of her mother's revelations. 'Isabella, are you listening?'

'Yes, yes, I am, but there was something else that you said.' Isabella was trying to pull her fuddled thoughts together. She'd had a glass of sherry before dinner, wine during it, then the brandy, and she normally hardly drank alcohol at all. But she'd felt that she needed its help to get through the evening entertaining Adele. She didn't want anyone realizing how unhappy she was; she didn't want them to know about Michael's infidelity yet. She had arranged a small dinner party to welcome Adele back from the Continent, a women's affair, Lucinda and Victoria were to come up to town for the meal and then stay the night afterwards. But during the afternoon Lucinda had telephoned in a fluster and called off for herself and her daughter, so it had only been Adele and Isabella at table. The chill of the Cadogan Gardens dining room had not daunted Adele who had talked non-stop about her foreign experiences, her tour of Europe, until the telephone call from her mother in America had interrupted her.

'You said something about Bill,' Isabella said.

'Well, yes, he's involved in all of this as well.' Adele slowed her speech deliberately, as if she were explaining something to a child, and her accent had become almost a drawl. 'Johnnie and Mary have been having an affair for years and years. Well, of course, there's been nothing physical since the accident, but that won't make any difference to my divorce. My goodness, when I think how I've suffered.' She paused, lost for a moment in private memories, then she went on, 'Anyway, what was I saying about Bill? Oh, I remember, Mother told him about Johnnie and Mary before she told me. That was typical of her, she always puts the boys first. Bill's filed for a divorce already – apparently he's got some pretty little English rose that he's just dying to marry. She's a girl he met through Michael, I think she's Michael's secretary or something.'

Isabella put her hands up to her mouth as if she was about to be sick and the colour in her cheeks had flared so quickly that Adele thought she must be ill. 'Isabella, Isabella are you feeling all right?'

'What was the girl's name? Was it Arabella?' Isabella asked.

'Yes, that's it, Arabella. Do you know her? Look, Isabella, are you all right, you look pretty ghastly.'

'No, no, I'm fine thank you. It's just . . . where is Bill now?' The implications of the knowledge she had about Arabella struck Isabella forcibly and she felt an overwhelming surge of guilt. All the doubts she'd had about Michael – none of them was true.

'Mom said she thought he'd be back in England anytime, that's why she phoned, I expect, a sudden realization that if Bill told me first she'd miss my reaction. Mom likes to watch other people's emotions.' Adele smiled grimly. She was old enough now to survive her mother's peculiarities and to forgive them. Thinking back, it hadn't been like that until after her mother's second husband had died.

'You'll have to excuse me, Adele.' Isabella had risen unsteadily to her feet. She had so much to do, but she wasn't certain where to start. She must find Bill first, though. 'Adele, where would you think Bill would go when he gets back to England?'

'Well I would have thought that was pretty obvious. He'll go back to that girl, won't he? His Arabella. I bet he just can't wait to tell her the news.'

The telephone rang out in the hall and Isabella looked down at her watch. It was eleven o'clock; she went quickly out to answer it before it woke the household.

'Isabella? Isabella is that you?' It was Michael's voice and she felt relief flood over her. Thank goodness she hadn't done anything to hurt him since their lunch together. Another day and she may herself have been talking about divorce.

'Hello, darling,' she replied. 'Is there any news?'

'Yes, I'm afraid there is, and it's not good. Look, do you know where Adele is?'

'She's here with me. In fact, she's right beside me now.'

'Then put her on the line.' Michael was abrupt in his concern, but it didn't matter to Isabella any more. He could be abrupt, angry, anything, because now she knew he was still her Michael.

Adele's brightness dulled as she listened to Michael. Arrangements were made to meet Bill off the train up from the West Country in the morning. Adele looked over at Isabella, and the pain she felt for her brother's hurt was very clear. She put the telephone slowly back on to its cradle. 'The girl's dead,' she said dully. 'She drowned in a boating accident. Poor, poor Bill, it's all over before it really started. Michael sent his love. He says he'll try and get back to Pencombe in a week or so. He was her commanding officer so he has to sort everything out. He wants us all to go down to Kent. He thinks it will be best for Bill.' Adele leaned against the wall. She looked tired, the nervous energy that had filled her all evening had drained away. 'Will you come with me to the station tomorrow?'

'Yes, of course.' Isabella put her hand out and touched Adele's arm. 'Bill's lucky he's got you.'

'Lucky? I don't know about that. If I hadn't ever married Johnnie then Bill would never have met that girl, and his wife would never have had an affair with my husband. Complicated, isn't it?' She gave a nervous laugh. 'I'll go to bed now, I think I'll need all my strength tomorrow. God, what do you say to a man who's just lost his future?' She turned and walked slowly up the stairs. Even in her sorrow her hips swayed elegantly, the droop of her shoulders was most fashionable.

Isabella waited a moment then went back into the drawing room to turn off the lights before going up to bed. She plumped up the cushions on the chairs they'd been sitting on, and smiled quickly at the silver-framed photograph of Michael on the sofa table. She tried to stifle the thrill of pleasure that was welling in her. It wasn't right, she thought, to be so happy in the presence of tragedy. The phone rang again as she passed it in the hall on her way to the stairs and she picked it up quickly. 'Hello?'

'I just wanted to say goodnight,' Michael's voice was tired through the crackle on the line, 'and to tell you I love you.'

'I love you too, darling,' Isabella answered and she went upstairs with tears on her cheeks, tears induced by joy and sorrow.

'But I don't understand.' Victoria's voice was muffled by her handkerchief. She was crouched down in the chair by the range in the kitchen at Reason Hill, as if she was terrified of attack. Her father towered over her.

'Luke insisted that you would.' He was struggling to contain the fury that was making the vein in his temple pulsate madly. Standing by the dresser Lucinda watched aghast. She had never seen Thomas shout at their daughter like this before.

'He's threatening to pull out of everything. No, by God, it's gone further than that. He is pulling out of everything. He's going back to America, throwing it all up and for what? Yesterday you come home, full of plans for your future together, this morning he phones me up acting as if it's all off. You'd damned well better tell me what the hell it's all about, my girl, or I'll . . .'

'Thomas!' Lucinda could stand it no longer. She rushed over to her daughter, gathering her into her arms. Thomas's hand fell back down to his side. He hadn't been going to strike the girl, but he'd felt like it. Too many plans would come unhinged for Thomas if Luke did as he promised. Whatever had his daughter done to upset the man so much?

'You should never have given in and allowed Luke's proposal.' Lucinda glared up at her husband from where she crouched on the floor beside Victoria. 'That man is nothing but an upstart, and he's far too old for her.'

'But Mummy, I love him.' Victoria's tear-stained face emerged from her handkerchief. 'Let me go to him, please, I know he'll change his mind, I can make him, please.' She looked up at her father and he saw that she understood whatever problem it was that she had to overcome.

'What is it?' he asked. 'What have you done?'

'It's none of your business.' Victoria stood up slowly, pushing aside Lucinda's clinging arms. 'If you'll just let me deal with it on my own, I can sort things out.'

Thomas stared contemplatively at his daughter. She had far more strength in her than he'd ever supposed. 'What will you do?' he asked.

'To begin with I'll phone Luke, I'd like to do that right away. Then I'll know what I have to do next. This business you have with him, Father, how important is it, really?'

Thomas considered his reply for a moment before giving it, then he spoke carefully. 'It's more important than it should be. I'm not a man who likes to admit I've made a mistake, but I've overstretched myself badly by anticipating Luke's money.' He ignored the sudden intake of Lucinda's breath. She was obviously scandalized at his revelations to their daughter.

'I shall do my best, Father. It isn't anything I've done deliberately, you know. Whatever you may think of me, I've never wanted to hurt you.' She walked out of the room, crossing the hall to go to her father's office. she closed the door behind her and then turned the key in the lock. She did not want them listening to her. She had no doubt at all in her own mind what had made Luke act as he had. She dialled the number of the hotel and asked for Luke's room. He answered the call on the third ring, only then did she realize how desperately she wanted to marry him.

'Luke, this is Victoria.' He didn't answer her, but there was no sound of him putting down the receiver, so she went on. 'My father says that you are going back to America.' She paused and then added, 'Without me.'

'You know why I am going back, Victoria. There is nothing more we have to say to each other.'

'Oh, but there is,' she spoke quickly, determined that he shouldn't sever the connection. 'Perhaps we don't know each other terribly well, Luke. I didn't think to begin with that our loving had to be based on knowledge, it was too quick for that, at least it was for me.' She paused, hoping he would encourage her, but she had to go on alone. 'I see now that I was being foolish. By not knowing each other it was impossible that our love could overcome the first hurdle put in its way.'

'This is not simply a hurdle, Victoria. Dimitrou has told me everything.'

'Dimitrou? Oh, yes, I thought it must be him. And are you prepared to believe what he tells you without talking to me about it? That doesn't sound like an astute man of the world to me, Luke.' She had put an almost teasing tone into her voice, but there was a thin film of sweat on her forehead. She was concentrating very hard indeed.

'I am going back to America, Victoria. Nothing you say

can stop me.' Luke had no choice. He needed to go back to oversee an important deal that he had in the offing, but he was convincing himself that it was his disappointment over Victoria that was making him go.

'Then will you come back for Christmas?' It was a month away, Victoria would have time to work something out by then. 'We all go to Pencombe for the celebrations, it's an incredibly happy time. Please say you'll come.' Victoria shut out memories of the cold draughty rooms, the family bickering. 'You said that you still missed England sometimes. There could be nothing more perfectly English than Christmas at a castle.' She laughed nervously, but the telephone line made her sound confident, and Luke thought over the suggestion. Perhaps he would come back.

'Christmas,' he said. 'Why should I come back for that?'

'Because I asked you to.'

'I'm afraid that's not reason enough.'

'Then come because you're English, because you belong here. Whatever you say about America, it's not your real home, Christmas is a time for being at home.'

'So, I should come back for England, is that what you think? Well perhaps,' he paused, and Victoria held her breath. 'Yes, I'll come to Pencombe for that. Get Isabella to write to me and make it a proper invitation. After all, I should hate to end up sleeping in the stables, however traditional it may be at that season.'

'You shall have nothing but the best, Luke, I promise you. The best room, the best place at table.' And the best invention I can contrive to ensure that I get you in the end, she thought. ''Til Christmas, darling.' She blew a kiss into the receiver.

'À bientôt, Victoria.' Luke's tone was dry, but admiring. He had to give her credit for trying, although she had missed her chance. She should have asked what it was that he'd been told: now he knew that everything Dimitrou had claimed was true.

Victoria went slowly back to the kitchen. Her parents were standing side by side, waiting for her.

'I hope you can survive until Christmas, Father,' she said, 'because shortly after that I anticipate becoming Mrs Luke Jones.'

Paul gave Timmy a gentle push into the room and closed the door quietly behind them. He put a finger to his lips as Timmy looked at him in disbelief. The hushed, tension-filled atmosphere enveloped them.

Timmy slowly took off his hat and clutched it in front of his chest. Over the past few weeks, since he had taken to the road with the travelling sheep-shearers, the battered felt hat had become a permanent fixture. It had required a cultural shock to make him take it off, and the surprise of finding a full-size billiard table in the back room of the edge-of-town bar had provided one.

The room was an oasis of quiet. The only sound was the run of the balls on the baize, and the sharp click of them colliding. It took a minute for Timmy's eyes to adjust totally to the gloom. Thick curtains had been pulled against the daylight, and a fringed light-fitting hanging over the table cast a pool of yellow on the green. Around the sides of the room several groups of men stood silently; occasionally one raised a glass to sip the amber-coloured beer, but for the main part they were unmoving, their concentration fixed on the play on the table.

Paul nudged Timmy away from the door. It was hard for Timmy to focus on reality. In size the room was almost identical to the billiard room at Pencombe, and while the rough wooden walls and shabbily-dressed onlookers could not be more different than memories of home, in the gloom Timmy could almost imagine he was back in

England. He felt a surge of homesickness. He wanted it to be green and leafy outside, and wet. He wanted to feel cold, to trudge through muddy lanes. It was November, he could almost smell the woodsmoke. Paul was trying to attract his attention, to focus it on the play, and in particular on one of the players.

Paul had sent the message that they must meet. Timmy knew already what would be said and he had prepared himself. After all, he had been aware that his friend was in love with the Irish schoolmistress before Paul himself had known it. All the red balls had been cleared off the table and the colours were being potted with ease. The man in the dusty black waistcoat who dominated the game was obviously a master at his trade, a professional. He potted the pink, and then, with an unnecessarily flamboyant stroke, the black. A ripple of appreciation, the rustle of money changing hands. Someone reached for the light switch and they were plunged back into reality. Timmy blinked. Any similarity with England had been dispelled in an instant.

'Come on.' Paul pulled at Timmy's sleeve to hurry him towards the door. 'Don't want to be last in the rush for the bar.'

Timmy followed slowly. He knew what Paul was going to say, but was happy to put off the moment of it being said. He'd made no plans for being on his own again. The shearing had been hard enough to occupy his thoughts and now he would have to make a decision.

The two men took their beers over to a table in a corner. It rocked unsteadily as they set the glasses down. The beer spilt over the top of Timmy's glass and made a spreading pool. He put a finger into it and drew patterns on the stained wood. 'You don't have to tell me,' he said. 'I only came here to wish you luck. She's the perfect wife for you, Paul, you'll be good for each other.' He smiled as he lifted the glass to his lips. 'Cheers!' he said, but he could hardly swallow. It was all too much: he was physically tired and emotionally drained.

Paul raised his glass in a silent acknowledgement. It made him feel worse that he hadn't had to say all the words he had prepared to tell Timmy how things were. They were silent for a while, just like most of the others there, drinking their beer was enough entertainment. Then Paul reached into his pocket and pulled out a bundled handkerchief. He passed it over the table.

'Have a look at what's in there,' he said. 'Don't wave it around, just take a quick look.'

There was something hard wrapped in the handkerchief; through the cloth it felt like a stone. Timmy fumbled, nearly dropping the bundle on to the floor and then held it beneath the table top to unwrap it. The stone was a nugget of gold, about the size of a hen's egg, irregularly-shaped. It looked almost like a painted pebble. He ran his fingers over the surface and it felt warm, almost greasy.

'Go on, put it away quick.' Paul sounded anxious. He didn't think anyone was watching them, but he couldn't really tell.

'Here.' Timmy went to pass it back, but Paul said, 'No, no, put it in your pocket. Go on.'

'What the hell am I to do with it?' Timmy didn't want the responsibility of acting as a guard for another man's wealth, and he knew Paul too well to suspect that it was a gift. There was too much of the Scot in his friend for that kind of gesture.

'It's our stake.' Paul was smiling now, glad that he was started on what for him was the purpose of his visit to town. 'I've provided that, you'll provide the skill, and together we'll take on the buckeroo in the backroom.'

'You're joking.'

'I most certainly am not. And before you ask, yes, Maureen knows all about this. In fact that rock in your pocket was given to her. Some old prospector crept into the village to die, Maureen found him somewhere to stay for the last few days, and he gave the nugget to her in gratitude. Touching isn't it? And don't scowl, Timmy, because if you'd smelt the old blighter you would have thought Maureen was a saint just to stand downwind of him, let alone battle for a bit of care and attention for the old devil.'

'Don't be an idiot, Paul. I'm not going to play on that table back there for anybody, and I'm certainly not going to let you stake me with that. You go and sell it and invest the money in some more sheep. God knows I know how you love the things.' He laughed, happy to be joking over a beer. Stake at the table indeed. But Paul wasn't laughing with him.

'I'm deadly serious,' he said. 'Maureen and I have talked it over. Neither of us can settle happily into married life thinking that we ousted you from what the two of us had agreed. There's no way that I can afford to invest in a new business now, and you're right, I'm learning to love the woolly creatures. This way we're giving fate a chance to redress the balance. It was fate that Maureen and I bumped into each other, out here in the wilderness, now it's up to fate to help you on your way, or at least luck. Lady Luck we'll settle for – fate's probably a bit too heavy. And anyway, I saw how you played in that hotel in Sydney, just after we landed. We don't need luck, we just need you to play as well as you did then.'

'You're insane.'

'Well, I'm not arguing with you there, but I will tell you one thing. If you don't do as I ask you'll make an Irish lady very sad. She's a very determined woman, you know. Oh, and by the way, she asked me to give you this.' Paul passed over the letter. It was dog-eared, having been read many times. Timmy had left it with his trunk. It was the letter from Meg. 'And Maureen says you'll forgive a woman's curiosity she's sure.' Paul had imitated the Irish brogue, Timmy felt his neck grow hot.

'She's read it?' he asked and Paul nodded.

'She says to go and fetch her. She reckons they'd make good friends. All you need is your fares, old man, and a bit left over for starting off when you come back. Come on, I'll be your first customer. Book me a flight now: you can fetch Maureen's old mother out from Sydney for the wedding. We'll do it in style, and make the old battle-axe love her son-in-law.'

'She'd be sick as a dog.' Timmy laughed at the thought of an old woman flying in a small transit plane. It would be ridiculous.

'Well, of course, there would be that benefit too,' Paul said, and they laughed together, the beer making them loud. 'Come on, be a sport.' They raised their glasses to each other.

'Lady Luck,' Timmy said solemnly.

'Lady Luck,' Paul replied, drinking to fortune, and the friendship that bound them together.

'You mean if she'd been found in time, she wouldn't have died?' Bill's voice was steady, without a tremor. He had suffered so much in the past few days that nothing seemed to touch him any more.

'I don't think it's a good idea to pursue this any further, Bill.' Michael didn't want to go into any more detail. The fact that Arabella had not died from drowning at sea after all, but from exposure after getting herself back to land, was difficult enough to face.

'But we must go into the details of it. After all, you yourself told me that you were her commanding officer. This whole matter must be cleared up, sorted out, blame apportioned.'

'Blame?' Michael stood up. The study at Pencombe had never seemed so cramped, so confining. Bill's calmness was unnerving.

'Yes, Michael, blame. There was no organized sea search after the wreckage was found and as far as I can gather no land search at all. Arabella had done her bit, she'd got herself out of the water and up that cliff. She'd dragged herself into shelter. If any effort at all had been made to find her she'd be safe now.'

'It was the lifejacket that put everyone on the wrong track, Bill. If we hadn't found that then we would have carried on looking for Arabella. The fact that everyone assumed she had drowned meant that we were only looking for a body washed up by the tide.' Michael put his hand up to loosen his shirt collar. It felt too tight and swallowing was difficult. 'There's nothing that talking about it will do to bring her back. I really wish you would leave it alone.'

'I'm sure you do, and I'm equally sure that I'm going to pursue this to the end. It was somebody's fault that Arabella died, and I intend to have that fact recorded.' Bill stood up stiffly, his movements staccato in their precision. He walked to the door and went out into the hall without another word. When he passed Isabella he did not acknowledge her.

'Isabella!' Michael called to her from where he stood in the study doorway. 'Come in here for a minute, will you?'

'Bill looks awful.' She waited to speak until the door was safely closed behind her. The house seemed full of listeners. Adele clearly sided with her brother in blaming Michael for Arabella's death, and William and Edward seemed to be always loitering in corridors, eager to pick up the facts that the grown-ups were unwilling to tell them.

'I'm not sure that he isn't a bit unhinged. He's desperate

217

to blame me for the girl's death.' Michael rubbed a hand across his forehead, his nerves were on edge. 'God knows, I'd give anything to be able to turn the clock back and not to have given the instructions to call off the search. But it's easy with hindsight. At the time everyone was convinced she'd been lost at sea. Bill himself added to that when he said how she would never wear a lifejacket.'

'You mustn't blame yourself, Michael.' Isabella went close to her husband, putting her arms around him, trying to give him comfort, but his body was stiff and unresponding. 'You'll make yourself ill, and then you won't be any help at all when Bill needs you, because he will, you know, he'll understand eventually and then he's going to need your help desperately. Don't take it all on your own shoulders, please, darling. Why don't we go out? Come on, let's go for a walk together, I'm desperate to get out of the house – all this gloom is suffocating.'

Michael nodded almost imperceptibly. He was having to work very hard at not being engulfed by a flood of remorse. The old, well-remembered pangs of guilt were very close. It would be too easy to allow it all to merge together: the desperation he'd felt during the war, the responsibility for the deaths of men he'd never seen, men who'd only been numbers on typewritten pages. He had been able to deal with the reality of death when he had been involved in it. On the beach in Turkey there had been death all around him. The men he had managed to save had been real, flesh and blood, as had the men they had been too late to help.

It had been Michael who had identified Arabella's body. She'd been like white alabaster, her cuts and grazes disguised by the mortician's skill. Too perfect for life. He couldn't cope with the unreality of any of it. 'Let's go now,' he said. Air, that was what he needed, fresh air. Isabella hurried along beside him, aware that Michael was facing a crisis that she had no part in; she was an observer and nothing more. The cold sharp air of winter brought no colour to her husband's pale face. He seemed oblivious of the wind blowing from the east that made her pull her coat tightly round her shoulders. The bare trees were suitably sombre against the steel grey sky. The heavy-coated sheep grazing on the parkland were also touched with grey.

It was a day that made a man look inside himself for comfort, but for Michael there was none. He was walking fast, taking long strides, hurrying away from his past. He tried to force his thoughts forward into the future. The land around him was less than immaculate, there were the brown, decayed stalks of docks in the short cropped grass. This was the Home Farm, part of the few hundred acres that would remain in Montford ownership. Next summer, if Isabella's plans worked, there would be trippers down from London, paying to see around the house and gardens, picnicking in the fields. It should all be pristine, a rural idyll that would entice them back again. He must concentrate. He could not afford to let the plan for saving Pencombe slip away from lack of effort. But he kept remembering Arabella's face. He knew it hadn't been his fault, but he felt guilty. Guilty, the word reverberated in his head and he suddenly stood still.

'I've got to talk to someone,' he said.

'About the accident?'

'About all of it. I've never told you.' He paused for a moment, staring unseeingly ahead. The wind stung his eyes, bringing the sheen of tears. 'I've never told you how bad the war was for me. I feel guilty even saying that. When you think of the others, the men who died, perhaps even worse, the men who were so badly injured. What life must be like for them, I can't even imagine. But I'm finding it almost impossible to cope with.'

'Do you mean what you went through in Turkey? I never really knew what happened, not all of it, but . . .'

'No, no, I could deal with that, I was there. It's all the times that I wasn't there that I can't stand. It's like a crushing weight that I can't get away from. I was a planner – don't you see? – an organizer. We sat in our ivory tower and plotted our way, we balanced the figures, as long as they lost more men than we did, it was a victory. It was all tactics, not real men at all. Until sometimes in the middle of the night I'd realize that for the soldiers out there it was all too real.'

'And Johnnie had such a glorious war.' The cynicism in Isabella's voice made Michael turn to her in surprise.

'What on earth do you mean by that?'

'Well, there was Johnnie, obviously living dangerously, being hailed as the conquering hero and it turns out that he was rotten all through. Don't look at me like that, Michael. You heard what Adele said as well as I did. And you remember what happened in the Boer War, don't you? After all, it was you that told me about it, years and years ago. Johnnie thought shooting the Boers no more than shooting game, and you hated him for it then.'

'I never hated Johnnie.'

'Yes, you did, Michael. And you loved him as well. Love and hate are sometimes very close.'

'Do you hate me then, Isabella? Do you hate me for being weak? Because I am weak, I always have been.'

'No, I don't hate you, my darling.' Isabella put her hands up to touch Michael's face, 'I love you and I always will. You're not weak, you're brave, brave and strong, but everybody needs help sometimes. Won't you let me help you, Michael? Please.' She stretched up to kiss him, tenderly at first, tentatively offering comfort, then she felt his response, his demanding need. They kissed with a new, intense passion and she felt his tears cold on her burning cheeks.

There was a resounding crash as Timmy's trunk was thrown bodily up off the floor of his cabin and hurled against the far bulkhead. Timmy leaned over the edge of his narrow bunk. He screwed his eyes up so that he peered through narrowed slits to follow the course of the rogue trunk as it careered backwards and forwards across the floor, responding to the rise and fall of the ship on the heaving sea. Rise and fall, the words echoed hollowly in Timmy's head, and he was sick again. Not that he had much left to be sick with. They were two hours out of Sydney and he'd started retching only a few minutes after they'd left port.

The taste of bile in his mouth was vilely bitter, but at least it covered the taste of the cheap brandy that had permeated everything, his clothes, his hair, even the blanket that he clutched at. It was easier if he kept his eyes closed. He lay back on the thin horsehair mattress. The two other bunks above him were empty. He could vaguely remember seeing their occupants earlier when they'd come down to the tiny cabin to stow their gear. If it hadn't been for his farewell drinking session with Paul then he too might have been smoking a quiet pipe in a convivial gathering of other travellers.

The trunk slammed suddenly against the side of his bunk, jarring his head so that the pressure inside it pounded mercilessly at his temples. He would never touch another drop of brandy again, never.

After a few more mad lurches the trunk wedged itself at an angle across the corner of the floor and a kind of peace fell. The noise of the waves thudding at the hull became a rhythm rather than an aggression. He began to feel a purpose to the rise and fall, he was going back to England, every wave mastered was a few more feet gained in the right direction. He began to dream, creating a make-believe world inside his head. He was playing a game of snooker on the table at Pencombe. The surroundings were those of England, but his hands were greasy from the lanolin-rich wool of sheep that were bleating outside the door, and through the jumble of animal noises Thomas was calling to him. He couldn't quite pick out the words. He was bent over the table, lining his cue up, aiming for a red ball sitting plum in line for the centre pocket, but Thomas kept shouting.

With a start he sat up, banging his head hard on the bunk above him. He was awake now, but the shouting continued, he rubbed at the crown of his head, trying to ease the pain and the confusion. Then he realized that the banging that he'd thought was in his dream was actually someone thumping on the door. He looked vaguely around him and managed to make sense of it all. His trunk had wedged the door closed and someone wanted to come in.

Getting up and out of his bunk was far more difficult than getting into it had been. He had to clutch for precarious handholds to heave himself upright. As he stood up he felt that the ship was falling madly downhill, then it stopped jarringly still for an instant and he teetered on his feet. He gripped at the door handle as the floor beneath him tipped and the ship began the laborious, painful climb upwards, to hang shuddering, poised for another fraction of a second before hurling itself once more down into the abyss. His head was clearing and he kicked at the offending piece of baggage, at first wedging it more firmly, then slewing it away from the door that swung drunkenly open towards him. There was no one there now. Presumably they'd given up trying to rouse him. He stared, bemused, through the open doorway then finally, moving slowly, taking care not to jar his head any more than was absolutely necessary he fixed the trunk so that it wedged the door firmly open. Then he heaved himself back onto the bunk.

This time sleep came swiftly, cleanly, absorbing him totally. It was the game in Australia that he replayed, the one that Paul had persuaded him into. He could see his opponent clearly. He seemed slightly larger than life, the stained black waistcoat that he wore like a badge of office showed every mark in the glare of the light over the table. There were stains on the baize too, but the cloth ran true enough. Timmy turned for a moment to smile at Paul, his friend and backer. Then he looked briefly at the gold nugget, his stake, formally placed beside the pile of Australian dollars that was wagered against it. In his dream, the balls loomed large on the tables, as they had when he'd played for real. He'd seen everything very clearly: the cue had seemed to move through oil, he had never played with such precision, and the smile had begun to fade on the face of the man with the waistcoat. The first two frames had gone to Timmy, easily, smoothly. He hadn't felt nervous or edgy, the beer had kept him bolstered up. He had a glass that he sipped on the rare occasions that his opponent played on the table, keeping the level of alcohol in his bloodstream gently topped up. Then the third frame and his concentration slipped. It was inevitable, he'd been playing too well. The fourth and the fifth went to his opponent and the atmosphere around him in the darkened room began to lift – the local champion was beginning to show his form.

The challenge was the best of nine frames and Timmy was down, two frames to three. He felt a tremor of fear then, low in his belly. He realized that he should have kept off the beer, he wasn't used to it. He must keep on believing he could win. Lady Luck, that was who Paul had said they'd need with them. He had to be lucky, and luck

223

only ran with the self-believers. He closed his eyes and breathed in slowly, counting to ten. He knew he could win, he must summon all the powers of concentration he possessed.

The champion bent smoothly to the table. Feeling the adrenalin of victory beginning to flow, he played by instinct, relying on the hours and hours of play stacked behind him. For once, his experience failed him. The pink that he went to pot bounced across the open mouth of the pocket. He stood up slowly, staring at the offending ball in disbelief. But it didn't really matter, he thought. He was up three frames to two, and twenty-six to seven. Let the outsider have another crack – he'd be back on the table soon enough. Timmy returned to the table with a surge of optimism. He was being given another chance and this time he would play it for all he was worth. He took the frame without his opponent ever getting back to the table. Three–all, then Timmy took the seventh frame, four-three. The local man's backers began to fret. It could have been disconcerting, the shuffling feet, the scarcely muffled coughing. But for Timmy it was all encouragement. He felt the benefit of the hard work on the farms that made his muscles move like silk. He was super-fit and he felt it. He played the last twelve balls of the final frame better than he'd ever played in his life. It was a display of perfection that silenced the room, a grudging admiration at the speed and certainty of his potting. There was a ripple of applause when he potted the final black. He stood up slowly, savouring the moment of victory. He turned, looking out of the light into the dark, looking for Paul, but the picture was fading.

He woke suddenly, his head crystal clear. The first thing that he saw was an arm hanging loosely over the edge of the bunk above him. It swung with the rise and fall of the ship, keeping in rhythm with the swing. There was a dull groan, obviously issued involuntarily. Timmy smiled, he felt fine, he felt wonderful. A waft of frying bacon crept through the cabin door. He was hungry, ravenous. He sat up gingerly, waiting for his head to ache, but there was nothing. His sins had been exorcized. The groaning from the bunk above him increased in volume, becoming a threat, and he threw himself quickly out of his bunk and opened the door to step into the narrow companionway. He was just in time. He heard the cascade as his fellow passenger was revoltingly sick all over the floor of the cabin. He shut the door quickly. He would find a steward and send him in to clear up the mess. Thank God he'd been able to afford a reasonable berth. He'd been tempted to go back steerage, hoarding his precious capital, but fortunately he'd been swayed by the celebratory brandy, otherwise he would never have been able to set off in search of a minion to make his accommodation habitable, or to pursue his intention of finding a decent breakfast.

He would get back to Kent in time for Christmas, using the return voyage to formulate his plans for his future. He smiled a greeting to a fellow passenger he passed who was also clutching at the slippery walls of the companionway to stay upright and received a muttered acknowledgement. The man's face was pasty white and Timmy felt inestimably superior, he had got his suffering over and done with already. The smell of bacon was becoming stronger, Timmy's spirits rose in exact proportion to the increase in the appetizing aroma. He felt very good, Lady Luck had smiled. It was a brilliant omen for his future.

Part Three

Faint heart faire lady n'er could win.
Edmund Spenser (1522–99)

Maude stared down unseeing at her hands that were white with flour. She held the rolling pin tightly, too tightly for the good of the pastry that she was pressing down on hard. There was a constricting band of pain around her chest and her breathing was loud, rasping. She had been peeling the apples for the pie when the memories had started. The big, round, shining green Bramley apples had been sent over from Mr Cade's farm, from Reason Hill, Lucinda's home. As Maude had slowly and carefully pared off the apple peel in one long strip, the smell of the orchards had taken her thoughts back to when, more than twenty years ago, she'd been Lucinda's maid. That was when they'd all lived at Linstone Park, just along the ridge from Reason Hill. As the peel had fallen in a tidy heap she'd remembered the old wives' tale, if the peel came off in one piece, then the love of your life was true and if you'd already met him, then it would fall in the shape of the initial of his name.

Maude's eyes had filled with tears: true love. It led them all astray. As she'd fetched the pie dish out of the cupboard and onto the table she'd thought about Lucinda's own true love, Thomas Cade. He'd been a handsome young man, and no mistake. For love of him Lucinda had thrown over Michael Montford, and the certainty that she'd be a real lady, all for what? True love. Then there was Miss Isabella, Lady Montford now. She'd loved Michael right from the start, and where had it got her? There'd been times recently that she'd been so unhappy she'd looked as if her heart was breaking. Now she was happy, too happy, and that wouldn't last, Maude's tears of premonition spilt over, dropping down on to the pastry. Maude had married for true love; she'd married her Mr Dove, moved to Pencombe, and God had given them a son. Maude's tears fell faster. Flashes of memories, like moving photographs crowded her mind. Herbert as a tiny baby, red and wrinkled. Herbert as a toddler, holding her finger to steady himself for a moment then launching himself away from her, always determined to be independent. Herbert going off to school in the village, his shoes too big for his skinny legs. Then Herbert a grown man. She'd had such dreams for him, such plans. And now, now that Herbert had died, so had love. Maude could no longer bear her husband to touch her. She shrunk from his embrace, where once she'd clung to him for comfort; now the thought of his loving made her skin crawl.

The pastry was oily, her hands were too hot, and she'd handled it too much, but she didn't care what they thought of her cooking. Praise had no meaning to her now. It was vengeance that mattered. Vengeance is mine, said the Lord, but Young Eli still came and went in his cocksure way.

The pain in Maude's breast flared as she bent to put the pie in the oven. The heat from the iron range hit her in the face and she blinked rapidly. Young Eli would burn in hell, she would see to it. She stepped back from the heat, wiping her hands slowly on her apron. She heard Dove come into the kitchen, coughing gently so as not to surprise her by his presence. When the killer of her son found justice, then perhaps she would once again find comfort in her husband's arms, but until then she was inviolate. She sat down on the hard-backed chair by the range. There was nothing to do but wait for the pie to cook.

Dove was quietly clearing away the mess she had made on the kitchen table. He performed the task humbly, grateful for a way of showing his care. He too was waiting; Lady Montford had explained to him that Maude was in a state of shock. She would get over it in time, Her Ladyship had said, and meanwhile it was best to keep her busy, so on Cook's afternoon off it was a good idea if Maude did a little baking; she must feel needed. Dove had been thankful for Her Ladyship's concern as he had been grateful to Master Edward for taking the blame for the accident that had killed his son. It wouldn't have been right for Miss Victoria to have to face up to all that questioning from the police.

Dove found he lived more in the past these days. He kept remembering how it was Miss Lucinda, Victoria's mother, that had got him the post of butler at Pencombe. He could remember Miss Lucinda and Miss Isabella learning to bicycle-ride, on the long gravelled drive at Linstone. That was when their father Eli Bradbury was alive. Eli was Young Eli's father, too, and Dove could remember the woman who'd been Young Eli's mother. She'd been a common little thing, but brave – so brave that they'd all cried when she'd died so that her baby would live. He could almost remember how bad her screams had been, and then the silence at the end, broken by the new-born baby's cry. That was how it would be when Maude came back to him. When it ended, there would be a new birth, a new life, a new beginning of their life together – it had to be; he couldn't face the thought that it would go on like this. He looked surreptitiously over at his wife. She was sitting forward on the edge of her chair, twisting her apron between her fingers, her lips moving silently as if she recited a litany. He ached to go to her, to put his arms around her, but he knew she wouldn't want it. He stood for a moment, watching her, loving her from afar, then he became aware of a smell, the acrid stench of burning. He hurried to the oven and pulled the door open, sharp grey smoke poured out, making him cough. He turned quickly at the cry behind him. Maude had dropped her head down

231

on to her hands and was rocking wildly to and fro. Her sobs sounded painful.

Victoria's hand was trembling. She put the lipstick that she was holding down on to the dressing table and stared critically at herself in the mirror. She was nervous and it showed. Her face was fashionably pale, and it heightened the strain in her expression. Her pupils were pinpoints even though she no longer smoked anything other than the occasional cigarette. Since coming back to live at Reason Hill she had been a model of decorum.

Luke was back in England and he would be coming to the farm today; in less than an hour she would see him again. He must love her, must be bowled over, she needed him now more than ever. Being apart had convinced her that she could not live without him, without what marriage to him would offer. They had written to each other, her letters overflowing with an enthusiasm for country life that she had never felt before. His replies had been polite, nothing more. Marriage to Luke would open a new and exciting future for her. She applied a little more face powder with a swansdown powder puff as she allowed her imagination to paint a glorious picture of life in America. It would be a new, wonderful beginning. She would be among achievers. That was what she had come to realize was missing in her life: it was the company of people fired with fresh ambition. Everyone was so aimless, her family and friends contented themselves with close horizons. They aimed at goals they could see, never those that needed imagination. There was a key to the life that could be hers, and it was Luke, therefore her love for him had grown into a passion that surpassed anything she had ever felt before. Mere physical attraction palled beside the emotion that she felt for the man who could create a shining world for her. She picked up the lipstick again, gripping it firmly, and applied a perfect Cupid's bow. The tremor in her hand was a thing of the past. She could feel a surge of excitement, she could get her way, it was up to her.

Luke frowned at the state of the driveway. It was potholed, full of puddles and the paintwork of the car would suffer. He, like Eli, had chosen a Bugatti as his ideal car, and this was not his first. He had owned a much earlier model, in America. One of those that Ettore Bugatti had designed in 1910. It had been a B type 13, with a 1.3 litre engine. The first of a new breed of smaller racing cars. He slowed down to a crawl, and the engine roared throatily, it was not suited to idling. By keeping to the edge of the track he avoided the worst of the holes, but every now and again a lurch and a splash told of the mud streaks appearing on the deep green paintwork. He had enjoyed the drive down from town, the power of the machine answering his urging, the open road ahead of him. He had missed the changing countryside, the all-enveloping atmosphere of England. On either side of the track the leafless apple trees stretched away, the grass that grew at their feet was neatly cropped. Thomas Cade kept his orchards in better repair than his driveway. The farmhouse appeared ahead of him, its red tiled roof welcoming against the grey skyline. There was more garden around it than he remembered, probably Lucinda had been responsible for that. Lucinda – she was the real bar to his marriage with Victoria. When he had returned to America she still haunted his dreams. The memory he had of her clinging to him when he'd saved her from the flood was strange because in it he saw himself as well as her. Like a Hollywood movie, they clung to each other. It should have been a story with a happy ending, but it had become confused.

There were no potholes close to the house. The drive opened up into a wide sweep of gravel overlooking the view of the Weald and he parked there. Turning off the engine he sat for a moment appreciating the silence. Soon the birds forgot his intrusion and resumed singing. Far below he could see the river, cutting through the winter fields as a thin silver line. So small, so insignificant from here, yet once it had been his whole life.

'Luke.' Victoria's voice surprised him; he had not heard her approach. She held out her hand to him. 'I'm so glad you came back,' she said. Luke could hear the insecurity in her voice. She looked very young and vulnerable. The confusion in his thoughts returned: he wanted to hold her, to take the strained expression from her eyes, but instead he shook the hand she offered.

'I'm looking forward to Christmas at Pencombe,' he said.

'Will you come in? I'm sorry but Mother and Father have had to go to the solicitor's in Ashford. I'm afraid they won't be back until this afternoon.' Victoria was willing Luke to come into the house. All her scheming depended on him wanting to make love to her. She must make him want her enough to forgive the fact that she wasn't a virgin. There was no one else in the house. They would be alone, perhaps for the only time before Christmas, she must make him want her.

Luke turned away from her, to look out over the view again. The river was calling to him. 'Get your coat,' he said.

'My coat?' Her voice was little more than a whisper. Her plan was falling to pieces right at the start.

'Yes, your coat. I'll take you to see my Kent. It's not the same as yours, Victoria; it's a world I don't expect you've ever known existed.'

It seemed unreal to Victoria sitting in a car that was quite identical to Eli's except for its colour. The inside was the same, the brown leather, the maple dashboard, but

Luke's car was green and Eli's red. Not that it belonged to Eli any more, of course. Victoria tucked her hair up into her hat as the wind streaming over the windscreen pulled at it. That car was Dimitrou's now. She could think dispassionately of her former lover now. He was handsome, charming, a beautiful man with no soul at all, and they were enemies. She had seen it in his eyes when they had last met, and he had made Luke leave her.

'Are we going to Yalding?' She had to shout to be heard over the rushing wind. Luke nodded his reply and Victoria understood then. He was taking her to where he had once lived. Surely if he didn't care a little for her then he wouldn't do that. She looked at his face as he concentrated on driving, the strong jaw, the prominent cheekbones, his expression was very serious and determined. She wondered suddenly if, after all, she had the strength to win his love.

The car slowed as it approached the village. Victoria looked at the handsome manor house she could just see over the substantial red-brick wall. She tried to see it with Luke's eyes, but could not decide how he must feel. When he lived here, all those years ago before she was born, he must have looked up to the owner of a house like that, to a man of obvious wealth and security. Today he could probably buy the lord of the manor ten times over. How must he feel? She looked again at his face, and to her surprise he was smiling. He turned to her as the car slowed.

'Let's walk,' he said, smiling so broadly that his strong teeth showed brilliant white against his tanned face. She felt a surge of pride that they would walk together in public. He was the returning, conquering hero.

It was a grey day, but at least it wasn't raining. They parked on a verge in front of yet another beautiful house. Victoria looked unseeingly at the handsome Georgian elevation. Should she take Luke's arm? It worried her that she didn't know how to act towards him, and Luke gave her no clue. He had walked to the centre of the road and stood there, breathing deeply as he stared towards the narrow stone-walled bridge ahead.

'I once rode across that on a horse that had almost killed a man.' He looked over at her, standing uncertainly by the car. 'I did that a lifetime ago – your lifetime, Victoria. It was before you were born, before your mother and Thomas Cade ever lay together.'

She could feel the red flush that ran up her neck. Behind Luke the village shop, its windows crowded with bags of flour and sugar, seemed to spy on them. It was a narrow road, people could hear his words. He began to walk then, going towards the bridge. She followed hesitantly.

'There was a hay wagon here,' he gestured with his hand as he walked, taking for granted that she was still with him. 'That damned horse took fright and bolted all the way up to Reason Hill. By the end of it we were both exhausted, but I won.' He laughed harshly. 'I won the day because he had to carry me home, and by nightfall he was nearly dead on his feet.'

Victoria shivered miserably. Crossing the bridge the winter wind was cold on her face. She tugged her hat down as far as it would go and turned up her coat collar. Still Luke walked ahead, his words blown back to her on the wind.

'That was the day that your father promised Reason Hill to Timmy. I was there, and my sister Jenny was there. She could tell you a thing or two about the bother that promise caused. See there.' He stopped suddenly and pointed downriver. 'You can just see the cottage. God,' he leaned both his hands on the parapet of the bridge, breathing in great draughts of the chill air, 'I never thought I'd be brave enough to face coming back to it.' He stood staring out towards the small cottage that he had shown her. It was insignificant, a traditional waterman's home. Only its solitary nearness to the river singing it out from any of the other labourers' cottages that made up the Tonbridge side of the village.

'Where is everyone?' Victoria was feeling unnerved. She hadn't seen a single villager since they'd arrived at Yalding, although she had a constant impression of being watched.

'It's a secret village,' Luke said. 'Except for high days and holidays they live out their lives in the back rooms. They plough happiest close to the hedge down here, Victoria. Do you want to wait here? Your shoes won't like the mud on the river path.' He turned back to her, ready himself to take the narrow slipway between two weather-boarded cottages that obviously led to the water.

'No, don't leave me. I'll come with you.'

Luke had already started forwards. Now that he was close to his past, he felt its pull irresistible. The river flowed sluggishly, low between its banks. The water was steel grey, reflecting the sky above. On the far side from them there were small, muddy beaches where the imprint of hooves showed that livestock came to drink. Stretching back from the bank were the water meadows. Looking over at the flat fields Luke thought back to the day of the hare coursing, over twenty years ago; it had been the day when he'd sold Thomas Cade four barrels of finest brandy. Luke had been a smuggler then, a criminal. And the day had started with a man being killed, a stupid, ignorant sailor who'd thought that he could get away with black-mailing men whose lives depended on secrecy. They'd brought the body to Luke. He stood very still, looking down into the slow-moving water. He could almost remember the fear he'd felt, the sudden knowledge that his days here were numbered. In those days he'd never been able to imagine a future other than his life on the river. And now, what was there for a future now? He turned slowly to look at Victoria. She was staring up at him, her face quite still.

'Come,' he said and put out his hand to her. She did not reach out to take it, so he took a step towards her and took her by the arm and she allowed herself to be led by him. She was overcome by a strange, empty emotion, it was as if sensation was suspended. All she was aware of was her slow, even breathing. They walked to the cottage. It was painted dark blue, with lank grass growing round the brick doorstep. As they got close they saw that the door and windows were boarded up. Luke led her silently past the home that had once been his, and carried on beyond the tumbledown sheds that had long ago housed his pony and chickens. Still they followed the river bank.

'When I lived here, I was a different man,' Luke said. He spoke slowly, considering his words. 'I did things then that I would not do now, but nothing that I am ashamed of.' They walked on in silence until they reached a low stone building, half sunk down into the ground it formed a wing for the lock gates spanning the river. Luke stepped down to the door. 'In my day it was padlocked,' he said. 'But then in those days there was something to hide.' He pushed the door open ahead of him and then stepped through, out of Victoria's sight. After a few minutes, when his eyes had adjusted to the gloom he called to her to follow him. She put a hand out to steady herself as she stepped down. The grey stone that she touched was damp, a dank smell of the river came towards her and she stepped unwillingly into the dark. She recoiled as Luke took hold of her. She did not want to be out of the daylight.

'If I told you what I did here once then it would be a secret that would tie us forever.' His whisper was loud in the echoing vault.

As Victoria became used to the light she could see the iron rails beneath her feet. Stone walls made a cavern around them. He turned to face her, holding both her arms he towered above her.

'Then tell me your secret.' She spoke harshly, accusingly. He was playing with her, as a cat would play with a mouse.

'Women betray trust,' he whispered, the words instinctive.

'You'll never know about me if you don't give me a chance, Luke. I won't betray you and I could be everything for you. Friend, lover, confidante, but you won't know unless you give me a chance. Trust me.'

'Trust?' His fingers were pressing painfully into her arms, but she didn't notice it.

'I've never known anyone like you before, Luke. I'm not afraid to admit that. Why can't you accept that you've never met anyone like me? If you think I'll betray you it's because you've been let down before. I'm not like that, I give everything or nothing.'

'Like you gave yourself to Dimitrou.' He hissed the words.

Struggling from his grip she hit out with all her strength. The slap of her palm on his face echoed around them. 'They were right,' she shouted at him, 'my parents were right. You're no gentleman, Luke. All your money hasn't bought you the right to speak to me like that.'

'I'm no gentleman and you're no lady.' He pulled her to him roughly, pressing her against his body. She forced her head back away from him, ready to shout again, her fury absorbing everything. Then his lips were pressing down on hers, forcing her to yield. She pushed at him with her hands, clawed at his hair and still he held her. He stopped kissing her suddenly. Their faces were very close, her hands still entangled in his hair. He stared at her silently as the world stopped spinning. Then she lifted her lips to his and this time they kissed as lovers.

Later they sat on the river bank, uncaring of the mud marking their clothes; it would brush off later.

'I hid a dead man in there once.' Luke nodded towards the eel trap that they had left. 'It wasn't me that killed him, that was some of the other members of the run, but they gave his body to me to get rid of.'

Victoria knew about the smuggling run now. Luke had told her as he'd held her in his arms in the dungeon-dark trap. They had kissed – nothing more – and yet Victoria felt that she had given more of herself to Luke than she had to any other man. It had been a total commitment.

'I waited for the summer flood,' Luke continued, 'then I took out the coracle, loaded down with the stinking rotten corpse. I wanted to dump it well downriver. That was when I found your mother, out on the river. She had been swept into the torrent along with the horse she'd been riding. Somehow I got her out of the water.' His mind was full of pictures that he didn't tell Victoria about. This time, more than ever, it was like watching a film. His love for Lucinda had only ever been imagined, he saw that now. 'It was fate, I suppose. We drifted near a barn that was stranded on an island in the flood, and your father was there. I left the two of them together, and that night you were conceived. I loved the river, Victoria, I've never loved another mistress like that, and now I see that the river made you for me.' He looked wonderingly at her, seeing suddenly how much of a miracle she was. 'Let me make you happy, Victoria. Come back to America with me – I have a whole world to lay at your feet.'

'I love you, Luke,' she said, and as she kissed him she heard the sounds of the river that had given her life.

'How on earth will you manage?' Michael stepped back from warming himself at the drawing room fire, he was appalled. He hadn't appreciated until Isabella told him that they'd had to put extra guest beds in the old nursery how large the house party would be this Christmas.

'I've got a couple of girls coming in from the village, Cook will do very well as she always does, and Dove can manage as long as none of us expects too much of him. I think it would be a good idea if you had a word with the boys. They take him too much for granted, William especially.'

'Well, dammit to hell, they should be able to take the staff for granted – come to that we all should be able to. This business with Maude has gone far enough.'

'There's no point in shouting at me, Michael. Times have changed: nobody has an easy relationship with their house staff any more. And poor Maude has every reason for being difficult.'

'You're too prepared to put up with things Isabella, and you look peaky, definitely off colour. I'm worried about you.'

Isabella looked up at her husband in surprise. She didn't feel unwell just then. Although she had been suffering from nausea at times, she thought it must be something she was eating that was disagreeing with her, but nothing more. How nice it was to see that Michael cared. She tucked the needle with which she was sewing neatly into the tapestry and laid her handiwork down on the wine table beside her. 'You're old-fashioned darling,' she said. 'You'll have to change with the times, too. It seems some of us wives and mothers are now supposed to be housewives as well, and I don't mind, I quite like it really.'

'Don't ignore what I said, Isabella, I don't think you look well. You should see the doctor – in fact, I insist on it.'

The door opened noisily as William and Edward came into the morning room.

'Father!' William was very red in the face, clearly

furious. 'Have you seriously given instructions that we're not to shoot over the Home Farm any more?' The two boys were fresh from the outdoors, their plus twos earth-stained. Isabella looked down and saw in exasperation that their shoes were leaving a trail of mud on the carpet.

'Get your shoes off,' she said, 'and please remember to take them off outside in future. I will not have you traipsing dirt into the house. Neither will I have you speaking to your father in that tone, William. When you have taken your shoes off you can come further into the room and talk like a civilized human being. Until then I suggest you keep quiet.'

William muttered furiously to himself as he tried to maintain his dignity whilst balancing first on one leg and then on the other to remove the offending footwear. Edward kept his head down as he performed the same gymnastics. He didn't want his parents or brother to see how funny he thought the whole thing was.

'Very well.' William advanced into the centre of the room. 'Have you forbidden us to shoot on the estate, Father?'

'Not totally, no,' Michael answered. 'But I don't want any more unsupervised shooting. You know my feelings about guns. They've been used too freely here for years. We'll certainly have a couple of proper shoots a year, rustle up a few beaters. That's enough for any man, there's plenty else to do for sport.'

'Like what?'

Michael breathed in deeply at the imperious tone in William's voice. He'd known the boy wouldn't be happy at the situation. That was why he had something up his sleeve, something to make Christmas a joyous, peaceful holiday by encouraging the boys out of doors without their guns.

'You'll find out soon enough. But in the meantime I

think you two can scout around and find something to clean up that mess on the carpet. And I want you to be particularly good at looking out for your mother over the next few days. We have a houseful of guests and as you know the staff is pretty stretched. We're all going to have to pull our weight.'

Isabella was amazed. The thought of Michael 'pulling his weight' in the house was quite astonishing, but if it inspired William to come down off his high horse for a while then it would be no bad thing.

'Who's all coming then?' Edward asked. He'd been too tied up in the end-of-term festivities at school to pay much attention to the letters from home that had outlined the plans for Christmas.

'Well, your Aunt Lucinda and her family, of course,' Isabella replied, 'and Luke Jones will be coming with them, so that's one more on that side that we don't normally have.'

'And Albert's wife,' Michael added.

'Yes, of course, and Maggy.' Isabella frowned slightly. The poor child had no more hope of fitting into Lucinda's concept of a Pencombe Christmas than a candle in a snowstorm. 'Timmy's back from Australia as well,' she continued, 'and then there's Bill and Adele and her daughter.'

Michael had been hoping that Bill would decide to stay away. After all his recriminations after Arabella's death had not lessened. If anything they had gained in their intensity.

'How about Eli?' Edward asked, his face deliberately innocent of expression.

'Yes, he's coming too,' Isabella said, 'although I must admit it surprises me. I would have thought he'd think we were far too dull.'

William certainly thought Christmas was going to be dull, but he had the sense not to show his feelings for once.

'We'll go and get something to clean up the mud then,' he said and the boys hurried out of the room. Boredom was already taking a grip on them. Edward wished he was back at school, William wished that he was old enough to do as he wanted, then, unlike the unfathomable Eli, he would certainly not spend Christmas at Pencombe.

The room was quiet after the boys had left.

'I hope the bird is as big a success as you think it's going to be,' Isabella said.

'Don't talk too loudly, I don't want to spoil the surprise.'

'You don't really expect them to come back and clear up the mess on the floor do you, Michael? I can guarantee you we shan't see them until suppertime now. William would die rather than show some signs of domestication.'

'But that's disgraceful. He'll have to be made to pay some attention to what I've said.'

'No, leave him alone, Michael. I really don't have the energy for the pair of you standing up to each other. The main problem is he's too similar to you. Edward you might have a chance with, but William is very much set in the mould.'

'If I didn't know better I'd say that you were subtly trying to get a message across to me, Issy.'

'Oh, but I wouldn't dare. I'm much too frightened of you to try and change you, darling.' Isabella laughed companionably. She and Michael were closer than they'd been in a long time. She had faced up to some of her husband's faults and overcome her dislike of them. It was a major step forwards in their relationship. She felt easier, too, about the future of Pencombe. Work was in progress to make a charabanc park between the village and the estate. She had supervised a general moving of effects and artefacts around the house, and the rooms on display to the public were now well-stocked with reasonable antiques. They were going to grow plenty of colourful flowers in part of the kitchen garden that they no longer needed so that the public rooms would be well supplied with cut blooms during the summer. She was beginning to think of the summer as 'the season'. Those warm months of the year now loomed large in importance as the time when they would all see if their plans would work and the tourists would in fact come.

A chill, dry wind gusted along the Pantiles towards Timmy, bringing with it the scent of winter, but he didn't notice the smell or the cold. It was a long time since he'd been to Tunbridge Wells. To keep his mind from the coming meeting with Meg, Timmy was trying to remember the last time he'd visited the town. It must have been before the war and he'd been not much more than a boy. In those days the shops in the Regency walk had seemed like so many Aladdin's caves, their Christmas windows had glittered enticement. Odd that it had been Christmas then, as well as now.

He was nearing his goal. Ahead of him the parade of shops ended in a flourish with a bustling tea shop that was the popular place for refreshment for the genteel ladies and gentlemen of the elegant town. He straightened his tie as he walked the last few feet to its door, his footsteps ringing loud on the flagstones. Stepping into the warmth of the tea rooms he left behind him the abstracted hurry of the last minute buyers of gifts, their hurrying figures dim in the gloom of early afternoon.

Inside the tea shop electric lights reflected back off several bottle-glass panes strategically placed amongst a multitude of windows. Timmy took a deep breath. He was uncertain how the meeting would go – suddenly he felt that Meg was unknown to him.

There was a tempting display of cakes for sale just inside the door, and around it a gaggle of middle-class ladies jostled for attention trying to buy some to take home. Timmy made his way through them, murmuring apologies for his intrusion, feeling out of place in the all-absorbing atmosphere of leisurely affluence. A black-dressed, frilly-aproned waitress hurried towards him, ready to show him to a table, but he hardly noticed her. Meg was there after all and she was no different from his imaginings. Seeing him enter she stood up and held her arms a little way towards him. He came up to her and let himself be kissed on the cheek, breathing in the warm feminine fragrance. She was so pretty, he thought, the cherry red coat she wore showed up the pink of her cheeks, the tiny fur collar lay against the soft white of her throat.

'You look well, Timmy.' Meg's eyes were bright, she was trembling with happiness. Timmy did indeed look well. He glowed with a sleek fitness he had brought back from Australia. He towered above everyone else in the shop, and while he felt awkward because of it, she felt proud. He was a real man, her man, the one she loved. He only had to be made to realize it.

'Sit down then.' She patted the chair, talking to him like a child, teasing him gently. 'I think we'd better order an extra plate of cakes to fill you up. My, but you've grown in Australia.'

Timmy smiled self-consciously. He looked surreptitiously around the room, expecting to discover that they had an attentive audience, but all the other patrons were busily occupied in their own conversations. He let himself relax a little. 'Have you been waiting long?' he asked.

'No, no, I've only just arrived myself.' Meg was never going to admit that she had arrived twenty minutes early for their appointment. She'd been so eager to see Timmy again.

'Thank you for your letters,' she said.

'I'm afraid they weren't very long. I was never much of a correspondent.'

'Oh, they were fine. At least they told me you still had body and soul together. I hope – ' she looked down at the tea cup in front of her, hoping she wasn't blushing too visibly ' – I hope you didn't think I was too forward suggesting we meet up here. But it seemed so silly. After all, Tunbridge Wells is very close to Pencombe. We'll be spending the holiday only a few miles apart. I just wanted to wish you Happy Christmas in person.'

'If you hadn't contacted me, Meg, I would have got in touch with you. I've something I want to ask you before I go back.'

'Go back?' Meg sat very still. All her fears returned. He was going away from her again.

'Yes, I'm going back to Australia, going back to stay. It's a new world over there, one with new opportunities. Just right for someone like me. I never really belonged here.' He looked around the room again, hearing the high-pitched, aimless chatter, seeing the opulence of the clothes. This was too soft a life for him. He needed a land that challenged – a people who offered more than small talk.

'Home is where the heart is.' Meg looked very serious. 'You do belong here in England. But for some reason you've set your sights far away. Don't dismiss all the years you've been happy here, or all the friends you have.'

The waitress came with their tea, putting down the plates of scones and cakes, finding room for the cream and jam, fussing over the placing of the tea pot and water jug. The clatter she made covered Timmy's confusion. He did not know how to reply.

'You mustn't run away, Timmy,' Meg continued, 'because running away would be turning your back on yourself. I could help you, all your friends could help if you were here.' Meg was clasping her hands tightly together on her lap. She was saying the words that her mother had told her must be said, but watching the hurt in Timmy's face she wished she didn't need to. 'I know some of the problems you've had, and I also know that there are others that you'll never tell me about. But whatever is in the past, running away won't make it go away.' She poured the milk and then the tea into their cups, covering the silence between them by being busy.

When she'd finished Timmy spoke. 'I don't think you're right that I'm running away, or perhaps that's not fair, perhaps I do think you're a bit right. But that isn't all of the story, not by a long way.' He took a scone from the plate she offered him, then some cream and jam. 'I believe that I could make a go of living in Australia, and it would be on my own terms. It has to be. It wouldn't matter two hoots there that I'm Thomas Cade's son, or that my uncle's a lord. That wouldn't make any difference to a farmer who needs supplies urgently enough to charter a plane to ferry them out. Then it will be my ability that means the difference between success and failure. Nothing more, nothing less.'

'So, you're determined to go to Australia?'

'Yes, I am. And I want you to come with me. I want you to come as my wife. Together we could do anything we wanted. There's so much space out there, room to grow.'

Meg sat very still. The words Timmy had spoken were the words she'd dreamed he might say for as long as she could remember. But not this way. She wouldn't leave England, she had no past she wanted to run away from, and the space that Timmy wanted sounded terrifying.

'Will you come?' Timmy couldn't fathom her expression. Meg had turned from pale to flushed, then back to pale again. He'd been abrupt and he knew it, but surely she loved him enough to understand how he felt about her.

'No,' she said, and he felt suddenly sick. 'Nothing will make me go to Australia, nothing at all.' All the fears she'd had when he was away came back to her. The thought of the terrible, poisonous snakes, of fierce, strange Aborigines with bones in their noses. There'd been a book at school with pictures that had remained in her mind. It was an odd, dangerous land, not safe for a girl whose world revolved around the afternoon tea dances. Out there there would be no one who'd appreciate her clever ways at copying the latest fashions. She could never leave her friends, never leave her mother, never. 'Can I pour you some more tea?' She spoke without a quiver in her voice although a consuming anger was welling up in her that Timmy'd dared to suggest she should leave everything she loved. She encouraged the anger, fuelling it to give no space for despair. He held his cup forwards to her, the intimacy of the gesture made her fingers tremble and she had to adjust her hold on the teapot, she was determined he shouldn't see how upset she was.

They finished their tea in near silence, speaking only in monosyllables, each of them burning with anger at the other's insensitivity. Timmy paid the bill and they parted at the door of the shop, shaking hands briefly without exchanging any of the seasonal greetings that were being voiced all around them. Meg walked quickly back towards the town. She and her mother were staying with friends who lived quite near the opera house. In her handbag the prettily wrapped present that she had brought for Timmy remained, ungiven. It would have been quicker for Timmy to have walked in the same direction, his car was parked at the far end of the Pantiles. But he was determined not to walk with Meg, and he took the long way round. When he got to the car it leaned drunkenly forlorn, the front nearside tyre was totally flat. As he stood looking down at it in the struggling light of a streetlamp combating the early dark the drizzle began to fall. He turned up his coat collar and pushed up his sleeves. It was cold and damp and Australia seemed like a great, warm, glowing beacon beckoning to him.

Luke held the telephone receiver in his hand for several minutes after he had finished making his call. He sat motionless on the edge of his bed; the affluence of the room around him should have been comforting, but he felt unhappy, insecure. Now that he had actually spoken to Dimitrou all the past jealousy had re-emerged. It was impossible to push it from his mind by summoning up memories of how it had been with Victoria on the river bank at Yalding. She was in the house right now, in his house, in another room that was only a few yards from where he sat. She was busy making herself more beautiful for him. Why did he have to torture himself? He stood up slowly and put the receiver back on its cradle, then walked over to the handsome mahogany cheval mirror and looked critically at his reflection. He had been proud of his looks until he'd met Victoria. Now he looked too intently at himself and saw age in the creases around his eyes. There was nothing he could do to alter the years between them. He was convincing himself that it was his money she wanted him for and nothing else. He had lived for so long only to make himself rich. Now, having achieved his ambition, the thought that Victoria may be deceiving him, might only want him for his affluence, was eating into him. She had to be perfect for him, had never to have loved before, it was a kind of test. Perhaps when Dimitrou arrived this afternoon he would be able to see the truth. As he walked out of the room his footsteps were muffled by the rose-pink deep-pile carpet that stretched from wall to wall in every one of the upstairs rooms and corridors. He found the silence oppressive.

In the conservatory a wrought-iron table was laid for lunch for two. It was covered with a cloth from Madeira, made of cream linen embroidered with brown and there were napkins to match. Highly polished rat-tail silverware reflected the winter light that shone through the freshly cleaned panes of glass. A small bowl of bronzed chrysanthemums made an informal centrepiece. Victoria bent over the table to smell them. They made her think of Reason Hill, they had a homely smell about them. She had been sad when they'd been used at Lord Montford's funeral. For her they were part of life, not of death. It was delightful to be able to eat in amongst the plants, she thought. There were ferns flowing over the edges of the terracotta pots sitting in regimented lines on the whitewashed staging, and more chrysanthemums growing in pots ranged close to the glass. It was pleasantly warm thanks to a coke-fired boiler that chuntered comfortingly behind a trelliswork screen.

'Isn't this delightful?' Victoria turned around quickly as she heard Luke's steps behind her on the tiled floor.

'I'm glad you like it. I thought you might appreciate the uniqueness of Christmas Eve lunch in a hothouse, and apart from that I intend to stock up on some heat before we go over to Pencombe. All the reports I hear confirm that it's likely to be cold there.'

'Who told you that, Luke?' Victoria was on guard. There was something about the way that Luke looked at her that was unnerving, as if he was scrutinizing her.

'Bill Macaul did. We met in town the other day.'

'I didn't know that you knew him.'

'You'd be surprised who I know, Victoria. Let's sit down, shall we? I am expecting a visitor this afternoon and I have some preparation to do for that.'

'This afternoon? But we're to be at Pencombe by six. That's when the village children come in to sing carols, and I'd hate to miss that.' Victoria fidgeted with her napkin. She was becoming convinced that something was wrong. She had been so surprised when her parents had allowed her to spend the few days before Christmas with Luke as they had been unchaperoned apart from the staff. She had been eager to come to stay at Luke's country house, but it had been an uneasy few days. Luke seemed to be watching her, waiting for her to commit some indiscretion. She had lost her appetite, even the tempting smell of the hot Vichyssoise that Luke had chosen to begin their lunch was not enough to make her feel hungry. She did little more than sip a few mouthfuls before putting down her spoon. 'Luke, is something the matter?' she asked.

He paused before answering, looking down at his bowl. He had to tell her some time. 'I've asked Dimitrou to come down here.' He looked up at her quickly, wanting to see how she reacted. The effect of his words was everything he feared it might be; Victoria started back in her chair as if she'd been slapped.

'How could you!' She spat the words out at him. Livid patches appeared on her cheeks. 'After everything you've said to me, how could you do that? I hate him, you know I do. What on earth possessed you?' She was shaking her head in disbelief; she could hardly believe it.

'I have to see the two of you together. You have to prove to me you don't care about him.'

'Don't care? Don't care about him? What do you think I am?' She stood up abruptly, pushing her chair back so that the metal legs screeched on the tiled floor. 'I've told you everything about myself, all my thoughts, my feelings, God, I've talked for hours over the past few days. I've told you everything and you've believed nothing.' She turned away from Luke. She couldn't bring herself to look at him. She felt desperation well up inside her, but something else as well — she felt fury, ice-cold anger. The anger was directed at Luke for his unreasoning insecurity, but it was not directed at him alone. Dimitrou she loathed, he'd used her and that she would never forgive, and Timmy had been weak: he should have seen what was happening between them and prevented it, she understood that now. She'd been young, immature, the fault had been his not hers. Not that she'd told Luke about that episode in her life. There were some things she would never tell him about.

She stood silently as the girl came in to clear away the soup dishes and lay the trout at their places. The anger had cleared her brain. She thought of her father. He had never been a help to her, always putting her mother first, whoever was right. And then there were her brothers, who lived in their own world of the land. Who had ever been on her side and hers alone? Her mother certainly hadn't and her Aunt Isabella was generally positively against her. She turned around slowly and with great deliberation sat down again at the table.

'If you require me to voice my feelings for Dimitrou in front of him then I will certainly do so.' She spoke carefully, her voice low and controlled. The trout on her plate looked delicious. She began to lift the skin away from the flesh. 'I hope that you will be satisfied by that.' She had always looked after herself and would continue to do so in the future. Whatever Luke required of her she would do.

'Perhaps that is what I need.' Luke spoke almost humbly, shamed by her ability to control herself. 'I'm not sure what I wanted when I telephoned him, I think it's simply that I couldn't face the thought of us going back to America with his presence still between us.'

'Whatever you think is right, Luke.' Victoria was totally in control of herself now. Faced with the challenge of meeting Dimitrou again this afternoon she felt fully charged with energy. They began to talk of other things, to discuss if they would continue with the lease of this, their English country house. Victoria had a clear grasp on her future role. She would now assume her position as maîtresse of Luke's establishments in her conversation. Luke spoke deferentially to her as she intended he should. They both ate well of the caramelized apple flan and fresh cream that was their dessert.

After coffee in the drawing room Victoria went up to her room to supervise the final packing of her clothes. She redid her make-up carefully. She was determined that she should look as perfect as possible for the confrontation with her past. The final effect of her appearance pleased her. She had chosen a slender wool dress of aquamarine, with a shawl neckline that accentuated the fashionable shortness of her bobbed hair. The long rope of pearls that she chose as her only jewellery reached almost to her waist. She added a slight touch of rouge to her cheekbones and it made her eyes seem very bright. When she was ready she went to stand by her bedroom window and looked out over the drive.

Victoria waited until she saw the red car wending its way towards the house. Dimitrou was driving and there was a passenger beside him. The car stopped and Dimitrou got out, stretched quickly and then walked around the car to open the passenger door. Victoria instantly recognized the girl who got out of the car. She had been with Eli the night that Timmy had brought Victoria back to London. How small the world always proved to be. She smiled slowly to herself. She felt totally in control of the situation, she would appear as chatelaine and Dimitrou could not fail to be impressed. Her smile faded a little as she realized that she did, after all, still want to impress him. But as Luke's wife she would have everything.

She walked serenely out of her bedroom, holding her

head high. Glancing at her reflection in the mirror on the stairs, she was delighted at the effect she had created. Now she simply had to get through the next few hours and the future would be hers.

'Dimitrou.' Victoria held out her hand. She had walked into the drawing room after the others had already gone in. She was determined to make an impression with her entrance. Luke watched her intently: the next few minutes were so important to him. 'And we've met before, of course.' She went over to shake hands with the girl standing to one side of the fireplace. 'You're a friend of Eli's, aren't you?'

'Yes, I'm Kiki.'

'Oh yes, Kiki, I remember your name. Won't you sit down? In fact why don't we all sit down? And I'll ring for some tea. It's quite a drive down from town, isn't it, and then of course you have to go all the way back again afterwards.'

'But we're not going back to London tonight.' Kiki spoke in the same trilling voice that Victoria remembered. 'Eli's asked us to spend Christmas with him.'

'But he'll be at Pencombe.' Victoria was surprised enough for her voice to rise several octaves. 'And we'll be there,' she continued. 'All of us, the family, everyone.'

'I'm sure it will be delightful.' Dimitrou smiled with the smile of the cat who had got the cream. He was overjoyed to see Victoria disconcerted. For a minute, as she'd entered the room, he'd thought she might after all manage to carry off her act as the *grande dame*. Now he could relax, and look forward to Christmas.

'Tea! Terrific!' Kiki jumped up from her chair as the tea trolley was wheeled in. 'I'm absolutely starving. We had to leave too early for a proper lunch. Shall I be mother? Or perhaps not.' She turned to look at Victoria, her lips curved in a smile. 'You should have the honour reserved for you, of course, Victoria. You be mother, or am I being a little premature?' Her high-pitched laugh hung in the air; Luke wished now he'd never invited the club owner to his home. He felt the room was defiled; he disliked the tawdry atmosphere brought by the girl with the too heavy make-up. He looked at the man he had assumed his rival, Dimitrou didn't fit in the particular Englishness of the room. He looked over at Victoria. She was doing very well, he could see that she was disconcerted — probably more than that, she was upset beneath the veneer of sophistication she was assuming. He was proud of her. He felt a glow of well-being, that was how a man should feel of his wife, proud. 'Perhaps,' he said, 'as we are all going to spend Christmas at Pencombe we should hurry through our tea. I understand that carols are sung at about six. It would be a pity to miss them.'

When they went out to the cars Victoria had made up her mind. They would not keep the lease on here. She would happily part now with the house that earlier on today she had thought she loved. Luke and she should have everything new for their married life together, new beginnings. She adjusted the fox fur around her neck. She didn't like it actually touching her face, but she knew that close to her skin it enhanced the perfection of her complexion. She was wearing a long, rust-coloured woollen coat which reached almost down to her ankles and she had on a cloche hat in a subtly darker tone of the same colour. Her shoes and bag were black patent leather. She felt she looked festive, yet restrained, she believed she was dressing as Luke would wish, and she was right, he was very proud of her, she was his ideal woman.

It wasn't until he heard the roar of the engine, felt its trembling power through his hands on the steering wheel, that Luke felt the urge to race. Beside them on the gravel drive the red Bugatti also roared into life. The men looked at each other. Manners dictated that Luke should gesture his guest to leave first. A perfection of good manners would mean that Dimitrou would decline the offer and allow his host the pole position, but neither of them felt constrained by convention. The gears engaged, the cars surged forwards, and side by side they approached the wrought-iron gates. Victoria let out a small cry of horror. There was nowhere near enough room for both cars to pass between the stone-built pillars at the same time. It was the cry that reminded Luke of Victoria's presence and made him slow down. If he had been on his own nothing would have stopped him from hurling himself, man and machine, into the narrow gap, but he pulled on the brake and Dimitrou powered through ahead of him. They drove down the drive, bonnet to bumper, at nearly fifty miles an hour. The peacefully grazing sheep scattered from the parkland bordering the narrow lane. There was no way that Luke could overtake Dimitrou now. Reaching the end of the driveway Dimitrou did not slow down to check if anything else was on the road through the village, but luck was with them and both cars joined the thoroughfare safely. The noise as they sped between the high-banked hedges beat on Victoria's ears. She was too excited to feel fear. They must get past Dimitrou. With all of her being she willed the car on; the flaming red car that had once been Eli's must be overtaken.

The cars stayed so close to each other as they raced along the main road from Dover to Canterbury that they might have been joined by an invisible link. Every time Dimitrou checked in his driving mirror the vague outline of Luke's head through the windscreen met his view. Their speed began to climb, fifty, sixty, seventy miles an hour. The two cars were at peak performance and each of the drivers urged every ounce of power out of their engines.

Victoria leaned forwards in her seat, willing the car on. The trees and hedges flashed past, blurred, indistinguishable, not that she spared a glance to the side, all her concentration was fixed ahead of her. They were driving dangerously fast when they entered the outskirts of Canterbury. With a clashing of gears Luke began to slow and the gap between him and Dimitrou lengthened. Victoria turned to him, about to shout he should go on faster, but then she saw Dimitrou was slowing down too. Luke had seen the road blocked ahead of them, and had simply reacted more quickly than his rival. They slowed almost to a crawl. A congestion of traffic in front of them was making its slow way towards the town centre. Victoria tugged at Luke's sleeve to attract his attention and then pointed urgently at a road sign over to her left, signposting the way to the London road. They could go round the city, outside the old walls. She held her breath as they edged forwards in the traffic queue. A little way in front of them she could see the left-hand turn. If only Dimitrou didn't take it. Luke watched intently, his shoulders tensing as he saw the possibility to gain precious miles on his opponent, but then he saw Kiki too point up at the sign. Luke pulled hard on the steering wheel and accelerated hard. He must get around Dimitrou's car, but it meant he was blocking the road on the wrong side. A black Ford came towards them, its horn blaring, the driver close enough to be seen mouthing obscenities, but they had reached the turn to the left, Dimitrou went round and Luke stayed beside him, trusting to luck that there was no one driving on his side of the road. He was concentrating too hard to hear the screech of brakes of the Ford that they left slewed across the road behind. Ahead of them it was all clear.

The great grey walls of the ancient city reared up on their right. Oblivious of the dangers of taking up the whole width of the road they hurtled forwards. The cars were identical, it was up to the drivers. There was a film of sweat on Luke's top lip. Victoria stared at him, urging him on, all her concentration joined to his. As the road began to rise, their car nosed ahead. Both the drivers were crouched low over their steering wheels, the power of the engines was part of them, and this time it was Dimitrou who allowed the threat of an accident to lose him position. They could see the van coming towards them, wide and shining like an enamelled beetle, looming ever larger. Dimitrou slowed fractionally and Luke forced his way in front, back on to the left-hand side of the road, Victoria let her head drop back and laughed out loud, laughed with the joy of victory.

Maude stirred the glassful of sherry slowly into the mince-meat. The fruit-rich scent rising from the earthenware bowl in front of her perfumed the kitchen but she was oblivious to it. She sang softly, repeating the same melody over and over, the words filling her brain, 'Bye, baby bunting, daddy's gone a-hunting . . .' She was alone, all of the others were upstairs listening to the carols, but she hadn't gone with them. She lost Herbert in a crowd; here, on her own, he was with her. 'Bye, baby bunting,' she sang again.

They had lit the fire in the hall and it roared up the chimney; the five-foot oak logs were licked by flame from the coal beneath and they crackled merrily. Right in front of the fire Isabella could feel the heat scorching the backs of her legs, while William, standing in front of her, was hardly touched by the warmth. That was the beauty of it all, Isabella thought, the contrast between the hot and cold, the warm family unit against the vast world outside. They were united at this season of goodwill towards all men. Even Eli's thoughtlessness at inviting his strange

259

friends, the nightclub owner and the girl Kiki, hadn't marred her happiness. Bill seemed to have relaxed. He had greeted Michael with affection and Adele was happily fussing around her daughter, new life was springing in the aftermath of disaster. It even seemed easier to think of Johnnie with forgiveness; Isabella had sent him a card, as she had done every year, and when she'd written the words 'with love', she had meant them. Eli was very dapper, wearing a bright red waistcoat, 'seasonal attire', he'd called it, and it suited him. The heavy gold watch chain that decorated the front had belonged to their father, Isabella wished suddenly that he was here with them all; it was years since he'd died, but he was often in her thoughts. She pictured him as he had been when he was faced by almost insurmountable problems. His wavy grey hair was in disarray and he looked like a flustered owl, approachable, consolable. He'd very rarely been like that, but it was a fond memory, an easier one to live with than that of the family autocrat, determined to bend his daughters' wills to his way.

The village children stood rigidly to attention in the centre of the hall. They were singing their best, throwing their voices up to the high vaulted ceiling where the smoke from the fire made curling grey wreaths. Christmas was the one time of the year that the vast room came really alive. Isabella and the boys had hung holly and ivy everywhere that there was something to drape it over. Even the suits of armour were decorated with red and green. But it was the people that made the difference, a crowd of happy, united people, singing for the glory of their God for, after all, it was a religious celebration.

Isabella felt a twinge of guilt. When she had been a young girl she had found her religion very important, a mainstay to her life. Now she was so busy, her time filled with her family, the house, plans for the future, that the

Sunday visit to church had become little more than a ritual, prized for the chance it gave her for quiet reflection, there was no guiding force in her Christianity any more. They had reached the end of 'Once in Royal David's City', and, with a self-conscious rustling of hymn sheets, the singers prepared themselves for their finale. It would be 'Away in a Manger', as always. Isabella felt her eyes fill with tears. She could remember William and Edward first learning the words, stumbling over the phrases, their eyes glowing with eagerness. Little children made it easy to appreciate God's gifts.

They all joined in the singing. Michael's voice was deep – he was not a good singer, but an enthusiastic one. She tried to distinguish William's voice and leaned forwards to look at him carefully. He was only mouthing the words, she was sure of it. She smiled. Poor William, he was so unbearably self-conscious of the fact that his voice had broken. Edward was singing loudly, he was still a treble, he turned to look at his mother, making sure that she too was singing. This was her family, their voices joined in celebration. After the last note died, she went quickly to Dove, encouraging him to pass round the mince pies and then busied herself in ensuring that all the children had a glass of orange squash. The grown-ups would have the mulled wine that Michael was ladling from a huge bowl. Toasts were given and exchanged all around, Christmas had truly begun.

Lucinda accepted Luke's Christmas kiss with a smile. She had proffered her cheek in some embarrassment, but this was a relationship she would have to get used to if she didn't want to lose Victoria. Thomas had shaken Luke's hand warmly, patting him on the back, eager to show that he welcomed the newcomer into the family. Albert's wife Maggy was given no such special consideration. She stood on the edge of the gathering, her figure grossly misshapen with the child she carried. If anyone other than her husband spared her a thought it would have been one of pity, but they would have wasted their sympathy, Maggy was supremely happy; she was a quick learner, and here was an opportunity for her to learn invaluable lessons. She adored Albert – he was worth two of any of the other Cade men – and she would make him a perfect wife. For Maggy that meant that she would help her husband to negotiate the hurdles between him and success. Albert dreamed of rolling acres populated with fat, happy cattle, all breeding stock, nothing would be slaughtered for meat. He wanted a big family, as did Maggy. They would have sons, lots of them, who could inherit his dream when it had become a reality.

Maggy watched them all, paying particular attention to the women. Lucinda's failing was easy to spot. She was a snob, she wanted a title, and a great big house like her sister. That was stupid because anyone could see that Isabella had to work hard just to keep the place going. What a waste, Maggy thought, because she could see that Isabella was very clever. What a waste of her energies simply to keep a crumbling, draughty house in the family. Victoria was different. For years Maggy had despised her, but now she could see that she had been wrong. Now the real Victoria had appeared like a butterfly from its chrysalis, but she wasn't a fragile creature that would fade away after a few short days, however much she looked it. Maggy watched her carefully. She would use some of Victoria's ways as a pattern. She saw how casually Victoria had taken Luke's arm. It appeared that she had done it unconsciously, and by so doing it showed how absolutely Victoria proclaimed her ownership of the richest man in the room. Maggy slipped her arm through Albert's and he looked down at her in delighted surprise. He was so proud of his little wife; she stood up to them all and however much they might ignore her, she was here by right. He squeezed her hand tenderly.

Eli sipped cautiously at his third glass of mulled wine. It was too hot: if Michael wasn't careful the alcohol would boil off. Of course that was probably his intention – Michael didn't approve of intoxication. Having categorized his brother-in-law as a potential teetotaller Eli proceeded to look around for amusement. Inevitably his eyes were drawn towards Kiki. He thought she looked smashing, the hem of her skirt was a good three inches above her knee and the vivid emerald green of her dress complemented his own waistcoat admirably. The fact that she had come with Dimitrou didn't bother him. He owed the man no favours, in fact, to the contrary, he owed him a punch on the nose.

Dove lay unmoving in the bed. The room was in almost total darkness. Only when the moon appeared fleetingly from behind the clouds could he see the outline of the window, and the shape of the chair with his clothes for the morning neatly folded over its back. It would be an early start. There were extra fires to lay, more boots to check. Breakfast would be a much grander affair than usual, and this year he had to cope without Maude's help. There was a space between him and his wife as they lay side by side on their marital bed. They never touched any more. To begin with he had suffered from the lack of affection – once or twice he'd longed simply for a woman to fulfil his bodily needs, but all that was over. Maude was so strange now that he was content to leave her alone.

He could no longer imagine a future. After Herbert had been born all his dreams and ambitions had centred on the boy. Now that he was dead there was nothing to project his mind forwards to. He let his thoughts drift aimlessly.

He was finding it difficult to get to sleep, he'd enjoyed the carols and felt absorbed by the jollity. Tomorrow there would be a general exchanging of gifts, no more than tokens really between the staff, but it was still something to be enjoyed. He had bought Maude a bed jacket for her Christmas present: it was made from fine pink wool and fastened with a ribbon tie at the neck, one of the village ladies made a little money for charity by crocheting them throughout the year. Long ago Maude had said that she thought they were beautiful, a real luxury she'd called them. This year, with no present to buy for Herbert, Dove could afford one for her, but the joy had gone from the giving. He drifted off to sleep eventually, and rolled inevitably towards the centre of the bed, where it dipped.

Maude had stayed awake, as she always did, until her husband began to snore. The moment he moved towards her she slipped out of the bed. The floor was cold beneath her bare feet, but she didn't notice it. She went from the room silently, her long white nightdress floating like a ghost through the shadows. She would spend the next few hours, as always, dozing in a chair by the dying fire in the kitchen. Towards dawn she would make her way back to bed. The secret hiding from her husband's body had become important to her. Every night untouched she counted as a victory.

Eli made his way carefully down the stairs. He was convinced that Kiki would have understood his veiled messages throughout the evening. When she'd spent the night at Cadogan Gardens they had ended up in the kitchen, and it was an ideal meeting place here at Pencombe in the middle of the night. They would be well away from the other, sleeping guests. Isabella had put Dimitrou in the same room as Bill, Eli was still laughing at the horror on the club owner's face to discover that he was being given a chaperone. Kiki had been provided with what was not much more than a broom cupboard in an annexe next to Victoria's room. There were people sleeping everywhere in the main part of the house, crammed into the rooms that had central heating – not that it seemed to make much difference. Eli had been more than happy to abandon his bedroom; it was almost as cold as the ice house down by the lake.

The kitchen door made no noise as it opened, the hinges were kept greased. There was an oil lamp turned down very low and it threw giant shadows across the room. Maude opened her eyes slowly. She had been dreaming, a muddled dream that she couldn't quite recall. Young Eli stood in front of her: was he part of the dream?

'Oh, Christ.' His muttered words convinced her he was flesh and blood, no apparition.

'Good evening, Master Eli,' she said, her voice high and wavering; to Eli's highly tuned sensitivities she sounded insane. 'Come for something from the kitchen, have you? Come for something to eat from old Maudie?' She stood up slowly, making no effort to pull her nightdress around her. The neck buttons were undone and the white cotton fabric slipped, revealing a bony chest. She moved towards the table and the nightdress opened a little more, showing a withered breast. But Eli didn't notice. He was watching her hands, as she reached forwards to where half a crusty loaf sat on a breadboard in the middle of the table. Beside the loaf lay the breadknife. Eli watched in awful fascination as the thin fingers stretched out and closed around the handle.

'I'll make you a sandwich,' she croaked. 'You always liked a sandwich of my potted ham didn't you, Master Eli? Right from the start when you were boys together, it was always your favourite, wasn't it?' Her head jerked up suddenly and she stared at him, the light from the lamp shining redly in her eyes, which were sunk in her face, but glowing with life.

'Yes, Maude, I always liked them.' Eli had to lick his lips before he spoke, they were dry. He felt his skin crawl; he wanted to run away from the woman in front of him, but his feet seemed unable to move.

Maude began to sing, crooning the words. It was a nursery rhyme. Eli had to concentrate trying to pick out the words, the tune, then he realized, it was 'Bye, Baby Bunting'. He watched her cutting the bread, his eyes drawn to the knife. She cut three slices, four, and then he realized that she was no longer aware of his presence. He could escape. He had begun to turn back towards the door when it opened and Kiki stood there, wrapped in an ivory negligée of silk and ostrich feathers, her lips pulling back in a smile. Then she noticed the other woman in the room and began to look puzzled.

'Who's there? Who's there?' Maude's voice cracked as she called out. 'Don't go leaving me, Master Eli, I've not done yet.'

Eli heard her footsteps on the flagstoned floor and ran towards the door. He turned quickly, clutching at Kiki, pulling at her to leave with him, but then he realized Maude wasn't behind him after all. He looked round and saw she had gone back to her chair by the fire.

'I'll see you tomorrow, Master Eli,' she called out. 'We've tomorrow and tomorrow, we've forever, you see.' She laughed then, a dry cackle that made Kiki clutch tightly at Eli's arm, pressing her body against him for comfort. They left the kitchen together, almost running down the long corridor. They kept hold of each other, each determined not to look back.

They made love frantically, clinging together, drowning the memories of the mad woman with an excess of pleasure. At last they fell asleep in each other's arms, entwined, entangled, but still, somewhere in his dreams Maude reached out to Eli and he cried out until Kiki stopped him with her kisses and they made love again in the harsh light of dawn.

'I think it would be nice if you showed the bird to Maude,' Isabella told her sons.

'Not "the bird", Mother, call her "the falcon", please.' William was most correct. The gyrfalcon sat on his leather-gauntleted wrist, its head encased in a leather hood decorated with tassels. The bird was calm, soothed by the dark.

'You don't really want us to show her to Maude, do you?' Edward was almost hopping around his brother in his excitement. He was longing to take the falcon out into the parkland. They had been given a lecture by their father on how not to let her off the leather thongs that he referred to as jesses, but he could hardly wait to see the beautiful blue grey and cream bird out in the open.

'Yes, I do,' Isabella replied. 'We all have to do everything we can to get her interested in something. The doctor said that it's impossible to guess what might work. She just needs to be triggered back into reality.'

'Well, I think she's potty, but I'll go with William if he wants, I'll protect him – she might turn violent, faced with the incredible Morag.' Edward stroked the bird's back as it sat motionless.

The boys went away quickly, determined to avoid another lecture from their mother. She certainly wouldn't have approved of Edward's use of the word 'potty'. They made their way down to the kitchen, but Cook shooed them away. She was much too busy for them, and no, she said, Maude wasn't in her usual place sitting by the range. They should ask Dove, he'd know where his wife was. Dove was busy with their father in the gun room; Cook knew that, she told them, because she had asked him to help her hold the turkey so that she could force the stuffing into it, but he'd declined the honour. They were to catalogue the shotguns this morning, he said. Lord Mont-ford was sending most of them off to auction early in the New Year. William turned pale. His father really was going too far, there was going to be precious little for him to inherit when the time came.

The gyrfalcon was becoming restless. She tried once or twice to flutter up off William's wrist but he held tightly on to the jesses. The bird irritated him. 'Do you want her, Edward?' he asked.

'Rather.' Edward had known that his brother would tire quickly of the novelty of the bird. That was why he hadn't been concerned when he'd gathered that their father's Christmas present to them was a shared one. 'There, there, pretty Morag.' Edward caressed the bird, 'his' bird he thought of it as already. They would become inseparable; that was how falconers should be. He would always walk with her on his wrist and look like a knight from the Crusades. He would train Morag to fly to the kill at his bidding. He would have liked to take her hood off, to look into her eyes, but he would wait a little longer, until William was totally dismissive of the creature.

They found Maude in the corridor outside the gun room. She was turned towards them, watching their approach, she had obviously heard them coming. It was uncanny, Edward thought, she was like a cat, a mangy, scabby old cat, with that same underlying ability to inspire fear. She held a finger up to her lips, 'We've got to be quiet,' she whispered.

'Maude!' William spoke loudly. She unnerved him and the only way to deal with fear was to act with bravado. 'Mother thought you would like to see our gyrfalcon.' He gestured to Edward to take the bird up closer to Maude.

'She was a Christmas gift to us from our father. She's a very fine specimen.'

Edward felt sorry for the old woman. Her face had softened at the pretty bird. She came shuffling towards them, dragging her slippered feet on the flagstones. 'She's really beautiful, isn't she, Maudie?' Edward held the bird up, showing off the fine plumage.

'Poor thing can't see.' Maude's voice was plaintive. She had stretched out a hand as if to touch Morag, but she left it poised, several inches above the leather hood.

'She has to wear that so that she doesn't get frightened,' Edward said. 'It keeps her quiet and you slip it off before she's to fly.'

'Can't see her eyes.' Maude's head was tipped to one side. She was whispering, her own eyes very bright, their pupils so large that her eyes seemed black.

Edward reached up to untie the hood. Maudie had been good to him, until she went funny. The leather helmet slipped off and the bird stared at them. It turned its head slowly, surveying them all, then it fixed its gaze on Maude.

'She likes you, Maudie.' Edward was amazed, the bird and the old woman seemed to be silently communicating. The door to the gun room opened without warning and the bird fluttered wildly, Edward clung tightly to the jesses and leaned his face away from the frantically beating wings.

'What on earth are you doing?' Michael came striding towards them, looking annoyed. The bird had startled him and he was not enjoying selecting which guns should go for sale. He was trying to convince himself that he was disposing of them for the safety of his family, but in reality he wanted the money that they would fetch.

Maude slipped silently away as Edward fumbled with the hood, trying to soothe the falcon whilst his father tried to calm his own temper. William stood motionless. He was looking through the open doorway, at the pile of neatly labelled guns lying on the desk. He took a few steps towards the room and then stopped. There was nothing he could do, he breathed deeply, trying not to lose control of himself, but it was impossible. He turned abruptly and ran away from them, back down the corridor. Edward and his father looked at each other in unspoken sympathy. Poor William – he was finding everything difficult these days.

Victoria stood as close as she could get to the fire in the library. She was alone, she had needed some time to think, to work out her feelings. To her astonishment she was beginning to dread the thought of going to America. The feeling had started when they'd driven up to Pencombe yesterday. They'd been absorbed into the family, she knew the pattern of entertainment off by heart, the carols on Christmas Eve, followed by a supper of cold baked ham. Lunch today would be late, starting at two o'clock and going on at a leisurely pace until well after four. The timing was Isabella's compromise. She wanted the children to have a Christmas dinner as well as the grown-ups. During the evening they would have a light supper, play a little cards, and eventually, inevitably, the men would gather in the billiard room and play snooker into the early hours. To leave England would mean to leave all of that.

Victoria stretched her hands out towards the heat, rubbing them together. The engagement ring that Luke had given her that morning gleamed. A deep red ruby surrounded by diamonds, it made her fingers look pale, the oval shape of the setting enhanced how long and slender they were. She shivered, feeling cold. The library was always draughty. There was a sudden rattle like gravel thrown at the window and she looked up, startled. The wind was gusting but surely it was too cold for rain. She went to look out, and there was snow falling, hard aggressive snow that littered the grass with tiny white pebbles. The wind blew it in miniature flurries, then as quickly as it had started it was over and the winter garden was still once more, the stone jardinières looking as if they were sprinkled with icing sugar. Her breath was steaming the glass and she rubbed at it with her fingers. She heard the door open behind her but did not turn around. She stood very still as Timmy spoke to her.

'I came to wish you luck,' he said. 'And to tell you that I'm going away too. We're both flying the coop. Funny, isn't it?' She heard him walk towards the fire and turned slowly to look at him. He was standing where she had been, staring down into the glowing logs. They hadn't been alone together since he'd driven her back from Boscastle. 'I asked Meg to come with me, but she wouldn't, she wouldn't leave her mother, wouldn't leave England. Luke's a lucky man.'

Victoria didn't speak. She couldn't: her heart was pounding much too hard. But it wasn't the sight of Timmy that was making her feel like crying. It was the thought of how close she herself had come to spurning the man she loved for the fear of going into the unknown. More snow scudded across the windows.

'She loves you, you know,' Victoria said.

'Not enough, it seems. I'd never thought of that side of it. I didn't see that she would think I was asking her to give something up, I just thought I was offering myself to her, and stupid though it might sound, I thought she wanted me.'

'You should ask her again.'

'Never!' Timmy looked up at her, his face flushed, 'I certainly won't put myself in a position to be refused again.'

'If you loved her enough you would.'

'It's not that I don't love her enough — if you believe

271

that then it just goes to show you don't know me at all. God, it's hopeless.'

Victoria turned away from the window. She walked towards Timmy who was glowering down into the fire.

'I understand you all right, Timmy.' She reached out and patted him gently on the shoulder. She felt so sorry for him: he was proud, too proud and it was a failing she recognized.

The door opened and Luke came into the library. He thought what a pretty picture they made, Victoria and her stepbrother. She had her hand companionably on his shoulder, and they turned to him, their expressions surprisingly alike, considering that there was no blood tie between them.

'Come and tell Timmy he's an ass,' Victoria said to him. 'And tell him he can come and visit us in America whenever he wants, because, after all, he is my big brother.' Victoria felt so happy, she leaned against Timmy for a moment and then walked towards Luke. She had found peace at last.

Thomas sat down heavily in the chair by the fire. He had eaten too much as always at Christmas, first the massive lunch, then supper. He enjoyed the ham best of all the festive meats, and always had an extra couple of slices too much; he sipped at his digestive brandy. All around him in the drawing room the family were chattering, enjoying themselves, and he was alone with his glass of Christmas spirit. So Victoria was actually going to marry Luke. He hadn't believed it would really happen at first, but the change in the girl was remarkable. He had to be pleased with the union, however much he was concerned at the difference in their ages. It was a relief for Thomas to be able to feel genuinely happy at his daughter's forthcoming marriage. For a while he had felt guilty, felt that he was selling her, because Luke was paying more than handsomely for the privilege of marrying Victoria. Most important of all for Thomas was Luke's new decision to buy the distilleries. Now there would be no link between Thomas and the illicit whisky running, and he understood that Luke was planning to put Eli in control of the British side of his enterprise. Thomas drained the drink in his glass, determined to quell the doubts that tried to surface. Every businessman worth his salt in America had an involvement somewhere in breaking the prohibition laws, Luke had said that over and over again. It wasn't as if Victoria was marrying a crook. Michael came over to him brandishing the brandy decanter and Thomas held his glass up for a refill.

'Penny for your thoughts,' Michael said.

'It would cost you more than that, Michael, a lot more than that.' Thomas smiled grimly. The alcohol wasn't dulling his senses effectively enough.

'It's that bad, is it?'

'Bad? No, it's not bad, a lot of it's good. I mean, just look at the change in Victoria.' They both looked over to where she sat on the arm of Luke's chair. She was chatting animatedly to Isabella who was smiling happily, relaxed and at ease with her niece.

'I gather Eli's going into some kind of business with him.' Michael was deliberately vague, he'd only overheard snatches of conversations about the proposed job so far and he wanted to know more.

'You'd better ask them about that, Michael. After all, I've got much too much on my mind. Don't forget I'm the father of the bride; I'll have a speech to make, and I think I'm more frightened about that than I've ever been about anything.' They both smiled at the obvious lie, then Michael's expression changed.

'When will you be able to complete on the land purchase then, Thomas?' he asked.

Thomas looked sharply at Michael. It was totally unlike him to talk about money in any but the most formal of environments. 'In due course, I should think, Michael, in due course.' It would take time to take over the freehold interest of those thousand acres which Thomas had been farming for years.

'But you will be able to complete? I feel very awkward about this. After all, you're family, but I've given you a lot of leeway already, I do want the funds early in the New Year and I wouldn't want to have to sue for them – after all, contracts have been exchanged for some time and . . .'

'Sue for it? What the hell are you talking about?' Thomas struggled to keep his voice low. 'Good God, Michael, this is Christmas Day. Why on earth are you bringing this up now?'

'I've let things slip long enough.' Michael's expression was fixed. He looked stern, aristocratic; Thomas realized then that his host had already had too much to drink. 'I know you don't think much of me as a businessman. None of you think much of me, come to that, but I've changed. I'm going to pull this place together by hook or by crook, and I'm getting out of the service, I've got that in hand. You only have to look at Isabella to see what a strain having me away has been on her.'

Following Michael's gaze Thomas looked over at Isabella. She had lost a little weight around her face and she looked tired, nothing more. Feeling herself under scrutiny she looked over at the men, smiling at her husband and brother-in-law talking over a glass of brandy.

'I'm surprised you're still here.' She raised her voice to cover the gap between them. 'I expected you to sneak off hours ago.'

'Oh, no. Don't encourage them.' Victoria was laughing.

'They'll all go and we'll be left alone.' The women were unaware of the tension between Thomas and Michael.

'Now, I've heard about this.' Bill came over from where he had been talking with Adele and Timmy. He looked down at the watch on his wrist. 'It's half past ten, and tradition has it that the gentlemen of the family see in Boxing Day over a few frames of snooker. Come on, Michael, Luke and I are new here, and of course Dimitrou, we mustn't forget our young friend.'

Dimitrou and Kiki were standing side by side close to the fire. They had little to say to each other, and both of them were glad of an interruption. Dimitrou walked away from her, going towards Michael and Thomas.

'Now you're not going to abandon us as easily as that.' Victoria stood up quickly, Luke too was preparing to rise, Eli was grinning, and even Albert was murmuring his goodbyes to his wife where they sat cosily on the small regency striped sofa. 'I vote we make a new custom, we'll all come. Now don't look so woebegone, we promise not to listen to any of your jokes – well, not to the rude ones anyway.' She laughed happily. 'You will come won't you, Mummy, Aunt Isabella?'

'You don't really mind do you, Michael?' Isabella asked her husband. He looked a little strange and she decided that he probably had a touch of indigestion, after all, the chestnut stuffing had been very rich, too rich really. She would have Cook do something different next year.

'No, I don't mind,' Michael lied. He felt there were too many people in the house, now he couldn't even find escape in the billiard room. He'd only play for a while, then go up to bed early. Everything was changing this year.

In the kitchen only Dove and Maude sat at the scrubbed table. The others had gone off into the village, to a get-together at a relative of Cook's. She'd taken pains to

275

explain to Dove that she would have asked him too, only she couldn't on account of his wife. The butler stared morosely into his brown ale. It didn't feel like Christmas, Maude hadn't bought him a present and he couldn't tell if she'd liked the bed jacket, because she'd scuttled away with it; he supposed she'd wanted to open it in secret. He'd worked hard today; there was always more to do when the house was full, and he was tired, tired and frustrated, he needed some fun. He wanted someone to talk to.

'Been busy today,' he said, knowing that Maude wouldn't answer him, but unable to bear the silence any longer. 'Lunch is always too late on Christmas Day. It would make my job easier if they had it at the right time. Or took it in the evening, civilized like. This way it's half one thing and half the other, doesn't really please anyone.' He poured the remainder of the quart bottle of beer into his glass. Cold comfort for a man, he thought, weak ale and no company. 'As for having to do the inventory this morning, that was a cheek. I couldn't believe it when His Lordship said I was to help him. Today of all days, not right. Not right to handle guns on God's day anyway,' he said piously.

'Saw the guns,' Maude said, startling her husband so much that he nearly let the glass tip over.

'You did, did you? And what were you doing? You shouldn't be in that part of the house.'

'Saw the guns,' she said again and he groaned. She was potty all right. They'd have to do something about it. It wasn't good having her around normal folk; she should be locked away. But that would have to wait. Tomorrow was Boxing Day, and he'd be worn out if he didn't get some sleep.

'You comin' to bed then?' he asked as he stood up, and she looked away from him, shaking her head slowly, then she began to sing. He hurried out of the kitchen, he couldn't bear that bloody nursery rhyme. He slammed the door behind him, cutting off the words, but it continued inside his head, 'Bye, baby bunting . . .'

'Doubles?' Bill asked Michael. He had already chosen a cue from the rack on the wall and was chalking the tip, clearly intending to play himself.

'Whatever you like.' Michael was listless, unable to summon up any enthusiasm.

The two men were slightly apart from the others; Bill appeared to be concentrating on the blue chalk in his fingers, but then he spoke. 'I'm sorry, Michael, I can understand now that I was wrong in blaming you. It was nobody's fault.' His voice was low, and Michael had to lean towards him to pick up the words.

Michael couldn't think what to say. He'd almost brought himself to the point of accepting the blame for Arabella's death.

'I'm going to stay on in England,' Bill continued. 'After all, there's nothing for me to go back to America for, I certainly don't want to see Mary and I can't face the thought of being Mother's little boy again. She doesn't need me there – I think it probably suits her to have me to write letters to. I'd like to carry on down at Falmouth if you'll have me. I need something to occupy my mind.'

'It won't be up to me any more; I'm resigning the post.'

'What on earth for? It's not because of what happened to Arabella, is it?'

'No, it's nothing to do with that. It's just past time that I did. Something has to happen about Pencombe and I can't leave it to Isabella any more.'

'No, well that I can understand, I know she's not been well.'

'Not well? Who told you that?'

'Adele did. She said that Isabella keeps on being sick, but then you'd know that.' Bill made a performance of smacking his forehead with his hand. He was beginning to realize that he'd been indiscreet.

'Doubles, you said?' Michael took a cue down from the rack. He was furious. Isabella had been telling everyone else except him how she felt. He walked towards the table, raising his voice to attract attention as he went. 'Thomas, come and play, and . . .' He paused looking at the other men in the room; there was Albert, Timmy, Luke, Dimitrou, 'Dimitrou,' Michael added, 'come and show us if you're any good.'

Dimitrou smiled slowly, enjoying being the centre of attention. He took his jacket off and unbuttoned his shirt cuffs, then rolled them up, revealing his well-muscled brown forearms. Kiki felt her interest in the game of snooker reviving and Victoria began chatting animatedly to Luke.

The four men stood around the table, and the light from the fringed lamp shone on them, lighting their faces theatrically. In the shadows of the room the others formed small groups, Eli passed around his cigar case and within minutes aromatic smoke was drifting up towards the high, vaulted ceiling. Isabella looked around at her guests. They all seemed happy and relaxed, well-supplied with drinks. The house party was working, she felt relieved and took a small sip of her brandy. Nausea flooded over her, and she closed her eyes. She wouldn't drink any more alcohol tonight; she had only taken a little wine at dinner, but it obviously wasn't agreeing with her. When she opened her eyes Michael was looking over at her. His expression was stern, almost disapproving, but then she realized he must have seen the look on her face when she felt ill, and she smiled reassuringly at him. He went back to talking to the others gathered round the table.

They spun a coin to decide who would break first. It was high in the air, turning gold and bronze when the door opened.

'Maude!' It was Isabella who saw her first, and she cried out in alarm, because Maude stood framed in the open doorway, her head haloed by the lamp in the corridor behind her, and in her hands she held a shotgun. For all her past weakness, it was pointed unwaveringly towards them.

'Maude, what on earth ...' Michael went to walk towards her, his hand outstretched to take the weapon.

'Don't! Don't come for me, Master Michael, or it will be you and not him.' She turned as she spoke and suddenly the gun was pointing directly at Michael's chest.

'Don't do it, Michael,' Thomas's voice rang out loudly. 'Do as she says, leave her alone.'

Eli was standing between Isabella and Victoria. All of his life had suddenly narrowed down to this moment. She'd come to kill him; he knew she had. He stared, fascinated, at the barrel of the gun. It gleamed as if slicked with oil and it moved slowly, almost imperceptibly, towards him. For an instant it hovered, pointing at Victoria, and he heard her sudden intake of breath. After all, it had been her who'd really killed Herbert, however Maude apportioned the blame, but no, the slow arc of the gun continued and eventually, as he'd known it would all along, it pointed directly towards him. He wanted to speak, wanted to make some clever remark, to sound unconcerned, nonchalant, but he realized that he could not open his mouth, his jaw was locked tight. He was unaware that the expression on his face was of disdain, a faint smile lurking at the corners of his lips.

'They were going to send the gun away.' Maude's voice was high, questing, deceptively weak, for the gun barrel was unmoving with the strength of her insanity. 'Master

Michael should have known better. He should have known that little Maudie wouldn't want that.' There was cunning in her face now, cunning and a kind of mad intelligence.

'Put it down, Maude.' Isabella's voice was little more than a whisper but it startled Eli and almost distracted him from the figure in the doorway.

'Lady Isabella.' Maude paused. She seemed to be thinking, remembering. 'You were good to Herbert,' she said, 'he liked you, not like Miss Lucinda, he didn't like her.'

Lucinda shrank back against the wall behind her. She could not take her eyes from Thomas, he was so desperately vulnerable, so close to that awful woman, and yes, Lucinda did remember how she'd been to Herbert. She'd been dismissive, he was nothing, less than nothing, until now. Suddenly he was a threat to them all.

'My Herbert was a good boy,' Maude's voice had risen querulously, 'worth more than the lot of you. He was good to his mother . . .' Her voice trailed off, she stood silent for a while and then softly, caressingly, she began to sing, 'Bye, baby bunting . . .'

Thomas was concentrating hard. He had sensed rather than seen his wife cringe back against the wall, and Victoria was too close to that damned Eli. The blast from a shotgun spread over a wide area; he couldn't take the chance. He was steeling himself, surreptitiously altering his stance, getting his weight forwards on to the balls of his feet.

Then Luke's voice called out, 'The police should reopen the case.' He was talking to Maude, projecting his personality across the table that was between them. 'It's not good that you're unsatisfied. You have a right to see justice done, Maude.'

The others turned to him amazed, but then realized that he was right. The woman was mad and could only be reasoned with by a mad kind of logic.

'I'll go and see them myself if you want,' Luke continued.

Thomas kept watching her hands on the gun. The thin finger holding the trigger was tightening convulsively, he could see it. And the barrel was wavering, imperceptibly but definitely. If she fired now Victoria might take the whole blast.

'Shall I go then? Shall I go and get the police now?' Luke's voice was loud, imperative. He was beginning to walk forwards, trusting to his dominance to overwhelm the woman. He too was aware of the threat to Victoria.

'No!'

Thomas heard his daughter cry out and realized that she was going to try and stop Luke. He threw himself forwards then, holding his hands out towards the gun, to grasp it, to throw the barrel up, to ward off the death that it threatened.

The blast echoed round the room, careering off the walls. Tiny, deadly pellets flew everywhere, ricocheting up off the slate of the table. Thomas was still going forwards, he was almost there, his hands were reaching for her, when he felt the blow in his face. Carried on by his own momentum he fell against her, knocking the gun from her hands. He fell against the door, his hands clasped up to his face; he thought 'Lucinda' and then the floor was rushing up towards him. He felt the warm, sticky blood that flowed beneath his fingers, heard Victoria screaming 'Luke! Luke!' and then the blessed dark received him.

It hurt Maude as Thomas pushed her to the floor so that she let go her hold on the gun and it flew away from her. She twisted awkwardly in falling and a stabbing pain shot up her ankle. 'Hurt Maude,' she whispered, 'hurt Maude.'

There was so much noise; her head was still ringing

281

from the blast, and there were screams, women's voices, and shouting. She could hear Master Michael shouting.

She must get away. She put her hands out to the wall, needing its help to get to her feet. Her nails scratched on the stone. The floor was cold, her legs were chilled, Maudie should take more care she thought. She turned away from the noise and the corridor stretched out ahead of her. She would go back to where it was warm beside the fire in the kitchen. Then she saw him, he stood with his hands up to his mouth, his eyes round with shock. A great feeling of revulsion for her husband swept over her. She began to run towards him, stumbling once as her ankle nearly gave way, but she wouldn't let it. She was strong, strong. He stood there, unable to move, transfixed by the chaos he could hear and petrified by the awful vision coming towards him.

She stood right in front of him, and still he couldn't move. Her eyes glittered, tantalizing him; he could no longer hear the shouts from the billiard room. Quite slowly and deliberately she stretched out her hands towards him and then lunged forwards. Her nails drew blood instantly, raking thick lines down his paling cheeks. She heard the shout behind her and she knew that the hunt had begun. She was the vixen, she understood that now, and with a cry she darted past her husband. He was defeated, now she must go to ground, find sanctuary; she could outrun them, vengeance would give her speed.

The moon shone off the frost-whitened cobbles. It was very still in the stable yard. She passed soundlessly, like a shadow. The last remaining hunter at Pencombe turned his head slowly, sensing her presence, but he was old, and beyond whickering for attention. She had seen where they'd taken the bird. Poor thing, like her, it was held in captivity. A slave she'd been, nothing more, over the years of service, with the issue of her body cut down in his youth for their amusement. She would take the bird with her, they could escape together. She fumbled with the bolts on the door, her fingers slipping on the icy coating, but they came free at last.

'Pretty bird,' she whispered, 'pretty one, Maudie's come for you, you knew I would.' She spoke low, softly, and the bird was calmed. It could see well in the dark and night held no fears for it.

She had seen how the boys held the creature by the leather thongs and she would do the same until they were both well away from this accursed place, then she would set it free. It would fly away – she could already see that moment in her mind, and it sent a rush of excitement through her body, warming her. She had to encourage the bird on to her wrist with soft, petting sounds with her tongue, cajoling it. Then suddenly it hopped, squeezing down into the thin skin of her arm with its talons, making her gasp with the sudden pain. But the poor thing didn't know any better, and she forgave it instantly. She pulled the door closed behind her, struggling to fasten the bolt again with one hand. They shouldn't find it easy to work out where she'd been. Now she must get to cover, and she knew where.

The wide stone walls that stretched out on either side of the house had watchtowers at each end. They were nothing more than conceits in the mind of the master builder who had added them more than a century ago. The house had never been truly fortified. The tower nearest the village was empty and was sometimes used as a trysting place for lovers. The other one was used as a log store – the green-cut high-piled logs were left there for twelve months to season – she could find shelter there.

The bird leaned forwards as she ran, but made no attempt to fly. It kept its head lowered towards its chest, its eyes scanning the night lands they moved through. The door opened easily and inside a shaft of moonlight showed the pile of logs, making a rustic staircase leading upwards. Maude clambered on the wood, scraping her shins but not noticing. There was a wide ledge running high up around the inside of the tower. She reached it thankfully and sat down, her legs dangling. Beside her a mock arrow slit gave her a view out over the drive. After a while her breathing eased and her head drooped forwards. She rested her left arm, the one the bird was on, on her lap, and the two she-creatures slept uneasily until dawn.

The sound of the two cars bursting into life on the gravelled sweep in front of the house cut across the peace of dawn. The frost on the grass had hardened and it crunched underfoot as Albert set off across the parkland. He looked back briefly to where Eli and Dimitrou sat in the cars. Michael had sent the young men out to start the search for Maude. Albert was glad to be given something to do, he couldn't stand being cooped up inside any more, Victoria was walking about the corridors like a wraith. She had been forbidden to go into the upstairs room where Luke lay. Thomas was on a makeshift bed in the billiard room as the doctor had said it was too dangerous to move him.

Eli stared out across the park. The woman must be found; until she was in safe custody he felt Thomas and Luke would continue to hover between life and death. The car engine began to idle contentedly, and he waved to Dimitrou. They had agreed on the circuits that they would make around the village, intending first to make an outer perimeter search, then as the village came to life, they would enlist help to begin beating the woods inside the circle.

The crunch of wheels on the gravel woke Maude. She

blinked slowly, trying to summon her thoughts. At first the view through the slit in the wall beside her looked hazy where the cars' exhaust fumes hung heavy on the cold air, but then her sight cleared. They were coming for her. She quivered and her nervousness communicated itself to the bird on her wrist. It twisted its head looking around their refuge, searching for the danger that it sensed was coming near.

'Hush, my pretty one,' Maude whispered through her dry lips. Her legs were cramped and she had to struggle to get down from the ledge. The first log that she trusted her weight to rolled over and she teetered dangerously, then she slithered rapidly down towards the floor.

The sound of the cars moving off made Albert walk faster. He didn't see what Eli and Dimitrou hoped to achieve. Like a wild creature she'd have to be flushed out. He was making for Colin Wood, it was the nearest patch of dense cover. A few acres of mixed woodland, made up of birches and the occasional oak, it was clogged with heavy undergrowth and was under half a mile from the house. There was a woodcutter's hut near the heart of it, he'd try there first. The noise of the engine backfiring startled him, and he looked back quickly. It had sounded almost like a gunshot. He'd been going to bring a gun out with him, but his mother had become almost hysterical at the sight of it, and so he'd brought only a stick. It was a solid piece of Irish blackthorn, dark-varnished, and he held tightly on to the thick knob in his hand, taking a kind of comfort from its substance. He scanned the land as he slowly turned his head back towards his goal. He looked along the wall, the tower and then down the green alley that ran beside it.

The tower. He stood still, looking back to the small square building with the steeply pitched roof. He should have thought of it before. He turned and began to walk towards it. It meant he was cutting back close to the drive and the sound of the cars grew louder. They came side by side, revving their engines like racing cars on a starting grid. Dimitrou had let Eli drive the red car that he had once owned, while he was in Luke's car. It had been as well, after all, that Dimitrou had been with them for the holiday, because he was the only one of them who'd known what to do instantly to help the two gunshot men.

Maude pulled the door of the tower towards her. A log had rolled down off the pile as she'd clambered on it, and she had to kick it away before the door would open enough to let her out. She pulled it closed behind her, remembering to cover her tracks. She stood for a moment to let her eyes adjust to the hard morning light and then set off, keeping close to the wall. The sound of the cars beckoned to her, she must see them before she set off across country. She must make sure that they were driving away from her. The bird fluttered, wanting flight, feeling a morning hunger.

'No, no.' Maude stroked its back absently. She was concentrating on the throb of the engines, trying to tell how far away from her they were, but the sound bounced off the walls making it difficult to judge its direction. 'We won't be long now, my pretty one,' she said.

She had reached the corner. She must be brave and lean forwards to see around it; she steeled herself for the moment, a little further, just another step.

'There she is!' Albert flung out his arm, pointing to the corner where Maude's white face had flashed into sight. At the same moment, the baying of a dog from behind her told of William and Edward with Bess on a lead. The retriever had scented the bird. The terrier Patch that had been running around their heels set off in pursuit of the quarry with a joyful bark.

Maude twisted frantically. She wanted to go back, back

to the house where it was warm and safe, she had a tremendous, overwhelming urge to return to the hearth. The dog came bouncing towards her. She watched petrified as its jaws snapped open and closed with its yapping, it wanted the bird. It was a killer and she knew it. She turned then and ran, ran out in front of the house. Albert was there, cutting off her escape to the park. He held out his arms on either side of him, like a man shepherding geese. He had the blackthorn stick out on the side furthest away from the wall. She was being herded back and she turned, desperate for space. The cars were rolling down the drive towards her, the newly risen sun glinted off their windscreens, and she couldn't see the men driving them. They were inanimate, inexorable machines. The boys came into sight then, around the corner of the tower. They stood still looking at their quarry, the bigger boy held the terrier in his arms. Masters William and Edward: she wanted to call to them, she wanted them to come to help poor Maudie, but something stopped her, she couldn't remember what, but there was some reason why they wouldn't help her.

'Bye, baby bunting . . .' she began to sing and it comforted her. She stroked the bird's smooth feathers. 'Daddy's gone a-hunting.' She began to walk slowly backwards, taking small, neat steps, placing one foot carefully behind the other. Albert stood motionless, as did the boys – 'her' boys, they were.

Then she saw William struggle with the dog in his arms. 'Damn!' The word came clearly across the frost-sharp air. 'Patch! Patch! Come back!' But he shouted in vain and the little dog bounded towards its quarry.

Maude turned instantly, fear giving her speed. She ran like the wind, she must get away, must save the bird.

Eli had almost been afraid to breathe, it had been so finely balanced, but in his mind he had begged her to come towards him, closer. She was coming closer and he began to accelerate, looking forwards, never to the side of him. She was coming to him.

The green car shot across in front of him, crashing into the bonnet with a grinding, jarring sound. There was a loud hissing and steam shot up from the radiator, the bumpers of the cars locked and their momentum carried them on together. Maude still ran towards them, looking back over her shoulder now at the little dog close on her heels.

'Stop!' Edward shouted. 'Maude! Stop! Maudie!'

But he was too late. She stumbled and fell beneath the turning wheels. As she felt herself falling she let go of the jesses, flinging her arm up to send the bird flying, sending it to freedom, high and away. Her last cry followed the bird up, up towards the heavens.

'I can't stand it any more.' Victoria pressed her knuckles hard against the corner of her mouth. She was desperately trying to keep a grip on reality. She had to see Luke, she couldn't believe he was alive unless she did.

'You can and you will, Victoria.' Dimitrou stood beside her, he too was seeking the warmth of the fire in the drawing room. They were alone together. In the wake of terror their enmity had ended.

'You swear to God you'd tell me?' she asked.

'Yes, I swear.' Dimitrou was shivering. He held his hands out in front of him and they trembled as he rubbed them together. 'He's going to be all right, I told you. But you mustn't see him; it's essential to keep his blood pressure low. Don't look at me like that. It's true, it's not just a music-hall joke. A man sees the woman he loves and his blood starts to pound. That would finish him now. His system needs time to mend, not long, a few days and you'll have him back. Come now, you're not going to throw a lifetime together away for the sake of a few days?'

'Then why are you shaking? It is because you're hiding something from me, isn't it? What is it? What won't you tell me?'

Dimitrou stared down at his hands. However hard he tried he couldn't control them. 'I'm not hiding anything from you. I'm shaking because I killed that woman. She was mad,' he said, 'mad, and I killed her. It's bad luck that, very bad.'

'It was her fault. She ran straight into your car, and anyway, if you want to take any responsibility you'll have to share it with Eli. He was as much to blame as you; in fact more so because he was steering towards her, Albert said so. Eli's not worried about bad luck, far from it. He looks like a different person since the accident. But what I don't understand is why you two crashed anyway. Couldn't you see where you were going?'

He looked round at her quickly, thinking that she must know why, but then he realized. He lived by a code that she didn't understand – she didn't comprehend why fate would want revenge on him for killing one of its innocents, one of the afflicted. Neither did she understand what had happened out on the drive. 'I couldn't let him do it,' he said. He spoke softly, feeling his way with his words. 'It would have been very wrong to let him run her down in cold blood, because that's how he was then, it wasn't anger driving him, it was a cold hatred. So I steered into his car, tried to push him off the drive. I didn't mean that she should die.'

'Yes, but why did you do it? Why did you stop him doing something wrong?'

'I did it because I felt I owed him a debt. That way I repaid it.'

'A debt?'

Dimitrou stared down at the flickering logs. If fate did

as he thought she might he could be close to death himself. Perhaps it was time for the truth.

'I used him, used him and you. I took his money and his car and then I took you. The trouble is – ' he turned and looked at her, wanting her to see the truth in his eyes ' – that I found out too late how I felt about you. No, don't look away.' He caught at her hand, holding it tightly. 'I loved you, I didn't understand before what the word meant. But you're brave, Victoria, and strong. Don't worry,' he smiled wryly, 'I'm not going to beg you to come back to me, or anything so melodramatic. I can see that you love Luke, and he's right for you now. But remember, if you ever need help, ever, Victoria, come to me. I shall care about you for as long as I live.'

Victoria stood undecided for a moment, then she accepted Dimitrou's words. 'I'll remember, Dimitrou,' she said, seeing for herself that he was serious.

The door opened and Dimitrou let go of her hand quickly. They were both staring into the fire when Isabella came into the room.

'Have you seen your mother, Viccy?' she asked.

'I think she's still with Father.'

'No, she's not with him, only Timmy's in there, and the doctor wants to have a word with her. Would you pop up for me and see if she's in her bedroom?'

'Yes, of course.' Victoria left the room quickly, puzzled by her aunt's request. It wasn't like Isabella to send someone off on an errand. Normally she would have gone looking for her sister herself.

'Dimitrou,' Isabella came across the room towards him. 'You know more about this sort of thing than we do. Perhaps even more than the doctor does. What chance do you think Thomas has?'

'He's still alive then?'

Isabella put her hand on the back of the chair beside her

for support. Dimitrou's question had given her an answer. She nodded dumbly. 'He's in awful pain,' she whispered.

'Then it would be kinder to put him out of his misery.'

'Oh, my God. Why? Why did it have to happen?'

'He sacrificed himself to save his daughter. If he hadn't gone forwards Victoria might well be dead now.' Dimitrou's face paled at the thought that it might have been Victoria lying on the floor in the great cold room, the life slowly ebbing out of her. 'What are they doing for him?'

'Trying to take the pellets out of his face,' Isabella shuddered, remembering the scene she'd just left.

'What are they giving him for the pain?'

'Nothing, the doctor says he's too weak for drugs.' Isabella started in shock at the sudden roar of fury that burst from the man beside her.

'The man's dying!' he shouted at her. 'Nothing will save him. Let him have some dignity, some peace, for God's sake. He needs morphine, as much as it takes to make it bearable for him. I'll tell them.' He made to push past her but she caught at his sleeve.

'No, don't you go,' she said. 'Michael's instructed them to do everything they can to save his sight. That's why they're trying to take the pellets out. He doesn't think Thomas is dying. I'll go, you stay here.'

Dimitrou pulled away from her, wrenching his sleeve from her grip, but then he realized they wouldn't listen to him, she was right. He turned back to the fire, keeping his back to Victoria and Lucinda as they came into the room.

'Lucinda.' Isabella went towards her sister, trying hard not to show the sorrow she felt inside.

'He hasn't, Thomas hasn't . . . ?' Lucinda couldn't put her fears into words.

'No, it's not that, at least . . . Will you come and sit down for a minute?'

The sisters sat side by side on the sofa and Victoria sat

on the floor, close to her mother's feet. Lucinda patted her daughter's shoulder, then began stroking her hair. Her eyes were wild, but her touch was gentle.

'Dimitrou, would you come and tell my sister what you've told me?' Isabella had taken her decision. It was Thomas they had to think of now; they must face up to the reality of his condition.

Dimitrou put all the care he felt for Victoria into his telling them. He was gentle, but firm. There was no disputing his logic. When he had finished, Lucinda's face had settled into lines of grief, but she was calm. She stood up carefully. 'I shall go and ask them to make Thomas as comfortable as they can,' she said.

'Would you like me to do it for you?' Isabella asked.

'No, thank you, but I would like you to come with me, and you too, of course, Victoria.' Lucinda was very dignified, she walked slowly between her sister and daughter. At the door she stopped for a moment and turned.

'Thank you, Dimitrou,' she said. 'Thank you for having the courage to be honest with me, I appreciate that.' Then she turned and went out, leaving Dimitrou staring after them. He saw now why Victoria was as she was: she came from a line of brave women.

They buried Thomas close to the single gnarled yew that stood sentinel in the small churchyard at Linstone. It was a cold, grey morning, the only heat in the stone-built church was from the crush of mourners. Family and friends joined with men who owed their living to the enterprise of Thomas Cade and Sons, farmworkers, warehousemen, and workers from the brewery. Mixed with their mourning was an underlying unease. What would happen to their jobs now that their employer had gone, so early, to his Maker?

Lucinda wore unrelieved black, but she had insisted that

Victoria should wear grey. She felt her daughter was too young for unrelenting mourning and she believed that Thomas would not have wanted Victoria to hide her beauty. After the service Lucinda accepted the condolences of the mourners who lingered in the churchyard, shaking their hands, listening to their words. She felt dazed; she had taken a sedative to help her through the morning, so that for the moment there was no empty future stretching terrifyingly ahead of her, but a blank wall that stopped thought and feeling.

At last the family went back to Reason Hill. Looking out through the darkened windows of the funeral car, Lucinda thought how small it all looked. Her home was like a doll's house, she saw it all as if from afar. Michael helped her get out of the car, he had been very good to her over the past few days – a rock to lean on. She patted his arm gently as he led her up the steps towards the front door.

'I just want to say a private thank you, Michael,' she whispered. 'Before the others come, I want you to know that I couldn't have coped without your help.'

Michael squeezed her hand in reply. It was impossible for him to talk; his throat was very tight, and he was finding it difficult to swallow. It seemed unbelievable that Thomas had gone for ever.

'Where's Isabella?' Lucinda stopped on the top step and looked back at the second big black car pulling up on the drive. She wanted her sister near. They waited silently until Isabella and Victoria came up to them. The boys were coming now too, Albert and Timmy, Eli, William and Edward, Tom and Jonathan. Lucinda sighed deeply as she went into the house. She felt that its walls were closing in on her. This was the most difficult place for her to be, there was too much of Thomas here. She would have rather been anywhere else than at Reason Hill, and yet it was her home. With Thomas gone there would be no move to Linstone.

Lucinda let Michael lead her to a chair in the drawing room. Over the last few years they'd used this room less and less. Family life had revolved around the big farmhouse kitchen. Lucinda looked helplessly at the chintz-covered chairs, the handsome Georgian tallboy with the shell inlays, the Pembroke table in the window. They were all so alien, so lifeless. The blue and white vase upon the table was empty, she hadn't been able to bear the thought of flowers in the house. Strange that the masses in the church had pleased her, she thought. Isabella came up to her with a glass of sherry. There was a small confusion as Lucinda's hand shook when she took the glass and some of the liquid dripped on to the chair. Isabella quickly wiped it up with her handkerchief. Lucinda stared at the damp mark it had left on the arm. It didn't really matter.

'I think Mummy would be better in bed,' Victoria whispered to Isabella. She was being careful to keep back out of earshot of her mother. 'Can't she have something to make her sleep?'

'A little later she can,' Isabella replied, 'but I think she should stay down here for a while. She'll want to be able to remember afterwards how it all was, it will be important for her.'

Victoria looked at her aunt strangely. She couldn't see why her mother would want to remember today at all, but perhaps that was something to do with being a member of a different generation.

'I've kept one car back to drive you all over to Pencombe.' Timmy had come quietly up behind them, and Victoria gave a visible start as he spoke. 'And I've sent the others away. That's all right isn't it?'

'Yes, that's fine, thank you, Timmy.' Isabella smiled gently at her nephew. His dark eyes looked tragic, they were sunk into his face that had aged overnight. 'Are we all here?' She looked quickly round the room, scanning the faces that she loved: funerals were so difficult, she thought; afterwards there always seemed to be so much time and so little to do.

Isabella was standing uncertainly, when there was a quiet bustle at the door behind her. When she turned she saw Maggy carrying plates piled high with sandwiches. She had not been at the service because Albert had felt that it would be too much for her. Instead the newest Mrs Cade had spent the morning preparing the funeral feast. There was a general movement in the room, everyone eager for something to do, glad to have something to occupy their hands, and truthfully the men, at least, were hungry. It was nearly half past one, and none of them had had a good breakfast.

Michael came up to his wife. He had been talking quietly with Lucinda, but now she was sipping at some tea, being cajoled into trying a sandwich. 'I've asked Luke's sister to stay the night here,' he said, 'she's more than happy to, and I think it would be a help for everyone.'

'What a good idea,' Isabella said. 'I'd been wondering if I should stay, but I would like to go back with the boys. Edward's taken it all very badly.'

'Well, he was fond of Maude, too, wasn't he? We should have done something about her sooner. When we first saw she was going off the rails. Poor soul, too late for her now, too late for everyone.'

They stayed for an hour: that seemed long enough for all of them. Lucinda said her goodbyes well. She hadn't cried very much at all, only shedding silent tears that she dabbed off her cheeks with a lavender-scented handkerchief. Thomas would have been very proud of his wife.

It was a quiet drive back to Pencombe. Isabella was beginning to realize that the pain of losing Thomas was going to be worse now that the flurry of getting ready for the funeral was over. There was only one good thing, her sickness seemed to have gone entirely. She wondered if it was the shock that had driven it away. Whatever had achieved the cure, it was a great relief. As the car pulled into the drive she patted Edward's hand. He was looking out of the window listlessly. Suddenly he stiffened. 'Dad, Dad. It's Morag,' he said. He was pointing to a well-grown oak, the first of the trees that dotted the parkland leading away from the village. Michael leaned towards the window to look out. The falcon was easy to spot on the bare branches. The wind ruffled its plumage and it sunk its head further into its shoulders. Even from a distance it looked miserable.

'You'd better go inside and change, boys,' Michael said, 'then we'll have a go at bringing her down.' He sat back against the seat and a great feeling of relief flooded over him at having something to do.

Victoria rapped loudly with her fist on the window pane. She wanted to attract Edward's attention as he stood on the drive below. It looked as if he was about to take the bird indoors and she wanted it to fly once more. She wanted to show Luke how it soared and swooped. At last the boy looked up, squinting against the glare from the sky. She mouthed the words at him, exaggerating her lip movements, wanting him to see what she was saying through the window. 'Make her fly again, go on, make her fly again.' She repeated the message several times.

Edward peered up at his cousin. He knew perfectly well what she wanted him to do, but he was enjoying watching her struggle.

'Come on then, let's see this creature that all the fuss is about.'

Victoria turned in delighted surprise, Luke was standing

close behind her; she hadn't heard him cross the room. It was the first time she'd seen him up since the accident.

'Oh, Luke!' She threw herself into his arms, hugging him close, tasting the salt tears that had come so suddenly. 'I love you, I love you . . .' she said and then her lips were pressed against his mouth.

'Steady on.' Luke was laughing and struggling for breath at the same time. 'Too much passion could undo all the good work.'

'I'm sorry, I didn't think . . .' Victoria was embarrassed for a moment, then she linked her arm through his. 'I can't tell you how miserable I've been,' she said.

'You don't have to, your aunt and uncle have kept up a running commentary on it.'

'I kept thinking you would die and I couldn't bear it. I think I would have killed myself if you had.' She clung to him possessively, and then led him close to the window. 'Come and watch her fly,' she said. 'It's the free-est thing you ever saw.'

Luke put his good arm around her shoulder. He wanted to hold her close, and he felt more secure holding on to something. He was putting a good face on it, but the wounds in his left arm and side still ached and his legs felt like jelly. His poor Victoria would have to come to terms with the fact that he wasn't immortal one day. It was inevitable that he would die before her. In all probability he would leave a young widow. Lying in bed had given him time to reconsider his relationship with Victoria. He had passed through all the possible emotions, and in the end he had accepted that they had to love, there was no way that either of them could survive without the other now. But it would be Victoria who paid the price for their loving when she would be, at the end, left alone. He pulled her closer to him and softly kissed her cheek.

'There, there she goes,' Victoria cried.

Luke looked out through the diamond-shaped panes to where the bird hovered high in the bright, pearl sky. Its wings fluttered incredibly quickly, faster than the eye could see. Watching the bird Luke could sense the power stored within it, the potential energy that was almost magically suspended in mid-air. Then in an instant the bird was falling, hurtling like a stone towards the earth, its wings tight back. It was a deadly bullet hurling itself at its prey. They sensed rather than saw the lure that Edward swung fly off from his hands. Close above the earth the bird twisted suddenly to one side, the mad fall became a glide, and feet first it cannoned into the shapeless lump on the ground. Instantly it began to peck savagely at the prey held fast by its talons. In the wild this would be the kill.

'She stoops to conquer,' Luke said the words softly.

'I didn't know you liked Shakespeare.' Victoria turned away from the window, looking up at him.

'That's what it means isn't it? The bird "stoops", plunging from the skies to the kill. That's what you did to me, my fair Victoria.' Luke was smiling, he felt steadier on his legs now, and in his arms was the woman he loved, who loved him in return. 'You stooped from your ethereal heights and pinioned me to the ground with your talons.' He took her fingers in his hands, bringing them up to his lips. He felt Victoria stiffen suddenly.

'Have you seen Dove's face yet?' she asked.

'Where Maude marked it? Yes, I have. He'll take those scars to the grave.'

Victoria leaned her head against his chest, closing her eyes, allowing herself the luxury of relaxing. She had been so tense since that awful night.

'I miss my father dreadfully,' she whispered.

Luke stroked her hair softly, holding her head against his chest.

'I just keep thinking I should have been a better daughter to him. I don't know if he ever knew how I really felt about him, I keep wanting him back, so that I can tell him.' Her words tailed off. All the memories of the times that she knew she had disappointed him kept coming back.

'He loved you, Victoria, that's the most important thing of all for you to remember, and he was very, very proud of you. He told me so.'

'When did you talk about me with him?' She asked the question querulously, almost envying Luke's past relationship with her father.

'We talked about you a great deal. I had to justify my position in your life to your father, and that wasn't done simply by talking about the money I have, Victoria. Your father put a great deal of thought into approving me as your future husband.' Luke was glad that none of the business deals that would have tied him in with Thomas had to be brought into the open now. In the cold light of day it would have looked as though he'd paid a price for his bride.

'Eli said that if Father hadn't thrown himself at Maude then I'd probably be dead.'

'Eli is right.'

Victoria shivered in his arms and then stepped back, looking up into his face. 'It's time you got back into bed,' she said. Her eyes were red, but her face was composed: she was learning to live with her loss.

Luke was thankful to lie down again on the warm bed. He felt ridiculously weak. He patted the space beside him and Victoria sat down close to him. She straightened the collar of his dressing gown and then smoothed the sheet that was turned back over the blankets. They sat silently, companionably, holding hands. After a while Luke closed his eyes and slept.

Victoria sat very still watching the man she loved sleeping. The strong lines of his face were relaxed and there was a faint tinge of grey around his chin. He was only shaving every second day because his skin was sore — the doctor said it was a reaction to the drugs he was taking. She felt she was taking an unfair advantage of him, as if she was eavesdropping on a private conversation, but she was drawn to the secrets that she felt his unconscious self might reveal. He was vulnerable, she realized that suddenly, the determination was something he applied. She wanted then to wrap her arms around him, to hold him close, to keep him safe. Instead she slowly disentangled her fingers from his grasp. She was smiling as she did it. She was going to spoil him, she would go to the kitchen and persuade Cook to produce something really special for his lunch. She looked back at him sleeping peacefully as she left the room and blew a silent kiss on her fingers before closing the door gently behind her.

'Australia!' Michael stared down in disbelief at the letter he held in his hand. 'Isabella, they've offered me Australia.'

Işabella looked up from her breakfast, 'And what exactly are they suggesting you do with it?' She smiled at her husband. He was running his fingers through his hair, looking the perfect picture of the astonished male.

'They're offering me a high-level diplomatic posting, I don't believe it! Listen here, they're saying that this posting is in response to a specific request. They've put in a few quotes from a letter sent to them from Australia — there's a bit about "in recognition of his especial bravery" — then there's how they want it recognized that the position is to be given as a, quotes again, "specific honour". Good God,' Michael laid the letter down on the plate in front of him. 'It's all about the Anzacs. That man we met in the Café Royal, do you remember?'

'Yes, yes, I do remember, Michael.' Isabella's head was spinning. A posting to Australia. It was unthinkable, unbelievable. 'What will you do about it?' she asked.

'I don't know, I've got no idea.' He ran his hands through his hair again and picked the letter up to re-read it.

'Australia.' Isabella said the word slowly, contemplatively. Timmy had talked a lot about the country, about the new start he believed he could make there. She looked carefully at her husband. His face had come alive, he looked young again; there was a good, fresh colour in his cheeks.

'Of course, I'll have to refuse,' he said.

'If you think that's the right thing to do, dear.'

'Well, there's no choice, is there? After all there's Pencombe, and the boys have to finish their time at school, then they'll have university, all that sort of thing. Still, it's a damned nice thing to have been offered, isn't it?'

'Yes, absolutely.' Isabella paused and then she added, 'I wouldn't turn it down immediately though, I don't think that would be politic. You ought to look as if you've at least considered the offer seriously.'

'You're quite right, I don't want to offend anybody. I'm really pleased you know, quite delighted.'

They went back to eating their breakfast. Michael opened the rest of his post, going through it carefully. There was beginning to be some activity on the land sale front and before long there would be money coming into the Pencombe coffers. Together with the proceeds of the gun sale it meant that he could retire his commission without their feeling the pinch too much. He'd tell Isabella soon what he intended, now that it was obviously going to be possible.

Isabella pushed her chair back from the table and stood up. 'I thought I'd go and keep Luke company for a while, Victoria won't be driving over from Reason Hill until this afternoon. What are your plans, darling?'

'Smaile's coming in.' Michael didn't look up from the letter he was reading. The factor would be arriving shortly

301

and he wanted to have gone through all the post before then.

'I'll see you for lunch then.' Isabella left the room briskly, she had quite a lot to get through. She hoped Luke was feeling strong this morning because there was a great deal that she wanted to talk to him about.

'It's just a feeling I had.' Isabella was enjoying her conversation with Luke, he was satisfyingly quick to understand her, and they were both indulging in a little fencing with words.

'You may well be right, Isabella, and if I agree that you are, I've no doubt that you have just the ideal temptation to make me stay in England.'

'Oh, yes, Luke.' Isabella smiled happily, 'I have absolutely the ideal temptation. One that I can assure you Victoria would never allow you to turn down.'

'Then I'd be grateful to you if you gave me first option on the offer, before you dangle it in front of your niece. I'm no match for her if she sets her mind on something.'

'How would you like – ' Isabella took a deep breath. Now it had come to the stage when she had to commit herself; after this there would be no turning back ' – how would you like to take over Pencombe? On a tenancy, that is, lock, stock and barrel as it stands today.'

Luke's eyes narrowed, he became very thoughtful. 'Is this about you and Michael?' he asked.

'Yes, it is about me and Michael, but not in the way it would have been a few weeks ago. Michael's been offered a diplomatic posting to Australia, a very good one. I think it's just what the two of us need, a new start, new places, new faces. The boys can stay on here at school, and I'm sure that Lucinda would be more than happy to keep an eye on them. Don't you see?' Her voice rose a little, she was determined that Luke would say yes, she knew how right she was. 'It would make everything perfect. You and Victoria could live here at Pencombe, Lucinda could take over the west wing and bring Jonathan with her – it's quite self-contained – and then William and Edward could come to her for their holidays. That leaves Reason Hill for Albert and Tom. There's more than enough room for them to share for a few years.'

'But I have business interests in America, Isabella.'

'Then why don't you send Eli out there? You'd already decided that he could handle the distilleries. If you trusted him with those then surely he could do whatever had to be done in America.'

'It's not the same over there, Isabella. It's not like it is in England, it's a hard New World.'

'And I believe that Eli could make a hard new man.'

Luke was silent for a moment then he said, 'You may well be right about that too.'

'Too?'

'Well, you were certainly correct when you said that Victoria would never let me turn down Pencombe.'

'Then you'll do it? You'll say yes?' Isabella's face was so eager that Luke would have laughed at her if there hadn't been so much at stake on his decision. All their futures had suddenly been thrown into a great big melting pot.

'Give me some time to think,' he said, and watched the animation drain from her face. He reached out his hand to her. 'You've done very well so far, Isabella, and you've certainly captured my interest. Now, I just have to see if I can live with the idea. You know you'd make a pretty good saleswoman. Perhaps you should change direction and go to America instead.'

'You will think about it?'

'Yes, I will, and I won't talk to Michael until you and I have talked again. There, that's saved you one last question, hasn't it?'

Isabella squeezed his hand tightly and then left the room. So much depended on his decision, but even if he did as she wanted there was still Michael to persuade. She went along the corridor to her bedroom. She would change her dress and freshen her make-up. There was no harm in adding a little allure to her plans. As a final thought she dabbed a touch of perfume at her temples and on her wrists. She smiled self-consciously at herself in the mirror, but all, she reminded herself, was fair in love and war, and perhaps this was a little of both.

Johnnie arrived at Pencombe just before lunch. On his instruction, the hired car pulled to a stop in front of the huge baronial doors in the centre of the north façade. It was an entrance that was only ever used by uninvited guests, those who didn't know that they should gain admission to the house through the small courtyard. But Johnnie had no intention of doing as everyone else did, he was going to make his reappearance as dramatic as possible. He pulled the wrought-iron bell pull three times in slow succession and the rarely used bells jangled uncertainly. It was Isabella who heard them first as she crossed the corridor from the drawing room towards the study. Michael became aware of the sound a few seconds later, as he was conducting the factor out to his runabout parked outside the buttery. There was something about the bells that made Michael uneasy. The small hairs on the back of his neck rose and he hurried Smaile out into the daylight.

Dove made his slow way towards the door. He put his hand up tentatively to his cheek. It had become a habit, touching the scar ribbons, before facing the scrutiny of others.

'Hello, Dove.' Johnnie held his hat out to the butler as he stepped quickly into the house. It was darker in the hallway; he'd felt uncomfortably exposed in the harsh winter light. 'Don't bother to announce me.' He went ahead, walking faster than the servant. His limp was pronounced, but he didn't feel any pain today: there was too much for him to look forward to.

Isabella saw him coming towards her. She stood waiting, unable to believe her eyes. In the gloom of the passageway, it seemed that time had changed her brother-in-law very little indeed. 'Johnnie,' she whispered.

'The fair Isabella.' He held out his arms and she stepped into them, holding him close. 'Don't squeeze too hard,' he laughed. 'Don't forget the old war wounds.'

She leaned back from him then and looked up into his face. He felt the shock that passed through her as she stiffened instinctively and then relaxed too quickly. She'd tried to cover the horror she felt but the effort was too late.

'Not a pretty sight, is it?'

'We've all changed, Johnnie, grown older . . .' She couldn't think what to say.

'You don't have to worry, Issy, I've got used to that kind of reaction by now. Have a good look – go on, don't keep turning your eyes away. Have a proper look, see what a face that's been through fire looks like.'

'Oh don't, Johnnie.' She wanted to draw away from him, but he held her firmly by the shoulders. It wasn't the scarring that made her want to run away, or the misshapen balance of his face, one cheek puckered and redly swollen, the other sunken and white. It was his eyes. The eyelids were pulled unnaturally tight, making his eyes seem almost oriental, but it was the expression, they were cold, dead and he looked at her without compassion, without pity. He wasn't Johnnie any more; she was in the arms of a stranger.

'Johnnie!' Michael's shout made Johnnie let go of Isabella and she stepped quickly aside, leaving the brothers to face each other. She wanted to run into her husband's arms, to hide in safety. Instead she stepped back against the cold stone wall and waited.

Johnnie held out a hand to his brother. It was encased in a black leather glove. Isabella felt her eyes irresistibly drawn to the outstretched hand. She kept trying to imagine what it must be like. Adele had told them that his right hand had been burnt almost to the bone.

'Johnnie. Good Lord, what a surprise!' Michael took the proffered hand in both of his own. 'Why didn't you tell us you were coming?'

'I thought you might not want me down here, and I didn't want to stay in London.'

'Not want you here? Why on earth did you think that? But never mind, you're here now and that's all that matters. Come on in front of the fire, you must be freezing.' Michael kept chattering on, trying to hide the dismay he felt. He'd imagined so many times what it would be like when Johnnie came home, and now here he was and Michael's overwhelming feeling was one of embarrassment. He couldn't feel pity for someone so composed, so self-contained.

'I'll go and tell Cook there's one more for lunch,' Isabella said. 'Pour Johnnie a sherry, Michael, and I'll have a lemonade. There's still some in the jug, I think.'

Johnnie followed Michael into the almost comfortable warmth of the drawing room that he remembered so well. 'So Isabella's on the wagon, is she? She'd do all right in America just now.'

'Do you find prohibition difficult?' Michael grasped at the suggested topic for some conversation. He felt very much at a loss for words.

'Difficult? No, I don't find it difficult. In fact I find it rather the reverse, but that's a long story, too long for before lunch.' Johnnie sat down heavily in a chair by the fire. 'Well, it hasn't changed much here, has it? Mind you, I gather you've been having a bit of excitement. Can't see the damage, though.' He peered exaggeratedly about the room and then laughed before sipping at his drink. 'God, this stuff's rubbish. Where on earth do you get it?'

'A bit of excitement? Do you mean what happened at Christmas?' Michael paused. He had been pouring out Isabella's lemonade; he couldn't believe that Johnnie could be referring to the shooting so casually.

'Yes, I do, not that anyone wrote to tell me, but I'd have to be pretty dim not to have seen all about it – it was all over the papers. Of course having a real-life drama in the home of a lord certainly helped you achieve the column inches. Should boost the old visitors no end come summer.'

Michael stared down silently at the glass in his hand. He felt the anger beginning to build inside him, but he wasn't going to let it take him over. He owed Thomas's memory far more than he could achieve with an explosion of temper.

Isabella came quickly into the room. Lucinda was following a little way behind her, and she wanted to make sure that Johnnie knew about Thomas – it would be so awful if he didn't. 'Johnnie,' it would be difficult to say this quickly, 'Johnnie, did you hear about . . .'

It was Michael who provided her with an answer, and it was very short, his voice hard. 'Yes, Johnnie knows all about Thomas.'

'And Maude,' Johnnie added, 'let's not forget poor Maude. After all, some of the accounts I read . . .' But he stopped there, because Lucinda came into the room and the transformation that came over him was astonishing for both Michael and Isabella to watch. He stood up slowly, carefully, apparently in some pain. He stood for a moment, leaning on the back of his chair. Then, as if with an enormous effort, he stood straight, holding his arms out towards Lucinda. 'My poor, poor Lucinda,' he said, and his voice was soft, almost breaking with emotion, 'I came as soon as I heard.'

With a sob Lucinda flung herself into his arms. She held on to him tightly and cried against him as she hadn't cried before. Johnnie had come back, come to comfort her. Johnnie who'd been her very special friend. After a while she dried her eyes, then she ran her fingers tenderly down his cheeks, 'Oh Johnnie, my beautiful Johnnie, why did this have to happen to you?'

Isabella watched in growing horror. It was as if the years had turned back. This was Lucinda and Johnnie, they'd been close, very close, never lovers but always friends, and together they had been devious and, at least as far as Isabella was concerned, dangerous. Johnnie had been determined to marry Isabella then and it had been on Lucinda's urging that he had tried to force himself on her. If it hadn't been for Michael he would have succeeded. Isabella shook her head, trying to clear the jumble of thoughts that Johnnie's return had aroused. Lucinda had changed so much over the years. When they'd all been young, she had been headstrong, determined that life should be lived for her enjoyment. She couldn't go back to being that shallow, pleasure-seeking creature again, could she? Isabella and Michael looked at each other, and the uncertainty that they felt was clear. It was as if the clock had been turned back.

Dove entered the room silently. 'Luncheon is served,' he intoned, observing with satisfaction that Master Johnnie had stirred them all up. He could do with some amusement after such a miserable Christmas.

'I have something to ask you, Lucinda. But before I do, I want you to know how important your answer will be to me.' Johnnie stopped walking. They had reached the copse and the trees sheltered them from the wind that was blowing from the east. The sun broke through the clouds and it was almost warm.

Lucinda kept her eyes lowered. She wouldn't say right away that she would marry Johnnie when his divorce became absolute, it would be in less than a year, but she would try and make him understand that as long as he was prepared to wait a little while then one day she would say yes, and gladly. She was never meant to be a woman alone, Thomas would never have wanted her to remain a widow and she and Johnnie had been meant for each other for a long, long time.

'When I first went to America I found life there very different from life here in England,' he said. 'Looking back, I think that probably the biggest difference was in the money that was spent on pure pleasure. I know that it looked as if Adele and I were spending pretty freely over here, but that didn't hold a candle to what it was like in Chicago. There everyone we mixed with was on a par — life had to be lived at speed; it was marvellous and I loved it. To begin with, that is.' He paused.

Lucinda said softly, 'You don't have to explain anything to me, Johnnie. I don't need a justification of how things went wrong between you and Adele.'

'I wasn't going to give you that, Lucinda. What I'm trying to explain to you and, God knows, I'm finding it difficult, is why I have a son you've never heard of.'

'A son? But . . .'

'No, don't ask me any questions yet, I just want to make you understand why I had to keep Benjy's existence a secret. The thing is . . .' He looked away from her, to the winter-bleak fields rolling off into the distance. 'I've got to trust you, Lucinda. You won't let me down, will you? Say you won't.' He clutched at her hand, squeezing it painfully

309

tight. 'We've been friends for so many years – you were the only person I could think of.'

Lucinda was beginning to realize that she had been wrong to assume that Johnnie's return had been to offer her comfort.

'Mary is Benjy's mother.' Johnnie almost choked over the words. 'We're desperately afraid that Bill will find out about the boy.'

'You mean you're worried that Mary will come badly out of her divorce? Come to that, if your Benjy's existence becomes public knowledge, Adele will have the most incredible evidence to use against you.' Lucinda's temper was rising. She didn't want to be party to a lot of sordid secrets.

'I want you to take care of him for me.' Johnnie hadn't realized that he was turning Lucinda against him. 'If we get him right away from America, have him educated in England, it would be the best thing for him. He's mixing with a rough crowd now, and I must get him away from them.'

'A rough crowd? How very charming.' Lucinda threw her head back, her eyes were blazing. 'You're intending for me to take some child whose existence I'd never even heard of, the result of an illicit union, some moment of passion that you probably can't even remember. A boy who by your own admission is going to be wild. You expect me to bring him into my family? How dare you, how dare you presume so?' Lucinda's cheeks were flaming, embarrassment at her misinterpretation of Johnnie's motives mixed with pure fury in defence of the morals of her own young.

'I've put it badly, I knew I would.' Johnnie watched Lucinda's temper in annoyance. He'd known she'd be awkward to handle, but there had to be a way to bring her round. The only thing he mustn't do was to tell her the truth, the real reason why he had to get Benjy out of America. 'I didn't mean that Benjy's a difficult boy, far from it, he's a sweet generous child, I meant that I was concerned for him in the future. After all, he's reaching an age where he's going to look for broader horizons.'

'How old is this paragon of virtue then?' Lucinda's curiosity wouldn't let her storm away from Johnnie as much as she would like to.

'He's twelve. His birthday was last month.'

'Twelve?' Lucinda's eyebrows rose in surprise. 'But that means he was born just before your daughter. My goodness, Johnnie – ' her eyes narrowed in amusement ' – what an amorous time you must have been having all those years ago.'

'The fact that Adele became pregnant was the way that we managed to keep Mary's condition hidden. We had to keep her away from the family when it began to show. Bill was easy, he was away for months at a time. In those days he was travelling all over the States, building up the business, so it was perfectly understandable for Mary to say that she wanted to spend some time holidaying in Florida. Normally Adele would have wanted to go with her, but by then she was expecting her baby and all she wanted to do was stay at home, close to her mother. It worked out very well, Benjy was born, Mary got her figure back, came home looking brown and happy, all without them ever knowing a thing.'

'My God, Johnnie, you've got the luck of the devil.'

'Well, perhaps.' He allowed himself a smile. Despite herself Lucinda was becoming interested; that had to be the first step.

'Does he look like you, Johnnie?'

And that question, Johnnie thought, was definitely the second step. 'Yes, he does. He's got my eyes, my mouth – at least the mouth I used to have.' He smiled and the scar at the corner of his lips puckered, but Lucinda hardly noticed how changed he was any more. For her he was the Johnnie he'd always been.

'I can't take him, Johnnie. How on earth could I explain a strange American child? You'd be more at risk of having him found out if he came to me, besides . . .' Lucinda realized the clinching argument, 'Bill's not going back to America. He's staying here in England, so you see,' she smiled happily now, she didn't have to refuse after all, 'you'll be quite safe leaving Benjy where he is. If you're worried about him keeping bad company then why don't you send him away to school? There must be somewhere civilized over there.'

'Oh yes, Lucinda, it's quite civilized in parts of America.' Johnnie smiled at Lucinda's snobbishness. 'But I don't understand. Why is Bill staying on in England? He's got their business to go back to, and then there's his mother – she'll want him to come home. I don't understand. What's keeping him here?'

'Well, in the beginning it was that stenographer girl, but he lost her because she died. I don't know why he doesn't want to go back to his own home now, apart of course from the situation with Mary. Anyway, he's going to take a lease on Cadogan Gardens, and he and Adele will share the house. And he's talking about some business interests in the docks; I've no idea what. You'd have thought he'd had enough to do with water, what with the accident at Falmouth. But he seems set on his plans.'

'Cadogan Gardens – is this Michael penny-pinching then?'

'It's not Michael who's arranged it at all; it's our indefatigable Isabella, and you know what she's like when she gets a bee in her bonnet. She's got Luke agreeing to take over Pencombe, and now all she has to do is convince her beloved Michael to take his posting to Australia like a good boy. She's even got me to agree to be a guardian to her boys, so there you are, there's another reason why your Benjy wouldn't fit into my newly reduced circumstances. I shall be moving into the west wing.' She gestured down towards the house. 'I'm not sure that I'm not being treated a little like a dowager.' Her mouth turned down at the corners, she was beginning to feel sorry for herself. 'But I shall learn to live with my loss in time.' She sighed, leaning a little towards Johnnie for comfort.

'Is that the time?' He looked down at his watch in exaggerated surprise. 'I hadn't realized. No wonder I'm starving. Come on, last one down to the house is a sissy.' He laughed as he spoke and held out his arm towards her. Lucinda felt thwarted and she smiled grimly. The weather was bleak, and a cold, bleak future seemed to beckon. She would not accept it: she was meant for better things. After all, her Thomas had always intended that she should be a lady. How very fortunate, she thought suddenly, that Johnnie had not encouraged her into making a commitment she should never have made. She owed Thomas's memory far more. After a while, when she had shown the world the depth of her grieving for her husband by a suitable period of mourning, she would find herself a companion to take her on in life, and she would make sure that he was someone very suited to her potential. She was quite charming to Johnnie as they completed their walk, and he went indoors feeling that Benjy was as good as promised a home in England already.

Timmy accelerated hard, leaving the village of Pencombe far behind him. He had spent most of the night rehearsing what he was going to say to Meg. Now he just wanted to be face to face with her.

It was annoying that both the Bugattis were still being repaired. When some of the shock of Thomas's death had passed, Timmy had gone down to the garage in the village to survey the damage to the two vehicles. They were parked side by side covered with a greasy tarpaulin, their temporary resting place the corner of a field bordering the garage forecourt. The stone building that now housed a mechanic and a boy looked just what it was, a converted forge. It provided an incongruous backdrop for the pair of elegant cars that would have been more at home in Park Lane. But the estate owned the site, hired the workers and took the profits, so it was logical for the work to be carried out there, although it would be slow. The job had to be fitted in around repairs to the estate tractors, demands for petrol, and the essential business of keeping the middle-class locals' tourers and runabouts in good working order.

Timmy kept rehearsing his speech. The more he repeated the words, the less convincing they sounded to him. He must think about something different. He tried concentrating hard on his driving, but there wasn't enough challenge in propelling Isabella's Ford along at a steady thirty miles an hour. What he needed was to be roaring along, goggles down, leather helmet on, then he could have felt the exhilaration of some speed. He slowed to a crawl behind a furniture removal van, it was far too wide for the road and he squeezed his horn several times, it should pull over. When at last it did he went cautiously around it: he had no intention of risking another accident to his aunt's car. The repair bill from the accident in Cornwall had been horrendous. He began to wonder if Victoria's ideas on how to convince Meg that she must go back with him to Australia might not be better than his own. His stepsister had suggested flowers, chocolates, a romantic dinner, sweeping the girl off her feet with tender words, a few hours dancing cheek to cheek. She'd also suggested getting Meg away from Brighton. She herself would invite her up to Cadogan Gardens she'd said. Aunt Isabella wouldn't mind, she approved of Meg, then Timmy could offer his beloved everything: London, the high life, the heady atmosphere of love and abandon. But the more Victoria had painted the picture of the perfect setting for a proposal, the more Timmy had shied away from it. He couldn't believe that girls really wanted all that tinsel, all the empty glitter. At least, he couldn't believe it about Meg. She was different, that was why he loved her.

He parked the car in front of the terraced cottage. He made sure that the handbrake was fully on, it was quite a hill. As he opened the front gate he felt a tremor of nerves. He felt sick, sicker than he'd felt flying over the Hun, but then he believed that his present mission was less certain of victory.

'Timmy!' Meg opened the door in response to his knock. She was wearing a blue and white checked apron over a simple navy dress. Her hair was fluffy, as if it had only just been washed, and her cheeks were pink. Timmy thought she looked quite beautiful. 'Oh dear,' she said, 'I look an awful mess, you should have warned me you were coming.' She began to run her hands over her hair, trying vainly to smooth it. 'Gosh, I must look a fright.' She stepped back, ushering him into the hallway. 'Mum's out and I'm baking, you'll have to come through to the kitchen.'

He followed her towards the back of the house, twisting his tweed driving cap in his hands. She was so much more composed than him, he felt he would never have the courage to say all the words he had planned.

'Sit down – I shan't be long, then I'll make you a cup of tea, and if you're very, very good you can have a fairy cake, a hot one straight from the oven. You'd like that, wouldn't you?' She was being very managing, trying to cover the fact that when they'd last parted it had been in anger.

'I'd like two better,' he replied and they laughed.

'You've got to tell me all about Victoria.'

315

Timmy watched Meg's hands as she efficiently creamed together some butter and sugar, then carefully beat in two eggs. He began talking, telling the story of Victoria's romance far too slowly for Meg who kept drawing him on with her questions. She wanted to know everything, how handsome Luke was now, because, of course, Aunty Jenny was a beauty and she was Luke's sister. Was Victoria any less Miss Prissy Boots since she'd fallen so madly in love? Where were they going to live? Dozens of questions kept Timmy occupied as several batches of cakes made their way into the modern gas oven that stood gleaming in the tiled space that had until recently housed a coal-fired range.

Meg chattered happily, keeping the subject well away from Timmy's recent loss. She'd sent a letter of condolence, and she thought the best thing now was not to bring the subject up until he did. She stole little looks at him when he wasn't aware of her scrutiny. He had lost some weight, not that he'd had any to spare, he needed feeding up. She felt she wanted to smother him with affection. But she wasn't going to let him know it, at least not yet. She'd had such an awful Christmas, she'd almost hated him after their meeting at the tea shop.

'You'd better wash your hands,' she instructed him. 'Everything will be ready in a couple of ticks. Come on, you can use the sink in here, and there's a towel on the back of the door.'

Timmy went to do as he was told and Meg went quickly out into the hall. She wanted to put on some lipstick and a little face powder; she felt as if her cheeks were burning. She looked critically at herself in the mirror in the hallstand. She'd been right, her cheeks were dreadfully red. She powdered over them generously — trust Timmy to catch her looking a fright.

She smiled suddenly at herself in the mirror. She loved

him, loved him madly, but she certainly wasn't going to let him know it, first he had a price to pay for taking her for granted.

'All ready?' she called out, and then went back into the kitchen. She'd taken her apron off. If she'd had more warning, they could have eaten in the front room, but now Timmy would have to put up with things as he found them.

'You've got flour all over your face,' Timmy said as he sat down. 'Would you like me to get the towel for you?' He started to get up again, and she stopped him quickly.

'Timmy, what does go on in your head?' she asked. 'Haven't you noticed that everyone, just everyone is wearing face powder these days? It's fashionable, you see.' She narrowed her eyes as she spoke, trying to show him what an ass he'd been. 'You know you should go up to town more often, it's being hidden away in the country that makes you act like a bumpkin.'

She spoke so naturally that Timmy didn't take offence at her insult. He was beginning to appreciate that perhaps he had been wrong, and Victoria had been right. Fortunately it wasn't too late to remedy that.

'Would you like to come and meet Victoria and Luke then, so that you can see the answers to your questions for yourself?'

'What, come up to Reason Hill?' Meg waited until she had swallowed her mouthful of hot sponge cake before replying. She looked contemplatively at Timmy: he was trying to get her onto his own ground.

'No, not to Kent, I thought it would be more exciting if you came up to my aunt and uncle's house at Cadogan Gardens. I mean we could go to some shows, do a bit of dancing, see the shops, that sort of thing.'

'Really?' Meg's face shone, even the powder couldn't hide her excitement.

Timmy helped himself to a third cake. Women, he had to concede, were better at understanding other women than men were.

'So tell me about Australia.' Johnnie was relaxed. He leaned back in his chair, surveying his brother across the expanse of desk between them. He was amused. This had been his own study for the few years that he and Adele had lived at Pencombe; then, on the rare occasions that it had been used, it had been perfumed with cigar smoke and there had been a well-stocked drinks trolley in the corner. Now it was austere, a room stripped for action, Michael clearly believed himself above bodily luxuries.

'I find it difficult to talk about. It was such a surprise, it came right out of the blue.' Michael spoke slowly, haltingly.

'What you really mean is that you're embarrassed to tell me what a hero you were, that's it isn't it? You're playing the shrinking violet. Well I wouldn't bother, it's all out in the open now, all your cloak and dagger stuff. I knew there had to be something behind it, the planning that you said you spent all your time doing was nothing more than a smokescreen and all the time you were our gallant saviour.'

Michael didn't like the tone of Johnnie's voice. It wasn't a sneer, but it came close.

'No, I'm not playing the shrinking violet. What bothers me is that I can't accept the post, it seems like throwing their gesture back in their faces.'

'Well, don't look at me to take over your place again, I've done it once and I'm too old now for cold, venerable houses, too old and too clever. Mind you – ' he paused and appeared to be struck by a sudden thought ' – if you really wanted to go, there might be something I could do.'

'No, no, I really can't. There's Isabella, for one thing,

318

she'd never agree to leave the boys. In time I'll be able to look back and be delighted at it all, it's just a bit difficult at the moment. What was it you wanted to talk about anyway?'

'I wanted to tell you that I've decided to "do the decent thing", and give Adele an easy divorce. To begin with I was all fired up to fight her tooth and nail, but I've cooled down now. There's no point in dragging all our names through the gutter – the gutter press, that is.'

Michael felt relieved. If Johnnie had wanted, the story of his affair with Mary could have become the scandal of the decade.

'My lawyer is going to suggest that we admit to . . . how shall we put it? A few indiscretions in my past with a young lady of only moderate repute. And I'll give Adele a more than generous settlement. I should think she'll end up quite happy about the whole thing.'

'I don't know what Bill intends to do.'

'I don't know exactly either, but I do know that he's agreed not to pull Mary's name through the mire. My mother-in-law came the old matriarch, she didn't want to give her friends too much to chew over. So there you are, Michael, there'll be no stink, just a refined, slightly sanitized odour, and we'll all be free to go our separate ways.'

'And you and Mary, what will the two of you do? Will you get married when you're free?'

'Good Lord, no! All that was over long ago.' Hearing the suggestion voiced out loud made Johnnie's mind up irrevocably. He would come home, home to England. He couldn't bear the thought of carrying on the macabre relationship with Mary any more. And with the Bertiolie family breathing increasingly heavily on his neck it would be a lot healthier outside America. He'd send for Benjy, it would be good to have the boy near him, and of course now that Adele was staying in London he could see some more of his daughter. She was growing into a very pretty girl. He became almost sentimental at the thought of having his children around him.

'No, I'll stay single to the grave now, old man.' And celibate, he added in his thoughts, there was no choice about that. 'You know, it bothers me, this Australian thing. There might be something I can think up. Do me a personal favour and don't turn it down for a few days. Let me just mull it over; it won't do any harm, even if I can't come up with anything.'

Michael felt touched by his brother's concern. 'All right,' he said, 'a few days, but don't lose any sleep over it. I'm resigned to refusing.'

The brothers went through to the drawing room to join Isabella for tea. Johnnie was pleased when, after a few minutes, Lucinda came in to join them. He waited for an opportune moment and then winked at her slowly. She looked perplexed for a moment and then smiled in understanding: Johnnie was up to something. It was like old times, and the jealousy that she'd kept hidden from herself for so many years, the feeling of how unfair it was that her sister had everything, the house, the title, came close to the surface. The tea she sipped tasted suddenly very good, the fruit cake that she bit into was delicious. She felt interested in life for the first time in what felt like ages.

'What you must understand, Isabella, is that he will never go to Australia if you ask him to.' Johnnie was being very forceful. He had Isabella in his power and he knew it.

'I don't see why.' She was trying to be defiant, but she had an unpleasant feeling that Johnnie had all the answers and she didn't like being alone with him. She sat very upright in her chair, feeling trapped by Johnnie's insistence. He stood by the fire, he was so still that he was menacing, he compelled her to listen by the strength of his argument.

'Because he won't want to be beholden to you. You of all people should know that, Isabella. If it's not his idea, then it's a bad one. He's always been like that.'

Had he? Isabella asked herself. Was it true what Johnnie was saying about her husband? She shook her head silently as if denying the validity of the accusation but she knew, deep inside, that there was enough of the truth in it to make her believe that Johnnie might well be right.

'I'll give you a way out.' Johnnie was feeling good, he sensed he was winning. 'I'll take over the scheme you've begun, and I'll carry it out just as you would have done. The only difference is that I'll say to Michael that I thought of it. You just go along with that, Issy, and we'll all be home and dry.'

'We?' Isabella seized on the word, she had to know Johnnie's motive for helping her.

'Well, you didn't expect me to interest myself in all of this for nothing, did you? I need a base here myself, I've decided to come back: I'm fed up with the life over there, a man needs to live amongst his own. I want to hunt, fish, do a bit of shooting, live the life of a country squire. I've been down in the village often enough now and they've stopped gawping. The ideal place for me to base myself is here.'

'But if you carry on with my plan then there will be nowhere for you. After all, Luke and . . .'

'I don't want to live in the house. It's too old-fashioned for me. No, what I want is for the estate to call in Pottifers in the village. It's a rotten tenancy, they pay little more than a peppercorn rent, and they're old – they don't need a big house any more.'

'Pottifers? But the Maddoxes live there. They've had the

house for ages, I think that Mr Maddox was even born there. Wasn't his father the tenant before him?'

'You can't be sentimental over them when you've been turning farmers off their land without a qualm, Isabella. Just look at it realistically. That property is going to fall down if some money isn't spent on it soon. It's a fine, late Georgian house. There are buildings like that in America and when they're worked on they become very comfortable indeed. It would suit me perfectly.' And I'll have a flat in town, he continued in his mind, and get in touch with that club owner Dimitrou, as Luke suggested. There's no reason why I couldn't start up a few ventures over here. With what I've learned I'll run rings round the insular English.

'I'd have to talk it over with Smaile.'

'I've done that and he agrees with me. He's drafted a letter, it only needs your agreement and he'll set the whole thing in motion. But you'll have to be quick, Isabella, or you'll miss the boat, and I mean that literally. Michael can't hang on much longer without giving a response.'

Isabella felt that the next few minutes were very important. She had to consider, to weigh everything in the balance, the good and the bad. She closed her eyes to help her concentrate. What was the most important thing: was it the future of Pencombe or her relationship with Michael? She must think of the boys. What they needed was a secure, happy family. It was a miserable dilemma that she was in; she had to decide either to stay in England and face an almost certain return of the problems in her marriage, or to go to Australia, leaving the boys at school. There was no way that she could disrupt their education by taking them with her. She sat very still. There was one new, inescapable factor that must tip the scales, one that she couldn't tell anybody yet.

'All right, Johnnie,' she said, 'we'll do it your way.' She

stood up and walked from the room. She hated having to hand everything over to her brother-in-law, but she believed that what he said was right: Michael would not accept Australia if the price meant having to accept that Isabella had provided it for him. He hated the new, independent type of woman, he was forever saying it, and sadly his refusal to move with the times meant that he was determined that his wife should more than conform to his ideas of womanhood. It had been her plans for Pencombe, as well as her mistaken suspicions about him and the girl Arabella, that had nearly ruined their marriage. Michael had never forgiven her for being the one to show him how necessary it was to sell off the outlying farms. She realized suddenly how close the two situations had nearly become. If she had shown that she could arrange the estate so that Michael could leave it, then once again he would have felt betrayed. She felt better having justified to herself letting Johnnie have his way, but she felt tired, she would have a short nap before going to change for supper. Then she thought she might have the energy to dress up for the evening. She hoped that life in Australia would be very gay.

'My goodness, Victoria, you look absolutely stunning.' Isabella looked at her niece in admiration. The girl was ravishing, her new-found confidence had made her into a true beauty. Luke had his arm around his fiancée's waist, his brown hand resting lightly on the shimmering silver fabric that seemed to dance with the thousands of tiny silver beads that swirled as Victoria twisted her body, showing the dress off for her admiring audience in the drawing room at Cadogan Gardens. She tipped her head to one side and the grey ostrich plume that blossomed from the silver-sequined bandeau around her forehead arched, echoing the bend of her slender silhouette.

'That outfit must have cost a fortune,' Meg whispered to Timmy. She felt eclipsed. Her own dress made from deep red shantung had been an eye-catcher in Brighton, but in London she thought it looked dowdy and old-fashioned. She looked down miserably. It wasn't nearly short enough: if she'd known she could have turned it up another two or three inches. Timmy slipped his arm around her waist and she shrugged it off quickly. It was one thing Victoria parading her husband-to-be, but Timmy and Meg had made no announcement of any future plans. Come to that, they hadn't even reached an agreement, Meg was still determined not to leave England.

'I do hope Michael won't be late.' Isabella checked her watch again. If they didn't set off soon they'd be late for the preview.

'We'll just go on to the gallery without him,' Luke said. 'He can follow us when he does turn up. Johnnie must have kept him talking longer than he ought. Don't worry, Isabella. You've got two stalwart gentlemen to protect you – or isn't that enough?'

'Yes, but you've each got ladies of your own. I want a man just for me.' Isabella was determined not to let the thought of Michael and Johnnie discussing the plan, her plan, spoil her mood. She had managed to convince herself that Michael was bound to accept the opportunity to go to Australia. Whenever her thoughts seemed in danger of considering him turning it down she became very bright, enthusiastic, almost girlish. She was looking forward to the evening. The exhibition was in a fashionable new art gallery just off Bond Street, and she was looking forward to it; it seemed ages since she'd accepted an invitation to that sort of thing. 'Frivolous entertainment' her father-in-law had once called the cocktail circuit that fêted new, up-and-coming artists amongst the titled and the affluent.

Isabella approved of her reflection in the long gilt mirror

over the fireplace. She was very pleased with her new dress. It might not be as *outrée* as Victoria's but it flattered her figure, and the jet-black watered silk complemented her golden hair that the stylist had rolled into a tight chignon at the nape of her neck. Compared to the short bobs of both the girls it was very sophisticated. Isabella was surprised at how seriously she had found herself taking the challenge of going out for the evening in the company of the two young girls. She hadn't realized before that vanity formed such an important part of her emotional make-up.

They were walking out into the hall when the front door opened and Michael came in. 'Good God!' He stopped still, looking at them, leaving the door still open and the freezing night air rushing into the house.

'For heaven's sake shut the door, Michael,' Isabella called to him. 'You're letting all the heat out.'

He closed the door slowly, still looking in astonishment at the vision before him. 'Isabella, Isabella,' he said. He was so obviously stunned by his lovely wife that the others burst out laughing.

'Michael!' Isabella turned very red. He was embarrassing her – embarrassing and pleasing her. 'Come on, you'll have to get a move on, we're late already.'

'You stay, Isabella,' Luke said. 'He'll never manage to get himself ready if you don't.' He felt very pleased. He had the most beautiful young woman in London on his arm, and from Michael's manner it was easy to see that he must have agreed to Johnnie's proposal and was going to do as they all wanted.

Isabella laid out Michael's clothes. They were all easily to hand in his dressing room and she certainly wasn't going to bother to call a maid up to sort them out. Besides, it would have spoilt the intimacy of the moment. Michael was bathing: he'd said he wanted to feel fresh for the evening.

'Do I need to shave again?' his voice came through from the bathroom.

'No, I don't think so, dear, you looked quite perfect to me.' Isabella laid the black tie on the bed beside everything else.

'And you look quite perfect to me.' Michael came back into the room. He was hot from his bath, pink-faced, glowing with health, the white towelling bathrobe heightened his colour. 'I must say, I was quite staggered when I came in just now. You look magnificent.'

'Magnificent? I'm not sure that's a word I like: it makes me sound a bit like a battleship.' She stepped forwards happily into his arms, feeling how warm he was, breathing in the comfortable, soapy smell of him.

'You're much too slim to be a battleship.' Michael let his hands run down from her waist, feeling how slim her hips were. He pulled her suddenly against him and bent to kiss her.

'Michael!' she pushed him away, realizing that he wanted her. 'Michael, we couldn't possibly; we've got to get to the gallery.'

'Don't be a prude, Issy.' He pulled her back towards him.

My hair, she thought despairingly, I'll never be able to do it up again. But then she closed her eyes.

They joined the others for supper in the Grill Room at the Café Royal. It was a perfect setting to follow on from a little light culture. The glittering dresses of the ladies reflected in the mirrors on the walls; the intimate opulence of the rococo decor was theatrically stimulating. It was a venue where the gentlemen vied with each other to be the wittiest, the most urbane, and brittle, clever chatter floated upwards on wafts of perfumed cigarette smoke.

The Montford party was one of the loudest in the room, Michael insisted that they would drink nothing but champagne. He stood to tell them that he and Isabella were going to Australia, and he didn't sit down until he had explained that they had missed the preview because of a lost shirt stud, only colouring slightly at the memory of the reality. The minute that Michael sat down, Luke got to his feet.

'To Michael and Isabella,' he said, raising his glass, and the others joined him in the toast. As Meg sat down again she was feeling as self-conscious as the others were relaxed. Victoria smiled at her, but it was a strange, knowing smile. Meg felt nervous, she didn't know the rules about this kind of evening.

'You know, it must be twenty-odd years since I came to that party they threw here for Rodin.' Michael leaned back in his chair, giving the waiter plenty of space to serve the Pigeon au Pimlico. 'We all poured out of here afterwards, chucked the horses out of the shafts of a hansom and then pulled him ourselves round to the club, God it was a splendid evening.'

'And I was so jealous of you,' Isabella said. 'When you got home we had the first row we've ever had.'

'The beauty of it is I don't remember a thing about that part of the evening.' Michael signalled for more champagne. 'I was absolutely tight. It's a pity you weren't around in those days, Luke, this place was absolutely wild. On another night there was Marie Lloyd chasing the head waiter around with a hat pin, swearing like a trooper that he was cheating her over a bottle of brandy, then flinging her arms round the neck of the manager. She was a remarkable woman – pure fire.'

'And I thought I was right to be jealous of you meeting the great artist himself. Now I find out that all the time you were with another woman, Michael!' Isabella was feeling wonderfully happy. It was such fun to remember the days when her passions had been aroused so easily at the opportunity that Michael had had to meet the famous sculptor. How furious she'd been at yet another example of how lucky men were. After all, Michael didn't even really appreciate art. She stopped laughing suddenly. A strange procession was making its way towards the table: an enormous silver salver and cover were being carried slowly, ceremonially towards them. But they already had had their meat course.

The waiter bearing the salver stood beside Meg, whose face registered near horror. She had no idea what strange rule of etiquette might be expected of her. She hardly breathed as the second waiter reverentially removed the silver lid and the salver was proffered to her. In solitary splendour sat one red rose. 'Mademoiselle,' the waiter whispered encouragingly, and she reached out tentatively to take it. She stared at the bloom, almost unseeing in her blushing embarrassment, then she looked at Timmy, whose face was strangely empty of expression. She looked around the table. The others were busily eating and drinking. She didn't quite know what to do with the flower, so eventually she laid it down beside her plate, and picked up her knife and fork. Just as she did so another silver salver appeared beside her. On it was a second rose.

She looked up at the mirror on the wall and felt suddenly sick; a line of other waiters stretched behind, they were all queuing up for her. There were twenty-three red roses in all; Isabella helped Meg clear a space for them on the table. Meg felt dazed; it was dream-like, no one at the table acted as if it were even in the slightest odd. In fact – she looked quickly around the room to check – no one in the room seemed to think it strange. They cleared the meat course, and brought on the dessert, a confection of meringue and flaming liqueur. As they were being served a waiter deftly arranged the roses in an ice bucket on a stand and placed them beside Meg. She kept looking at Timmy and at last he leaned towards her. 'This is the message,' he said, passing her a small white envelope. She took out the gold-rimmed card that it contained and read the words on it, 'To the twenty-fourth rose in the room, all my love, Timmy.'

Meg felt her cheeks flaming.

'Eli!' Michael stood up to welcome the newcomer. The champagne had made him almost unsteady on his feet.

'All set.' Eli grinned at Victoria, who got up slowly, languorously, like a silver cat. She beckoned, crooking her finger at them to follow her, and they all trooped out of the room, through the marble foyer, towards the night-bright street.

'Coats,' Michael bustled about, ignoring Isabella's questioning looks. She realized then that she and Meg were the only ones not 'in the know': something odd was going on. The two Bugattis were pulled in by the kerb, the red and the green. Dimitrou sat in the driving seat of one, Eli got into the other. Meg said in an odd voice, 'Those are my trunks from home in the cars. Where . . .?' The small cavalcade moved slowly off and they began to walk beside them on the pavement. Timmy took hold of Meg's arm. He started to whistle softly and then louder as they heard the music.

There was quite a crowd watching the Gaiety girls dancing to the music of the man on the piano. Meg looked on in open-mouthed astonishment. The steps around the statue of Eros formed a stage: there must be twenty, thirty girls dancing, kicking their legs in time to the music, they were singing too, and the growing crowd was joining in.

'So.' Timmy put his arm around Meg's shoulders, his head was tipped back, he was laughing out loud, and the white silk scarf thrown around his neck fluttered on the evening air as he turned her round to face him. 'All this is to prove, that you are never, never again to take me for granted.' He laughed again as he gripped her round the waist and began waltzing in time with the music.

'Timmy, Timmy, have you gone mad?' Meg's head was reeling, the lights were spinning past. 'Oh my goodness, Timmy,' and then she was dancing too, lifting up her neat little feet, skipping round, as they laughed and laughed.

'Come on then, Issy,' Michael took his wife firmly by the hand, 'I'm not being left out.'

'What on earth?' she gasped as he pulled her into a clear space, it was all unbelievable, the crowd was singing, almost drowning the piano. 'Good Lord, Michael, did you arrange all this?' She threw an arm up, encompassing the lights, the dancing and the music.

'Me? Oh no, not me, my dear, we have my brother to thank. Now, don't look like that, Issy, and don't talk, save your energy for dancing.' He whirled her around and the crowd closest to them cheered at the handsome lord and his lady, so happy, so radiant, so in love.

It was Eli who started them joining the chorus line, pushing and encouraging Luke and Victoria first, and then the others joined in too, and the line snaked round and round, they kicked until their legs ached, sung until they were hoarse.

Timmy stood still so suddenly that Meg would have fallen, if he hadn't been holding her so firmly. 'Now,' he said, bending over her, making her feel very small, 'now, will you admit that you love me?'

'Admit?'

'Yes, that's right, admit it now, Meg, or I'll stop the music, and then I'll ask you again, in front of them all.'

'Oh, you wouldn't.' She clutched her hands together in

front of her, her face showing the horror she felt at the thought of all those people listening.

'But I most certainly would. Shall I?' He turned as if to shout to the man at the piano, the man wearing a yellow and purple striped waistcoat.

'No, no,' she cried at him, shouting to be heard above the music, 'I love you, Timmy, I love you.'

'And you'll come with me to Australia?' He was still laughing, still so sure of himself and she knew then, that she had to be with him, wherever, forever.

'I'll come,' she cried, and there were tears on her cheeks, tears of happiness, 'I'll come with you to the ends of the earth.' And then they kissed and a cheer went up and the car horns burst into life, keeping time with the music.

Johnnie stayed out of the bright lights watching. He'd got his way, all of it. Michael had fallen into his hand like a ripe plum. Now Timmy was disposed of, too. The little girl in the red dress was allowing herself to be walked towards the piano, they were all gathering into a knot. The sickly sweet notes of a love song rang out in the street, there were car horns too, a general, mad air of fantasy, all created by him, his imagination had brought it all to fruition, but he didn't want to share in the aftermath, the surfeit of congratulations. He saw the girl turn to kiss Timmy, watched in a kind of pain as the pair clung to each other. Silly little thing, he thought, she'd been swayed by the wine, the night and the music. He stifled a rising pang of envy and turned. He would go away from this, this parody of life.

He swung his cane as he walked, and it touched the pavement making a strange rhythm, the uneven fall of his footsteps, the click of the ferule. The streets he walked were dark, there were few seekers of pleasure abroad. It was nearly midnight, time to have found a place to pursue

331

their enjoyment indoors, or to have given up and gone home.

'Got a light, dearie?' She stepped towards him out of the darkened doorway, her kohl-rimmed eyes bright in her pale face. The coat she wore was long, almost reaching her ankles. It was made from old crushed velvet and faded in patches but in the dim light it was tawny, cat-like. A cloud of stale scent engulfed him.

'Need a bit of company?' she asked. Her voice was harsh, common, but it didn't repel Johnnie. She was gaunt, dirty, but there was a spark, deep in her eyes. 'You look a real swell.' She waited then, holding her cigarette a little way towards him and he reached into his pocket for a lighter, wondering suddenly if she had a man-friend with her, and he was their intended victim. As if reading his thoughts she said, 'I could do with some company myself. I'm all alone and it's not good, is it, dearie? Not good to be alone in the night.'

He was about to answer, about to smooth-talk his way into a sordid adventure, when he remembered. For a moment his hideous past had slipped his memory, but the poison of it flooded back.

'Alone, alone are you?' he cried. 'I'm not surprised. You're a slut, a filthy slut, you stink of the gutter. Go on, get back into it where you belong.' He raised his cane as if to strike her, knowing as he did so that the rush of his fury was ending. He felt suddenly desperately close to crying.

The man from the shadows stepped out behind Johnnie, and her bright eyes narrowed as she saw the gleam of the blade. He stabbed down once, twice: he was an expert at death, he'd learned to be that in the war. They wasted no pity on the sack-like bundle that fell without a sound on to the pavement. They were Londoners: they knew the ways of the River Thames, and the tide was starting to ebb. They'd have to be quick to get rid of the body before dawn.

It was as the man slid the body over the edge of the boat and into the oily water, that he remembered. 'A message from your friends,' he said, whispering the words for fear of them carrying on the dank air. But greater still was the fear that gripped at his belly, he was working for men to whom life was cheap, and death was very, very easy. 'Mr Bertiolie said as you were to be sure to know, they sees everything, everywhere.' He muttered the words like a benediction as he stooped to reach the thin pole lying in the bows. The body turned over slowly, floating, as bodies will, face up, and the man leaned out of the boat, poking with his stick at the bubbles of air trapped inside the clothing that would slow the sinking. For a short while, Johnnie's face swam palely white, his brown eyes staring upwards with a childlike innocence, then, with a final swirl, the river closed over him. The man rowed back to the slipway, his muffled rowlocks dripping with the river fog.

Isabella turned up the collar of her black velvet cloak. The lights of Southampton sparkled in the distance, reflecting off the night sea in a path of light. It was impossible to judge how quickly they were sailing away from the shore, but they must be making a good speed. She could feel the power of the engines making the deck throb beneath her feet. It would have been easy to cry, as she sensed rather than saw the nightbound coast of England slip away. She turned as she heard Michael coming back towards her. He'd said he'd gone back to their cabin to fetch his gloves, but when she looked down at his hands he wasn't wearing any. His eyes were very bright and she thought that he too was close to tears.

'The boys will be all right,' she said.

'Of course they will. They won't even spare us a thought

333

until half term, and Lucinda has so many plans laid to keep them busy at Pencombe that we'll be lucky if we get a letter even then.'

They stood side by side, leaning on the rail, looking down at the silver, black sea.

'It was odd, Johnnie slipping off like that,' Michael said. 'He must have found it difficult, all that fun and laughter; it must have reminded him too much of the past. I wonder when we'll hear from him again?'

'Oh, he'll turn up when we least expect him – you know Johnnie.'

A few quick jazz notes drifted past on the wind, flung from an open porthole. The music stopped as quickly as it had begun.

'If they'd kept on playing, I'd have asked you to dance,' Michael said.

'And I'd have accepted.'

'Do you remember that last evening at the Café Royal?'

'I'm hardly likely to forget it; it's not every day that a nephew gets engaged, especially not in that distinctly spectacular manner.'

'Have you seen them since they came on board?'

'No, I think they're taking the fact that they're in the honeymoon suite very seriously.'

Michael laughed, 'I thought that was a very nice gesture of Luke to make.'

'Very nice? Good heavens, I think it was more than that, have you any idea what it must be costing him?'

'Fortunately, none.' Michael put his hand into his coat pocket. He felt for the small leather box that he'd gone back to the cabin to collect. He had a gesture of his own that he wanted to make.

'Michael,' Isabella turned to face him, 'I have a confession.'

'Confessions are for penitents, my dear Isabella, and

somehow I've never thought of you as that. I have a much better idea. Why don't you forget all about your confession and let me give you something nice instead?' He brought out the box, and held it towards her on the palm of his hand. 'Here you are, my darling, this is with my love.' He paused a moment, and then he added, 'And with my thanks.' He wouldn't let her confess to being the originator of the plan to lease Pencombe to Luke; it was much easier if that fact was never openly discussed between them.

Isabella opened the box slowly. She had a sudden suspicion that Michael must know everything, but, looking up at his face, it was impossible for her to tell if she was right. Michael watched her as she took the tissue paper out of the box, revealing what lay on the velvet cushion beneath. She drew in her breath quickly, they were beautiful, dazzling. The earrings were fashionably long, brilliant diamonds in a white gold setting, the pendants were of blue topaz that matched exactly the necklace that she had around her neck.

'So that's why you asked me to wear this tonight.' She put her hand up to her throat. As if time had stood still she remembered the instant, all those years ago, when Michael had given it to her. With the jewels had come his love, his proposal of marriage and his life.

'I know I'm difficult sometimes,' he said. 'But I love you, I really do.' He took the box from her hands and took out the earrings, holding them for her to put on.

'I had no idea . . .' she said.

'But of course you didn't, you have no idea how secretive I can be when I want.'

'Well I've been secretive too.' Isabella's voice trembled, this was so important, 'I had something to tell you that I wanted us to have time to share. I . . . I've found some things hard to understand.' She reached out to him, taking his hands into her grasp, squeezing them tightly. 'But I finally understood when I read the words that you wrote to the boys. It was a beautiful letter, one I'm sure they'll keep all their lives. Any man would be proud to live by those ideals, Michael. The quote you used, "But some love England and her honour yet", it's Tennyson isn't it?'

'Yes, it's something I remembered from my own school days. I don't know why it came to mind, but it said what I feel, how I still feel.'

'I can see that now.' Isabella stepped forwards into her husband's arms, 'I've been keeping something from you.' She could feel the smile on her lips, as he could hear it in her voice. 'We have two beautiful sons, Michael, and I am very proud of them.' She paused, she wanted to choose her words with care. 'This time I think our baby will be a girl, and I'd like, I'd very much like, to call her Honour.'